What others are sa
Katrina D. Hamel's Div

"Powerful, imaginative, stirring! Here is a *Judah Ben-Hur* type story, but this time, it's about the wife of Simon Peter (*Beth 'eshet Shim'on*). Get ready for a unique, substantive, and emotional journey down a stream that flows cleverly from, around, and through the Gospel of Matthew: Like the parable of the 10 virgins at a wedding feast (now helping to narrate the very touching wedding of Beth to Peter, and also much later in the story); Or like the scholar at the crucifixion —"My God, my God"—saying without a beat: "It's a psalm!" Unlike many current stories, this one tries to respect the vision of our first Gospel (without first mixing them all up into a Gospel stew!). *Dividing Sword i*s not only a model of Bible story-telling, it is worth reading and then sharing."

—Gary D. Collier (Ph.D.), Director of the Institute for the Art of Biblical Conversation and author of *The Forgotten Treasure: Reading the Bible Like Jesus* (1993), and of *Scripture, Canon, and Inspiration* (2012).

"Katrina Hamel has written a story that is familiar and yet new. Working mostly from St. Matthew's Gospel, she has told the story of Jesus from the point of view of an unassuming woman, Beth, the wife of Peter. Even though we know the story, each chapter brings a new surprise. Hamel takes the abbreviated account in the Gospel and expands it using the knowledge we have about ancient Palestinian culture. Two generations ago, Dr. Frank G. Slaughter wrote a long series of novels based on the Bible. His books are now mostly forgotten, and it is time for a new generation to have an update of such biblical interpretations. Hamel is the one to do it. This well-written book provides insight and reading pleasure, and we can look forward to reading other works in a long series."

—Rev. Richard Davies (Ph.D.), Dean Emeritus, Martin University. In retirement he researches and writes about Pauline Studies, Patristics, Historical Theology and Theological Studies.

DIVIDING
SWORD

KATRINA D. HAMEL

This is a work of fiction.
While the characters are fictitious, the story of Jesus is based on historic events.

Scripture quotations taken from the New American Standard Bible® (NASB),
Copyright © 1960, 1962, 1963, 1968, 1971, 1972, 1973,
1975, 1977, 1995 by The Lockman Foundation
Used by permission. www.Lockman.org

Dividing Sword : a novel / by Katrina D. Hamel — 1ˢᵗ ed.

Summary: Based on the Gospel of Matthew. Driven apart by a revolutionary rabbi, Beth
and her cousin Reuben find themselves on opposite sides as Jesus of Nazareth divides
their families, their hometown, and their very faith.

[1. Historical Fiction. 2. Christian Fiction. 3. Faith – Fiction. 4. Crucifixion – Fiction 5.
Women disciples – Fiction] 1. Title

ISBN: 978-1-9990338-0-4

To my children: Caleb, Micah, Isaac, and Sadie.
May the Light of the Lord forever shine in your hearts.

CONTENTS

PREFACE

I delved into the gospel of Matthew in a way I never have before, and this book is the result. A Bible class led to a short story, and those brief paragraphs led to this novel, a work of fiction that seeks to explore the wondrous good news that the gospel writer presents us.

To honor that gospel writer, I have done my best to stay true to the account that he presents; to use his stories, and to try to see Jesus' ministry through Matthew's eyes alone.

I don't pretend to fully grasp the Gospel of Matthew. It is a work that always yields something new. My interpretations of his gospel will be found throughout, and I don't expect you to agree with all of them. In fact, I am sure that someday I will come back, shake my head a little, laugh at that idea I used to hold so dear, and move forward in new knowledge. Bible study is like that.

Scriptures found within this novel are paraphrased and incomplete, and can in no way replace the book of Matthew. It is my ardent desire that when you read this story you are drawn back to the Bible, to seek the truth that lies therein.

1

Veil of Innocence

The air rippled under his feathers as the raven mounted the wind and soared high over his domain. In the heights, he could not see the borders that broke the once whole land into three territories, governed by puppets held over unwilling subjects by the iron fists of Rome.

Suspended beneath the clouds, the raven did not discern between Jew and Gentile, nor did he understand the vast separation in culture, customs, and belief that split the little country into jagged bits that pricked and cut each other without mercy.

All the raven saw were the lands that in ancient times had been promised to the descendants of Abraham—craggy mountains and grassy slopes, harsh wilderness and fertile fields of sprouting vines and grains, trees and wildflowers nudged to new life by the spring sun.

With a glittering eye, the raven saw a long road. The road went through valleys, hugged canyons, rose to the heights, and then sunk once more, sometimes even and cobbled, more often rough and almost impossible to trace. The road was traveled by a steady flow of people. Their journey had been long, and sometimes dangerous. Where the people were going, the raven didn't know, nor did he care.

He was more interested in filling his belly.

The circling ravens overhead should have been a warning, but Beth and Reuben were innocent to the dark omen. The cousins broke away from their traveling group and raced ahead, each determined to be the first to set eyes on the city walls.

Their friends and family fell behind them; old and young moved steadily by foot or on donkeys, some with rugged carts. They were but one group in a massive country-wide pilgrimage headed to the festival. They were near the end of their three-day journey from the north.

The children were eager for their very first view of the city where the mighty King David had ruled in the distant past, in the glorious years of their forefathers.

A shepherd with his long staff drove a flock of sacrificial lambs ahead of him on the grassy plain beside the road. Beth could hear the bleating over Reuben's laughter. Disappearing around a bend in the road, a merchant caravan of camels plodded, their loads swaying. Only a small hill stood between them and their first view of the city of Jerusalem. Deaf to calls behind, the children dashed far ahead, fueled by the fresh spring day.

They stumbled to a stop.

Reuben flung out an arm and caught Beth's sleeve. Unable to tear their eyes away, they fumbled and found each other's hand.

Gaping and frozen in place with horror, they stared up at a contorted face. Flies buzzed over sunburned limbs that were spiked to a splintered cross. Crusted blood ran down his forearms and dripped from his feet to the packed dirt below. The man's chest rose and fell sporadically. He was unable to pull a full breath through his swollen lips. Fresh blood oozed from his wounds as he strained, trying to raise himself to take a breath. His glazed eyes rolled, unfocused. The smell of the man made Beth's stomach roil. Her nose burned with the coppery scent of blood and the sour stink of urine.

Nailed to the cross were letters on papyrus, but Beth couldn't read. In this case, she didn't need to. The message was clear. This man had been an enemy of omnipresent Rome.

An inky raven came and perched over the man's shoulder, turning its glinting eye this way and that, deciding if it was time to begin his feast.

A shifting movement startled Beth as she noticed a trio of Roman soldiers keeping guard. Two were sprawled on the ground, but the third stood with a wide stance and his muscled arms crossed over a dull metal breastplate. He watched the two children with mild curiosity on his scarred face.

"Run back to your family," he said. His voice rang with authority.

Beth wanted nothing more than to obey and escape from this horror. She tugged on Reuben, whose wide-eyed gaze was still fixed upon the cross. He didn't move. She bit her lip to keep from crying as she yanked his arm once more, hard.

"Come on!" she hissed at her cousin. Reuben tore his eyes away. Together they fled back around the turn in the road.

They collided with Zebedee, who was coming to find them. Their uncle was broad of chest, with unusually long, thick, and curly hair tied back at the nape of his neck with a leather thong. Panting, the children flung their arms around the kindly man's waist, and Beth took comfort as his large hand rested on her back.

"What is it?" he asked in his deep voice.

Reuben looked up at his uncle, his expression full of bitterness. "There's a cross, with a rebel." It was the first cross the cousins had ever seen with their own eyes, though every child had heard whispers of the horrible fate that awaited a traitor to Rome.

Zebedee's eyes hardened as he gazed at the road ahead, and his voice rumbled like thunder. "What? They should have been emptied before Passover!"

Beth's mother, Tamar, bustled towards them. She wore a frown on her face and Beth's baby brother on her generous hip. The rest of the travelers from Capernaum were not far behind.

"There's a cross up ahead," Zebedee grunted to Tamar, sparks in his eyes. Tamar looked at her daughter with concern, and Beth tried to swallow the ache in her throat. "It's right by the road. We'll have to pass by it."

Tamar pressed her lips together until they formed a thin line, then puffed out her breath. "Well, there's no helping it. Even at Passover, they can't let us forget." She clicked her tongue and turned around to warn the others so they could shield their children.

"Come, Beth!" her mother called over her shoulder.

Beth obeyed at once, Reuben hastening with her as they wove

their way through friends and neighbors to find their families.

Reuben came up to his parents and two younger brothers first, and the cousins shared a look before Beth pushed deeper into the moving throng. Tamar came up to her husband, Benjamin, and spoke to him in clipped tones as he led the soft-eyed donkey beside him. Spread over the donkey was a harness that held two large baskets on either side, baskets that still smelled of fish. One held their traveling supplies, and the other basket held Beth's two-year-old sister, Hannah.

Tamar passed little David to her eldest daughter. Beth held her baby brother close. She drew in the sweet scent of his downy head greedily, trying to wash away the stink of human waste and the tang of blood. Tamar took Hannah into her arms, and drew her mantle round her little daughter, shielding her from witnessing the grisly scene.

The crowd pushed ever forward. Like a wave, silence rolled back from the front until the only noise was the shuffle of footsteps and the rattling of wheels. Beth felt her heart pound as she came around the bend once more and heard the piercing cry of the ravens.

She tried to avert her gaze. She lifted her chin, and with narrowed eyes she fixed her gaze down the dusty road to where it led right through the large gates of Jerusalem—the city she had longed to see with her own eyes for as long as she could remember.

The enormous Northern Gates were thrown wide, and from this distance, she could see a blurry mass of people funneling into the city. She forced herself to notice the bulky, yellowish stone walls. She looked over the walls and saw towers that rose into the sky—the overbearing feature of the Roman garrison. That blight on the most Holy City was called simply the Antonia. She shuddered. She didn't want to think of Romans just then. A glint caught her eye, and her gaze shifted so she could see the top of a gleaming, white and gold structure, a building so dazzlingly beautiful it could only be the Temple.

The pilgrims pushed forward in their unnatural hush. Beth clutched her brother to her chest and tried to ignore the agony beside her. Her gaze wavered, and then, almost against her will, her eyes stole up and looked at the dying man just as they passed.

His breathing was even more ragged now. His muscles trembled. How much longer could he endure? Beth realized she was holding her breath, and let it slip out.

The soldiers glared as the pilgrims passed. Beth wondered if they expected trouble with the Passover festival so near. It was a festival of freedom after all. With her heart in her throat and her stomach knotted, she did not feel free.

At last they were past the torturous scene. Little by little, conversations resumed and her pulse slowed.

Beth's extended family left their traveling companions a little before the city and walked the rough road to Bethany.

Beth's father, Benjamin, her Uncle Zebedee, and Reuben's father, Ebenezer, were brothers, fishermen all. Zebedee was eldest. He had inherited his wealth and his valuable boat from their prosperous father. Her father and Ebenezer had also inherited a boat each, but Ebenezer, for reasons not clear to Beth, had lost his boat and was obliged to rent from the guild.

Their cousin, Simon, was a Pharisee and shopkeeper. He had a good-sized house in the town of Bethany, just two miles from Jerusalem. Simon's home would be full of relatives now, all come for the yearly Passover and Week of Unleavened Bread. As they ducked under the doorway, Tamar and Benjamin greeted their distant relations joyfully. Beth followed them inside and found the house was packed full of noisy bustle. Unnerved still, Beth huddled near her mother.

Tamar found a seat with the other mothers. All the women talked at once, their daughters clustered around them. Beth wondered how anyone could understand anything, but heads bobbed all around. Her mother took David from Beth to nurse him while Beth minded Hannah. As usual, the determined toddler kept trying to wander off. Benjamin went to the courtyard with the other men. Their voices carried into the house as they shared the news from their respective areas.

Beth's mind was full, but she knew her mother wouldn't wish to discuss the horror she had seen. Beth chewed her lower lip and wished she could speak to Reuben away from the others.

A little while later, Beth discerned a shift in the mood and conversation. Families began filing back outside, and Beth wondered where they were going. Reuben left with his family. He gave her a small wave as he passed. With a swoop in the pit of her stomach, Beth realized it was nearly time for the evening sacrifice in the

Temple. She was used to stopping to pray at the time of the evening sacrifice in her hometown far to the north, but perhaps from here, she might be able to hear the shofar blow.

She looked up as her father came over, smiling. "Would you like to go and see the Temple, my girl?"

Beth felt her heart skip a beat, and nodded. "Yes, Papa!"

They left Tamar with the two little ones in the house, busy in happy conversation. Beth followed her father out the door and over the mountainous ridge. Her heart pounded, and it had little to do with the sharply ascending road.

They paused atop the Mount of Olives and looked down over the city. "Stop here for a moment, my girl," Benjamin said. He wrapped his arm around her shoulders, and she leaned against him. Standing together, the father and daughter could see over the low Eastern Wall and into the Temple Courts. The Courts were an enormous raised platform lifted above the rest of the city.

Her father said, "From here, you can see everything. If your eyes are good, you can see over the Golden Gate, over the gates to the outer and inner courtyards, and perhaps even through the Temple doors. If you had the sight of an eagle, you could perhaps see to the curtain of the Holy of Holies itself."

Beth felt a surge of ancestral pride and awe. She wrapped her arms around her father in a sideways hug.

"It's so beautiful!" she breathed.

"It's the most beautiful Temple in the world!" her father exclaimed, tipping back his chin and raising a hand to the heavens. "As it should be."

Beth had heard the Temple described to her again and again by her father. He had detailed the rooms and their purposes and told her all about the careful way the priests performed the rites and sacrifices. As she saw it with her own eyes, she thought it was more wondrous, and more enormous in scale than she had ever imagined. Her entire town could fit upon the Temple Mount, with room to spare. The vast number of tiny people that milled in the courts staggered her mind.

They could have stayed and gazed in wonder for hours, but the Temple sacrifices were precise, so they hurried on. They descended the Mount of Olives and crossed the valley. Fearful she would be separated from her father, Beth kept her hand within his as they joined the great crush outside the Eastern Golden Gate.

Beth looked upwards in amazement as they passed through the thick city walls. The gateway alone was far larger than her house.

When they emerged on the other side, they were under a colonnade that wrapped around the entire complex—a roofed area supported by double columns. She looked up once more and saw the underside was elaborately engraved wood. The area sheltered many merchants and noisy animals. The din was overwhelming.

People streamed into the vast Court of Gentiles from the many large gates. Two gates were to her left, below the Royal Stoa where her father had told her the client king liked to entertain overlooking the spectacular Temple. Four more gates stood opposite her, and to her right was the infamous Antonia fortress, with a little gate allowing easy access for soldiers. The entire courtyard was paved in multi-hued, intricate stonework. In the Temple even the floor was beautiful.

She caught all that in a moment, then her gaze was fixed upon the dominating feature before her—the Temple itself. It was a marvel to behold, gleaming with gold trim and dazzling white marble. This was the place where God met with His chosen people.

Her heart soared with eagerness. She was about to speak to her father, but then her gaze was caught. Pushed out of the way was an old man dressed in rags. His milky eyes were almost hidden in deep wrinkles, and he held a beggar's bowl in his shaky hands. Near him was a middle-aged woman sitting on the intricate tiles, her legs twisted and deformed. Beth's joy drained away and her stomach wrenched. Here, so close to the one true God's Temple, how could there be the poor and the sick?

Beth tugged on her father's hand until he looked down. She tried to voice her questions, but tears rose and the words stuck in her throat. She gestured to the beggars. Benjamin glanced at them, then at his daughter. Her father smiled at her. He wove his way to the beggars and dropped a hard-earned coin into each bowl.

"Peace be on you," the old man whispered, and the woman bobbed her head with a small smile. Beth felt a little better, and she smiled again.

Benjamin led his daughter over to where people waited to pass through a narrow opening in a low balustrade. This was where the Court of Gentiles ended.

"What does that say, Papa?" Beth pointed to an engraved sign.

"No man of another nation is to enter into the barrier and the enclosure around the Temple. Whoever is caught will have himself to blame for his death which follows." Benjamin rested a hand on her hair. "The Temple's only for the Jews, my dear. We are the Lord's chosen people."

They made it through the narrow gate and climbed the steps that led to the Temple's inner courts. They crossed through another gateway into the first court, the Court of Women. It was full of people in preparation for the evening sacrifice and prayers. On the western side was a large, ornate gateway that led to the next courtyard, and men climbed more steps and went up to the Court of Israel. The gate between the Court of Women and the Court of Israel was thrown wide to reveal the Temple building on the highest platform with the large stone altar before it. The area directly around the Temple was the third courtyard, the Court of Priests. Beyond that courtyard, only the priests went into the Temple itself, and only the High Priest ever entered into the Holy of Holies, the most sacred place in the entire world.

Standing in awe of her surroundings, her inner turmoil melted away as she stood in the courts of the one true God. The pagans had their own temples, with figures of men or beasts that they sacrificed to. But none of those gods were real; they were not like Israel's God.

"We can go no further." Benjamin lowered his head to speak to her. "But we will listen to the prayers and the songs here, won't we?"

Beth saw that her father was happy. He beamed and nodded at the others around him, and they smiled at him too. Beth was in the midst of more people than ever before in her whole life. Young and old, men and women, all were gathered for worship. Commoners stood side by side with the wealthy. She stared at the man in front of her. She had rarely seen such fine clothes. His garments were embroidered in the Greek style, and he wore thick rings on his smooth hands.

"Beth!" a voice called, and Beth glanced back as Reuben pushed through the crowd with his father and two younger brothers scrambling to catch up. "I'm glad you came. Isn't it more glorious than we ever imagined?" Beth smiled to see her favorite cousin. Reuben's eyes widened, and he pointed over her shoulder. "Look," he said. "That must be a rabbi with his disciples."

Beth turned and saw a man with a faded beard and a striped shawl over his shoulders. Several young men clustered close before him, and he appeared to be instructing them as he pointed at one of the enclosed, smaller side courts.

Beth saw Reuben's face grow wistful as he said, "They're so lucky."

A long, rich shofar blast rose and filled the Temple Mount, echoing from a corner tower and rippling over the entire city. A hush fell. It was time for the evening sacrifice. Beth knew that on the enormous altar the priests were ritually sacrificing a lamb, as they did every morning and evening.

A priest, dressed in his spotless white robes and turban, appeared and stood before them in the gateway. Men of the priestly tribe of Levi came and lined the steps. The priest led the people in prayer. In one voice the crowd chanted the prayers by memory. The shofar blew again and they all knelt on the ground and pressed their foreheads to the beautiful stone floor before standing to their feet again. Beth had never prayed among so many people at once, and the vibration of the multitude of voices pulsed through her like an extra heartbeat. The Levites began their songs, and Beth soaked in the lilting melody with a hand pressed to her chest. A man jostled her as he passed. A glint caught her attention, something silvery. Even with the loud music, she heard the splatter of thick drops of blood hitting the stone. Her eyes widened as she stared at the wealthy man in front of her.

"Papa!" she cried out, wanting to flee but paralyzed with fear.

The wounded man turned towards her with glassy eyes, blood bubbling between his lips. He fell sideways, blood blooming on his embroidered robe. He convulsed, clutching his chest with twitching, jeweled fingers. Beth tasted bile.

Benjamin gripped her shoulder so hard it hurt. He tried to pull her away, but the crowd was too close. A woman screamed, interrupting the prayers, and the music broke jaggedly. People turned to look, crying out and pulling back. Within seconds the whole courtyard was in turmoil, people pushing past each other in their haste to flee.

Beth felt like the world spun around her. She was hoisted up and carried away by her father.

"What's happening, Papa?" she cried out, wrapping her arms around his neck.

"I don't know, my girl, I don't know." His voice was grim, and his head swiveled back and forth.

They were held back by people in front and pressed forward by people behind, all squeezing towards the nearest gate. Everywhere Beth looked were white, fearful eyes. She was relieved to see Reuben and his family manage to escape the courtyard ahead of them.

"If the man with the knife was here in the courts, then he's a Jew, isn't he?" Beth whispered.

Her father's eyes flicked to her face, but he didn't answer. Beth buried her face in his shoulder, feeling that the world was a violent, bloody place. When she lifted her head, they were through the gate. Temple guards appeared, holding their long spears upright. Roman soldiers were also marching from their garrison, hands on their sword hilts.

"You there!" a Roman demanded, drawing his sword and pointing it right at Beth and her father. "Are you armed?"

"Of course not," Benjamin answered, setting Beth down and putting an arm around her. Beth clung to him as the fleeing crowds buffeted her. "I am here with my daughter."

The soldier's cold eyes flicked to her, and Beth flinched beneath the hatred. She hid behind her father. The man swung his sword to another Jew and repeated the question.

Beth's father clutched her arm, and they rushed out of the Court of Gentiles and back through the Golden Gate. They ran until Beth was panting with a stitch in her side.

They paused to catch their breath at the top of the mount. Her uncles and cousins were there, waiting for them. She was surprised to her cousins James and John were excited rather than scared.

"You're safe!" Reuben came and grasped her hand as the adults spoke to each other in low voices.

She realized she was trembling and squeezed his fingers. His face was ashen, his eyes wide, and she wondered if she looked just as fearful. Her first visit to the Holy City had not been as she expected.

She peered down upon the magnificence of the Temple, still glinting in the setting sun. It was empty now. Everyone had fled except the Temple staff. The emptiness was haunting. As she gazed at the gleaming white marble and the dazzling gold, almost too bright to look at, she knew something more than worshipers was missing.

Every Jew knew it.

In Moses' day, the Shekinah—the presence of the Lord--

descended and filled the Tabernacle. Why didn't the Lord come down to be with them anymore? Why was He so far away? He had promised to be their God and they were to be His chosen people, like a bride joined to a good husband. Why had her ancestors been unfaithful to Him? Was that why there was so much pain and suffering in the world? It was more than her child's mind could understand.

That night, curled up in the crowded upper room with her aunts and cousins, Beth listened to the layered sounds of breathing and tried to find her bearings. Her safe childhood world had tilted, and the veil of innocence had slipped to reveal a bloody side to the world she had thought safe and beautiful.

She felt the need to make water, so she rose from beside her sleeping mother. She tiptoed through the crowded room and went down the stairs.

On her way back to bed, she saw a lamp was lit in the lower room of the house. She paused to peek inside. The men were sitting in a circle and speaking in hushed tones.

Beth listened for a moment and realized with a lurch in her stomach that the men were discussing what had happened in the Temple.

"The courtyard is being purified. What a disaster," Reuben's father, Ebenezer, said with a shake of his head. "I think they must have chosen the inner courtyard purposefully, to send a message. Perhaps the assassin was from the Essenes. They are still not pleased that a foreign ruler rebuilt our Temple."

"Perhaps," another man replied, drawing his hand down his long beard. "But that does not seem quite their way. The Essenes have withdrawn to their hidden places in the wilderness, waiting for the Lord to send their Teacher of Righteousness."

"It's the bold teachings of that Judas the Galilean, mark my words," another man cried out. "I heard him once, preaching against the sin of paying taxes to Rome. He called it allegiance to their false reign, selling ourselves in slavery."

Benjamin shook his head. "I just hope we don't have another failed uprising like we did when King Herod died. They are still rebuilding Sepphoris after the disaster with Judah ben Hezekiah." Heads bobbed all around the room. Benjamin's face was grim, and he clutched his hands together in his lap. "My wife was born near there, and her family was either killed or sent away into slavery when the uprising was crushed. Her grandparent's quick-thinking saved her life."

Beth pressed her hand over her mouth. She hadn't known that. To discover that her mother had a past of suffering felt strange. Her mother was like all the other mothers. She cooked, sewed, taught, and cared for them. Beth couldn't imagine her as a little girl running for her life.

"That was a dark time, truly." Zebedee reached out to put a hand on Benjamin's shoulder. "Rebels were crucified all over this country. I heard the total was two thousand men hung up to die."

Beth swallowed hard. A single victim had been torturous for her to behold. She tried to imagine two thousand dying men. That many crosses would be a stark forest of death.

She trembled and fled from the conversation, creeping up the steep stairs into the upper room. She wound around prone forms. How could they sleep so peacefully, knowing all the cruelty that existed in the world?

Long into the night she tossed and turned. The memory of the hungry raven at the cross pecked at her, and she wondered if she would ever be able to forget.

2

LIFE OF A FISHERMAN

Beth's laughter was contagious. Though smaller, she was faster and was quickly gaining distance. She glanced over her shoulder, her expression teasing. Reuben chuckled as he chased her swishing hair through the tall grass, the sun glinting off the dark waves. Fifteen feet ahead, she disappeared. He crept forward with his arms swinging back and forth, eyes sweeping to see where she was hiding.

He saw a pair of bright laughing eyes obscured by wide blades of grass, and she let loose a giggle as he crowed, "Ah ha!"

He sprawled beside her and they lay on their backs, panting. The sky was a rich blue that made it hard to tell whether it was far or near. The grass smelled hot and ripe.

"Does your mama know you're out here?" Reuben asked.

"Of course," she replied.

Yes, of course, Beth had asked before slipping out for a few minute's freedom. Beth never did anything disobedient. Not like Reuben.

"Didn't you ask?" she tilted her face to look at him, her thick brows furrowing.

"Not exactly," he admitted. "If I ask to play for a while, Papa takes it as a sign that I'm bored and need more chores."

Being thirteen meant a never-ending list of things to do and not enough time to do them. If he fished in the daytime, he was lucky

13

to get an hour or two for himself. If he fished at night, he ended up sleeping through the day and missing school. Ebenezer couldn't seem to believe that any son of his preferred study to fishing.

"Oh, Reuben," Beth chastised with a tone so gentle it rolled off him without effect. "If you want your father to treat you like a grown-up, you need to bend to his will sometimes."

"Easy enough for you," Reuben said, ripping off a stalk of grass and tearing it into bits. "Your father is perfect."

Beth laughed, "He's good, yes, but no man is perfect." She paused a moment. "Your father is always nice to me."

"Yes, well, you're you," Reuben laughed to hide his peevishness.

She was the good one of the family. The one the aunts praised and the uncles wished was their own. Not like him. His father wanted his firstborn to be just like him. It didn't matter that Reuben's younger brothers were miniatures of Ebenezer; his papa was determined that Reuben would be a fisherman too.

Just like his grandfather had been. And his great-grandfather.

"Beth," Reuben said, making his tone purposefully casual. "Do you think I'll ever be able to become a rabbi?"

Ever since that first, disastrous visit to the Temple, Reuben had been unable to shake the picture of himself in a Pharisee's shawl. He was called by God; he just knew it.

"Of course!" Her confident tone pleased him. "Well, as soon as you convince your papa."

His hopes withered. "Yeah, that's all."

Beth reached up a hand and pulled a head of grass down so she could rub the ripened heads off with her fingertips. "Give him time."

"Reuben!" a voice roared over the grassy field and the children started. "Where are you, boy?"

His heart leaped into his chest. He was caught. Reuben scrambled to his feet. "I'm here, Papa."

"What do you mean by running off without asking first? There's work to be done! Get home!"

Beth rose beside Reuben, her expression nervous before her angry uncle.

"Ah, Beth dear," Ebenezer's expression softened. "You should run on home too. See if your mama needs any help."

"Yes, Uncle," Beth said at once, and she began following the snaking trail they had made in the grass.

Reuben followed without a word. He kept his head lowered as if he was shameful of his childishness, but on the inside, his chest was hot with frustration. He had been working like a slave for days. Surely he had earned an hour of freedom!

Ebenezer followed Reuben right on his heels. It gave Reuben the feeling of being chased. He didn't like it. They strode into Capernaum, and Beth hastened away to her own house on the other side of town.

Nestled near the shoreline of a freshwater lake, the long and deep Sea of Galilee, Capernaum was of moderate size, full of fishermen, farmers, and tradespeople, built on tradition and stalwart commitment to the Jewish way of life.

They came to Reuben's house. A low stool was set up in the tiny courtyard. Reuben was pushed into it.

"There's a tear in the net, see?" Ebenezer held up the net and jabbed a finger at the broken strands. "It needs to be fixed before tonight. Make sure you check the rest too."

Reuben groaned. The net felt miles long. This would take the rest of the day. Ebenezer sighed tiredly and scrubbed a hand over his short beard.

"We all need to pull together if we're going to make it, you know?"

Reuben did know, though he didn't like it. His father left him with his string and the heap of nets. Reuben sighed and set to work.

Ebenezer disappeared into the house, and Reuben could hear his father talking with Reuben's little brothers. Laughing with them. Reuben gritted his teeth. When had his father last laughed with him? He couldn't remember. He always felt like a chunk of raw clay when he was with his father, being pounded and trod under the potter's foot to soften it. So it could be made into something—whether the clay wanted to, or not.

Reuben barely finished the net before supper. His stomach growled as he shuffled into the dim house to eat the thin stew his mother had prepared. He sat between his little brothers, Zeb and Ben, and shoveled food into his mouth.

The closer it came to dusk, the more he felt like running out the door and hiding again. Today, more than ever, he rebelled against his fate. He hated fishing. It was exhausting, back-breaking, cold work. And for what? After Ebenezer paid the guild to rent his boat and set money aside for taxes, there were hardly any coins left, not even enough for the family to afford the fish they caught.

This was the life his father wanted for him? Reuben cringed at the thought.

Now Daniel, the local scribe, he lived well. Daniel lived in the nicest house in town. Reuben often watched the dark-robed man move through the synagogue. Everybody nodded at the wise, aging scribe. Everyone asked Daniel's opinion in the discussion of scripture.

Reuben looked across at his tall and broad father. He wore the simplest of clothes. His sandals had been repaired so many times they resembled nothing more than patchwork. Nobody bowed their head to Ebenezer in the synagogue.

Reuben sopped up the last of his stew with his bread. His supper didn't satisfy. Nothing would satisfy until he was following his true calling.

The low sun peeked through the small window of their humble house.

"Time for work," Ebenezer said with a grin, clapping his hands on his knees.

"Can I come?" Zeb and Ben cried out in unison.

"Not today, boys," Ebenezer said. "We're taking out the dragnet. I'll be too busy to watch you."

"Aw, we'll be good, we promise!" Zeb protested.

Reuben handed his bowl to his mother with the subtlest shake of his head. Why were they so eager to be fishermen? Fishermen were common. Nobodies. They didn't do anything good for the world except put fish on the table of those rich enough to afford them.

"Not today," Ebenezer's voice was firm, and the boys quieted. When their father anchored his mind, a gale-force wind wouldn't shift him.

Reuben helped his father carry the net down to the shore. Beth was there, helping her father load baskets into the boat. She wouldn't fish with the men, but she helped prepare the boat and often returned to sort the catch.

"Hey, cheer up," Beth elbowed Reuben as he stowed the net at the bow. She put her head near his and spoke under her breath, "At least you get to stay up with the grown-ups. Mama will be sending me to bed with Hannah and David like I'm a little child." He appreciated that she was trying to cheer him up, though he'd rather have her pity than her encouragement.

"Beth, my girl!" Benjamin came up and swept Beth up into his arms. Though she was thirteen, he could still lift her like a doll. "Be a good girl for your mama. Tell her I'd love a hot porridge when I get home!"

"Yes, Papa," she said and kissed his cheek. She skipped for home, pausing once to wave before disappearing into town.

Beth was hardly out of earshot before the teasing and jokes began. While they held their tongues with a young lady present, they didn't care if their coarse jokes made Reuben's ears burn. Reuben gritted his teeth and bore the brash laughter as the men finished readying their boats.

"I see Uncle let little Reuben come along," John said as he mussed Reuben's hair into his eyes.

Reuben shoved off his cousin's hand. His cousin was only a little older but was at least three inches taller. Wider too. James was older yet, and he laughed and talked with the men like he belonged. Reuben felt like a little tag-along.

"Cast us off, boy!" Ebenezer barked the orders to Reuben, even though it was Benjamin's boat they were riding in today. Yes, a tag-along who was expected to do the work of a man. He untied the boat from the pier. He heaved the boat and jumped in before it drifted too far.

Benjamin sat at the rudder, and Ebenezer lowered the sail. The wind caught the thick white fabric and pulled them forward. The shallow-keeled boats moved fast enough atop the water, but with their wide base, they were cumbersome to steer.

The men shouted across the water to each other, but Reuben didn't pay much attention. The sun dropped below the horizon, and the sky turned from dusky hues to cold darkness. He didn't like working late into the night with only the distant stars for his light. Better a well-trimmed oil lamp, and a good scroll.

Too soon, they were letting out the long dragnet between the two boats. The two boats sailed parallel to the water's edge, stretching the net wide. The boats turned towards the shoreline, and the net was dragged between them, trapping fish and pulling them to the pebbly shore. Reuben sighed when his father ordered him out of the boat. He cringed as he jumped into the waist-deep water, sloshed to the rope, and helped heave the net out of the water. He had to fetch the baskets and sort the catch. The slippery fish flopped everywhere, leaving a smelly, scaly residue on his hands.

"Not bad, not bad," Ebenezer said looking over the baskets. "Let's go again."

They loaded up and prepared to go again.

Reuben clambered aboard his uncle's boat. Benjamin was already seated, rubbing his temples.

"What's wrong?" Reuben asked. His uncle looked weary, and yet they had hardly begun.

Benjamin laughed, though it sounded strained. "I'm just feeling my age tonight, that's all."

Reuben didn't doubt it. Decades of hard labor aged a man before his time. Yet another reason to despise the trade.

Benjamin shook his head like a goat flicking off flies as he gripped the rudder. Soon the net was stretched out again, and they were pulling the trapped fish to the shoreline.

"Ho there!" Ebenezer called out. "Off course a bit there, Benjamin."

The little boat was steering into the corralled fish, instead of straight to shore. Reuben glanced back to his uncle in confusion. He felt his heart skip a beat. Benjamin was slumped against the side of the boat, his eyes bulging in the starlight as his mouth hung slack.

"Uncle!" Reuben cried out.

He stood in transfixed horror as his father pushed by him. Ebenezer huddled over Benjamin, blocking Reuben's view. Reuben heard his father shouting to Zebedee, "Come quick! Something's wrong!"

The fear in the usually brash voice of his father struck fear in Reuben like nothing else. He craned around his father and saw Benjamin's face was strangely drooping—like it was melting. The stricken man tried to speak but groaned out something garbled instead.

Zebedee's boat pulled up alongside theirs. "What's going on?" his booming voice demanded.

"He's been struck with something," Ebenezer cried out. "A sickness, or a demon, God forbid. He can't seem to move or talk!"

"Lord help us!" Zebedee gasped when he was near enough to see Benjamin's face. "Get this boat turned around and get him home.

Now!"

Ebenezer had to shift Benjamin out of the way to take control of the rudder. "You sit with him, Reuben," Ebenezer commanded, his voice taut.

Reuben sat on the wet bottom of the boat beside his uncle. As he pulled Benjamin's head to lay on his chest, his uncle's face tipped up to the stars the fisherman knew so well. Reuben put his arms around the burly man, relieved to feel his chest rising and falling. He was sick, but he wasn't dead.

Reuben thought that Benjamin was the nicest of the three brothers. Benjamin liked to laugh, but never at someone else's expense. He was happy to let Reuben ramble on about something new he had learned, even when Zebedee was teasing and Ebenezer was bored. Benjamin was a good father to his three children, both patient and kind. Reuben's arms tightened. What would Beth feel when she saw her father like this?

Ebenezer reached the pier and began shouting for help. The boat was lashed to the paling and Benjamin's large form was carried by four men up towards the town. Reuben wanted to hang back. He didn't want to see his favorite uncle sick like this. Yet, he didn't want Ebenezer's shouts to be the first warning Beth and her mother received. His father had the tact of a bull. Beth deserved better. He ran ahead of the men, his bare feet slapping on the dirt road that led to Benjamin's home.

He paused outside the closed door. What would he say? His mind was as blank as a new scroll, but the men would be hot on his heels, so he gulped in a breath of cold night air, rapped twice, and threw open the door.

Beth's home was like his. The work space was on the ground level, and the sleeping and living space raised above.

Reuben called, "Aunt Tamar?"

He heard a shifting movement, and his aunt's face looked down over the edge with wide eyes.

"Reuben! What are you doing here?"

Reuben opened his mouth to blurt it all out, but he hesitated when Beth's face appeared as well. "Something's happened," he said, his tone as gentle as he could make it while his heart was galloping like a runaway horse.

"What's happened?" Tamar demanded, her tone rising with

concern.

"Uncle Benjamin, he's uh, well he's sick," Reuben stammered. He could hear the men's voices as they approached the door. Reuben's eyes fell on his cousin with pity. "I think it's bad."

Ebenezer led the men as they burst through the door, and the house was filled with shouting and exclamations. Tamar, somewhat prepared by Reuben, still began to cry as she hastened down the ladder and tried to take hold of her husband. The massive man was now as helpless as a babe.

Reuben glanced upwards and saw Beth hadn't moved. Her eyes were liquid orbs as she stared down at her papa.

Uncle Benjamin was put to bed, and one of the men rushed to Magdala to fetch the nearest physician. The whole time Benjamin kept trying to speak, but the words were all wrong. Half his body didn't work anymore. His mouth was twisted, and tears began to leak down a drooping eye. It was scary for Reuben to watch.

With so many people bustling around the room, Beth was pushed to the background. She sat wild-eyed near her little brother and sister, who by some miracle were sleeping through the commotion. Reuben sat with her. She was one of those he loved best in the world. Shouldn't he know what to say to her?

His mind tumbled. Was there any comfort he could offer? The children were no strangers to death and suffering in the world, but this was different. This was Uncle Benjamin. In the end, Reuben simply took Beth's hand and held it as they watched Benjamin weep and Tamar rock back and forth and moan.

The physician came near dawn. The man poked and prodded, clicked his tongue, and shook his head.

"There's nothing to be done," the man said, speaking to Ebenezer and Zebedee. "Either he will get better, or he'll die. He's in the Lord's hands now."

Tamar wailed.

The physician left. Soon after, the elders arrived to pray over Benjamin. Then they left too. Benjamin fell asleep, his breathing labored. The family sat and kept vigil.

The sun rose and life began outside the house, but inside everything felt smothered.

Hannah and David awoke, but one of the neighbor women came to whisk them away. She tried to take Beth and Reuben. Beth's mask of sorrow broke into an expression of panic.

"We're staying," Reuben told the neighbor, lifting his chin.

When his mother came to fetch him home, Reuben refused her as well, gripping Beth's hand tighter.

Benjamin's house was connected to Zebedee's by a courtyard. Zebedee's wife, the children's Aunt Naomi, brought bowls of hot barley porridge sweetened with dates for everyone—everyone except Uncle Benjamin.

They ate mechanically, watching Benjamin's chest rise and fall.

The day moved slowly. Reuben did everything he could for Beth. He brought her water, offered her food, and kept vigil with her, even when his eyes grew gritty and his back ached and he wished he could just lay down and sleep.

Benjamin slipped deeper and deeper into sleep. His breathing became shallow, and sweat beaded on his brow. As the sun moved towards mid-afternoon, he gave a jerk, and everyone jumped. He began to seize, half his body convulsing, his limbs flailing and striking those nearest to him.

Beth wailed in fright, "Papa! Papa! Somebody help him!"

Nobody could, though Reuben would have done anything to stop Beth's heart-rending cry and the choking sobs as she crawled across the room and tried to hold her father down.

When the seizure passed, so did Benjamin.

3

PATHS OF OUR LIVES

The sun was setting in the sky, but it was rising in his heart, warm and full of promise. When had he ever felt such eager joy? Reuben's steps were light as he left the scribe, eager to share the news with Beth.

A year had passed since his Uncle Benjamin had died, and while much had changed, much was still the same.

He strode back through Capernaum with his arms swinging. Reuben passed the new synagogue building, nodding to several men who sat on the dark, stone steps. The synagogue was the heart of the Jewish community. It contained the community records, the mikveh, a guest room for travelers, and was also the classroom for the boys of the community. Ezra, his teacher, looked up and raised a hand in greeting to Reuben.

Reuben passed the despised tax booth, closed for the evening. The corrupt tax collectors were gone home; no doubt to count their cut of the profits. The open-air market was also quiet, except for a few children enjoying a last moment of playtime in the hazy, purple twilight, before they were summoned home.

He turned his back on the water and hurried down a dirt road toward the small houses crowded close together. Reuben saw hills rising behind the simple homes, and beyond those hills was the mountain range that encircled much of the Sea of Galilee. The freshwater lake was at the bottom of a deep depression, the climate around the lake lush and hot.

Reuben saw Beth sitting before her house, her younger brother dozing on her lap. Benjamin had added his home onto the patriarchal dwelling when he had taken a wife for himself. Ebenezer, however, had preferred to rent a small house down the street. Now that he was older, Reuben suspected his father had been eager to get out from under the shadow of his successful elder brothers.

Reuben grinned when he saw Beth. She was small for fourteen, with thick, straight brows, a small chin, and expressive eyes. She was crafting a basket in the waning light. A cozy glow came from her open doorway, and he could see Tamar and little Hannah at work inside.

He felt his smile trying to split his face as he broke into a run and crossed the remaining distance, throwing himself down beside her, the house at his back.

"What are you doing here?" she asked in surprise. "Shouldn't you be getting the boat ready?"

Reuben looked back to the basalt gravel shore, to the triple pier where the local fishermen were loading nets into small boats. Reuben felt a twinge of guilt, but the boats could wait.

"I'll only stop a minute. I have to tell you about the best news!"

"Oh, I'll bet I can guess," Beth teased. "Did Ezra manage to scrounge up a new scroll for you to read? As if you haven't read every single one for miles around."

"Very funny, but no. It's far better than that." She looked at him with gratifying curiosity. Drawing a deep breath, Reuben's words tumbled, "Daniel the Scribe told me he's been impressed with my understanding and zeal for the law. For the past several months he's secretly been working on my behalf, writing letters to Jerusalem. Can you guess why?" He didn't wait for his amused cousin to respond before charging on. "He's been trying to find a place for me to study with one of the Jerusalem rabbis! Can you believe it?"

Her mouth fell open. "That's wonderful!"

"Today, a letter came from an esteemed rabbi." Beth's eyes widened with anticipation, and Reuben's grin broadened until his cheeks hurt. "Daniel's explained my situation—that I have no money

23

for fees, but a great desire for learning and study. He also told them that I have memorized the six hundred and thirteen laws laid out by the elders." He realized he was bragging and stammered, "N-not, not that I'm proud." The corner of Beth's mouth curved into a teasing smile, and she raised an eyebrow. "Anyhow," he pushed on, "the rabbi had written to say that I may join him as a disciple." Reuben searched Beth's face, hoping and believing that she would be pleased for him. She alone knew how much he longed for such an opportunity.

"Oh, Reuben! You've worked so hard. You truly deserve this."

Her words were exactly what he needed to hear. His eyes stung and he glanced back to the water's edge to collect himself. The familiar view was enough to stifle his joy. As he looked on the docked boats, he knew with a sinking feeling that not everyone would be pleased for his opportunity.

Beth hesitated before asking, "Is your father okay with this plan?"

Reuben snorted. "I haven't told him yet."

He wanted this happy moment first—before his father threw cold water over the whole idea of going to Jerusalem. The more years that slipped by, the more Ebenezer was obsessed with restoring his lost inheritance: the boat he had lost due to his own mismanagement.

Reuben picked up a rock and tossed it. "My mother will support me," he said. "And because I have the approval of a synagogue elder, Father will have to let me go. I think."

He felt a churning in his stomach. This opportunity was a blessing he had only dreamed of, yet it was going to cause no end of family strife.

Beth knew it too. She looked at him with sympathy. "Still. What about when you come home? You will come back, won't you?" Her voice hitched.

Reuben was warmed by her affection, and smiled at her, appreciating his gentle cousin more than ever. The rest of his family might be upset when they heard his news, but Beth would always be there for him.

"Of course I will. This is my home, after all. Maybe I'll be able to take over from Ezra when he is ready to retire." He pictured himself with a striped Pharisee's shawl over his shoulders, sitting in the new synagogue with rows of eager boys at his feet. He grinned and turned back to Beth. "After I'm done with my training in Jerusalem, I'll come back. Until I'm approved to be a teacher, I'll take up a trade."

"But not fishing." Beth tilted her head.

"Definitely not!" he cried out, then glanced around to see if anyone had overheard. In a lower tone, he stretched his arms wide and said, "Do I look like a fisherman, Beth?"

He was built nothing like his father, who was barrel-chested with thick, muscled shoulders made for casting nets. Reuben was stretched and narrow. He didn't look like a fisherman at all.

Beth chewed her lip, her large eyes cautious. "Perhaps not yet, but you're still young."

"We're fourteen, Beth. The paths for our lives will soon be set. I don't want to be trapped in a trade that I hate. Father has Zeb and Ben. Why can't he be satisfied with two fishermen sons?" He felt his ears burning with frustration.

"Perhaps he will be content with them," she soothed. "I think it's natural for a father to expect more from his firstborn. Perhaps with time ..."

"Time will change nothing." He lifted his chin. "But I can't let my father hold me back. I want to be a teacher of the law and a member of the Pharisees more than anything. Surely God will be pleased with my zeal and will help me, even if my father doesn't."

He looked back over the water. Most of the boats had already left the dock. His father would be furious, but just then he didn't care. Those boats would not be his fate.

A soft movement caught his eye. Beth was setting aside her basket. Gratefulness surged again. He was glad that he had her to share his dreams. She had filled the space a sister would have occupied in his heart. Beth was the one who looked up to him and always took his side.

A protective swell rose as he looked at her. It was only a year since Uncle Benjamin had died. The powerful man's abrupt end was a painful reminder that nothing was ever certain in this world.

Zebedee, as the eldest brother, had stepped in to care for his brother's widow and her three children. He hired men to fish with Benjamin's boat, keeping the craft to be passed on to little David someday. While Reuben's father, Ebenezer, was backward and simple, Uncle Zebedee had a nose for business. His sons, James and John, were brash but clever, and they promised to be as successful as their father.

With Zebedee's assistance, Tamar was able to feed her bereaved family. To help supplement their income, Beth and Tamar sent their weaving to the larger, urban market of Jerusalem where it was sold in cousin Simon's shop. They were able to get good prices for their Galilean linen.

Reuben knew Beth's face, manners, fears, and hopes as well as his own. He knew her shy ways, and that she did not have many friends among the other village girls. Hannah was six, hardly the age for a confidante. He felt his first worry at leaving. He knew Zebedee's honor would ensure Beth's physical needs were met, but would she have a friend?

"I'll miss you," he said, and she looked up with surprise.

She smiled, her expression sweet, as always. "I'll miss you too," she said, but then dropped her eyes and fussed over her brother's tunic, smoothing some folds. "I may have some news of my own." She was hesitant to speak, and Reuben tensed, though not sure why. She glanced up through her dark lashes and her voice was soft. "It's not final yet, but Mama told me that things will soon be set for my betrothal to Simon Peter ben Jonah."

Reuben stared, and for a long moment could say nothing at all. He was surprised to feel a tug of something like jealousy.

A married woman left her family home and went to that of her husband. Her duties would be to her husband and her home. Would she still have time to sit and talk like they were now? He doubted it. Beth was his best friend. Whenever he needed someone to talk to, she was there. When she was married nothing would be the same.

He frowned, shaking his head as he realized he should have read the signs. While he had been busy speaking with his teacher, Ezra, he had seen Peter and Tamar chatting after synagogue. Peter had kept staring at Beth while she blushed. With a twist in his gut, Reuben now understood why. Peter wanted to steal Beth away from her family and tie up her affection all for himself. Reuben felt a burst of anger. He knew he was being unreasonable, but he couldn't help it.

Looking over at his best friend, he saw her searching his face, anxious for his approval. His anger dissolved into shame. She had been so happy for him, even if he was going far away from her. She was selfless to the core. He had to be the same. He spoke around the ache in his throat, exerting himself to smile.

"Beth, that's wonderful," he forced the words from his tight throat.

"I'm glad you're happy," Beth said, but she gave him a small smile of understanding. Though she could not read letters, she read Reuben with ease. "You'll always be my best friend. You are as much my brother as David." She looked down at the little boy in her lap. After a long pause, she murmured, "It's kind of hard growing up, isn't it?" She glanced back up to his eyes. "But now, you get to fulfill your dream of going to study in Jerusalem. I'll get to live my dreams too, though they're smaller."

He realized they had never talked about Beth's dreams. Just his. He felt a twinge of conscience but pushed it aside.

Beth's affections were as constant as the rising sun. When he came home, she would be just the same: his best friend and most stalwart supporter. Nothing could change that.

He shook off his worries and grinned. "Has Peter convinced you to speak to him yet?"

The crease between Beth's brows smoothed as she laughed.

"We've spoken a few times. He seems kind. Peter brought his father from Bethsaida, and they had a meeting with Mama and Zebedee to discuss a betrothal. They have agreed on a bride price. Jonah will return in a few weeks time with the legal agreement."

Reuben was quiet for a long moment, unsure of what to say next.

"So-o-o-o," she asked, ducking her chin. "What do you think about Peter?"

Reuben drew to mind what he knew about Simon Peter. He knew Peter to be in his mid-twenties, a hardworking and smiling fellow, popular with many of the other fishermen.

"He lives with his brother, right?"

"Andrew. They moved here to avoid paying the extra taxes."

After the death of the old king, the land had been chopped up into territories. Ruling power was currently divided between two of King Herod's sons, Antipas and Philip, and the portion once held by a third son, cruel Archelaus, had been taken away and given to a Roman governor. The city of Bethsaida was now under a different ruler than the other fishing towns, and so the Bethsaidan fishermen had to pay taxes to bring their fish to the Magdala port where they would be salted and sold in barrels to be shipped far away, even as far as Rome itself. This frustrating tax had prompted many fishermen to move.

Beth was continuing, "Peter and Andrew have their own boat, a gift from their father."

Reuben was impressed despite himself. He knew all too well how costly they were.

"And will he take you back to Bethsaida, to his father's home?" He feigned mild curiosity, but his heart raced as he waited for her answer.

Beth shook her head, her eyes round at the idea. "No, thank the Lord."

Reuben hid a sigh of relief. Though he knew he was soon leaving, he didn't want to return and find her gone. As eager as he was to begin his schooling in Jerusalem, it was a comfortable feeling to know home would be just as he left it. Almost.

Beth continued, "Peter will keep his house here, and the bride-price is for him to take my mother, sister and brother under his roof as his own family. I won't have to leave my family, and Mama won't need to remarry."

Reuben lifted his brows in surprise. It was an incredible blessing to fall on the widow and her three children. Truly God's mercy was on them. He leaned forward.

"Your marriage will ensure happiness for you all," Reuben said.

Beth looked away, and he couldn't see her expression in the dusky light. Her voice was small as she said, "I'm nervous, I'm not embarrassed to tell you. But, I am pleased I can do this for Mama. She's suffered more than any of us since Papa died. I feel this is my duty, so I'm trying to be happy." She cuddled David a little closer, seeming to draw comfort from embracing him. "Mama has felt like an outsider since Papa died. Zebedee and Naomi are kind and generous, but she feels like a burden on them." Beth's voice hitched, and Reuben could tell how her grief had scarcely faded in the year since she lost her father. She lifted her face. "Peter is a good man, kind and hardworking. I think he will make a good husband."

"And you deserve no less," Reuben said, feeling a rush of peace about the whole thing.

He wouldn't have to worry about her being lonely. She would be well-cared for, and he was sure she would be loved. Who could know Beth and not love her? She would be married, and he would be trained as a Pharisee.

His earlier excitement returned in full force. He was heading toward three years of sitting at the feet of one of Jerusalem's finest rabbis. His heart warmed. He would become a wise and prestigious rabbi someday.

He lifted his chin with a jerk as the sun disappeared. He scrambled to his feet. His father would have sharp words for him, and Reuben shifted his weight, unwilling to meet his father's anger. He stalled. "Say, did you hear of that highwayman? Barabbas, I think? I overheard some of the men saying he and his followers have started attacking wealthy Jews and those who do business with Romans."

Beth's usually soft voice was sharp in the darkness, "Who is he to us? Whatever you do, or whoever you meet when you're gone, stay away from men like him. They preach national pride, but then murder, steal, and stir up people until Rome comes down and crushes not just them, but the innocent as well."

Reuben put up his hands and couldn't help but laugh at the dove scolding him like an angry magpie. "Whoa, calm down!"

David shifted in her lap, and Beth ran a gentle hand over his cheek to soothe him. "Sorry," she said in a quieter tone, though her voice was still thick with passion. "My own little experience with revolutionaries was enough for a lifetime. I would die if I had to see someone I loved on a cross." She looked up, and her large eyes implored him. "I mean it, Reuben. Stay away from anyone who even whispers the word 'revolution'."

"Of course I will." Reuben was solemn.

He fully understood her reluctance. He had never forgotten that first man he had seen nailed up to die. In the quiet moments before sleep, he had often wondered how long it had taken the man to find relief in death, and then how long it had been until the ravens had picked his bones clean. All that suffering for the sake of rebelling against the unjust Roman occupation.

He shook off the dark thoughts. "That's not how I plan to help bring our freedom. If we want God to restore our country to us, we need a return to purity. The Lord will bless us when we turn faithfully back to His laws."

Beth's tone was admiring as she said, "The Lord will use you for good. I'm sure of it."

Reuben stood a little taller, determined to be everything his cousin believed he could be, and more.

Hoping this would be one of the last times he set foot in a fishing vessel, Reuben took a few steps towards the lake where the rising moon was casting a ghostly light over the bobbing boats. He called back over his shoulder, "I think we'll both have full and interesting lives."

"With things as they are in the world, hopefully not too interesting." Beth's voice was little more than a whisper, and it hardly disturbed his pleasant dreams of the future.

4

LAMPS AND VOWS

"Are you sure I'm ready?" Beth whispered to her mother with a tremulous voice.

Tamar scanned her daughter and plucked a loose thread from her new dress, a long-sleeved, creamy white tunic that hung from neck to ankle. Beth brushed her hands over the soft fabric. She and her mother had woven it with a pattern of stripes along the sleeves and at the hem. They had no jewels, but over her waist-length hair and shoulders was a long, pale pink veil, which Beth would use to cover her face demurely before the groom arrived.

The groom! She was sick with nerves. Even after the long year of waiting, she didn't feel prepared to be a wife.

"Let me go through my marriage box again." Beth turned to the chest stuffed with items she had made for her marriage home.

She opened the lid but slammed it shut again, unable to focus or concentrate. She stared with longing around the little room. Their house was small, with the upper level for family and the lower level for the goat and four chickens. This room was where Beth had slept since girlhood, where she had helped her mother give birth to David, and where she had kissed her father goodbye. Today she would bid it farewell and never sleep here again. The thought made tears well up, so she turned back to the wooden chest for distraction.

Tamar laughed and caught her daughter's hands as she began to sift through her neatly packed marriage chest. "Peace, daughter. All is ready. Now all we need to do is wait for Peter to come for you."

Beth and Peter had been betrothed nearly a year ago, signing a contract that was as binding as a true marriage. For the next year, Beth had waited and prepared, but she didn't know when Peter would come and take her home as his wife. Always she was packed and ready to go, just in case.

Beth had kept her eyes and ears open, and in the past few days, she had seen Peter buying large vats of wine, and copious amounts of food. She had recognized the signs and knew the time was coming. For weeks Beth had gone to bed nervously wondering if the time had finally come. Tonight, when she was washing the supper dishes, Andrew had appeared outside the door.

"Be ready tonight!" he had hollered, and Beth had stared at her mother in shock for a full minute before she rushed to prepare herself.

Now she was ready, having ritually purified herself by washing in the mikveh at synagogue before dressing in her new clothing. She had ensured that her chest was ready. The groom would come at any time he pleased, and she had to wait for him to come for her. Beth nodded to her mother and took a deep breath to calm herself. She walked to the small window, lifted the curtain and looked out.

"It's dark now," her voice trembled.

Her seven-year-old sister Hannah was watching her in fascination, but little David's eyes drooped and his head bobbed.

Beth paced some more and then, unable to stop herself, went to the window and peeked out again.

"I see the lanterns!" she gasped.

A procession was coming down the street, heading towards her home. Someone blew the trumpet, and Beth felt a thrill race up her spine. Ten young girls with lanterns were waiting outside Beth's front door, and they held their oil lamps up to light the way for Peter as he came with Andrew, who was acting as the groomsman. Behind them was a gathering of wedding guests, each with lamps of their own. Beth backed from the window, her hands trembling. She pressed cold hands to her hot cheeks. Peter was coming for her.

She heard a soft knock on the door, and Beth sucked in her breath and stared at her mother.

"Go, my daughter," Tamar shooed her with her hands.

Giving up on taking deep breaths, Beth crept down the ladder, tip-toed to the door, and sucked in her lower lip as she pulled it open. She saw Peter. He reached out his large brown hand, and she saw her small one placed in his as her mother and his parents looked on with approval.

As the moon hung overhead, Peter escorted her across town. It felt like a strange dream. The night air was sweet and warm; it stirred her head covering. She heard laughter behind her, and happy voices, but the sounds strongest in her ear were the rustle of her new husband's clothes and the fall of his footsteps. He led her down the dim streets to his own home. It was a large house built with cut stones, designed in the modern style with a courtyard in the middle. Beth's new home was on the northern edge of town, with clear views of the Sea of Galilee out front and the hills in the back.

With the lamplight gleaming in his eyes, Peter went into his home first. She drew a wavering breath as he brought her under his roof. Beth's chest of belongings was carried in by two young men, and Andrew directed them upstairs. She felt her stomach lurch when she saw the lamps flickering against the walls on the upper level; she knew they were coming from the room Peter had prepared for her.

Peter's family gathered near him. Tamar, carrying sleepy David and with Hannah squirming by her side, came and stood by Beth. Her uncles Zebedee and Ebenezer stood nearby with their families, showing their support for the wedding. The guests filed in behind them, filling the large room, but Beth did not look at them; she felt a blush rising to the roots of her hair.

Peter spoke to Tamar. "Everything is as we have agreed. I've built rooms to hold my wife's family, taking them as my own."

Tamar nodded, her face radiant with maternal happiness.

Andrew, grinning, turned to the guests and called, "The bride price has been accepted. Peter will take his new wife to the bedchamber!"

The house filled with cheers and the usual jokes. Beth peeked upwards and saw that Peter was looking bashful too. It comforted her a little. Andrew escorted them up the newly-built stairs to the bedrooms. A window in the hallway looked down into the courtyard, and Beth glanced out. She saw the courtyard had been set up to host the wedding feast, a party that would continue for days.

Andrew led them to the open door of the lamp-lit room and waved them in with a flourish and a grin. Beth lifted her veil higher to cover her hot face.

Peter had draped a canopy over the room, creating a close and romantic bower. Beth's nose twitched at the smell of incense. The windows here were shuttered, and on a small table was wine, two cups, and fruit. The dominating feature was the low bed with a long bolster at the head and a striped brown blanket. Beth swallowed hard. Peter followed her into the room, and with a wink, Andrew shut them in and hollered to the crowd downstairs, who whooped and went into the courtyard to begin the wedding feast.

By morning, Beth was fully Peter's wife.

They joined the celebrations the next day as the happy husband and blushing wife. Beth and Peter sat at the head table, where Andrew made sure they were well supplied with food and drink while friends and neighbors brought them wedding gifts. Beth spoke with her mother-in-law and her new sisters for the first time, enduring their appraising looks and pointed questions until Peter rescued her. She breathed a prayer of thanks once that she would not be moving into her father-in-law's household as was traditional.

In a lull, Beth's mind traveled to Jerusalem. She wished Reuben could have attended her wedding. It had been a year since she had seen him last. She sighed. First Papa had died, then Reuben left. She felt a little left behind in Capernaum. Her mother had mischievous Hannah to care for, and quiet David to draw out from his shell. Beth was easy to overlook.

Her eyes sought out Peter. In the private corners of her mind, she hoped Peter could fill the empty places in her heart. She saw his easy smile and her heart fluttered. She believed she could love him.

The synagogue elders were invited to the wedding feast. Among the handful of elders were the dark-robed scribes, Daniel and Philemon, as well as the Pharisee teacher, Ezra. They were just presenting their gift of two flapping chickens when Beth noticed the unnatural silence that swept over the guests. She looked across the courtyard and saw a clean-shaven man in a short tunic, a little wooden box in his hands.

"It's Marcus!" a guest whispered.

Beth knew that Marcus was the semi-retired Roman centurion

who lived on the large estate south of Capernaum. He was charged with keeping an eye on the important trade-route and had several Roman soldiers under his command. His emperor had sought to reward him for service by giving him an estate, but Beth knew farmers who had lost their lands in the gifting.

The tension was strong among the guests as they wondered what they should do with this Gentile in their midst. The women averted their eyes and the men clenched their jaws. David, feeling the tension but not knowing what was the matter, left his playfellows and hid his face in his mother's dress. The synagogue elders alone smiled and nodded at Marcus, for he had won their favor. In a gesture of goodwill, he had given money for the new synagogue to be built, and they were wise enough not to forget it.

"Peter, why's he here?" Beth whispered.

Peter was silent, but put a hand on her shoulder as he rose to his feet. Marcus glanced around the room at the staring guests. Ignoring the thinly veiled hostility, he smiled and walked forward. Despite his easy expression, Beth could see the tension in his shoulders as he walked amid the silent people. She found she could pity him a little; surely he had wished his Emperor had granted him lands in his own country, with his own people.

"Peter and Beth," Marcus said, and Beth was startled that he knew her name. "I salute the newlyweds, and have brought you a gift."

Peter accepted it. He opened the pretty box and his eyes widened with surprise. He passed it to Beth, who looked inside and saw two silver bracelets.

"A generous gift," Peter said, his smile a little stiff.

The courtyard remained silent.

Marcus looked around himself and said to no one in particular, "I simply wish to honor the new couple."

"And we are honored," Andrew said, gliding forward.

He gestured for Marcus to come with him, and he supplied him with a cup of wine. Beth was happy to see a few of the elders went to speak with Marcus, and the rest of the guests began to relax and conversation resumed.

After the feast days were finished, the guests returned to their homes. Peter's family kissed him goodbye and returned to Bethsaida; his mother tearful at parting from her eldest son. Beth breathed a sigh of relief to see them go.

Tamar, Hannah, and David moved into one of the bedrooms in Peter's home, now a part of his family and under his protection.

Beth was pleased with the house and set straight to work making it a home. She and her mother found space upstairs for the loom, and in her mind, Beth was already planning her first weaving in her new home. On the lower level of the house was a clay oven to prepare meals in the rainy winter months. Beth placed her small grinding stone upon the roof beneath a canopy where the dust would not be bothersome. Downstairs, Peter and Andrew had taken down the walls for the old bedroom and created a large, open room—a cool place to rest and mend their nets after their hard days and nights on the water.

All the rooms in the house had windows that faced the courtyard, where they kept the chickens and the goat and strung the lines to dry the laundry. There was a second oven in the courtyard; they would cook outdoors during the summer so that the heat did not overwhelm the house. On the south side of the house was a little garden plot in which Beth and Tamar were eager to get planted with herbs, lentils, and greens.

Beth quickly stopped missing her childhood house as she fell in love with her new home.

Months passed, and Beth was satisfied and content.

Beth heard footfalls behind her as she stood in the courtyard taking down the washing. The afternoon sun was thrown against the stone walls, casting them in a warm hue.

Two large but gentle hands ran down her upper arms, sending a tingle through her. Her husband's hands slid down and around her waist, encircling her, drawing her close against him. He leaned forward, his breath near her ear.

"Are you pleased with your new home, sweet wife?" Peter whispered.

"I am, dear husband," she tilted her chin up, twisting her neck so she could see his face.

He wasn't particularly handsome, but the mingled warmth and vigor in his expression made her heart race. She felt a blush on her cheeks. A husband was a protector and provider for his family, and sometimes that was enough. Tender affection between a man and his wife was desirable, but often a marriage was little more than two people working for a common goal.

The Lord had seen fit to take her papa away, but he had not forgotten her. He had sent Peter to care for her, and love her in her father's stead. She had lost her best friend when God called Reuben to study in Jerusalem, but God had given her a new friend in Peter, one who was growing more dear to her heart every day.

Beth spun in Peter's arms, still holding one of his tunics. She hugged him with her face pressed into his chest. She felt him bow his head to kiss her hair. She was blessed, utterly blessed.

She whispered, "I will be happy to spend all my days here as your wife, raising our children and caring for our home."

He set a finger on her chin to kiss her lips, a kiss she responded to eagerly.

Andrew called out for him, and he returned to the house.

Beth hugged her husband's laundered tunic to herself, feeling joy washing over her. She breathed the scent of sunshine on the clean wool and felt peaceful and content, anticipating long years of quiet living with her husband and family.

5

NEWS OF A PROPHET

"It's not too late to change your mind, you know," Simeon said. "I thought you valued the strength of conviction." Reuben glanced upwards to his mounted rabbi, daring to tease a little.

Simeon raised an eyebrow. "Not when the convictions are wrong. Jerusalem is the place for you, not some rural fishing village."

Reuben ignored the slight against his hometown. Surely this northern area did look humble and common to a wealthy landowner who kept a house in Jerusalem. Simeon wanted to see the community Reuben was so eager to return to, and he was willing to leave his other students at home to do so. He seemed intent on using his powers to convince Reuben to return to Jerusalem and his patronage.

Simeon, seated on his sleek horse, looked down and said, "Your town must be larger than that crass village we just passed."

Reuben glanced back to Magdala, the bustling port city full of trade and business, one that housed both Jew and Gentile. Magdala was at the heart of commerce around the Sea of Galilee. Set near the shore, with many piers thrust into the water, and boasting a large covered market, the town Simeon was quick to disdain was situated on an important crossroads of Roman-built roads.

"I'm afraid not," Reuben said.

He began to feel uneasy at Simeon coming to see his humble birthplace. Thankfully, Simeon would be staying in the scribe Daniel's large home. The idea of hosting Simeon in his father's one-room house was mortifying.

Simeon sniffed but continued his appraisal without further comment.

Reuben was gratified that Simeon was willing to continue as his patron. As he neared his rural home, he began to feel a growing, uncomfortable doubt that he was being foolish to let the opportunity of a Jerusalem career slip out of his grasp. Homesickness had consumed him these last few months; three years was a long time to be away from home. Yet, now that home was so near, the yearning felt foolish.

"To be honest," Reuben said, clearing his throat. "I've been rethinking my original plan to stay in Capernaum."

"Ah ha!" Simeon's expression was triumphant. "You could do great things in Jerusalem—with my guiding hand."

"You think too highly of me," Reuben deferred, though he warmed at Simeon's good opinion. Simeon was sparing with praise, and that made it all the more valuable.

Reuben looked ahead to where Capernaum was coming into view. How could he choose? If he went to live in Jerusalem with Simeon he might never return here again. But how could he stay in Capernaum wondering what his life might have been?

"May I spend some time back at home before I decide?" he asked Simeon, and his rabbi looked down from his horse with a thoughtful expression.

"It is hard to sever our first roots," he strung the words out as he tilted his head to the side. "I believe I understand your difficulty in committing to a career away from your family." He gave a small smile and his voice was brisk again. "Very well. Take a year. Return to your old life and see if it holds all that you require."

Reuben grinned and quickened his pace.

"Ah, you have returned at last! Peace be on you, Reuben." Daniel set his hands on Reuben's narrow shoulders and kissed his newly bearded cheeks. "Welcome home. You've been gone so long I thought you decided to stay in Jerusalem." He chuckled, and Reuben's smile felt lopsided as Simeon raised an eyebrow. "You find me a little more wrinkled since you left, eh?" Daniel joked, clapping a hand on Reuben's back with a laugh that ended in a wheeze.

Daniel did look like the past three years had been hard on him. His beard was thin and white, his hands had more spots, and the corners of his red eyes sagged, even as he smiled. Reuben, of course, did not point any of that out to his aging friend, one who had worked so hard to find Reuben a coveted place. Instead, Reuben turned and introduced Simeon.

"We've met before, many years ago of course," Simeon inclined his head.

"How long has it been? The years all swim together." Daniel laughed, setting one spotted hand on Simeon's shoulder, and taking Simeon's other hand with warmth.

Simeon stiffened under Daniel's grasp.

The country scribe continued, "Though I don't remember the exact year, I clearly remember the day I met the promising rabbi who was just opening his home to students. You made an impression on me, Simeon." He wagged a finger with a toothy smile. "That is why I wrote to you, on behalf of this one here."

He waved his hand at Reuben, his crinkled eyes beaming. As he took his hand from Simeon's shoulder, the Jerusalem rabbi's shawl slipped, just an inch.

Simeon frowned and rearranged his prayer shawl with its long fringe and tassels. Prayer shawls in the Temple services were common, with their blue threads woven through the tassels to remind one of his relationship to the one true God. A Pharisee, however, wore his shawl always, symbolizing his constant devotion. Simeon liked his striped shawl to be pristine, smooth, and level at all times.

Reuben had learned that everything Simeon did was methodical, and it showed in his upright posture, trimmed beard, and tidy attire. The single mar on his proper appearance was a puckered, pale scar that crossed his broad forehead. Reuben had never worked up the courage to ask its history.

Reuben looked between these two different men that had helped lead him on his path—clever, modern and ambitious Simeon against the rural, warm and joking Daniel.

"Well, we're glad to have Reuben back. We'll need a teacher for our children, in a few years perhaps, and learned men to shepherd our community. I'm happy you decided to return home." Daniel patted Reuben on the back, and Reuben's smile stiffened.

Daniel led the men from the courtyard into a side room, and they removed their sandals and washed carefully in the pharisaic way before seating themselves around the low table. Reuben sighed in relief as he wiggled his weary toes.

Daniel's widowed sister, Leah, lived with him, and she brought the men a platter of bread. Daniel blessed the loaves, and they all took a bite. Leah returned with a pot of stew. Already on the table was a dish of olive oil and another of vinegar, a bowl of fresh curds, and some figs. She then left the room to let the men talk.

Reuben tore a piece of bread and dipped it into the pot of lentil stew. It was seasoned and cooked to perfection, with chunks of tender lamb. Eating meat regularly was only for the wealthy, and Reuben had enjoyed his share in the upper-class home of his rabbi.

"How are things in your quiet, little town?" Simeon's tone was cool as he also took a bite of food.

"Well, you've come at an interesting time," Daniel said. Simeon's eyebrows shifted a hair in disbelief that anything interesting could happen in Capernaum. "There's a new prophet, and several of the local men have gone to hear him speak. It has the town in quite a stir."

Reuben's ears perked up, and he had to clamp his jaw to keep quiet. Simeon preferred his students to be silent until invited to join the conversation.

"People are always eager for news of a prophet," Simeon scoffed.

Daniel raised his bushy brows. "This one though, they're calling him Elijah."

Reuben's lips twitched. This had to be the prophet he had heard of. He had appeared not long ago in the wilderness, and his fame was spreading. The Jewish people believed that the famous and powerful prophet of old, Elijah, would return to them someday, preparing the way for the chosen Messiah. If this prophet was real, he was the herald of a new era for the people of Israel.

Despite Reuben's best efforts to look collected, Daniel noticed Reuben's expression and smiled with understanding as he said, "He speaks often of a kingdom of heaven. He preaches repentance, which is admirable. On top of this, he rejects common clothing and instead wears animal skins. He eats what he can scavenge in the wilderness, mostly locusts and honey, I hear."

"Oh, I know of whom you speak," Simeon said with an airy wave of his long fingers. "This is the man who performs ritual cleansing in the river, correct?"

"Yes, it is." Daniel looked up with a surprised smile, seeming pleased Simeon was already appraised of the new prophet. "Word has reached Jerusalem then. I shouldn't be surprised." He chuckled. "Many people in this area are going out to see the prophet in the wilderness, and be immersed by him in the river."

Ritual cleansing in a mikveh, a divided, deep stone bath where the water was always circulating, was common these days, a way for the people to purify themselves. A man or woman would go into the water, speak the blessing, and submerge themselves completely. It was not to cleanse the body but reflected an inner desire for purity. A mikveh immersion was done at special times in a person's life. The mass baptisms of this "Elijah" in the river Jordan had caught the attention of the religious leaders.

"Have any of our Jerusalem brethren gone out to hear him speak?" Daniel asked.

Simeon replied, "As I was preparing to leave Jerusalem, they were selecting some of our party to journey and see him. If they find his message satisfactory, they will be baptized in the river as an example for the common people."

Daniel raised a brow. "What do you believe?"

Simeon smirked. "Every couple of years a new revolutionary rises up, crying out for a restored Israel. The man may have the gift of prophecy, or he may just be another desperate fool trying to be something he is not, to accomplish something he can not. To the downfall of many. It has been four hundred years since a true prophet walked the earth. I tend not to accept every zealous orator who camps out in the desert."

Simeon's doubt cast a shadow on Reuben's youthful hope. Too many rebellions had failed. What they needed was the promised Messiah, a true, Jewish king to lead them. Simeon was the wisest man he knew. If Simeon was right in his doubts, and this prophet was false, Reuben didn't want the people to take up weapons and break the delicate peace.

Daniel's beard twitched and his eyes were troubled. "Yes, yes. A true prophet would be a gift. A false prophet, only a curse."

Daniel finished his meal in contemplative silence, and Simeon and Reuben did not disturb his reflection. At the meal's end, the old man leaned away from the table and said, "Perhaps we should go as well. We could meet our brethren from Jerusalem and hear what this prophet has to say for ourselves. Then we'll know if we should denounce or embrace his words. What do you say, Reuben?"

Reuben's heart lifted, and his weary muscles were forgotten. "I say yes!" he cried out.

Simeon's eyebrows shot up towards his scar, and Reuben shrunk in his seat, berating himself. With as much dignity as he could muster, he tried again, slower.

"It's always good to witness with our eyes, instead of trusting the opinions of others."

Daniel smiled behind his hand, and Simeon said dryly, "Wise words, indeed." He looked at Daniel. "You will need to leave tomorrow if you want to be there at the same time as our brethren." He paused a moment. "I will go with you. It will take me near to Jerusalem once more." He nodded, then as an afterthought he added, "If that is not displeasing to you, of course."

Daniel clapped his hand on Simeon's shoulder again in his familiar way and chuckled, "Why should I object?"

Simeon's lips thinned, and he stiffened away from the more open man. Reuben felt embarrassed. As a child, he had always thought of Daniel as so wise and polished. Now the man seemed rural and ... common.

Daniel continued, "Very well. We'll leave first thing in the morning. Simeon, you are my guest of course, but I think we should invite Reuben to stay here too, so we can get an early start."

Simeon agreed and Daniel closed the meal with a thanksgiving prayer.

Reuben rose to his feet and spoke to his elders, "If it's all right with you, I think I'll go and see my family."

"Ah yes," Daniel said, but then he creased his already lined forehead further. "Have you made peace with your father?" Simeon raised his brows, and Daniel explained in an unnecessary whisper. "There is little support from his father for Reuben's chosen path."

Reuben suppressed a snort. Outright animosity would be a better choice of words.

"No, I haven't," Reuben admitted.

His father had not replied to a single letter nor sought him out in Jerusalem during the festivals.

Daniel pursed his lips and peered hard at Simeon. His eyes flickered as he sifted through decades of memories. "If I remember correctly, you had your share of difficulties as you began your career. Your father wanted you to be as he was, a Sadducee. I remember there was quite the uproar."

Simeon's face reddened as he gritted his teeth. Reuben looked to his rabbi with surprise, but Simeon turned his face away. Reuben flushed with embarrassment at Daniel. The scribe should be less familiar with a rabbi of Simeon's caliber. Still, he couldn't help feeling grateful to Daniel for unearthing this bud of comfort. It was nice knowing that he and Simeon had this in common. If Simeon had been able to rise above his father's displeasure, surely he could too.

Daniel, oblivious to Simeon's suppressed anger, turned his wrinkled eyes on Reuben.

"I had feared things might still be tense," Daniel said. "When I heard you were returning home, I took the liberty of making arrangements for you in regards to a trade. I believe you have no inclination for fishing?"

Reuben shook his head vehemently.

"Well then," Daniel said, clapping his gnarled hands together and rubbing them with satisfaction. "I have passed my scribal business onto Philemon. Unsteady hands you see. No, no, it's just a part of life, isn't it? Anyway, Philemon needs an apprentice, and you need a trade. It won't pay much, but you'll get room and board."

Reuben's throat thickened with gratitude, and he stammered out his heartfelt thanks, which Daniel waved aside with pleasure.

"Cheer up, young man. Some of your family will be happy to see you. Beth asks for news of you every week."

"Beth?" Simeon asked, swiveling his head to bore his student with his piercing dark eyes.

Reuben knew at once that Simeon was worried about an attachment tying his pupil to Capernaum. Reuben was quick to reassure him.

"Beth is my cousin. She married a local fisherman nearly two years ago." He had received the news in a letter from Zebedee. He had been neck-deep in his studies but had taken the time to write a letter of congratulations to his cousin. He thought it must have given her pleasure to receive a letter of her own, even if someone else had to read it to her.

"Oh," Simeon said, his expression smoothing. He began to rise. "I shall come with you."

"No!" Reuben cried out, horror flooding him. Simeon frowned and Reuben fumbled for a reasonable explanation. "My father never replied to my letter. He might not be expecting me."

It was a feeble excuse, and Reuben was sure Simeon saw right through it. However, the rabbi sat back down.

"Very well," Simeon acquiesced. He eyed Daniel with a subtle, resigned sigh.

Reuben was hesitant to leave Simeon and Daniel alone together. It was clear the men were not destined for friendship. Still, it was better to risk coming back to a sour rabbi than to live with the embarrassment of Simeon seeing his humble home and his uncultured parents.

The hour was growing late as Reuben left Daniel's large and comfortable home. As he strode through Capernaum, he walked with his chin high. He smiled at people he knew as they called out greetings to the clever boy who had returned a scholar.

It was nice to be welcomed back, yet as he turned the corner on a narrow side road and saw his childhood home, his shoulders drooped. With a dissatisfied sigh, he looked on a little stone and mortar building crammed in between two other equally plain houses. It was smaller than he remembered, humble in every way. Thank goodness Simeon was not here to see it.

The front door, like all the doors in town, was open this time of day. Drawing a bracing breath for courage, he ducked under the low doorway and stammered out a greeting. He looked up and saw his mother's joyful face beaming down at him.

"Reuben!" she gasped.

He climbed the ladder, and she rushed forward to throw her arms around him. Reuben breathed deep her familiar scent of cook fires and bread, and his chest warmed with a feeling of home. She stepped back and looked him up and down, dashing happy tears from her cheeks. Reuben swallowed and cautiously glanced around the room at the rest of his family.

His father was sitting cross-legged on the floor. He did not rise.

Zeb and Ben came forward with an easy confidence to see their long-absent brother. At the sight of their smiles, Reuben relaxed.

"My word, what is Mama feeding you?" Reuben exclaimed, clapping a hand on their shoulders.

Both of his younger brothers were now a little taller than him, and they looked more like young men than the boys he had left behind.

Reuben chuckled. "Zeb, you look ready for your first beard."

Zeb grinned and rubbed the sparse stubble with pleasure. Both of his brothers were darkly browned with calloused hands. Under his grip, Reuben could feel corded muscles forming across their shoulders from long days and nights casting nets.

Reuben gathered his resolve as he turned from his smiling mother and brothers. He sat across from his father. Reuben tried to talk, but his father was distant and coolly polite—as if his son were a stranger.

It mortified Reuben, choking off his words.

"Have you eaten?" his mother asked, fluttering around him.

"Yes, don't worry." Reuben smiled at her.

Ben sat near his father. "Are you home to stay, or going back to Jerusalem?"

"I am here for a while, anyway," Reuben said, looking at his father's averted face, feeling the choice between Capernaum and Jerusalem was already tipping for the Holy City. "I won't be staying here though, Mama, so don't worry about that." He kept his eyes on his father as he continued, "I'm going to study under Philemon as a scribe, and I will live with him as his apprentice."

He hoped that for once his father could be happy for him.

Ebenezer's eyes flicked to meet his son's gaze, and his blank expression became scornful. "So you've once more decided all on your own, have you? No need to ask your father's blessing? I see you haven't changed."

Heat crept up Reuben's neck. Maybe he should have asked his father first, but what good would it have done? It sure hadn't helped the last time.

His voice was cool. "I see you haven't changed either." His father snorted and looked away.

This was going nowhere. Reuben stiffly said his goodbyes and rose to his feet.

"Will you come and share Sabbath with us this week?" his mother cried out as Reuben strode stiffly for the door.

Her eyes were longing, and her hand reached out for him. Reuben glanced at his stony father. Ebenezer would not meet his eyes. Ben and Zeb shifted uncomfortably.

"Perhaps." Reuben shrugged. He had no desire to spend an entire day under his father's roof, but he was sorry he was hurting his mother.

He left the house, and under a low, red sun, he strode away. He had known better than to expect a warm homecoming, but it still hurt to feel like a stranger in his own family. He swallowed several times, feeling as if something sharp was stuck in his throat. Could he live in Capernaum when his father treated him like this?

Reuben left the narrow street and passed the tax booth. His lip curled. The tax dollars were collected by his countrymen but sent on to Herod Antipas, who used Jewish money as tribute to the Roman Emperor—the real power behind the ruler.

As it was late in the day, the men in the booth were closing up shop. Reuben would have passed by, but his casual glance at the tax collectors made him stop in his tracks.

"Matthew?" Reuben gasped.

A young man in the booth looked up, and Reuben saw that it was indeed his old friend and classmate from his youth. His brain told him he should walk on by. Speaking to a tax collector was likened to speaking to a harlot, but his heart and feet pulled him to the booth almost of their own will.

"Reuben!" Matthew exclaimed. "You're back."

He extradited himself from the booth. His partner, a handsome and polished man several years older than Matthew, smirked like he was enjoying a joke.

Reuben held out his hands. "Matthew, what are you doing?"

Matthew rubbed the back of his neck. Reuben noticed that he was wearing fine clothes and had a large seal ring on the hand that rested on his waist. Reuben's shock melted into disgust. Matthew was clearly enjoying the spoils from over-taxation already.

Matthew answered with his eyes averted, "Working."

Reuben scoffed. "Stealing, you mean. What happened? I never would have thought someone like you would be tempted by wealth."

As boys, they had both loved to study and learn, and young Matthew had seldom been without a borrowed scroll.

Matthew drew a deep breath. "Not all of us were fortunate enough to be plucked out of a fishing boat and land in the house of a patron."

Reuben fumbled for a suitable retort, but Matthew continued with his eyes cast to the ground. "My father was sick. I couldn't afford the medicines and the physician's bills. I was unable to leave him and go out to fish, so we had no money to pay the taxes. We were about to lose our house when Aaron took pity on me and suggested my name to Marcus, who let me have this job. I was able to hire a servant to care for my father properly until he passed away."

Reuben felt a sliver of pity for Matthew's difficult circumstances, but the idea of working for the oppressors and taking hard-earned coins from his own people to give to foreigners overwhelmed all other emotions.

"But why continue after your father's death?"

Matthew raised his hand, palm up, and then let it fall.

He sighed. "And do what, Reuben? Tell me, what should I do? If I took a boat and returned to fishing, would any of the other men work with me? Should I toil alone, scrape together a few coins, barely have enough to eat, with only rags to wear? I'm a leper to the people in Capernaum. They'll never forget. This is who I am now." His voice was fatalistic.

Reuben thought him a coward, and he raised his chin. "Better to scrape by an honest man than to live in luxury as a crook."

"Yeah?" Matthew clenched his fists at his side, his face darkening. "Easy for you to say. Everything you needed the past three years has been handed to you: that fine linen robe, the shawl around your neck, those sandals on your feet, the food in your belly, even the knowledge in your head. You've been spoiled, Reuben, and forget what it's like to work all day just to put bread on the table."

Reuben drew up to his full height. "If you continue this life, I can't be your friend. If you can admit your sins, I'm sure the synagogue will forgive you and welcome you back."

"Welcome me?" Matthew threw back his head and laughed mirthlessly. "Not until they had publicly whipped me and made me pay heavy fines. Even then, they'd never forget."

Aaron came out of the booth and put his hand on Matthew's shoulder, "Matthew is not without friends. He doesn't need you. In this modern world, money goes further than honor."

Matthew raised his chin, but his eyes were uncertain. His Jewish longing for righteous honor was still strong in him, despite his new career. Matthew's mouth twitched, and his expression was closed.

"Goodbye, Reuben. I hope your rich rabbi gives you all that you desire."

Reuben spun on his heel and marched away, refusing to look back over his shoulder. He seethed with frustration that his friend could be so stubborn. First his father's coldness, and now Matthew's fall to shame—this homecoming was not going as he expected. Reuben sighed and tried to calm himself as he approached Peter's house.

The front door was still open, and Reuben went forward and called out a greeting. Peter came forward. Reuben could see that Peter didn't recognize him. Had he changed so much?

Reuben smiled. "Don't you know me? It's Reuben ben Ebenezer."

"Reuben?" Peter squinted his eyes, then widened them and beamed. "It is you! You've grown! You look like a true Pharisee now. Come in, come in."

Peter stepped back as Reuben touched the mezuzah on the doorpost and entered.

The main room was spacious, with woven rugs and matting spread over the dark stone floor. This appeared to be their family living space. He saw a low table with cushions, a shelf with clay pitchers, jugs and serving dishes, and a basin for washing up. In the corner was a fishing net spread out for repair. The air was fragrant with hearty spices, and the walls danced with lamplight.

He saw Beth rising to her feet from the table, letting the mending in her hand tumble to the wooden surface.

"Reuben, is that truly you?" she gasped. She hurried to him and took one of his hands with both of her own. "He's finally home!" she said with a laugh to Peter.

Reuben set his other hand over both of hers, feeling his stress slipping away. His emotions were soothed by her pleasure in seeing him. He glanced her over.

She had not gained in height, coming just to her husband's shoulder, but her hair was thick and smooth, her fresh face had matured some, and her cheeks had color. Peter was taking good care of her. He glanced at her middle but saw no sign of pregnancy.

"Did I hear Reuben is here?" Tamar's voice came from upstairs, and soon he saw her familiar, soft figure. She hurried forward and hugged him.

Hannah charged forward with a bold, "Hello!"

David shyly came up behind his sister, keeping Hannah between him and Reuben. David reminded Reuben of Beth at that age.

Reuben glanced around once more, but there was no evidence of a baby in the house. It seemed Beth and Peter had not been blessed with a child of their own yet. For some reason, that pleased him. He was glad that not everything had changed, at least not yet. He put that thought aside and greeted his younger cousins.

Tamar gestured to the cushions around the table. "Come, tell us all about your time in Jerusalem."

They seated themselves and Beth brought watered wine and pottery cups. They all beamed at him, and Reuben felt his heart warm from being welcomed by the pleasant family circle.

He told them of Simeon and his fellow students, and some of the things he and seen and done in Jerusalem. They were perfect listeners, attentive and curious.

"I haven't been back a day, but we're heading out in the morning. At dawn we journey to see the prophet, the one the people are calling Elijah."

"Really?" Beth glanced at her husband with an affection that pricked Reuben with sudden jealousy. "Peter and Andrew went out to see him as well, and they were baptized by him in the river. Andrew stayed behind with our cousin, John, to hear more of what the prophet has to say."

"Did he?" Reuben's curiosity overrode his other emotions, and he let loose a flood of questions.

Peter held up his hands to stem the assault with a chuckle. "We were impressed with him, and his message. I think if you're going in the morning you'll enjoy seeing and hearing it firsthand. It would be better than I could tell, I'm sure."

Reuben nodded, seeing Peter's wisdom.

They talked until late. Peter even postponed going down to his boat so he could stay for this welcome home visit. Reuben was flattered. Ebenezer would never have done such a thing for a guest. Reuben began to think he might grow to like Peter.

When Reuben left to return to Daniel's house, he tipped his face to the stars and thanked the Lord for good friends. The scales between Jerusalem and Capernaum were wavering again.

As the sun rose the next morning, Daniel's household gathered and prayed the Shema.

Reuben did not regret his enjoyable late night, but his head was sluggish from lack of sleep. He ended the prayer with a huge yawn, and his face heated as Simeon frowned at him. Once they were outside, the dewy morning air soon revived him.

They retraced the steps that Simeon and he had covered just the day before. Daniel was on a donkey due to his age, slumped like a sack of grain. Wealthy Simeon rode his horse with back straight and chin high, and Reuben's youthful stride took the miles on foot.

Daniel noticed the birds, unusual shaped clouds, and spoke of simple, common things with pleasure. Reuben enjoyed conversing with his old friend but noticed Simeon was looking away, clearly bored. Simeon's mood dampened Reuben's enjoyment, and he grew quieter.

The new prophet was preaching in the Jordan wilderness. Born from a trio of rivers, the Jordan River poured down from the mountains, spilled into the Sea of Galilee and funneled back out to snake through the land into the Dead Sea. Long ago it had been this river that Joshua had crossed to bring the people into the Promised Land. When the priests carrying the Ark of the Covenant had touched the rushing river, God had held back the water so His people could cross on dry land.

The place this new prophet had chosen was along an unpopulated section of the river, about a day's walk from Jerusalem. It was almost a two-day journey from Capernaum, and so the men had to overnight at an inn.

As they neared the Jordan River the next day, it was impossible to become lost. A steady stream of people traveled to and fro on a new path through the coarse, low brush. The common folk gave the trio of Pharisees deferential nods. Reuben felt proud to be a part of a well-known and respected party.

"I think we've found the place," Reuben said as they began to pick their way down the gradual slope, the rocky soil crunching beneath his sandals.

Trees grew up along the life-giving river, some stretching their limbs out to trail their leaves in the swirling coolness. Reuben surveyed the crowd clustered around the bank ahead, craning his neck for his first view of the new prophet. A man was standing in the rushing river, plunging a woman beneath the surface. Reuben's heart gave a heavy beat as he realized this was the baptizing prophet everyone had been talking about.

Simeon pointed. "We timed our journey well. I see our brethren."

Though Reuben was eager to push forward to see the prophet up close, he dutifully stayed on Simeon's heels. They picked their way around the water's edge and joined the small group of Pharisee teachers and lawyers standing apart from the crowd. With what felt to Reuben like agonizing lethargy, they exchanged pleasantries while standing in the shade.

A little ways away, Reuben's quick gaze noted a group of Sadducees, the rival party who held the power over the Temple Courts. Their party was the cream of Jerusalem, the wealthy elite. It was from them that the High Priest had been chosen.

He noticed a few of the Sadducees eyeing Simeon and wondered if they were still bitter from the rabbi's defection to a rival party. Though it was all years in the past, tradition ran deep.

The polished Sadducees and Pharisees were in stark contrast to a rugged group of sun-darkened men that stood near the shore in simple, dusty garb. Many had the same wild hair and unkempt beards as the prophet in the river. They must be his disciples, Reuben decided. He could see his cousin, John, among the young men. What did Uncle Zebedee think of this?

A voice cut through Reuben's musings.

"Simeon!" Nicodemus' tone was surprised. "I thought you were off to Capernaum. You seem to have gotten lost." He chuckled, and Simeon gave a ghost of a smile in return.

Nicodemus was one of the few Pharisees chosen by the chief priests to sit on the Jerusalem Sanhedrin, a group of prestigious and learned men who oversaw the people and judged cases brought to them. Reuben had often thought that Simeon was either jealous or thought himself superior to Nicodemus. Perhaps, he wondered as he looked on them now, Simeon was both.

"I see your favorite student." Nicodemus winked at Reuben. "But I don't see the rest of your usual disciples."

"I have left them in Jerusalem," Simeon said with a shrug. "If a man loses a sheep, doesn't he leave his flock and go after it?" He looked at Reuben pointedly.

Reuben dropped his eyes, trying to suppress a smile. Simeon had often held up Reuben's keen questioning, unparalleled memory, and dedication to his studies as an example to the other young men under the rabbi's care. While Reuben did not enjoy the narrowed eyes from his fellow students, it had been wonderful to have his talents noticed by one so hard to please.

Daniel, observing this exchange closely with an expression that made Reuben flush, waved a knobby hand towards the river. "Well, shall we?"

Reuben went forward with the others. He truly hoped this was Elijah returned. It would be amazing to live in the days of a true prophet.

As the Pharisees moved towards the water, the Sadducees noticed and elbowed their way ahead. Reuben suppressed a smirk. The common people stepped aside as the Pharisees and Sadducees pushed their way to the front.

The prophet was speaking to a middle-aged man wearing his sleeveless inner tunic, both men up to their waists in the river. His voice was sharp and clear and carried well over the crowd.

"Repent!" the prophet commanded. "The kingdom of heaven is near."

He took the man by the shoulders and plunged him under the water. With his thin brown arms, he heaved the man back up to his feet. The man struggled to get his balance, and the prophet braced him until he steadied, then clapped him on the back. He turned his wild, bearded face toward the crowd. Reuben felt a quiver of eagerness rush through him as he waited for the prophet to speak.

The prophet's keen eyes blazed as his gaze encompassed the Pharisees and the Sadducees who had arrayed themselves at the front of the crowd.

"You brood of vipers!" His words cracked like a whip, and Reuben flinched. "Who warned you to flee from the wrath to come?"

Reuben felt the crowd's eyes boring into his back, and was shocked at this greeting. What had they done to this wild man? The prophet wasn't finished with them yet.

His wiry, taut arm was pointed at them as he cried out, "Bear fruit in keeping with repentance! Don't think you can hide behind the family tree of Abraham." He bent and plucked a stone from the bottom of the river and held it outstretched towards them. "From these stones, God is able to raise up children to Abraham. Judgment time has come, and the ax is falling! Every tree that does not bear good fruit is struck down and cast into the fire."

He threw the stone near the water's edge, and droplets were sprinkled over those closest to the shore.

"I plunge these faithful into mere water," the prophet spoke. "Another is coming after me, who is mightier than me. He will baptize you with the Holy Spirit and with fire!" Spittle flew from his lips as he raged, and Reuben drew a step back. The prophet roared, "He is coming to sift the wheat from the chaff. The wheat he will gather into his barn, but the chaff he will burn up with fire!"

It was clear from his angry gaze that the prophet considered the Pharisees and Sadducees before him as the chaff, useless husks that were beaten from the grain and lost to the wind as the winnower sifted his grain. Reuben's face flushed with anger.

The religious teachers turned as one from the prophet, their faces stony. They refused to answer the wild man, deeming his challenge unworthy of a response.

Reuben's eyes flicked to Simeon. His rabbi's lips were pressed together and his eyebrows were low over his dark eyes. Simeon pushed his way back through the people to where he had tethered his horse. Reuben hastened to catch up. As he passed Nicodemus, he saw with surprise the man was not angry, but deeply thoughtful as he gazed on the fiery prophet.

The Sadducees gathered themselves into a little whispering knot, but the Pharisees took to the path, buzzing like angry bees. Reuben helped Daniel get settled on the donkey and then shouldered his bag and waterskin.

Reuben's mind was full as he joined the long line of Pharisees ascending the slope to the road. He was indignant at the brash way the prophet had brushed off the religious leaders. Yet, despite his anger, he was frustrated that he hadn't been able to hear more of what the wild man was teaching. All this walking for one caustic speech!

Disappointment filled him. Surely a man who had so little regard for the law-abiding Pharisees was not the prophet they were waiting for. Reuben would have to wait for the true Elijah.

With a dejected sigh, Reuben paused and looked back. The wild man was talking to a man on the shore, holding his hands up in refusal. A breeze carried the words up to Reuben.

"I need your cleansing, and yet you come to me?" The fiery man's voice was incredulous.

The other man, whose face Reuben could not clearly see, replied, "Allow it this time, for it is fitting to fulfill all righteousness."

The baptizer relented, and the other man waded in and was doused in the Jordan River. As he was brought dripping to his feet, Reuben heard a rumble, low like thunder, and was startled when a curious light fluttered from the sky and lit upon the second man. The baptizer stared in awe up at the heavens.

Reuben turned and hastened to catch his group, muttering to himself, "What a strange reflection from the water."

6

FOLLOW SOMEONE ELSE

"The prophet's been arrested!" Andrew cried out as he charged into the house.

Beth jumped in alarm at the outburst, dropping her bowl. The pottery shattered, and leafy herbs tumbled across the stone floor.

Peter rose from the stool by his nets, looking concerned as he went to the brother he had not seen for several weeks. Andrew's clothing was dirty, his hair disheveled, and Beth thought he looked thinner than before. Beth glanced down at the mess by her feet and sighed. She grabbed her broom and began to sweep up the sharp shards of pottery. Tamar came in from the courtyard to see what was going on.

"Are you all right?" Peter asked, setting a hand on his brother's shoulder. Andrew nodded, but his expression was heavy.

"I am, though I hate to think about how he must be suffering." Andrew rubbed his dusty face with both hands, looking worn.

He glanced up with a small smile for Hannah and David as they came near him, both of them wearing matching, worried expressions.

"But what happened?" Peter glanced at the children and lowered his tone. "Was it the Romans?"

Beth gathered up the greens into a new dish with trembling fingers, straining her ears.

Andrew shook his head. "Herod Antipas' men came and threw him into prison."

Beth set the new bowl down on the table. The soft thud was the only sound in the room. She didn't bother to hide her sad sigh, and Tamar murmured a prayer. In her short eighteen years on this earth, Beth had learned that arrest usually meant torture, and often death. Everyone was silent, digesting the bad news.

Tamar was the first to revive. She hurried back out to the courtyard to check on the meal. Andrew went to wash his hands and face, pouring water from the tall water jug into a basin. Peter and the children seated themselves around the table. Beth stood alone, rooted to the spot. Did this arrest mean the prophet John was not the Elijah after all?

Peter drummed his fingers on the tabletop, then slapped his palm on the wood in frustration, making Beth jump again.

"But why did Herod Antipas arrest him?" Peter asked. "Was he threatened that a desert prophet might rise up and take his throne?"

Andrew dried his hands on a coarse strip of cloth. "Nothing so grand as that. It was because John was brave enough to do what those in power won't. John told him that it is unlawful for him to have Herodias as his wife." He tossed the towel back down and knelt at the table.

Tamar brought the clay pot. The fragrant spices didn't tempt Beth's appetite as usual. She sat in her usual spot and bowed her head for the blessing. Afterward, everyone sat and looked at each other. No one reached for the food.

Hannah's brow puckered as she tried to understand. "Why can't Herod Antipas have Herodias for a wife? What's wrong with her?"

Peter glanced at Tamar, leaving it to her to decide how much to reveal to the innocent young girl. Hannah was ten-years-old and as inquisitive as ever.

Tamar passed around the platter of bread, giving her youngest daughter a measuring glance. "Herodias was the wife of Herod Antipas' brother, and that brother is still alive."

"Oh." Hannah's eyebrows shot up, and she looked at Beth, her mouth and eyes matching circles.

Beth couldn't help but smile at her sister's ridiculous expression, but her amusement was fleeting as other emotions pushed their way forward. Her stomach soured as she thought of their corrupt ruler.

The tetrarch of Galilee might have a few drops of Jewish blood in him, but it did not seem enough to curb his selfish, worldly desires.

Peter huffed through his nose, shaking his head. Beth saw his frustrated emotions and felt for him. Andrew saw too.

"A prophet must speak the truth, no matter what," Andrew said to Peter, his tone a little defensive.

Peter bobbed his head, his mouth grim. "I know. I'm just sorry the man was arrested. I had thought ... I had hoped ..."

"I know." Andrew craned his head and rubbed the back of his neck.

"So what will happen to the prophet?" David asked, eyes wide and fearful. "Will he be crucified?"

Beth's stomach lurched.

Andrew reached over and put a hand on the boy's shoulder. "I doubt it. Word has it, if John recants, Herod Antipas will let him go. Apparently, he believes John is a true prophet. He's likely too afraid to kill him."

"Besides," Hannah said with a shrug, sticking a bit of bread in her mouth and licking her fingers noisily. "Jews don't crucify people like the Romans. We stone criminals to death."

"Hannah!" Beth exclaimed as David's eyes grew wide.

Neither child had ever beheld a man upon a cross, and Beth hoped that it would stay that way.

Tamar frowned at her careless younger daughter. "That is hardly helpful."

Peter sighed, still talking to Andrew. "From what I saw of the prophet, he's the type to stand his ground. It isn't likely he'll be freed."

Andrew nodded, but admiration washed over his face. His tone was proud as he said, "I agree."

Natural hunger asserted itself, and the mood shifted. Andrew began to sniff the spiced stew and his expression relaxed. He ripped a barley loaf in two, taking a large bite. The others began to dip their bread into the savory stew as well.

Andrew looked at his brother. "No matter what happens, I'm proud to say I heard the prophet speak with my own ears, and I was baptized in the Jordan by his hand."

"What will happen to his followers?" Beth asked, thinking with pity of the many men who had thought John was the herald of the coming Messiah. "Did they try to arrest you as well?"

"The soldiers beat a few of the young men who tried to stop the arrest, but John told us not to fight them." Andrew stared at the bread in his hand and pondered aloud, "In fact, it felt like he wanted us to stop following him."

Peter looked baffled. "What?"

Andrew nodded at his brother. "He told us to follow someone else."

Five voices at once asked Andrew, "Who?"

"I don't know his name," Andrew admitted. "But I know he's a cousin of the prophet, a man John baptized in the Jordan a week or two ago." Everyone leaned towards Andrew as his voice became hushed. "It sounds crazy, but when John lifted the man from the water, a light came out of heaven and landed on him, gentle as a dove. The cloudless sky rumbled like thunder, and I swear I heard, 'This is My beloved son.'"

Beth felt a strange flutter in her chest. When the scriptures spoke of the coming Messiah, he was often spoken of as God's son, His anointed one.

Peter raised his eyebrows. "Are you sure?"

Andrew jabbed a thumb at the door. "Go ask John ben Zebedee if you don't believe your own brother. He was there with me."

Peter still looked skeptical. "If you really saw it, why didn't you run after the man?"

"I might have, but he left before we could comprehend what had happened. He just walked off into the wilderness and didn't come back." David stared with his mouth hanging open at this strange tale. Andrew reached over and tousled the boy's hair as he said, "If the man is anything like his cousin, I'm sure we'll hear of him before long."

Peter and Andrew left the house as the sun was sinking. They walked together down to the pier, carrying the newly-repaired nets. Andrew had refused to stay behind and rest. He claimed he was looking forward to casting for fish again. They would fish for several hours before finally coming to join the rest of the family in slumber.

Beth watched them as she leaned against the door frame with her arms wrapped around herself. From where she stood, she could see Herod Antipas' pleasure boat being rowed down the shoreline by a dozen slaves.

The bow was pointed towards his lakeside palace in Tiberias. The heavy craft was wide and slow, designed for leisure. Instead of sails, there hung a scarlet shade canopy, the fringed edges fanning in the breeze.

It was too far to see clearly, but she imagined she could discern the tetrarch's form reclining on a cushioned seat beside his forbidden wife, Herodias.

Beth rubbed her arms as she felt an unaccountable chill brush against her. Why should a man and a woman like that go free while a good prophet was locked up? The world was upside down.

With Andrew home, things slipped back into their old rhythms, and Beth was almost able to forget the prophet languishing in a pit somewhere far away. Weeks passed, and summer arrived in full force.

Beth discretely fanned herself with her hand as she entered the synagogue on the Sabbath morning with her family. The cool stone building was a relief after their muggy walk. She was wearing her good dress, the same one she had worn for her wedding. Her hair was combed and hung free down her back, and her light summer shawl was draped around her head, signifying her as a married woman. The fresh feeling from her wash in the lake yesterday was swiftly fading in the summer heat.

The synagogue was large and open, with pillars supporting the flat roof. Windows were high to let the heat escape, but their narrow openings allowed indirect light to filter in.

On three sides of the synagogue were tiered benches filled with the men, women, and children of her community. No babies were seen in the synagogue, as mothers were not permitted to carry their children outside of the home on the Sabbath. The elders considered carrying anything to be work, and work was forbidden on the day of rest.

She smiled and nodded at Reuben, who sat beside the retired scribe, Daniel. He grinned back. Beth sat between Peter and Hannah.

The synagogue official, Jairus, came forward and stood at the small stone altar near the center of the room. The older men took turns leading worship, and it was his turn this week. From a small closet in the wall, a thick, heavy scroll wrapped in fine cloth was brought forward and set upon the altar. This was their Torah, precious and holy. The Pharisees taught, "When one could not worship in the Temple, prayer and studying from the Torah is the equal of the Temple sacrifices."

"The Lord our God is One!" Jairus called aloud.

The congregation stood together and prayed the Shema and the Benedictions. Then he sat in the teacher's seat and read from the Torah, from one of the five books of Moses. It was in Hebrew. The lilting words slipped over Beth's mind without taking hold. She did not speak the ancient language of her forefathers; neither did most of the other women. A few women turned to each other and whispered to pass the time.

Daniel, sitting on one of the benches, nodded, his chin nestling into his beard as he dozed. Reuben sat beside him. His eye caught hers and they shared an amused smile like when they were children. It felt good to have him home.

A paraphrase of the text in Aramaic followed, and Beth straightened up as she listened. Then, a section of the prophets was read, Jairus turning the large scroll until he found the proper place. Again, it was in Hebrew. Beth sighed and leaned back. The prophecy was interpreted for them. It was a common favorite, for it spoke of hope for the future--a time when the Israelites were free once more.

"The people who walk in darkness will see a great light.
A light will shine on those who live in a dark land . . .
For a child will be born to us; a son will be given to us;
And the government will rest on his shoulders;
And His name will be called Wonderful Counselor, Mighty God,
Eternal Father, Prince of Peace.
There will be no end to the increase of His government or of peace,
He will establish the throne of David and his kingdom,
And uphold it with justice and righteousness,
From then on and forevermore."

After the Torah was rolled closed and swathed in its protective cloth, Jairus said, "We have a new-comer to our community, a man from Nazareth. He asked to give the sermon this morning."

A man rose up, and all eyes turned on him. Many were a little wary of a stranger in their midst.

Beth glanced to the side as a motion from Andrew caught her attention. He was on the edge of his seat, leaning forward and staring at the newcomer as if he was trying to recognize him. She followed his gaze back to the Nazarene.

The man was in his early thirties, Beth guessed. His dark hair and beard were neat. His clothing was simple but well made, and his worn sandals showed he had walked a great deal. His brown eyes swept over his audience, and he smiled at them as if he had waited a long time to meet them all.

He sat in the teacher's seat and taught with a clear, even voice. Several of the men began nodding their heads as he spoke with confidence about righteousness.

In her own humble opinion, Beth thought the man spoke well.

Just before he finished he paused. "And I say to you," his eyes captured them all. "Repent! The kingdom of heaven is near."

He got up and returned to his seat, and whispering broke out in the room.

Andrew turned to Peter. "I think that's the man I saw at the river."

Beth's whole family looked at the Nazarene with wide eyes.

After the closing prayers, Andrew scrambled to his feet and followed the newcomer out the door. Peter turned to Beth and chuckled a little, but lines of concern were between his brows.

Andrew returned home the happiest Beth had seen him in a long time.

"I've been at Zebedee's house," Andrew said by way of explanation. "That Nazarene was the man I saw at the river. His name is Jesus, and he's taken a small house here in town."

Tamar wagged her long spoon at Andrew. "He seems like a nice young man, but he doesn't quite strike me as 'a beloved son of God.' Be careful, Andrew. This is not the first time a sign appeared to mark a leader. Signs can be misinterpreted, to the downfall of many."

They all looked at Tamar with concern, watching the emotions playing over her face. Peter and Andrew had heard of the terrible fate of her family in Sepphoris.

Tamar felt their eyes upon her, squared her shoulders, and went back to stirring her pot.

Beth chewed her lip and studied Andrew's excited face with worry. Her mother's family had thought a revolutionary would lead them in glory. Instead, he had led them to their doom.

The Nazarene was the talk of the town as he was witnessed over the summer months speaking to the people on the steps of the synagogue, under a tree on the outskirts of town, and even on a hilltop south of Capernaum.

Many of the townspeople did not approve. A mysterious prophet off in the wilderness was one thing. A would-be-prophet in their home town was something altogether different.

Andrew and John ben Zebedee often went out to hear Jesus speak about the same kingdom that had drawn them to his cousin by the Jordan. Andrew would come back and tell Peter all that Jesus had said, encouraging him to come and listen.

With growing frequency, Peter began to go and sit with the Nazarene. Beth saw it with trepidation.

The summer heat eventually waned, and it was time for the autumn harvest. Women went out to the fields with the men to help with the olive picking, and the community olive press became a noisy gathering place.

Shading her eyes from the sun, Beth stood at her front door and squinted against the glimmering water. Her mother came out from the house and also drew her hand over her eyes, one hand on a generous hip. Only a few boats drifted on the lake, their square sails catching the fickle wind as they worked together to chase fish into the wide nets spread between them. Peter and Andrew's craft was tied at the pier with the rest of the Capernaum boats. The two men were nowhere to be seen.

"Perhaps I will send David to search for them?" Beth thought aloud.

"I'll go!" Hannah said, skipping out the door.

"I think not," Tamar said, shooing her back into the house. "You and David need to finish your chores."

Hannah thrust out her lower lip but obeyed.

"And I should go and finish supper," Beth admitted.

Despite her words, her feet did not move. She shook her head and frowned. The men had never been so late before. They must all be bone-tired by now. What was it about the Nazarene that kept them so enthralled?

Beth lifted her chin as she recognized a figure coming towards them. "Look, here comes Uncle Zebedee. He'll know where they are." Zebedee walked with a bounce in his step that belied his growing years.

"Good day! Have you seen my sons?" Tamar called out.

"Ah, yes I have!" Zebedee responded with his rumbling voice as he approached. "I've been with them all day. Well, ever since we returned from an unfruitful night of fishing. We saw Jesus teaching near the shore, so we brought our boats closer so we could listen. The man is a gifted speaker. Droves of people came to listen, so many that he came and sat in Peter's boat to speak to them. After he was finished talking to the crowd, we sat with him for quite some time. I have never met one like him. He is half my age, yet has a wise answer for every question."

"You've been caught in the Nazarene's net as well?" Tamar teased.

"I have!" Zebedee chuckled, unashamed. "As the sun began to sink, we realized the time. Peter wanted to continue the conversation, so he invited us to dine here, at his house."

"Here?" Beth exclaimed, and her mind flew to her cooking pot. Would there be enough for the unexpected company?

She jerked towards the front door, anxious to improve the meal for guests, but a sound from the road made her stop. She looked past Zebedee and could see the small group approaching.

Too late. The simple meal would have to do.

Naomi strode beside her two sons wearing a basket on her arm. She was a short and sturdy woman with thick, silver-gray hair and a no-nonsense face, but she always had a glimmer of pride in her eyes when she was with her family. Naomi swatted at her sons, James and John, as the rowdy youths teased and wrestled. Peter and Andrew were deep in earnest conversation with the newcomer.

Seizing the opportunity to escape their chores, Hannah and David ducked out the door to see who was coming, and then dashed ahead to greet the group.

As they drew closer, Beth wiped her damp palms on her dress. The group stopped before the house and greeted Beth and her mother. Beth glanced at her wild cousins. James and John were slightly older than herself, but their brash and rough nature had kept her from enjoying the same sort of friendship she had enjoyed with Reuben.

"Here's a mouse for you to meet," James teased, looking at her with a crooked grin.

Naomi cuffed the back of his head, her mouth set in a thin line. Beth felt her face flush, which made greeting the Nazarene even more difficult.

"Tamar and Beth," Peter said, ignoring James, "I am pleased to introduce Jesus of Nazareth, the wondrous man who has opened my eyes!"

The sons of Zebedee chortled at Peter's boisterous introduction, and even Jesus laughed. Jesus turned his face and smiled at the women. His warm, brown gaze met hers. She saw kindness and humbleness in his eyes, yet a power resided in the depths that startled her. She realized she was staring and jerked her chin away.

They went into the house. The room was dim and shadowy after the bright sunshine. Beth and her mother bustled around finishing the meal. Hannah was eager to be helpful but generally got in the way.

"Where will you go?" John asked, leaning towards Jesus.

"Everywhere!" Jesus said, his eyes sparkling with eagerness. "The cities around the Sea of Galilee for starters, and then onward from there. Nazareth maybe. Perhaps I'll make it down to Jerusalem as well." The men were all nodding. John couldn't take his eyes off Jesus, seeming to loathe having this adventure pass him by.

Beth hid a small smile, relieved to hear the man was leaving. She didn't like how Peter and Andrew were always with the stranger these days. If the Nazarene left, things would go back to their usual routine. Her heart lightened at the thought.

She brought a basket of bread to the table just as Jesus looked around at the other young men and said, "Come with me. You have all heard me many times over the summer, peppered me with questions, and seem eager for more. Follow me as my disciples."

Beth felt her stomach twist. Surely Peter wouldn't think of accepting. She tried to catch his eye, but it was as if she was invisible.

"Yes, rabbi!" Peter cried out. Andrew, James, and John all clamored their agreement.

Beth spun away from the table to hide her face, her jaw dropping. What was happening?

7

THE CALL

"Beth, come get the pot," Tamar snapped from the courtyard as Beth stood frozen to the spot, feeling ill.

Not wanting to draw attention to herself, she forced her feet to move. The mother and daughter finished bringing the food to the table. Beth worked automatically, her mind spinning.

As soon as everyone was seated, Peter leaned towards Beth. "Did you hear? We leave tomorrow to travel with Jesus."

He turned away before she could reply. Beth saw his overflowing joy. He was eager to leave. Too eager. She clutched her hands under the table.

Tamar was astonished and plied the men with questions. Beth stared at the tabletop, picking off a sliver of wood with her fingernail.

While the conversation swirled around her, Beth was lost in her confused mind. She ate without tasting, forgotten by everyone else. The phrase, 'fishers of men' kept popping up, and she couldn't gather what it meant. She wished she could find her voice and demand a proper explanation.

Tamar was a good hostess, making sure everyone had enough of the simple bread, stew, and figs. When she learned that Jesus had given up the little house he rented, Tamar invited Jesus to stay with them that night. Jesus accepted.

Beth slipped away under the pretense of preparing a place for the young rabbi to sleep. She tarried on the upper floor, wanting to be alone with her thoughts. What did Peter mean by running off like this? Had he forgotten his duties as a husband, or was he tired of her already? When she couldn't hide any longer without it seeming strange, she drew a bracing breath.

As she plodded back down the stairs, she heard the men discussing the kingdom of heaven. She nearly stumbled. The phrase reverberated through her mind like a blast from a shofar—half thrill, half terror. Was Jesus truly going to take the message of John on the road, carrying it town to town? John had proclaimed the kingdom in the wilderness, and now he was languishing in prison, his life in the hands of a corrupt client king.

With wobbly knees she returned to kneel at the table, staring around at the happy faces. They were oblivious to the danger they were all facing. She clenched her hands so hard her nails dug into her palms.

As the men talked routes and roads, Beth's heart sank further. It sounded as though they would be gone for many weeks, or perhaps months. It wasn't unheard of for a married man to become a disciple, but Beth had never dreamed of a day when Peter would leave his fishing boat—and her.

She had almost everything she had ever wanted. The only thing left would come in its own time—a child of her own. She wished she could grab ahold of everything at that moment, secure it in her heart, and stop this new rabbi from capsizing her little world.

Late that night, after evening prayers and when the house had gone to sleep, Peter and Beth lay down on their shared bed. With her stomach full of butterflies, Beth faced the wall, lost in her worries. She traced a crack in the plaster.

Peter was speaking of the wonders of Jesus, his words a low hiss that Beth didn't bother to discern. She became aware Peter had paused, and Beth realized that he had asked her a question.

"Sorry, what?" she asked, rolling over and trying to hide a little sigh.

"I asked what you thought of Jesus." Peter was lying on his side with his head propped up on one elbow.

Beth plucked at the blanket. "I don't really know him. He's a stranger to me." Her hint had no effect on her husband.

Peter's voice was rapt. "He was speaking by the water today, and his words stirred my very soul. Crowds are flocking to him. Everyone is amazed at his teachings. He will be a great rabbi, famous no doubt. Yet he wants us, simple fishermen, to be his disciples." He rolled onto his back with his arms behind his head. She could see him smiling. She tensed when he asked, "What do you think?"

Beth chewed her lip. She remembered when Peter had returned from his trip with Andrew to see the prophet, John. He had been full of almost equal enthusiasm, gushing for hours of what he had heard. Peter had almost remained behind with his brother, but as a married man, he had felt his duty to return to Capernaum and his livelihood. Why did he feel different now?

She was hesitant to voice her concerns, but Peter persisted in asking for her opinion until he wore her down. A flood of worries gushed out.

"How will Jesus preach about a coming kingdom and not end up in prison with John? How do you even know that he's worth following? He speaks of a kingdom, but how will he bring it? Are you prepared to join an uprising, become a zealot trying to undermine Rome and Herod Antipas' rule, refusing to pay your taxes, and bringing danger on your head and all who know you?"

"Beth," he chuckled patronizingly like he was reasoning with a child.

Anger rose up in her. She snapped, "You don't understand! You can't do this in secret. Herod Antipas' palace is visible from your fishing boat."

He reached for her, but she shifted away. She didn't want to be soothed; she wanted him to understand.

"You're overreacting." He sighed with impatience.

She covered her face with her hands and groaned. He knew she was a worrier, but he couldn't blame her resistance on that. What Jesus was doing was dangerous. Tears pushed their way forward, despite her best efforts to contain them. A sob escaped.

"I can't see you go to prison. I can't see you on a cross, I won't!"

Peter pulled her towards him. At first she resisted, tensing her body, but as another sob convulsed her shoulders, she softened. He drew her into his arms. She cried for a moment, and he said nothing. She knew he didn't agree with her. He didn't see the danger. How could she make him understand? She drew a deep, wavering breath.

"Even if he is all that you believe, it doesn't need to be you," she whispered. "You can let him go and stay here. With me."

Peter didn't answer for so long that she thought he had fallen asleep. She lifted her head to check and saw he was staring at the ceiling. His eyes flicked to hers, and she could see his determination. Her heart sunk. He wouldn't change his mind.

His words were calm. "Jesus is different than the men you fear, those failed revolutionaries. I can see it already. He speaks with such … power. He isn't like our teachers. He's not even like the prophet, John. The things that he says about the kingdom are amazing. He's not raising an army, at least not yet. He seems more concerned for us to be prepared for a kingdom that is coming—whether we want it or not."

"But Peter, how do you *know*?"

"I just do."

Impulsive man! She groaned, flopping back down. He wasn't going to change his mind. He would leave tomorrow, no matter how she felt. Tears burned, but she blinked them away. Peter was the head of the household and it was his decision. What could she do?

He had been so good to her these years of marriage. She loved him. Her anger softened under the weight of her affection. She curled towards him and ran her hand over his bare chest.

She struggled inwardly and the silence dragged on. How could she deny Peter this when he had done so much for her?

She felt an overwhelming sense that she was closing the door on a dream she had treasured as she whispered, "If you feel you should go with Jesus, I will accept it."

Peter took her hand and kissed her wrist with a low laugh. "I have the best wife!"

He rolled over and burrowed his bearded face in her neck. Despite herself, she laughed as it tickled, and he covered her giggles with kisses. For a time, he swept away her fears in a wave of passion.

In the dark of the night, Beth held onto his words as the fears seeped back in. Peter's even breathing told her he had fallen asleep. She reached out a hand and drew it over his cheek. How long would it be before they shared this bed again?

Before the sun dawned Beth was up again, rubbing her gritty eyes. Her mother rose with her. They took all the flour Beth had ground yesterday and baked unleavened bread in the oven. Beth wrapped dried date cakes. Sweet and full of energy, they made a perfect traveling food.

"Too bad we don't have salted fish for them to take." Tamar frowned as she bundled the food into a bag.

"They will be buying food on the road, I suppose," Beth said, and pressed her lips together.

She wasn't sure where the funds would come from. Their little clay jar had few coins in it. She looked at her mother and swallowed hard. "It sounds as though they will be gone for some time."

Tamar glanced at her daughter with a knowing expression. Beth was sure her mother understood the anxiety she felt. Beth had never been good at hiding her emotions.

"Let the men have their excitement," Tamar said as she patted her daughter's arm. "All good men need to express their zeal for the Lord in some fashion or another. For some reason, I trust the Nazarene. I don't think he will lead them into harm's way. I'm sure all will be well and they will return in a few weeks, ready to settle back into a quiet life here."

Beth hoped her mother was right.

The sky was streaked with pale, gray light as Beth heaved up her tall water jug and left the house. She returned with it balanced on her head, and she and her mother filled two water skins. Another skin was full of wine.

The men rose soon after. James and John came by with their parents. Their noisy voices announced their presence long before they were at the door. Together with Jesus, the family knelt and prayed to the one true God.

After the blessing, they shared breakfast. Beth could hardly swallow. She soon gave up the effort and allowed her sister to finish her share.

As the men talked of plans that had nothing to do with her, she felt as if she was fading into the walls, and loneliness plucked at her heart. She felt left behind, even though her husband sat just across the table.

"Ah, to be young!" Zebedee boomed as he clapped his eldest son on the shoulder. James winced playfully under his father's large hand and turned to his brother and gave him a far greater wallop on the back.

"To be young!" he crowed as the smack reverberated around the room.

John roared and leaned over to retaliate when a fierce stare from his mother made him shrink comically back into his spot. Everyone but Beth laughed at the boyish antics of the brothers.

Naomi shook her head at Jesus. "I hope you know what you're getting into with these two trouble-makers!" she said while smiling with deep affection.

"I think I do." Jesus grinned.

He prayed a brief prayer of thanksgiving as the meal ended, then he rose and went outside. The rest followed him.

Outside the door, the men shouldered their bags. The fresh morning scent began to invigorate them. They shifted their feet, eager to be on their way.

Jesus said farewell and thanked the women for their hospitality. Beth thought that his eyes lingered on her face. Did he see the doubt she felt? He gave her a smile of encouragement and opened his mouth to speak to her, but she turned her face away. She did not want to speak with the man who was taking her husband away from her.

Beth was embarrassed that she was the only one to shed a tear, one that Peter wiped away with a thumb before he kissed her goodbye.

Then they were gone.

"They'll be back soon," she told herself as she gripped her skirt in both hands. "Things will be as they were."

Peter did not leave Beth and her family unprovided for. He had asked Zebedee to use hired men to fish with his and Andrew's boat. The income would be less, but it would be enough to support the women and children.

Zebedee was a good businessman, and as the days went by, he often stopped by with a few fresh fish for their table. Though Beth and her family were taken care of, they all missed the men as they gathered around the table. Beth gave up trying to sleep alone and invited Hannah to share her bed as when they were both children.

Weeks passed, and they didn't return.

Word trickled into Capernaum with the passing traders, always the best source for news. Jesus appeared to be amassing an even greater following than John the Prophet. Stories of his wondrous miracles were spreading far and wide. Beth sniffed when she heard them. They were no doubt exaggerated.

Beth still held her private doubts and worries about Jesus, and all her quiet moments were filled with prayers for Peter's safety.

Fall harvest finished. Many of their friends and neighbors journeyed to Jerusalem for the Day of Atonement and stayed for the Feast of Booths.

The Day of Atonement was a solemn day of fasting and introspection for the entire nation. The High Priest would don his priestly garments with the jeweled breastplate and turban. The bells on the hem of his garment would tinkle as he went into the Holy of Holies, swinging incense. The people in the courtyard would wait with bated breath for him to emerge safely. Then they would know that their sins had been atoned for before God. A goat was sacrificed, and the priest laid his hands on another goat before it was led far from the people, symbolizing the removal of their sins.

Then, five days later, the pilgrims would camp for a week in simply constructed booths made from tree boughs, creating temporary villages all around Jerusalem, meeting family and friends. The Festival of Booths was always a joyous and thankful celebration. It was a time to remember when their forefathers lived in tents in the wilderness. Once more in the Temple there were sacrifices and special assemblies.

The festival days came and went, and Beth and her family fasted and went to the synagogue on the Day of Atonement. They constructed their booth in the courtyard with leafy branches, but as the shrunken family circle knelt under the temporary shelter to eat their supper, Beth felt like all the joy was missing from the festival.

The winter rains passed without her husband's return. Beth lay awake at night wondering where he was, if he was warm enough if he missed her. Always she carried an ache in her chest, a tight fist of stress that made it hard to breathe easy.

Her father had left her without warning. One sickness had swept him away, the sudden illness leaving in its wake heartache and uncertainty. If her dear Papa could be hale and hearty one day and dead the next, she knew Peter too could be snatched away in a heartbeat.

Spring bloomed around the Sea of Galilee, and the crops of winter wheat and barley turned ripe and golden. Without the men, Beth and her family stayed in Capernaum for yet another festival, instead of journeying to Jerusalem for the Passover and the Week of Unleavened Bread.

Even Tamar grew anxious for the men to return. She didn't speak of it, but Beth could tell.

Beth knelt on the roof beneath a sheltering canopy, grinding barley in her hand mill. Her arms ached and sweat beaded on her forehead, yet she didn't slow. Perhaps, if she worked hard enough, she could grind the fear and the bitterness from her heart.

A noise in the distance drew her attention to the south end of town. She frowned and rose to her feet as she saw a shadowy mass. It took her a moment to understand it was a sea of people. She stared at the noisy, milling medley of men and women. Children dashed around enjoying the excitement.

A motion next to her house caught her eye, and she saw her neighbor standing on the street to see what was going on.

"Sophia," Beth called out. "Do you know what's happening?"

Her neighbor turned her face upwards, shielding her eyes, "It's that prophet, Jesus of Nazareth!"

Beth felt her heart give an enormous leap, Peter was home! Forgetting her grain and her mill, she scrambled down the ladder and called out, "Come on, hurry! They're back!"

Tamar and Hannah knew at once who she meant, and dropped their work to follow Beth outside. Tamar gripped skipping Hannah's hand, trying to contain her energetic daughter. Beth was smiling so hard her cheeks hurt from months of disuse. The crowd was near the synagogue. The students were standing on tiptoes with the teacher, Ezra. Tamar called over to David, who happily left his class and ran up to join them.

The number of people in the noisy crowd was staggering. Beth's mouth dried at the sight of them. Seeking her husband, Beth sucked in her breath. She wavered a moment before joined the milling throng.

She had never been comfortable with crowds since her first visit to the Temple. The press of people made her break out in a cold sweat, and left her breathless. The faces of so many strangers began to blur together, and her pulse hammered in her ears.

"I can't!" she gasped.

She stumbled back from the press of people, panting, frustrated by her weakness. Tamar noticed Beth's retreat and joined her.

"Don't worry, I'll find them," Hannah cried out.

She charged ahead, diving into the crowd like the other excited children. Beth had often wished she had her sister's easy confidence. Hannah emerged moments later, face beaming, dragging Peter with her.

Beth's heart skipped when she laid eyes on him. He was thinner and travel-worn, but his gaze was bright and his stride strong. His eyes met hers and the flash of his teeth from within his beard brought back her smile.

He hastened forward and embraced her. The tighter he held her, the more the bands of anxiety loosened. She sucked in a deep, full breath for the first time in months, drawing in the scent of sunshine and sweat on his tunic.

Peter spoke tenderly to her as she buried her face in his chest, feeling safe, secure, and loved. After a long moment, she was able to stand back and smile at him, and he cupped her cheek. A tear slipped down her face and into his palm.

Jesus came forward with James, John, and Andrew, as well as a few others that Peter introduced as fellow disciples.

The camaraderie between the group was strongly apparent, and Beth felt a new, uncomfortable space between her world and her husband's.

Drawing the women aside, Peter spoke to Tamar and Beth. "Jesus has decided to stay in Capernaum for the summer. I hope you don't mind, but I have offered him our home for as long as he likes."

"Of course we don't mind," Beth said, but the happy hope of life returning to normal was shattered. She struggled to keep the smile on her face.

They found room in Peter's large house for several of the other disciples as well, all of them grateful for a comfortable place to stay. The crowds dispersed and Capernaum was quiet once more.

The large group sat late to supper, Tamar and Beth having thrown together a hearty meal.

"You'd never believe all the things I've seen," Peter exclaimed as Beth served the guests. "Jesus has drawn crowds from Syria, all over Galilee, throughout the Decapolis, and from Judea. We were in Jerusalem and beyond the Jordan."

The other men chimed in, sharing stories and laughing at inside jokes Beth didn't understand. She felt on the outside in her own house.

She excused herself as soon as she could without being rude, and escaped upstairs to a quiet corner. She buried her face in her hands, feeling her hopes sinking around her as laughter rose from below. She just wanted to return to her simple, peaceful life with her family and Peter.

As they bedded down for the night, Beth was keenly aware of the presence of strangers sleeping nearby. Peter was still bubbling over.

"I am so happy to be home with you, my love," he said. "I have so much to share with you. My words can't do Jesus justice. You need to come and see and hear him for yourself."

"I will, sometime," Beth demurred, staring at the roof.

Peter fell asleep almost at once. Beth rolled onto her side and watched his chest rise and fall. He was back at home at last, lying here beside her. He was the same, dear man that she had married, so why did she feel he had changed? Something had happened to him out on the road with that Nazarene.

She wriggled closer to him, curling over his chest. She wrapped an arm around him, holding him tight, determined to never let go of him again.

8

THE MEEK AND THE GENTLE

Jesus went out the next day. Beth was thankful that the other young men went with him and the house was quiet. Knowing Peter was nearby was a comfort, but she had declined going out with him. He had looked disappointed as he turned away, but she pretended not to notice.

"Easy, Beth, you are supposed to knead the dough, not pulverize it," Tamar chided with a laugh as she came in from the courtyard with a basket of freshly baked bread.

Beth looked down at the mess of dough and sighed.

Tamar began to wrap the warm loaves to keep them clean and fresh. She eyed Beth; the look on her face was speculative.

"Now that Peter is home, perhaps you will get with child," Tamar said.

"Mama!" Beth's face heated.

"What?" Tamar widened her eyes innocently. "You haven't been discouraging him, have you? The other women in town are beginning to wonder why you haven't become pregnant yet."

Beth felt a stab of irritation. The Pharisees and elders could learn something from the local women. Nothing, not even the smallest matter, was beneath the notice of Capernaum housewives.

"Things will happen in their own time," Beth said primly to her mother, but she spoke to herself as well.

She had her own worries that she hadn't conceived a child after three years of marriage. Of course, Peter had been gone for most of the past year. She glanced at her mother, who was still studying her.

"And no, I haven't been *discouraging* him," Beth said.

"As you say," Tamar said with the hint of a teasing grin. She changed the subject, catching Beth off guard. "Are you going to see cousin Simon today?"

Tamar began to measure spices into the pot to prepare a lentil stew. Beth smoothed both her dough and her emotions, feeling her face cooling. She could hear Hannah in the courtyard, singing to the goat while she milked her.

Tamar continued, "I would go, but I feel the start of a headache coming on." She dabbed the back of her hand to her forehead. Beth scanned her mother with a twinge of concern.

"No, I'll do it," Beth said. "I think the walk will do me good."

Beth was glad to have the subject of her empty womb put aside. She set the dough to rise in a large bowl on the shelf and dusted off her hands. She and her mother prepared a basket of food, including some of the fresh bread.

"How strange life is sometimes," Beth commented as she covered the basket with a cloth. "For years our cousin Simon helped us, and now he depends upon our charity. I'm glad we can repay him, but I wish it was for another reason."

Tamar clicked her tongue in sad agreement.

A little over a year ago, a man swathed head to toe in a long cloak had arrived at their doorstep. He had revealed himself as their cousin from Bethany. He had contracted leprosy. Because of the impurity of his disease, he had been forced to shut up his store and his Bethany home. Lepers were supposed to keep themselves away from the people. It was the law.

There was a leprous community he could have stayed with near Jerusalem, but Simon was a Pharisee and a prominent businessman. Pride had kept him from staying near his own town to be stared at, pitied, and feared. He had fled instead to his distant relations and anonymity.

"Leprosy is a terrible curse," Tamar said with a sigh, wiping a bead of sweat off her brow. "The way it takes away your life, you might as well be dead already."

She clicked her tongue and shook her head again, and Beth had to agree. She looked around their home, thought of her family, and reminded herself to be grateful for all her blessings. Especially now, in these uncertain times.

Beth tossed her light shawl over her head and left the house with her basket. It thudded against her thigh as she walked west to the outskirts of town, and then up into the low hills sprinkled with wildflowers. A few lepers lived in a handful of dry caves, separating themselves as the law commanded. When she arrived, she called for Simon.

Another voice, raspy and female, answered her from the shadowy mouth of the cave. "Simon is not here."

Beth was concerned. "Where did he go?"

"To see the so-called Miracle Worker." The voice was jaded.

"Jesus of Nazareth?"

"Oh yes, news reaches us, even here. Simon will be disappointed. Only God can heal us now. Cursed we are, cursed. Simon will be back by nightfall, mark my words."

Beth was surprised. Simon had never once left the caves, not even to attend synagogue. A corner was set apart for lepers, but those seats were never taken.

Beth called out again, "Are you sure he went to see Jesus?"

"Well perhaps he went for a stroll down to the market," the voice replied, thick with sarcasm.

Beth flushed but stood outside the cave as if waiting for the raspy voice to tell her what to do. She glanced back to Capernaum and felt a strange tingle move down her back.

What was it about Jesus that had roused Simon's faith? She hosted Jesus within her own house, yet she had never gone to see if the rumors of his miracles were true. She was struck with the absurdity of it and laughed aloud.

"Glad someone is having a nice day," came a mutter.

Peter had told her Jesus could heal, and Peter had always been truthful before. Somehow, she had thrown up a wall and refused to listen to what he told her about Jesus. She bit her lower lip, holding it in her teeth. She could go and see for herself if Simon's hope was well placed.

Yet, the idea of going among so many strangers made her pulse fly. She shifted from foot to foot. Simon had much more to lose than she did by stepping out in faith, and his bravery illuminated her cowardice. Drawing in a deep breath, she resolved to go and see for herself.

She was surprised when the decision to go see Jesus lit a spark of light inside her heart. She hadn't realized the desire to see Jesus at work had been growing in her.

Beth took two steps down the hill, then paused on impulse and emptied the basket at the customary place. She called to the dark cave, "Here, you can have this!"

She turned and skipped down the slope, feeling a strange buoyancy. She spoke to a few neighbors along the way, asking for directions to the Nazarene rabbi. Her long walk ended with her standing at the base of a tall hill on the south side of town in the valley of Gennesaret.

Prosperous crops and tidy farmhouses filled the valley, but swaying summer grass and blooms held sway over the tall hill. Jesus was seated at the top. His voice carried down the slope so that even at her distance she could still hear him. There was a group of people close to him, sitting right at his feet.

She searched and was able to pick out Peter with Andrew, James, and John. She even saw Zebedee and David. The rest of the crowd spread over the hillside.

She felt she should go up to Peter, but as she stepped towards the hill, a stranger assessed her with curious eyes. She hesitated, her palms pooling with perspiration.

As she wavered at the bottom of the slope, a movement caught her eye. She turned and saw a man wrapped from head to toe with his face upturned. Thinking she knew who he was, she went to him. She stopped a few paces away.

"Simon?" she called.

He jerked as if struck, and turned to her. The cloth around his face slipped.

She was unable to stop a gasp as she beheld his disfigured face. The entire left side of his head was bubbled with oozing sores. His diseased ear and his nose were eaten nearly away. The hair on the side of his head was sparse and coarse. He did not look at all like the healthy man she remembered hosting them in Bethany. Yet, his eyes were glistening with joyful tears, and the right side of his mouth curved upwards into a marred smile.

Seeing her reaction, Simon remembered who and where he was.

"Have you heard him speak?" Simon asked, pulling his coverings over his face. "In all my years I have never heard anyone speak like him, not even in the Temple courts. Listen, cousin, listen!"

Beth opened her mouth to question him, but Simon shushed her and flapped a bandaged arm towards Jesus. Puckering her brow at his overwrought eagerness, she turned her attention to Jesus.

Jesus was speaking, "You think you know those who are blessed, don't you? Well, let me tell you who is truly blessed.

"Blessed are the downtrodden, for theirs is the kingdom of heaven!

"Blessed are those who mourn, for they will find comfort.

"Blessed are the gentle, for the earth will be their inheritance!

"Blessed are those who hunger and thirst for righteousness, for they shall be satisfied.

"Blessed are the merciful, for they will receive mercy.

"Blessed are the pure in heart, for they will indeed see God.

"Blessed are the peacemakers, for they will be called Sons of God!

"Blessed are those who are persecuted for righteousness, for theirs is the kingdom of heaven.

"Blessed are you when people lie about you, insult you, and persecute you because of me. Rejoice and be glad! The prophets received the same treatment."

A whisper passed over the hill like the wind in the grass, and the people stared at each other in amazement. Jesus looked at his ardent followers with a smile. He spoke to his disciples, "You are the salt of the earth. Do not lose your saltiness, but bring God's flavor to the world. You are the light of the world. Shine that light before men so they may praise your Father in heaven!

"People say many things about me. I want you to know this: I have not come to abolish the Law, but to fulfill it. Keep the commandments and teach others to do the same, and you shall be great in the kingdom of heaven. Annul one of them, and you shall be least. If you want to enter the kingdom of heaven, you must surpass the righteousness of the scribes and Pharisees."

Beth saw several heads snap to attention as he mentioned the Pharisees. She followed the gaze of the people and saw Daniel was sitting with the scribe Philemon, Ezra the teacher, and her cousin

Reuben. All four men rose to their feet with dignity and faced Jesus.

Beth felt a twist of anxiety in her stomach. She sensed conflict was coming. She glanced at her cousin, Simon. He was a Pharisee as well. What did he think of Jesus' harsh words? It was hard to tell when his face was concealed beneath his ragged clothing.

Jesus did not quaver before the line of angry men but launched into a long speech about the laws. He spoke to his followers specifically, but anyone could hear. He took the laws they knew, stripped away shallow, surface piety, and struck to the heart of each law.

As Jesus spoke, the common men and women bobbed their heads, looking excited, eager, and infused with zeal for the Lord.

Beth's own heart was stirred, but greater was her alarm. Who knew the laws better than the Pharisees? Yet, Jesus challenged the Pharisees' teaching without fear. Jesus spoke on many topics while the four men stood like stone pillars.

She twisted the corner of her head covering in her hand. Surely the four Pharisees noticed Peter as he sat near the man who spoke not against the pagans, but against the spiritual leaders of their own people. The fact that Peter sided with this new, revolutionary rabbi was making a huge statement to their friends and neighbors. Beth clenched her fists and pressed them against her flipping stomach as she watched Jesus hack away at the Pharisees' righteousness. She felt the same way she did when Peter was away fishing and a dark storm-cloud rolled over the waters.

Jesus finished his long speech. He shook his head with a small smile, like a man trying to reason with a friend determined to do a foolish thing.

"Don't look for shortcuts," Jesus said. "Don't try to bend the law to suit your selfish desires."

He paused, and the only sound was the demanding cry of a baby. The crowds waited breathlessly.

Jesus cast his eyes over the people, took a breath and continued. "Why am I telling you this? Why am I talking to you about divorce and oath keeping? You need to be careful. Don't practice righteousness to look good for other people. If that is your purpose, you'll have no reward with your Father who is in heaven. Do you make a big show of your righteousness, parading around like an actor in one of the theaters, only pretending to be pious?"

His voice lowered, his tone was earnest as he said, "Don't put on a show! Do your good deeds in secret, let only your Father see what you do, and He will reward you. It should be the same when you pray. Don't be like the hypocrites, those play-actors of faith. They love to stand and pray in the synagogues and on street corners to be heard by men, don't they?"

She noticed low chuckling and head nodding in the crowd. They had all witnessed a puffed up prayer, eloquent in phrasing but empty in feeling.

Jesus addressed his disciples, "When you pray, go into your house. Go into an inner room. Close the door. Pray to your Father, and your Father will reward you. Remember, it isn't about looking good for others. When you fast, don't go around looking sorrowful, hoping that someone will notice and praise you, for that is all the praise you will get. Wash your face, anoint your hair. Fast in secret, and the One you are fasting for, your heavenly Father, will reward you."

Over and over Jesus was telling them not to be like the hypocrites, the Greek word for actors. From what he said, with the public prayers and the public giving, Beth had the uncomfortable feeling that he was speaking of all the elders, the leaders in the synagogue, and prominent Pharisees and Sadducees, maybe even the priests. The common people had no wealth to make a show about. No one listened to them as they prayed on the street corners.

Jesus was speaking authoritative, spiritually revolutionary words, and the Pharisees were bristling with indignation.

When John the Baptizer had spoken out against Herod Antipas, it had landed him in jail. Those in power did not tolerate mockery or condemnation. Did Jesus think that he was immune from the same fate as John?

"Therefore," Jesus said, "Be perfect, as your heavenly Father is perfect." Those who listened sat stunned, trying to understand. He smiled at them, raising his arms as if to embrace them all. "In everything, treat people the same way you want them to treat you, for this is the Law and the Prophets."

Daniel moved closer to Jesus, his steps slow, his beard white upon his chest. Though he was retired, he still wore the dark robes of a scribe.

"Now, young Rabbi," Daniel granted him the title, but his chiding tone sounded like he was speaking to an unruly child. "I understand your zeal for the law. I have felt youthful exuberance in my day. Indeed, much of what you have said is true. But we teachers are all in this together, aren't we? We are tasked with guiding the people and leading them into righteousness. Who gave you the authority to say your way is right and ours is wrong?"

Jesus met Daniel's gaze. "A tree is known by its fruit. Do you pluck grapes from thistles? Do you harvest figs from thorns? A bad tree cannot produce good fruit, and every tree that doesn't produce good fruit is cut down and thrown into the fire. Only those who do the will of my Father in heaven will enter the kingdom."

Beth's lips parted in amazement that Jesus dared to speak in such a fashion. Many in the crowd looked shocked.

Jesus' bold words were not finished yet. "Many will say to me on that day, 'My Lord! Did you we not prophesy in your name, and in your name cast out demons, and in your name perform many miracles?' And I will say to them, 'I don't know who you are. Depart from me, you who do not keep the law in your heart!'"

Beth furrowed her brow as she tried to understand. Was Jesus placing himself as a judge over the people? The people will come to him and speak to him as a lord, and he will cast judgment for their righteousness?

She felt uncomfortable at a mortal man making such a claim, but the words did more than cause discomfort for the Pharisees on the hill. Swelling with anger, the four pharisaic men turned their backs to Jesus and made their way down the slope in a snaking line, muttering.

Jesus' words chased them down the hill. "Everyone who hears these words of mine and acts on them may be compared to a wise man who built his house on a rock. And the rain fell, and the floods came, and the winds blew and slammed against the house, and yet it did not fall, for it had been founded on the rock. Everyone who hears these words of mine and does not act on them will be like a foolish man who built his house on the sand."

The Pharisees disrupted as many as they could on their descent, but Jesus' authoritative words rang over their heads. "The rain fell, and the floods came, and the winds blew and slammed against that house, and it fell—and great was its fall."

Jesus folded his hands in his lap to the sound of enthusiastic praise.

Beth was surprised to find herself clapping with the others, caught off guard by the vitality she felt from simply listening to Jesus' teachings.

Like a heavy thundercloud pushed away by a fresh breeze, the teachers of the people stormed away from the mount. Last of all came Reuben. Her hands stilled and gripped her skirt.

Beth still couldn't believe how much he had grown in their years apart. With his striped prayer shawl draped around his neck, he looked wise and learned. He now wore the dark robes of a scribe. He had to hold back his youthful step to match pace with his elders, but they all wore matching frowns and lowered brows.

Beth waited until the older three had passed, then hastened up to speak to her friend, a tentative smile breaking on her face. As she greeted him she felt awkward, like when they had been children and she had witnessed him being scolded.

Reuben looked up the hill, glaring at Jesus as he sat on the hilltop. "What do you make of this man, Beth? I hear he is a guest in your home." His eyes flashed, and she shifted her feet.

What did she think of Jesus? He spoke well, and his teachings were invigorating—and bold. She didn't have the impulsive nature of her husband. She needed time to weigh her thoughts. She glanced up the hill at her husband and stalled.

"Peter speaks highly of him," she said.

Reuben's eyebrows lowered at her words. "The elders are not pleased with Jesus. We've heard him speak several times now. He takes liberties and sets himself up as more than a common rabbi. He's becoming increasingly insulting." He looked at the stiff, retreating backs of the elders. "He may be harmful to the people."

Beth swallowed hard. She knew Jesus' words were authoritative, blatantly authoritative in such a way that the town elders would strongly disapprove. She didn't like the idea of being at odds with the leaders of her community.

"Perhaps it's not as obvious to you," Reuben said, straightening his prayer shawl with a little unnecessary show. "But he's teaching the people a different way, one that is appealing to commoners because he makes it sound so simple. He doesn't hold to the sacred traditions of the elders, and most of these gathered here—" he spread his hands wide, "—don't have the education to know the difference."

Beth pressed her lips together with a blush, unsure how to reply. She was one of those without education, and she had to admit to herself that she was intrigued by this kingdom of heaven where the meek and the gentle were blessed.

Her heart clenched at the thought of war, yet Jesus' words were not outcries against the injustices of the Roman oppressors, but teachings for the Jews on their own faith. If Jesus was bringing revolution, she sensed it would be different from what they had seen in the past. She scanned her countrymen on the hillside and desperately hoped so.

Her riotous emotions about Jesus' teachings were newly fledged. She wasn't sure how to express what she felt. Reuben was waiting for her to reply, his expression calm and poised, a credit to the Pharisees' discipline.

She knew he expected her to agree with him. There was a time when she would have agreed with anything he said.

Her eyes flicked back up the hill to her husband, her exuberant fisherman. Peter expected her to side with him. Her eyes flitted back and forth between Reuben and Peter like a bird trying to hop away from a snare.

Before she could say come up with something neutral to say that wouldn't offend either man, Reuben noticed Philemon waiting for him. He stood a little taller.

"I have to go. We'll talk soon." With a small smile, he clasped her hand for a moment.

She puffed out a breath of relief as she watched him hasten after the other Pharisees, smoothing his fringed shawl again.

She pressed her lips together. He had changed in their years apart, and in more than appearance. She couldn't define exactly how he was different, but he was. It was like his three years with his rabbi had burnished him with a polish that didn't seem to match their hometown. She glanced down at herself. She hadn't changed at all. She felt no different than she had as a girl of fourteen. Beth chewed her lip and watched as Reuben passed Simon with a wide berth.

When Beth turned back to the hillside, Jesus was making his way down the hill, people parting for him. Several young men followed close behind, Peter, Andrew, James, and John among them. Chatty Zebedee was talking with neighbors, David tucked by his side. The hillside was stirring as people rose and gathered their belongings and family members.

Jesus and his close followers pulled away from the crowd, and

Beth took a step to join Peter. She jolted as someone shouted,

"Watch out! It's a leper!"

Simon hastened past the crowd with limping steps, his tattered bandages swinging with his lurching steps. He did not slow, nor did he pay any heed to those who were cringing and rushing away from him. He went straight to Jesus. He bowed down on the ground, his diseased hands outstretched.

Simon cried out, his voice pleading, "Lord, if you are willing, you can make me clean!"

The plaintive request tore at Beth's heart, and she crept closer. Could Jesus truly could do what Simon believed? What would it mean if he could? Her heart began to pound so hard she felt it would burst right out of her chest.

Jesus looked at the prone man whose face was turned to the dirt, one reviled and unclean, untouchable. Crouching before Simon, Jesus reached out his hand and cupped Simon's face, lifting it. Beth sucked in her breath at Jesus' daring.

Gazing deep into Simon's glistening eyes, Jesus' tone was gentle. "I am willing."

Simon cried out, and with her own eyes, Beth saw the leprosy recede and disappear, leaving clean and glowing flesh in its wake. His hair darkened and thickened, and his nose and ear reformed. Beth's knees felt weak and she held her breath as Simon began to unwind the garments that covered his head and limbs. His fingers were whole, the skin on his arms and legs was clean, free of leprosy.

Beth had never heard of such a thing happening, and here it was, a miracle before her eyes. Simon bowed before Jesus again, tears unchecked as he thanked Jesus again and again. His gratitude moved Beth to shed tears of her own. Simon would have his life back. Jesus had given him an unbelievable gift.

"Tell no one," Jesus said. "Go and show yourself to the priest as Moses commanded."

Simon rose to his feet. He took Jesus' hand and kissed it, and then he immediately raced towards Capernaum, his pace undignified but full of childlike delight as his cleansed bare feet slapped against the stone. Beth stared after him, her mind reeling.

Jesus followed Simon down the paved road, chuckling as he watched the man dash away. Beth roused herself and slipped into the small group to stand with Peter. He was surprised to see his wife.

"So you came after all!" Peter asked. He studied her face. "What did you think?"

Beth glanced at Jesus, her throat thick. Simon was healed. All uncertainty melted away like the mist before the dawn.

"I saw it, Peter. I saw Jesus' power. My cousin is healed, and I can hardly believe it."

Peter's eyes widened as he ducked to look in her face, and a tentative smile split his beard. "But, you *do* believe, right?" Peter reached out and grasped her hand, his eyes probing hers.

Beth nodded as emotion thickened her throat. "I have to."

Peter tipped back his head and laughed aloud. "I knew you would if you just gave him a chance!" Other disciples looked over. Beth blushed and tried to shush her husband as she covered her toothy smile with her hand. Peter settled his laugh into a hearty grin, and the couple shared in their marvel as they walked into town.

Beth's mirth died the moment they entered Capernaum. Her stomach tightened as she saw the Roman centurion, Marcus, marching straight for them. Beth drew closer to her husband. Marcus had been friendly to their people, but he was still a Roman. A word from him and Jesus and those who followed him would be cast into prison for sedition.

How much had he heard about Jesus and the kingdom he professed? Was he coming to seize them now?

Beth grasped Peter's hand, clutching it as tight as she could. She would not lose him!

"Calm down," Peter murmured to her. "He is alone and unarmed."

Beth tried to be more rational. The semi-retired soldier was not wearing his short sword, but everything from his keen gaze to his upright stance proclaimed him a man of authority.

"What does he want?" Beth whispered.

The polished soldier stopped before Jesus. He was older than Jesus by twenty years at least, a foreigner with close-cropped hair and beardless face. Jesus was dressed like his countrymen, with a calf-length tunic and loose-fitting overcoat. They stood in the center of the Roman-built road as two opposites—devout Jew and foreign military leader.

Beth could feel the tension from the men around her. Jesus stood at the front of his disciples calmly, with hands at his side.

"My Lord," the centurion implored, pressing a fist to his chest and bowing his head in deference.

Beth saw Andrew and Peter share a surprised glance. The centurion would expect the citizens of Galilee to bow to him, not the other way around.

Marcus said, "My servant is lying at home paralyzed, and suffering greatly."

Beth felt a pang of painful memory. It was a sudden paralysis that had caused her father's untimely death. Benjamin had entered his boat healthy and strong, but he was carried out of it unable to talk or move.

She felt a wrench in her heart as she thought of her cousin restored to health. She realized what could have been—if only Jesus had been here for her father too.

Jesus did not hesitate, but replied at once, "I will come and heal him."

Beth's eyes widened. A follower opened his mouth, his angry face clearly showing his protest.

Marcus shook his head, holding up a hand as he spoke, "My Lord, I am not worthy to have you come under my roof. Just say the word and my servant will be healed."

Jesus stood as if stunned, then he clapped Marcus on the shoulder and turned to look at his followers with a delighted smile. "Do you hear that, my brothers?" Jesus said. "I have not heard such faith from anyone in Israel!" The men shuffled their feet, feeling chastened and insulted. Jesus seemed to know their thoughts. "Many will come from all corners of the world, and sit with Abraham, Isaac, and Jacob in the kingdom of heaven. The unbelieving sons will be cast out into the darkness where they will lament and weep."

The same protesting man snarled, "These pagans welcomed, and the sons cast out?"

He glared at Marcus, shaking his head. He turned and strode from Jesus, clearly a follower no more. The other men murmured to one another, digesting this strange proclamation.

Jesus turned back to the centurion. "You have believed. Go. Your servant will be healed."

Marcus bowed with gratitude and spun on his heel to march away, chin high, free of all doubt.

Before Beth could fully comprehend what had just happened,

Hannah came flying towards them, her hair billowing around her tear-stained face. Beth felt a tremble of fear and she stepped forward.

"What's wrong?" she demanded.

"Beth!" Hannah sagged with relief when she saw her sister's face. She rushed forward to grab her hand, tugging her forward. "I've been looking for you everywhere. Something has happened to Mama. Come on!" Tears ran afresh down the child's face as Beth stood in shock. "Oh, come on! She's in so much pain!"

A cold hand gripped Beth's heart. She had already gathered up the bones of her father, how could she lose her mother too? Grasping her sister's hand, she raced for home. She prayed she would not be too late and then ran faster. She hardly noticed Peter at her side. Beth heard more footsteps beside her, and a corner of her mind realized Jesus was coming as well. She felt a spark of hope.

The short distance felt like miles. A stitch caught her side, but she ignored it. Beth was gasping for breath by the time she ducked through the open door. Her eyes were sun-blind, but she stumbled up the shadowed stairs. She could hear her mother moaning in pain from her room. She found her lying on her bed, curled up, her skin damp with perspiration.

"Oh, Lord!" Beth wailed as she dropped to her knees and pressed the back of her hand to her mother's flushed skin.

She was burning with fever. Her mother's eyes were squeezed tightly shut, and the muscles in her neck were taut. How had this sickness come on so quickly and so strongly?

Beth cried out to the room at large, "She had a headache this morning, but that was all, I swear!"

The image of her father's face swam before her, his mouth slack, his eye drooping. He had made strange noises, unable to speak, and it had frightened her beyond words. Now her mother was writhing in pain, oblivious to Beth's touch.

Jesus came beside her, frowning with concern. Beth sucked in her breath. Could he do it again? Could he heal her mother with a touch, like he had healed Simon? Jesus crouched and grasped Tamar by her hand.

Beth gasped as she witnessed the sickness leave her mother. It drained away like water from a cracked jug.

Joyful tears sprang to Beth's eyes. He was doing it! He was healing her.

As the fever left, Tamar's breathing calmed, and her body eased. Her eyelids fluttered, and she stared at Jesus as he helped her rise to her feet.

Beth wilted on the floor. Her head tipped back as her lips parted, drawing in a breath. She brought her hands to her chest, feeling her heart galloping.

Tamar glanced back to her rumpled bed with surprise; she appeared a little dazed. She smiled at Jesus. "You did something, didn't you?" Tamar raised a brow.

Jesus smiled, and Tamar nodded once.

She took Jesus' hand in her own. Tamar's voice grew thick. "I'm honored to have you in our home, Rabbi. If you ever need anything, please ask."

Before Jesus could answer, a noise drew Tamar's attention to the others who were gathered in the room. Hannah was bouncing up and down with her hands pressed over her mouth, her eyes gleaming and round. The men were nudging each other in marvel.

"Ah, you've returned." Tamar smiled at the young men, brushing her hands briskly down her skirts. "You must be starving. Let me get you boys something to eat."

Beth wrapped her arms around her middle and laughed, and the men joined in.

9

"WHAT KIND OF A MAN IS THIS?"

The noise was overwhelming. Beth fought the urge to press her hands over her ears and waded deeper into the crowd of people that pooled before Peter's house. Some were eager for healing, many were only curious bystanders wanting to witness another miracle.

"Jesus, my daughter cannot hear!"

"Rabbi, please will you heal my son?"

"My husband has a demon. Can you help him?"

With her newfound faith, Beth believed Jesus could help them all. Considering what he had done for her cousin and her mother, how could she not believe? Though she was sure that Jesus was a righteous prophet gifted with powerful miracles, she was still uncertain what this belief required of her.

In the glow of her newly kindled faith, she had rashly volunteered to help Jesus today. The sea of curious onlookers pushed so close to the house that those who were weak or ill could not make their way to Jesus. The rabbi had sent out his followers to bring them to him. She had been so caught up in her gratitude that she had stepped forward with the other believers.

Her hasty offer felt foolish now. She was buffeted by elbows, flailing among the clamoring crowd like a rudderless boat. She wrapped her arms close around herself like a shield. Her shoulders hunched.

What was she doing here? What could *she* do to help? The press of strangers and the smell of unwashed bodies in the heavy summer heat made her gaze drift back to the house.

Yet, it would be embarrassing to retreat now. She hadn't even helped one person. She ducked her chin and crept through the waves of people, searching.

Beth inched around a portly man reeking of bitter spices and saw a woman craning her neck, trying to see over the crowd. The woman's face drooped with fatigue as she supported her son, a boy about Hannah's age.

Beth bit her knuckles as she saw the oozing and stained bandages wrapped around both his arms and hands. The feeble breeze drifted her way, and the stench of putrid infection made her breakfast rise in her throat. Beth cast her gaze about, hoping Peter would be nearby to handle this. She could not see him, or anyone else she knew.

The woman noticed Beth was watching her. Seeing hope she called out, "Help me, please! I need to see the rabbi."

After one more glance for someone, anyone else at all, Beth squared her shoulders and pressed her way to the woman. Relief flooded the woman's face when she saw someone willing to help her.

Beth cringed as she drew her arm around the boy's waist to hold him upright. He burned with fever. Was the fever catching? Panic rose in her throat, making it hard to breathe. How could she do this?

Beth brought the image of Jesus touching Simon's diseased cheek to her mind and held it there. She took a slow breath, trying not to draw in the stench of putrid flesh through her nose.

"He fell in the fire two weeks ago," the mother explained as she and Beth began to make their way through the crowd, slow step by slow step. The boy's head lolled forward as he stumbled in a half faint. "He's not recovering. I fear he will lose his arms—or die." The mother choked off a sob. Beth's heart went out to her.

"Jesus will help. Don't be afraid." Her encouragement fell back on herself, and she took a full breath and called out, "Please, let us through!"

People turned and saw the suffering boy. They began pulling back in pity or revulsion. The three made their way to the front of the house where Jesus was standing just outside the doorway. Jesus noticed Beth come forward, and his gaze fell on the mother and son with compassion.

The mother cried out, "Rabbi, please, will you heal my son?"

Jesus stepped forward at once and reached out his hands. They were strong and calloused from years of labor, yet gentle as he laid them on the boy's dark hair.

Beth felt the youth steady. He lifted his head. His brown eyes focused and found Jesus.

All of a sudden, he cried out in happiness, lunged forward and threw his arms around Jesus with instant trust and love. Jesus hugged the boy to himself, his face lit up with equal joy.

Beth wiped away a tear that pushed itself forward. Maybe leaving the safety of the house had been worth it, just to see this moment. She knew full well the world was full of cruelty and pain. As Beth had grown, she had learned to accept suffering as the way things were. Jesus, it seemed, did not.

"Praise God!" the mother cried, tears running down her face as she beheld her son in the strong embrace of the rabbi. "He is merciful to His children!"

The boy released Jesus. As the crowd marveled, he shrugged the soiled bandages from his arms, the limbs whole and agile.

Peter and James carried an elderly man to Jesus. As Jesus healed the man, Peter stepped to Beth with a teasing, boastful expression.

"Told you," he whispered. She twisted her lips to hide a smile and shook her head. He chuckled, and then grew more serious. "How have you been holding up?"

"I've been struggling," Beth admitted, wiping sweat from her brow. "I'm not like you, able to make friends with anybody and everybody."

"It's good to see you trying, my shy little dove." He pinched her chin with a grin.

The day wore on while Jesus healed all who came to him. The crowd continued to swell, the noise increasing. Capernaum felt overrun.

"What's going on here?" a loud voice demanded in a foreign accent, sharply cutting through the excited crowd.

Silence fell. Faces turned, and Beth saw three Roman soldiers with feet planted wide, hands on the hilts of their swords. They stood on the edge of the crowd, their narrowed eyes sweeping over the gathering.

"We aren't doing anything wrong," a man snapped, and several of the men muttered in agreement.

The exultant mood of the crowd darkened as if a cloud had slipped over the sun. Beth gripped her skirts in her fists, inching back to the safety of the house.

"Leave them alone!" a commanding voice rang over the people. Beth saw Marcus striding towards the soldiers. "This is a religious gathering, not a riot."

The soldiers scanned the crowd with lips pressed together. Beth saw that some of the people looked willing to make trouble, if but one of them would rise up. Their blood was stirred by the great signs of power that God was displaying through this new prophet.

Marcus crossed his arms over his chest. "Move along," he commanded the soldiers. They clapped fists to their chests and stomped away with many glances over their shoulders, hands still resting on sword hilts. Marcus nodded once to Jesus and marched away.

Beth sagged in relief. She turned and slipped into the cool, dark house. With trembling fingers, she filled a cup of water. Was it always like this around Jesus, a mix of wonderment and fear?

She heard steps approach. She turned and saw it was Peter. He accepted the cup she offered and quaffed it. She saw beads of sweat on his neck as his Adam's apple bobbed. Her clothes were sticking between her shoulder blades. The heat was growing more and more oppressive.

Peter wiped the back of his hand across his mouth. "Jesus has decided that he's done for the day, but the crowds are still growing. He's sent James and John to prepare a boat. He wants to go to the other side of the sea for a break. It might be better if the people have time to cool their heads, if you ask me. Don't worry, we won't be gone long." He leaned in and kissed her goodbye.

Beth stepped forward as his lips left hers. She hated the thought of him leaving again, even just for a day.

She looked around at the safe, familiar room. She felt so much pleasure in being Peter's wife. All her joy these past years had been wrapped up in her duties and this home.

Yet, inexplicably, her eyes were drawn to the open door, where the bright sunlight was dappled by the shifting movement of the crowd. She was safe in the house with her familiar routines, but another world glimmered beyond that door. Peter was moving towards that world, chasing the hope of a kingdom of heaven. She felt a flick of panic. She didn't want to be left behind.

"Peter?" she called. She licked her lips as he paused, then summoned her courage. "Would Jesus let me go as well?"

Peter's eyes lit up. "Really? You want to go out there with him?" He tilted his head as he asked her, "To places you've never been, with men you hardly know? Are you sure?"

Beth chuckled, tucking a hair behind her ear. Her husband knew her so well. "I can't deny I'm nervous." She reached out and took his hand in both of hers. "But *you* will be there. If you're working towards a kingdom of heaven, I will work with you. If you want me."

"Want you?" Peter dropped her hands and wrapped her up in such an exuberant hug that she was lifted off her feet. He laughed and spun her around until she was laughing too. "I want to share this with you, more than anything!" He set her down. She breathlessly caught her balance as he darted out the door at once shouting, "I'll ask him right now."

Straightening her mantle, Beth grinned.

She began to gather a bundle of food for the journey; none of them had eaten since morning. If Jesus refused Peter's request she would send it along with the men.

As she worked in the silent house, she heard laughter from outside the door and Jesus' disciples chatting. She remembered the disciple's easy comradery and their inside jokes. They were a tight-knit group, and she was on the outside.

She pressed a hand to her stomach as butterflies danced. The other disciples had been together for months. She had only served one day. What would they make of Beth joining her husband? Would they think her strange, or too forward? Perhaps this was a mistake.

She slumped to her knees and stared down at her palms on her lap. Was this the right choice? Her heart was a sail catching the wind, but an anchor refused to let it launch.

She didn't want to be left out and left behind, so why did part of her hope Jesus would refuse her and tell Peter that his shy little wife belonged at home?

Peter bounded back into the house. "Jesus welcomes you along, Beth."

Beth knew she should feel happy, but it was fear that prickled up her arms. Tamar came down from the upper floor of the house, her face confused. "What's going on?"

Peter explained, oblivious to Tamar's displeasure.

The maternal face measured her daughter. Her expression was unreadable as she replied curtly, "If that's what you wish, Peter."

Beth wrapped her arms around her middle and implored her mother with her eyes. She wanted to explain herself, but she could hardly make sense of her own emotions. Peter was already out the door, so she gathered up the bundle to her chest, ducked her head, and hastened after him.

Her mother's disapproval added another cord to her anchor. While there was nothing morally wrong with a woman going out with her husband, women didn't go gadding about when there was a home to be cared for.

Beth and Peter followed Andrew down to the large center pier. James and John were already in Peter's boat, sitting with three other young men who were guests in Peter's house: Thaddaeus, Judas Iscariot, and his friend Simon the Zealot. Thaddaeus was much like the other men Beth knew, but the other two were different. Judas was charismatic, handsome, and well-liked. His friend Simon the Zealot was a quiet, deep-thinking young man. The two friends often conversed in the evenings, mostly against the Roman occupation. Beth saw their heads were together again as they waited in the boat.

Jesus was coming, the crowd on his heels. As he made his way to the dock, a few newcomers pleaded to go with Jesus. Jesus spoke to them for a moment, and they stepped back, uncertain.

Jesus and his loyal friends clambered into Peter's boat, spacing themselves evenly. Beth accepted her brother-in-law's hand and was the last into the gently rocking, shallow-keeled craft.

Memories of time spent with her father flooded her mind as she found a place to sit. She remembered how she would run down to the pier to greet him and help sort his catch into baskets. Would he have approved of her going out with Peter and Jesus? Her father had been a devout man. He had loved to tell her the stories of their people, about the heroes and prophets. She remembered his longing expression as he spoke of their rich history—as if he wished he could have been a part of it.

As she dwelt on her papa, her mind calmed. She looked over the lake and smiled. She was sure that if he were still alive, he would be sitting right beside her, eager for the kingdom Jesus preached.

Andrew unfurled the square, white sail, and four of the men pulled out oars and began to row away from the dock.

Beth opened her bundle and began to distribute the food to the hungry men, eating a barley cake herself. The men were appreciative. Beth was happy she was contributing a little something with her presence.

She glanced back to shore. The crowd had spread out to watch, unwilling to let Jesus out of their sight.

A cold wind whistled across her damp back, chilling her. The breeze was a relief on the sweltering day, and the vessel shuddered as the sail filled and they gained speed.

"Where shall we go, Jesus?" Peter called from the rudder.

"Let's go over there," Jesus said, pointing across the inland sea to the area called the Decapolis.

The disciples looked at each other in surprise and concern. The Decapolis was set on the eastern shore of the Sea of Galilee and spread over a large area, encompassing ten major cities. Beth could see two of the cities from her seat in the boat. The citizens were mostly Greek foreigners who worshiped false gods. Why would Jesus go there?

Peter steered the boat to port about a hundred feet from shore, preparing to hug the shoreline and sail around the perimeter of the deep lake. No one liked to sail in the middle of the inland sea where the depths sunk into blackness. The sea was chaos, not to be trifled with.

"No," Jesus said. "Go straight across."

Peter hesitated but adjusted the rudder to obey. The disciples eyed each other with concern and held their tongues. Beth's stomach plummeted as she felt the seafloor fall away beneath the boat.

Jesus ate his meal then slumped back on the heap of nets at the bow of the boat under the small wooden deck, drawing his coat over his head. He was clearly exhausted.

"Shh!" John hissed at them all in a loud whisper. "He's asleep. We should let him rest."

"Then stop making so much noise," James hissed back, smacking John on the back of the head.

John made a face. Teasing aside, the men fell silent, and the only noise was the swish of the oars, the gulls overhead, the creak of wood, and the snap of the sail.

Soon they were well into the lake. Beth saw with trepidation that they were further from shore than any other boat. Beth gripped the side with white knuckles, trying hard not to think of the fathomless depths below. Peter was on the right side of the boat at the rudder, his chest lifted and his chin high.

Beth took comfort in the presence of her strong husband. He would take care of her. She remembered how in the first months of their marriage he had taken her for a picnic on this same boat, feeding her fresh fruit as she leaned back against his chest. She remembered feeling him draw in the scent of her long hair and how she had felt treasured.

A shadow swept over them, blocking the hot sun and ruining her pleasant memory. Beth looked up and saw dark, menacing clouds rolling across the sky.

"This doesn't look good!" Peter called forward, then glanced back over his shoulder at Magdala.

Beth followed his gaze. From here, she could see how Magdala was at the end of a narrow pass that sliced through the mountain ridge. As the weather soured, she could see the wind whipping down the pass and striking the water, churning the smooth surface into two-foot waves. The wind continued to grow. It ripped at their clothes and the sail stretched until it was taut as a drum.

They sailed on, and Peter's face lost its confidence as the waves rolled higher and higher, lifting the shallow craft and slapping it down with a splash.

"We need to get to shore. Now!" he yelled. He began to call out instructions, but the wind sucked away his words and the other men shook their heads in confusion.

The experienced fishermen among them leaped up and took over the oars, trying to help Peter bring the boat to land. The unwieldy boat stubbornly fought them.

The hair on Beth's arms stood up as the sky grew dark with an unnatural twilight. The waves churned into a froth. The sail became a hindrance rather than a help, jerking the boat before the unruly wind.

Andrew and James dropped their oars, jumped up, and tried to furl the sail as the wind lashed them, dragging their clothes and hair.

As the heavy cloth fought them, a wave washed over the side.

Beth yelped at the cold splash and watched with choking fear as water swirled around her ankles. The waves rose even higher still, higher than Beth had ever seen them. They were at least five feet tall, and the boat was fully in their power.

John scrambled to help the other fisherman manhandle the ropes to raise the sail as Peter screamed out orders for the other men to take up the oars. Lightning slashed the sky, and Beth cringed at a crack of thunder.

The skies opened up and water poured over them. She gasped as she was drenched with cold rain, and her teeth chattered.

The men were all shouting now. Those on oars were swinging them wildly.

Shaking water out of his eyes, Peter gripped the rudder with both hands, the sinews on his arms bulging with the effort.

Beth felt helpless. It was all she could do to keep her balance as the boat lurched, pitching one way, then the other. Her fear rose with the waves, and she pushed away the image of sinking into the black depths and disappearing forever. Hot tears of fear joined the icy rain running down her face.

"Peter!" she screamed over the wind. "Do something!"

He looked at her with fear in his eyes, and her stomach twisted. She knew he was doing all he could to save them from drowning.

Oh, why had she ever left the safety of the house?

She heard men shouting at the front of the boat, and saw Jesus rise. She had forgotten he was there. How was he sleeping through this storm?

"Save us!" several of the men cried. "We're going to drown!"

Jesus faced them all from the bow, and called over the wind, "Why are you afraid, you of little faith?"

He turned, and Beth could hear him yell something into the wind.

At that moment the clouds broke, the wind vanished, and the waves began to calm, like a sleepy child after a tantrum.

Beth drew in deep, shuddering breaths as a hush fell around them.

The clouds dissolved as a glorious sunset painted its hues across the water.

They stared at each other, gasping for breath. Unable to find words, they sat silent and still, absorbing what had just happened as the waves shrunk until the water was gently lapping against the boat. If they weren't sitting in six inches of water with rain streaming from their hair, it would have been impossible to believe the storm had been real.

Beth heard Thaddaeus whisper to Andrew, "What kind of a man is this? Even the wind and the sea obey him."

Beth stared at Jesus and wondered the same thing.

They bailed out the water, and Andrew untangled the ropes and set the sail.

As they drew near to shore, Peter said, "I believe we've come to the country of the Gadarenes. Those are the tombs up ahead."

Up high, above the trees near the shore, the stony hilltop was pocked with gaping black holes, caves that had for centuries been filled with bones.

When a person died they were anointed with oil and spices, then tightly bound in linen. A year later, the family would return and gather up the bones into special urns. This transition marked the end of their mourning. Many generation's worth of bones were in those tombs.

Jesus nodded. "That place will be fine. Let's stop there and rest."

Beth was apprehensive about stopping beneath those yawning black holes waiting like hungry mouths. The dead were unclean. Even though the tombs were high above, she didn't like to be so near.

With a shudder, she remembered a story Zebedee had told her and her cousins when they were children, a ghostly tale of angry spirits that haunted the Gadarene tombs, screaming and causing damage. She twisted the end of her dripping wet head-covering as they sailed towards the looming hill.

The men sat oppressed by the ominous caves as well, silently watching James and John toss a line and hook into the water, attempting to catch their supper. They caught only a handful of fish between them.

Peter brought the boat as near the shore as he could, to a narrow strip of pebbly beach cut short by the steeply rising hills.

The men climbed out first, splashing into the waist-deep water. Andrew secured the boat to the shore with a long rope, and Peter passed out the dripping nets to the other men. They would need to be spread out on the shoreline to dry. A heap of wet nets would swiftly rot.

Peter helped Beth over the side of the boat, and she sucked in her breath between her teeth as she plunged up to her chest. Peter smiled encouragingly at her and took her hand, helping pull her to shore.

The sun was low, and the storm had chased away all the heat. They were a shivering, miserable group as they scrounged for dry fuel for a fire. The only wood Beth could find was soaked through, and it was fully dark before they managed to make a feeble, smoking fire.

The fish were speared on sticks and held over the flickering flames. The men huddled around in a close circle, rubbing goose-pimpled arms and shaking their clothes to speed their drying. Everyone spoke in a hush. Only Jesus was at his ease.

After a mouthful of fish each, they wrapped themselves in their damp outer garments, laid down on the rocky ground, and attempted to sleep. The fire sputtered out, and the stars wheeled overhead. Beth shivered and was miserable.

Someone screamed atop the hill.

Beth and the others jerked upright, all except for Jesus. He appeared to be sound asleep, again. Beth scrambled across the pebbles to Peter, the rocks digging into her palms. She dove into his arms.

"We should go!" she whispered.

The men hissed at each other, but none of them wanted to be the one to wake Jesus just because they had heard a scary noise. After much whispering, they finally decided they would just need to forget the haunting scream and go to sleep.

Beth lay in Peter's arms with her ears straining to hear another wail from the hilltop. None came, but she lay awake for a long time. She shifted a sharp-edged stone away from her hip and thought longingly of her snug bed back at home.

From the tossing and turning she heard, she was not the only one sleeping fitfully.

The pale morning dawned at last, and they all rose stiff and cold to a comfortless camp and nothing to eat. They knelt together and prayed the Shema as the sun rose over the sea, pebbles digging into their knees.

Beth stretched with a groan and began to search for more promising firewood. Tamar, Hannah, and David would be up as well. Her stomach rumbled. Back in Capernaum, her family would be enjoying a warm breakfast. She suppressed a sigh.

A noise came from up the hill, and she knuckled her sore lower back and looked up the heights. A few men were driving a large herd of pigs. The beasts rooted at the ground with their snouts, scrounging for their breakfast. Clearly, these herdsmen were not Beth's countrymen. Pigs were lawfully unclean, unfit to eat or be used in sacrifice. The Greeks, however, thought quite the opposite. These pigs would end up on pagan altars, a portion of the animal burned to a heathen god and the rest was taken home to feed their family.

"What's that?" Judas pointed up to the tombs in alarm, and everyone turned to see.

Two low shadows moved towards them, alternating between a crawling, twisting movement and a wild run, their heads wrenching unnaturally.

Beth fled to hide behind Peter, and all the men retreated several steps.

"They're men!" James exclaimed as they drew closer.

"Sort of," John corrected.

The men had long hair to their waists, matted and filthy with debris. Their faces and beards were smeared with mud, making their gnashing teeth and wild eyes harshly white by comparison. They had cuts and scrapes all over their spindly limbs, some red with blood, some scarred and weeks or perhaps years old.

Peter held his arms out like a shield, Beth behind him. His voice was higher pitched than normal as he said, "Should we scare them off, Jesus?"

Jesus raised an eyebrow at Peter. "Are you afraid?"

"Isn't everyone?" Peter exclaimed without hesitation.

Beth trembled. She was terrified.

The two monstrous men came and fell before Jesus. The disciples all looked ready to leap into the water and swim for the boat.

Together the two men cried out with one, terrible voice, "What business do we have with each other, Son of God?" Beth saw Peter and Andrew share a look of amazement at the appellation as the wild men continued their wailing, one-voiced cry, "Have you come to torment us before the time? If you are going to cast us out, send us into the herd of swine."

Jesus didn't hesitate, but commanded, "Go!" and the two men collapsed. At that instant, the hillside was alive with squealing pigs.

Beth clung to Peter's arm and gasped as all the swine raced down the steep slope, shrieking with piercing screams. They charged into the sea where they thrashed and squealed until they had all drowned, their bodies bobbing in the water.

The disciples stood stunned.

The herdsmen who had chased the beasts down the hill wailed and pulled at their clothes in dismay. When they saw Jesus with the wild men kneeling at his feet, they cried out pleas for help from a pagan god and fled back up the hill.

Jesus crouched and spoke kind words to the two men, and he healed their wounds.

The disciples slowly relaxed. They murmured to each other as their eyes were dragged again and again to the bobbing, lifeless carcasses, the sound of the two men thanking Jesus over and over again loud in their ears.

No one asked Beth's opinion, but her wonderment of Jesus continued to grow. Jesus had shown how God's power triumphed over the pagan gods by destroying their sacrificial beasts. It reminded her of something a prophet of old might have done.

She discreetly took a long look at the two wild men. These men did not look Jewish, and yet once more, Jesus had healed them.

"How long do you think they were like that?" Beth whispered to Peter.

Peter glanced at the men and pursed his lips. He shook his head in amazement. "From the look of them, I'd say years," Peter said. "That scream last night must have come from one of them."

The two wild-looking men went into the sea and washed. The mud gone, Beth saw their bones protruded beneath taut flesh. They were nearly starved to death.

Andrew and Thaddeus both gave up their outer robes to the men. James and John sloshed out to the boat to fish for a meal.

Beth was trying to find the driest wood among the pile they had collected when she felt eyes on her. She glanced up, then dropped her gaze when she saw one of the men staring at her from the sunken depths of his skull-like face.

"You, a woman, follow him?" He gestured to Jesus, who was talking with Simon.

She didn't answer at first, unwilling to speak to a strange man. She glanced up and saw he was still watching her, hunger for truth in his starved face. She summoned courage.

"I do."

"Who is he?" the man asked, and now his companion also stared out at her beneath his wild hair.

Beth chewed the inside of her cheek. Why didn't they ask one of the men? Why ask her? Perhaps they were worried the Jewish men would refuse to speak with Gentiles. She had been raised not to speak to Gentile men, yet Jesus had seen fit to show them kindness. She hesitated, and they searched her face, waiting.

She drew her courage and replied, "He is Jesus of Nazareth."

"Yes, but *who* is he?" He waved aside her simple reply. "The demon who was inside of me called him the Son of God."

Beth scooped up a few pieces of wood and rose to her feet, the men's eyes boring into her as she stood. She looked over at Jesus. His outward appearance was not unlike the other men, yet he was different from any person she had ever met. He was as astounding as the prophets as old.

She turned back to the men, then shyly dropped her eyes, speaking to the pebbles between them. "All I can tell you is what I've witnessed with my own eyes." Her cheeks warmed as she glanced up and saw they hung on her every word. She lowered her gaze again. "I've heard him teach with wisdom and authority. I've seen him heal people from horrible sickness and disease. He's helped both Jews and Gentiles—a Roman centurion even." She stretched an arm out to the water. "I've seen him speak and calm the wind and the sea." She made herself lift her chin to look into their eyes. "I have seen him cast out demons with a single word."

Beth knew she had left out something important, the key phrase that Jesus had taken up as a banner from John. Despite her fear of revolution, she felt she needed to add, "I've heard him prophesy a coming kingdom—a kingdom of heaven. He has called people to repent and prepare themselves."

The men nodded, and their wide eyes released her and stared at Jesus with awe.

She glanced at Jesus and was startled to see he was watching her. He smiled at her and she flushed. Had he overheard what she said to the two men? Did he think the little housewife had overstepped?

She saw Peter gazing at her with admiration. He leaned closer and said, "You spoke well."

Beth brushed aside the compliment and knelt to prepare the fire.

"Hardly. I only told them what I know. There is so much about Jesus that I don't understand." She followed her husband's eyes back to the two men. They still stared at Jesus with wonderment on their ravaged faces.

Peter reached down and squeezed her shoulder. "Perhaps it is enough. You've helped them understand who helped them."

"I don't think they needed my help to see who Jesus is." Beth shook her head as she arranged the sticks. "They have their health as a testament to his power."

Peter just smiled at her and walked away. She set to work building the fire, finding comfort in the familiar task.

Later that morning, the people from the town above came down the hill. They had all heard what Jesus had done to their pigs and that the demon-possessed men bowed at his feet. They pleaded with Jesus to leave.

The healed men wanted to come with Jesus, but Jesus sent them home to their families. Beth watched them climb the hill, now washed, dressed, and healed. Surely the whole Decapolis would be stunned to see the demon-possessed men healed and in their right minds. What would the two men tell the people about Jesus?

Beth sloshed out into the water to return to the boat, cringing as she was soaked to her armpits once again. Andrew helped pull her into the boat, and she peered back up the hill. The gaping tombs were not so frightening anymore.

Jesus, carrying his leather sandals above his head, heaved himself dripping into the boat with his followers, and they sailed back to Capernaum on a calm sea.

Beth turned her face to the warm sun, feeling the breeze caress her face and dry her clothes. She had seen some amazing miracles, but she was still eager for the safety of home.

10

BLASPHEMY

Reuben crept around the back of the building. He pressed his back to the stone and leaned around the corner to take a peek. Peter's house was quiet. No multitudes swarmed. Did that mean the rabbi was gone?

"What are you doing?" a voice came from close behind him, and Reuben jumped.

With a hand pressed to his pounding heart, he turned to face his cousin, Hannah. "You shouldn't sneak up on people!" he gasped.

"Then what are *you* doing?" she asked, raising an eyebrow.

Reuben fumbled for a reply and Hannah laughed, seeming to find amusement in his awkwardness. It reminded him uncomfortably of how his cousins James and John used to tease him.

"Come on, Reuben, aren't you a little old for hide-and-seek? Who are you hiding from anyway?" Hannah shifted to look around the corner as well.

"Jesus," Reuben blurted, then bit his tongue.

"Jesus?" Hannah turned back to him, her expression radiating disbelief.

"No-I-didn't mean—" Reuben stammered, frustrated that he was bumbling before a child. He closed his eyes, drew a slow breath through his nostrils and puffed it out his mouth, the way Simeon had taught him.

When he opened his eyes, Hannah's facial expression hadn't changed. Her gaze flicked him up and down, mischief glinting in her eyes.

Reuben tried again, slower, controlled. "All I meant to say is that I'm trying to avoid Jesus of Nazareth."

"Why?"

"The man is pretentious and I'm tired of listening to him," Reuben snapped, then pressed his lips together. Why was he explaining himself to his half-grown cousin? He tried to smile, but the expression fell flat. He shook his head and sighed. "I'm just trying to drop in and visit Beth."

"It's about time, too." Hannah crossed her arms. "It's been ages since you've come by. It's almost like you never came back from Jerusalem at all."

"I've been busy with my apprenticeship. Learning to be a scribe is a difficult task." Reuben was annoyed his tone sounded defensive. Why couldn't he modulate and control his voice like Simeon?

"Really? It's got nothing to do with you avoiding Jesus?" Hannah waved her hand around herself, indicating how they were standing in the quiet street behind a house, looking for all the world as if they were hiding.

Reuben cleared his throat and straightened his shawl, feeling foolish. It was true, he had come the back way. He wanted to see if Jesus was at Peter's house before he strolled up to the front door. Though he wanted to visit with Beth, the thought of that pompous rabbi using his presence to insult the Pharisees again, degrading his rabbinical party in front of her, was enough for him keep his distance. He refused to be humiliated again.

He frowned, tired of hiding behind the house talking to Hannah. "Is Jesus there now?"

"No." Hannah shrugged.

Reuben nodded once and strode past her. She fell in behind him as he made it around the corner and ducked into the house without any hint of Jesus or his multitudes. He grinned, feeling triumphant.

He was greeted by the surprised faces of Tamar and his mother. They were sitting at the table with a small plate of food and two cups between them, obviously enjoying a visit. Beth was nowhere to be seen.

Hannah ducked in the door on his heels and winked at him. "Beth's not here either, though." Reuben felt his face droop and Hannah added with a grin, "She's off with *Jesus.*"

Reuben gritted his teeth. Why did the man need to hover in Capernaum? Couldn't he find another town to pester? One on the other side of the world, if he could manage it.

His mother rose to her feet, beaming, and he fixed a smile as she came forward. "My son! So you've pried yourself away from your writing desk at last. I never see you these days." She pressed him to her chest.

He allowed it for a few seconds, then broke the contact, stepping back with a stiff smile. His mother's neediness was an uncomfortable tie to Capernaum, a string that bound him just when he was beginning to realize he wished to leave and go back to Jerusalem and Simeon.

His mother's face fell a little at his coolness, and Reuben flushed with a twinge of shame. He could take the time to sit down for a weekly afternoon visit with her. Philemon would surely understand. He shuffled his feet.

Yet, he was so busy with his studies. They had to come first, didn't they? What was more valuable than the scriptures? What was more praiseworthy than devoting oneself to learning the Torah? Once he was a qualified scribe, ordained by the Pharisee elders, and given permission to take on students, then he would have time to sit and visit with his mother.

Tamar eyed him with pursed lips. "You've been spending too much time with your nose in the scrolls, Reuben. Look at him, he's getting thin, and his eyes are red." She wagged a maternal finger. "You'll ruin your eyesight spending too much time hunched at your desk."

Hannah sat at the table with a chuckle, picking up the corner of a sweetened wheat-cake to nibble. "If he does go blind, Jesus could just heal him." Her eyes danced at Reuben's indignant expression.

He had heard all sorts of tales of Jesus' supposed healing power circulating through town. He had yet to witness it for himself.

Hannah popped another bit of wheat-cake into her mouth, grinning as his aunt and his mother looked him up and down like two over-eager physicians.

Why did Hannah have to tease him? Reuben shifted his feet, feeling a sharp pang for his only other female cousin, the one who used to be his closest confidant and his most stalwart supporter. He came here to talk with Beth, not his mother, and certainly not Hannah. He needed to open his heart to Beth, share his hopes for the future. She would understand his need to return to Jerusalem. She would be proud of him for the opportunity.

But she was gone. Gone following some stranger from Nazareth. Reuben clenched his fists as he remembered the enthusiastic praise for Jesus chasing him down the hillside.

A noise outside interrupted Reuben's bitter musings and the women's appraisal of his health and fitness. Reuben stepped back out the door, his stomach dropping as he looked up the street. It was the man himself.

Jesus was leading a multitude of people and walking right up to Peter's front door.

His mother and aunt forgotten, Reuben fled the house to escape the encounter. Just before he slipped behind the neighbor's house, he saw Philemon walking on the outskirts of the people. Reuben hesitated. Why was Philemon with Jesus? Philemon saw his student and raised a hand in greeting, coming forward.

When Jesus stopped moving, he was instantly swarmed with people, all clamoring around him. Philemon stood with Reuben, a little ways away from the rest of the multitude. Close enough to observe and hear, but not so near that they would be taken as supporters.

"Visiting your family?" Philemon asked politely, nodding to Peter's house. "Isn't Jesus staying there?"

The question was mild enough, but Reuben heard it as an accusation. His fingers twitched, so he folded them together in front of him.

Philemon didn't seem to notice his discomfort and said, "I've been following Jesus this afternoon, trying to witness him healing for myself. Have you had the chance?"

"No." Reuben shook his head. "Though I have seen the after-effects."

He had seen his cousin Simon with his own eyes, his leprosy miraculously cleansed. He was glad his cousin was healed, yet he found it unsettling. He eyed Jesus. If it had actually been Jesus who had done it, where did the man get such power?

A movement caught Reuben's eye, and he saw a group bearing a man on a makeshift stretcher, each holding a corner of his mat. As they passed by Reuben, he saw the man's spindly legs were shriveled and twisted unnaturally.

"Paralyzed," Philemon said knowingly. He cast Reuben a speculative grin. "Maybe now we'll get to see what sort of power Jesus has."

He and Philemon moved closer as the paralyzed man was brought through the crowds and laid at Jesus' feet.

Reuben saw Beth in the crowd, hovering near Peter, giving nervous glances to the strangers that pressed close. She must have felt his eyes on her, and she looked up. She smiled at him across the people, and he grinned back. He was tempted to go to her and draw her away for private conversation, but curiosity got the better of him.

Reuben watched as Jesus gave those who had borne their paralyzed friend approving nods. Then he knelt near the man. He smiled with compassion as he set his hand on the paralytic's shoulder.

"Take courage, child," Jesus said, and Reuben held his breath, waiting for the miracle. Jesus smiled. "Your sins are forgiven." The man's face crumpled into grateful tears.

Reuben blinked. As he realized what Jesus was saying, he felt hot anger bubble up in him.

Philemon whispered through gritted teeth. "His sins are *forgiven?*" He glared at Jesus. "Blasphemy!"

Jesus, still kneeling by the paralytic with a comforting hand on his shoulder, looked their way. Reuben felt his gaze like heat from a flame. Jesus couldn't have overheard them, yet his eyes snapped.

"Why are you thinking evil in your hearts?" Jesus asked, and every eye turned on the two scribes.

Reuben felt his ears burning. He saw Beth staring at him with wide eyes. This was exactly what he had wanted to avoid.

Jesus' voice carried over the multitude. "Which is easier to say, 'your sins are forgiven' or 'get up and walk'? So you understand that the Son of Man has authority on earth to forgive sins—" he looked down on the paralytic "—Get up! Pick up your mat and go home."

The paralytic stretched out his legs, the tendons loosening, the muscles reforming as he put one foot to the ground, then the other. He stood upright, whole and healed.

His friends stared at him with wide eyes and open mouths.

"He's standing!" one of the young men crowed to the other, though they could all see the miracle unfolding before their eyes. "Uriah, you can stand!"

Uriah's face was lit up from within. He nodded to Jesus once, his eyes shimmering. His expression was laden with meaning. Jesus nodded back to him with a wide smile.

Uriah reached down and picked up his thin mat. The crowd murmured as he rolled it up and tucked it under one arm. Chin high, face set in serene happiness, Uriah padded back through the crowd, heading to his home.

As Uriah passed, the people began to cry out, "Praise God!" until the cry was echoing off the hills. The celebrating friends chased after Uriah, whooping for joy.

Philemon and Reuben did not join in the praise. Philemon turned his back on Jesus and beckoned Reuben to draw closer.

"I think it's time our brethren in Jerusalem heard what is going on with this prophet," Philemon said. "Write to your old rabbi and tell him everything." Philemon darted an angry look over his shoulder at Jesus.

Reuben also took a peek, but his eyes went to Beth. She was looking at Jesus with something akin to awe. Her admiration for Jesus felt like a punch to the gut. He lost all desire to share his heart with her.

"I'll write him now," Reuben said, swallowing hard. He set off for home with a clipped gait, frustration rising in him. Just because Jesus did miracles, the usually cautious Beth had thrown away all reason. And she wasn't the only one. The whole town was caught up in a fever for this Nazarene.

He rubbed a hand over his face.

Reuben arrived at Philemon's house. He kissed his fingertips to brush the mezuzah on the door frame, kicked off his sandals, and stormed into the familiar, pleasant workroom.

The room held two desks, one for Philemon, and one for himself. Each low table had a cushion before it to pad their knees as they knelt. On the shelves in the room were all the implements of their trade: rolls of papyrus, pots of ink, sealing wax, quills, wax tablets, and oil lamps. A small chest hid empty mezuzah and phylactery boxes, waiting to be filled with scripture.

A year into his trade, Reuben was already starting the meticulous work of copying out the selected texts, a proof of his skill. Not a jot or tittle could be out of place when one wrote down the Holy Texts.

Reuben gathered what he needed and knelt at his work table. He opened his pot of ink with trembling fingers. That would never do. He needed a smooth, steady hand just now. He shook them out, trying to calm his anger.

Yet, the image of Jesus' accusing eyes kept rising to the forefront of his mind. Once again, Beth had witnessed Jesus ridicule Reuben and the men Reuben worked with. Reuben shook his head and grunted with frustration, scrubbing at his eyes with the heels of his palms. He drew a deep breath through his nose and let it out through his mouth.

He looked around and reminded himself of his growing skill as a scribe. He was talented and clever and would be someone important someday.

Keeping his thoughts in that more pleasant vein, he dipped his pen into the ink and began to write to Simeon. He told him all about this new prophet, Jesus. He told of the miracles he had witnessed and the careless way that Jesus brushed aside the traditions of the elders.

He spun the quill in his fingers as he stared at the papyrus, the wet ink shimmering. He had wanted to talk to Beth today, to seek her advice. When he had come back home after his three years of discipleship, he and Simeon had agreed on a year's trial to see if Capernaum truly had enough to offer an ambitious, scholarly man.

The year was nearly up. Reuben knew now, more than ever, what his heart desired. What was keeping him in Capernaum? Surely not the stiff relationship with his own family. Beth was busy with her husband and home, and now she was infatuated with a showy, new rabbi. Reuben gritted his teeth as he remembered her expression of awe for the Nazarene.

With a glance around the room to be sure no one else was near, he dashed a few sentences more, excitement surging through his fingertips.

You were right, rabbi, as you always are. Capernaum is not the place for me. I cannot reach the level of learning I desire here, and I regret my choice to leave you. If you are still willing to continue your patronage, I will accept your invitation to return to Jerusalem and be your disciple once more.

He felt a pang of guilt as he penned the words. Philemon had truly taken him under his wing and embraced him into his family. He had given him a trade and freed him from needing to return to fishing. He would be forever grateful to the man.

Still, how could he remain in his hometown when his family could not appreciate his hunger for the law? Why couldn't they see his mind as a gift, as Simeon did? Why couldn't they be pleased for him, a fisherman's son, given the opportunity of living in sight of the Temple? He had given Capernaum a year and found it wanting.

Shaking off thoughts of his family, he rolled and sealed the papyrus and let his mind fill with happy daydreams for the future.

He waited two weeks before a reply came. A dark-skinned trader delivered a sealed scroll and a satchel, and Reuben paid the man for his trouble.

Retreating to a private corner of the house, he broke the seal with clumsy fingers, hoping that this was the summons he waited for.

To my student Reuben,

You did well to inform me of this Nazarene. I too find his words and deeds disturbing. I have shared your letter with the Sanhedrin and they are keenly interested.

As to the other matter, I would be pleased to have you return to me and resume your studies …

Reuben's heart soared.

… but with this new development, I believe Capernaum is where you should be for the time being.

Reuben's heart sank like a stone.

It is fortuitous for me that one of my own is situated to give me regular and exact reports about this new prophet. The Sanhedrin is desirous that I continue to keep them apprised of the situation as it unfolds. It seems my patronage of you already has its rewards.

However, I will not have you fall behind in your studies. There are a few scrolls I wish you to read. The first ...

The letter continued with a lesson plan for Reuben to follow, but with no mention of a possible return to Jerusalem or future promises to give him comfort.

Reuben dully examined the scrolls in the accompanying satchel. They were copies of the greatest writings of the most esteemed Pharisee teachers. Usually, he would have been elated to have this treasure trove at his fingertips, but a lesson plan was not what he desired. He wished to be back with Simeon in the exciting city, meeting wise and influential men, sowing seeds that he would reap in future years when he began his career.

Reuben shoved the satchel aside, regretting that he had said anything at all to Simeon about Jesus of Nazareth. If it wasn't for that man, Reuben was certain he would be packing his bags for Jerusalem this very moment.

11

FEAST OF SINNERS

Reuben stormed through the market, frowning at the simple wares and produce for sale. In the Jerusalem market he had seen colorful silk from the Far East, lush melons from Egypt, baked delicacies that made his mouth water, as well as trinkets, jewels, spices, silver and gold serving dishes, and delicate glassware. He turned up his nose at the common fare available in his hometown, a market even smaller than Magdala.

"I'll take all of it, the whole lot!" a familiar voice said, and Reuben looked over.

Matthew was standing in front of a table of freshly baked bread, digging coins from his moneybag. He tossed down the money. "See that it's delivered to my house, will you?"

The woman behind the booth gathered up the coins with an elated smile for Matthew. She saw Reuben's eyes on her and ducked her chin. Matthew was a tax collector. Even doing business with him was frowned upon.

Matthew noticed her downcast eyes and turned to see Reuben standing just a few feet away. Matthew's face lit up. Reuben cringed as the man hastened forward and grasped his arm.

"Reuben!" Matthew said with gleaming eyes and a huge smile.

"You're just who I wanted to see."

Reuben yanked his arm away as he took a step back from his unusually giddy childhood friend. "Are you drunk?"

Matthew chortled. "No, not unless you can say that I'm drunk on happiness. I'm having a feast tonight at my house. You should come! Please say you will."

Reuben furrowed his brow. What had come over Matthew?

Matthew's servant boy came up, leading a yearling lamb. "Will this do, my lord?" the boy asked.

"It's perfect, just perfect!" Matthew said. "Take it home to the cook. I want it roasted to perfection for supper tonight." The boy led the docile animal towards Matthew's house.

Reuben crossed his arms and watched as Matthew bought several skins of wine, slinging the sloshing bags over his shoulder. He began purchasing some figs from another booth, oblivious to the townspeople's wondering whispers and curious stares.

Aaron, the other tax collector, stomped up. "Matthew! What on earth are you doing? We need to get back to work."

"No, sir!" Matthew crowed, gathering up the basket of figs on his already laden arm. "I'm never going back to work there again."

Aaron put a fist on his hip. "Seriously? Jesus asks you to go with him, and just like that—" he snapped a finger in Matthew's face, "—you're going to drop everything and follow him?"

Matthew stood and faced Aaron squarely, his chin high. "Yes."

Reuben raised his brows, shocked at what he was hearing. Matthew had left his job as a tax collector? Reuben felt a momentary surge of pleasure for Matthew, but it was rubbed away by jealousy and distrust. He had asked Matthew to leave his trade, yet Matthew had refused. Why would Matthew take the advice of a stranger, but ignore that of a childhood friend and Pharisee disciple?

"So what now?" Aaron asked, eyeing Matthew up and down. "What will you do to support yourself?"

"I have no idea," Matthew laughed again, his shoulders shaking with mirth.

Despite his protests, Reuben was sure the man must be drunk; he was being so ridiculous.

Matthew said, "But for tonight, I'm having a feast to honor Jesus." Reuben sucked in his breath and clenched his fists. A feast in *Jesus'* honor? Matthew was still brimming with enthusiasm. "You should come, Aaron! I've invited all our friends."

Aaron raised his eyebrows. "All our friends? Even our, ahem, seedier companions?"

Matthew nodded, oblivious to the dark glare Reuben was aiming at his back. Matthew had dared to invite *him*—a scribe and Pharisee apprentice—to share a feast not only with Jesus, but with tax collectors and people of low repute?

Reuben drew up to his full height. Aaron looked over Matthew's shoulder and saw Reuben's face. He grinned, seeming to find it amusing.

Aaron twisted his face into a crooked smirk and replied while still staring at Reuben, "I'll be there. Nothing could keep me away."

Reuben spun on his heel, his errands forgotten. He had to go and tell Philemon and Daniel everything he had overheard. If Jesus was flouting the purity traditions by sitting down to dine with known sinners, the elders needed to know about it.

Reuben spent the day waiting in a mood of bitter dissatisfaction. As soon as evening fell, Reuben, Daniel, and Philemon strode down the dim street to witness the feast for themselves.

Reuben's pulse was quickened, though he wasn't sure why. He felt a sort of thrill, heading to confront Jesus. The man had embarrassed him twice. It was time he returned the gesture.

Matthew lived in one of the newest, most expensive Capernaum homes, with a large courtyard filled with ornamental plants and a little pool of water with a splashing fountain—a feeble imitation of Roman opulence.

The serving boy greeted them at the door and took them to the upper room where the walls reverberated with talk and laughter. True to what Matthew had said, Jesus was reclining at the table, the guest of honor at a feast of sinners.

Reuben was sure to note all who were in attendance. He saw with displeasure that his noisy cousins, James and John, were there, the loudest and brashest of all the guests. He saw Beth's husband and brother-in-law. Reuben pressed his lips together. For her sake, he wished the men back at their nets.

Aaron saw the three Pharisees enter, smirked, and raised his cup to them before taking a long draft.

Matthew, still intoxicated by happiness, turned to the men in surprise. He came forward, his arms open in welcome.

"Men, I am honored!" Matthew said. "Please, come and sit. This is a joyous day." He looked at Reuben in particular as he smiled.

Philemon turned his face away with disdain and spoke not to Matthew, but to one of Jesus' disciples who was sitting nearby.

His voice was cold and carrying. "Why is your teacher eating with the tax collectors and sinners?"

A hush fell over the room. Reuben saw James and John glaring at him, but he was no longer a short little boy easily intimidated by them. He was a scholar, and he was in the right. He lifted his chin.

Matthew dropped his welcoming arms. His smile slid off his face as he realized the Pharisees were not there to celebrate with him. The usual sadness began seeping into his eyes, and the familiar sting of rebuff slumped his shoulders.

Jesus himself answered, also loud enough for the entire room to hear. "It is not those who are healthy that need a physician, but those who are sick. Go and see if you can learn what this scripture means: 'I desire compassion and not sacrifice'." Philemon puffed up his chest as Jesus continued, "I didn't come to call the righteous, but sinners."

Daniel worked his mouth, his wrinkled eyes flashing with the zeal of a much younger man. He turned to the other two and growled, "I think we've seen enough."

He turned his back on the feast, leading the way out of the room. Philemon turned with a snap of robes. Reuben took one last glance before following. The sinners were all looking at Jesus in marvel.

Matthew held out a hand, and despite his better judgment, Reuben paused. Matthew spoke with pain and confusion in his eyes, "Why aren't you happy? Aren't you pleased for me? I've left my job. I'm not a tax collector anymore."

Reuben's voice was sharper than he meant it to be as he said, "Of course I'm happy you are no longer a traitor and a thief." Matthew's face jerked as if he'd been slapped.

Reuben felt compelled to give his childhood friend some solid advice. "If you've truly set that evil life behind you, then you need to get better friends. Put these men aside. Don't welcome them to feasts." Reuben lowered his tone as a dozen eyes turned his way. "And I would think twice about rubbing elbows with Jesus. His teachings are inflammatory. He is trying to make trouble, mark my words."

Matthew drew his hand over his mouth before speaking. "I'm still not good enough for you, am I?"

What could he answer? Reuben sighed, turned away, and strode out of the house, passing the surprised servant boy carrying a tray. He caught up to Daniel. Philemon was further ahead, his gait clipped.

"The man has charisma, I'll give him that," Daniel said with a shake of his head. "I've seldom seen a man draw the common people to himself so easily." He paused. "It never ends well, especially for the people." Reuben knew the aged scribe had lived through his fair share of failed rebellions.

"Then we need to protect them!" Reuben cried out. "Who will protect our people, if not us?"

"True." Daniel nodded, taking Reuben's arm to lean upon. "Though I struggle to decide how. So many regard Jesus as a prophet and will not listen to reason. We can't have Jesus beginning a doomed revolution, drawing Herod Antipas or Rome itself down on our heads. The peace is so delicate that the slightest spark will set this entire region aflame." He pressed a shaky hand to his temple. "Worse yet, we can't have him deceiving the people spiritually, leading them away from the truth of the traditions. I will need to think about this."

Reuben needed to ask a question that had been preying on his mind, but he was afraid of seeming foolish.

He glanced around to make sure no one would hear him as he whispered, "How can a man break the traditions of the elders with every turn, yet seem to have such a powerful gift?"

Daniel's creased eyes were measuring. The joking, jovial man was as serious as Reuben had ever seen him. "Don't be swayed by theatrics. Not all power is from the Lord, remember. He's not the first to have the gift of power, and he's not the first to use it badly. His words will be his downfall. We just need to get the people to hear, somehow."

The next morning Reuben sat glumly at work with Philemon, wishing he was away in Jerusalem. Shuffling steps at the door broke his moody reverie, and he looked up. Jairus, the synagogue official, stumbled into the room, his face drenched with tears.

Reuben dropped his quill in surprise.

Philemon rose to his feet with wide eyes. "What's happened?"

"My daughter," Jairus slumped against the wall and dragged his hands through his already disheveled hair. "She's dead!"

Reuben began to say, "I'm so sor—"

Jairus cut him off with a slice of his hand. "I need to find Jesus, he can heal her. Where is he? Do you know where he stays?"

Reuben and Philemon shared a look. Philemon stepped forward and tried to reason with Jairus, but the man was too distraught. Finally, when he saw nothing else would do, Philemon told him where Jesus could usually be found. At once, the man left.

Philemon frowned. "Set your work aside. This is not going to end well." Philemon's eyes blazed with righteous anger. "Jairus is clinging to false hope. It will make his grief all the stronger when Jesus fails. Somehow the Nazarene has performed many miracles, but *this*—" he shook his head, "—is far beyond him."

It looked like most of Capernaum was at Jairus' house, overflowing the courtyard and lower rooms and milling around the street. Professional, paid mourners summoned the people from far away with their plaintive wailing, their cries mingling with the flute players. Reuben and Philemon wove their way through friends and neighbors to find the family members. The two men bowed their heads and quoted comforting scripture.

The men were shown the body of the little girl. He and Philemon carefully kept from touching her or the mat she lay on. Touching a corpse made one unclean for seven days. Her skin was waxy and pale, her lips gray. Reuben recognized her. He had seen her playing with the other children and drawing water with her mother at the well. It saddened him to see a life cut short, but it was a hard world for children, and many did not reach adulthood.

Reuben left the house as soon as it politeness allowed, drawing a deep breath of fresh air through his nose.

They were outside the house for over an hour before they saw Jairus rushing forward.

"I can't believe it," Reuben spoke low in Philemon's ear. "Jesus actually came with him. He must not realize she is truly dead."

Jesus was hard on Jairus' heels, his disciples close behind him. Reuben saw Beth was once again with her husband. For some reason, her face was full of hope. Reuben frowned, but he managed to arrange his face into a neutral expression when Beth looked his way.

Jesus came right up among the mourners and spoke with his

familiar authoritative tone, "Leave, for the girl has not died. She is asleep."

Reuben joined the jeering laughter. He had seen the corpse himself. Jesus was doggedly insistent. Jairus, with his beard soaked with tears, commanded the wailers and musicians to be silent, and then he ushered everyone out of the house. The mourners shook their heads at Jesus and grumbled.

Jairus welcomed Jesus into the house with wild eyes, his hands pressed over his heart. The man believed Jesus could do something to reverse his daughter's death. Reuben could have cursed Jesus for his callous insensitivity. Jairus was a well-respected elder in the synagogue. He didn't deserve this mockery. The poor man would mourn twice as hard when his hopes for healing were crushed.

Reuben smothered a satisfied smile as he pictured Jesus' face as he beheld the corpse. The man would be embarrassed and stammering excuses. Jairus would know the truth. Then the people would mock Jesus. It was about time the Nazarene was humbled.

Jesus was only gone a moment. When Jesus stepped back into the sunlight, Reuben was about to sneer when his expression froze in shock.

The crowd gasped as one. The girl was standing at his side, her little hand in Jesus' large brown one.

Reuben felt his stomach drop in shock. He rubbed his eyes in disbelief as he saw her cheeks were flushed with a healthy glow. She fidgeted under the weight of so many staring eyes.

Jairus' wife sobbed. She ran to her daughter and drew her to her breast. Joyful tears ran into her daughter's hair. Jairus wrapped his arms around both his wife and daughter, crying praises to God.

The disciples of Jesus were beaming. Beth took Peter's hand in both of hers and leaned against his arm, her face radiant.

It soured Reuben's stomach.

The flute players stood shocked and the professional mourners looked awkward and unsure of what to do. Slowly the people began to speak words of awe and praise to God, the voices joining together until one of the flute players lifted his instrument to his lips and began to play a joyful song, and the mourners began to dance and laugh at this unexpected event. People began breaking away from the mourning-turned-rejoicing crowd, racing away to spread the news. Philemon and Reuben looked to each other in bitter bafflement.

Reuben crossed his arms. "Well! This news is going to spread. I wouldn't be surprised if Jerusalem itself was buzzing with it by the end of the day. The people will call *him* Elijah now."

Long ago that prophet, too, had raised a child to life.

He and Philemon turned to go, no longer needed. As they worked their way back to Philemon's house, occasionally passed by another excited witness, Reuben was quiet. He was trying to decide how he felt about this miracle. He was glad the girl wasn't dead; he wasn't hardhearted. Yet, he did not like Jesus being the one to raise her up.

He tried to reconcile the Jesus who had miraculous power with the Jesus who dined with sinners. The man aligned himself against the Pharisees and trampled on the traditions of the elders. Those traditions were the result of careful consideration of the law. Moses had received the law from God, a code of righteous living to set the Israelites apart from their pagan neighbors. The scribes and lawyers had studied and reasoned for untold years to ensure that the law was followed in every aspect so that the people were always obeying and honoring the Lord. How could a man who was so callous toward the traditions do something as miraculous as what Reuben had just witnessed? He had heard Daniel's opinion on the matter. Reuben glanced to the side.

"Philemon," Reuben said tentatively, and Philemon slowed his pace and allowed his apprentice to walk beside him. "I need to ask, how do we *know* that we shouldn't heed Jesus' teachings? How can we be absolutely certain that we should set ourselves against him? What if he is Elijah returned? What if he is the Messiah?"

Philemon looked unconcerned. "This is not a simple question, but the answer is clear to an educated mind."

Reuben nodded, wanting to show his wisdom to Philemon, even though he was still confused. He was ashamed of his niggling doubts, and the worry that maybe, just maybe, Jesus was a true prophet after all. Reuben was not the sort of man who could just take what his teachers said at face value. He needed to be convinced and know for himself.

He took a deep breath and tried again, choosing his words carefully. "So what do we say about today? People will ask us, is this the Messiah? What he did today was powerful. We saw that girl dead, and we saw her brought to life with our own eyes. If that was a trick, it was masterfully done."

Philemon held up an ink-stained finger. "Yes, but you must look at the whole picture. Don't get caught up in the emotion and the show. You must keep a firm rein on your mind. You have seen how he has set himself against the traditions and the teachings of the elders. Ask yourself, 'would a true prophet do that?' The scriptures tell how to discern if a prophet is true. Find and study this tonight:

"If a prophet arises among you and gives you a sign or a wonder,
And the sign or the wonder comes true when he says,
'Let us go after other gods (whom you have not known)
And let us serve them,'
You shall not listen to the words of that prophet.
The Lord your God is testing you to find out
If you love the Lord your God with all your heart and all your soul."

Philemon leaned towards Reuben. "Now, how does that help you understand?"

Reuben remembered this verse well, though it had sat neglected in his mind for so long. Now that Philemon had blown the dust away, he felt a sense of calm security wash over him.

Reuben grinned. "Of course. That is the exact verse I needed." Philemon smiled with a gracious nod. Reuben clasped his hands behind his back, drawing an easy breath. "Moses himself told us that a person can seem like a prophet, and even do signs and wonders, but if what he wants you to do is not of the Lord, then he is false. His power is not from the Lord at all."

Philemon nodded with a smile. "Just so, Reuben. Later in that same passage, it says that such a prophet should be put to death. What makes this Nazarene so dangerous is that he is trying to say that he *does* follow the Lord. Jesus, in his mantle of false goodness, can do a lot of damage. You must guard yourself, disciple-scribe, against this test the Lord has set before us. Do not let your youthful emotion sway your mind. Remember to heed your elders and the teachings you have been taught."

"Yes, Philemon," Reuben said.

If Jesus was set against the will of the Lord, then God could not let him stand. Reuben vowed to stand for God and fight against this false prophet at every turn.

The idea excited him.

12

SON OF DAVID

"Have mercy on us, Son of David!" The plaintive cry broke through the noise of the crowd, rippling over the people as heads swiveled to see who dared use such a title for this traveling rabbi.

Beth looked up and saw the source. Two ragged men shuffled forward, each grasping a gnarled staff in one hand. The older of the two, with a bare head and wispy gray beard, grasped the back of his younger companion's tunic. The man at the front reached forward with trembling, searching fingers.

Beth didn't recognize them. How far had these blind men stumbled in the dark, coming to find the one who could offer them hope?

Zebedee, who was walking beside her, also turned with raised brows. He had fished for several hours the night before, coming home as the sun rose for a hearty meal and a few hours of sleep. He would take a long nap again in the afternoon, but for now, he had come to see his sons and their rabbi.

The crowd watched the blind men in interest, and a murmur of excitement rippled as the title was passed from mouth to mouth. "Son of David?"

Beth knew the prophecy. They all did.

They were almost to Peter's house, and Hannah was bobbing outside the door, absorbing it all.

Beth smiled. Tamar must have given the eager girl strict instructions to remain at home, or her sister would already be running to greet them. Hannah stepped to the side as Jesus took the arm of each of the blind men and led them inside, away from the pushy crowd. Peter and several of the disciples followed, but Jesus shut the door on the swarm, who turned, disappointed, and milled around on the street.

Beth took the chance to sit with her back against the sun-warmed house and rest her weary feet.

Zebedee stood straight-backed, hands clasped behind him, bouncing on the balls of his feet with happiness, his gray-streaked curls dancing with the beat.

"Now I know why Jesus called so many fishermen to help him." Beth chuckled as she turned her face upwards to her uncle. The man, despite only a few hours of sleep, was still looking hale and ready for anything. "You fishermen are made of strong stuff."

Zebedee was pleased, and he laughed like rumbling thunder. "Perhaps we are. Don't you forget, my girl, you are the daughter of a fisherman. Your father's strength is in you." His eyes twinkled beneath his thick brows, and she smiled around a sudden lump in her throat.

"Not in me. Hannah perhaps." Beth deflected with a laugh as Hannah spun over, brimming with life and enthusiasm.

"Is it true?" Hannah clasped her hands in front of her sister, gleaming eyes wide. "Is Jesus the Son of David? Is he the one everyone's waiting for?"

Beth hesitated, feeling unqualified to answer. She looked to Zebedee for guidance, but his gaze was far beyond them. He began a rumbling, chanting recitation, a prophecy which the sisters recognized at once.

"When your days are complete and you lie down with your fathers,
I will raise up your descendant after you,
Who will come forth from you,
And I will establish his kingdom. He shall build a home for My name,
And I will establish the throne of his kingdom forever."

As the last word fell from his lips, Beth jumped as the door was thrown open.

From the shadows of the doorway, the blind men crept out. Their heads swiveled as their starved eyes soaked up the amazed crowd, the birds wheeling in the sapphire sky, and the sparkling Sea of Galilee. The two men stared at each other with wide smiles, and then they leaped down the street, whooping like young boys. They raced past the cluster of Pharisees. The three scribes pulled back their dark robes and glared like birds of prey.

A glinting eye filled Beth's mind, and she swallowed and pushed the image away.

Reuben was between the older scribes, his face grim. Again, Beth was struck with the changes in her cousin. Gone was the eager and curious-eyed cousin of her youth. In his place was a scowling young man with crossed arms, ink-stained fingers, and bitter eyes.

Was this the same boy who had raced through the tall grass to escape his chores? Was this the best friend who had poured out his heart to her and looked to her for praise and encouragement?

She chided herself for her inattention to him. She had been so busy that she had hardly spoken to him these past few months. She hoped he didn't feel as though all his family had abandoned him. Ebenezer was open in his disapproval of his eldest son. He now insisted his wife and sons honor his feelings and keep their distance, shunning Reuben for his refusal to bend to his father's will. The result was that Reuben had been set adrift, a painful place for a firstborn son.

Beth rose to her feet to speak with him, but she was stopped as Jesus came out of the house. He set aside two abandoned walking sticks, smiling to himself. He turned as someone in the crowd called his name.

"Please, help my uncle!" the young man cried. "He's possessed by a demon and can't speak."

Jesus went at once and cast the demon out. With only the power of Jesus' words, the mute man spoke. Beth had never seen Jesus fail to heal someone, and his powers never failed to stir her heart to hope for a better future for the painful world. Beth looked at Reuben again. He didn't seem to share her pleasure.

The Pharisees were muttering among themselves—even kindly Daniel looked bitter. Beth moved a little towards the religious leaders.

Reuben's eyes flicked to her. He broke away from his group and came towards her, casting a doubtful look back at his companions.

Beth and Reuben paused a few feet away from each other, and Beth felt an unaccountable awkwardness. This was her cousin, the best friend of her childhood. Why was it so hard to think of what to say? She shuffled her feet and tipped her head to catch his eyes with a smile. His expression was stony.

"Did you ever think you'd see miracles like this?" she asked. "Jesus' power is amazing!" She gestured to the healed man, who was now dancing without inhibition.

Reuben's brows sunk low. He glanced at the reveling man and sniffed in disdain. Beth puckered her brow, trying to understand his reluctance.

"I don't agree." Reuben's voice was flinty. "He is casting out demons with power from the ruler of demons."

Beth gasped, drawing her hand over her open mouth. Anger heated her face, and she moved her hands to her hips.

"You can't possibly mean that," she said. "Look at this crowd, look at their joy. The praises from their lips are for the Lord. Would the devil do that?" He wouldn't meet her gaze, and the coldness seeping from him was a chill on her bones.

She wanted to shake him, but instead, she said, "Reuben, think about what you're accusing him of. His message is repentance and preparing ourselves for the kingdom of heaven. Why would a demon teach such a thing?"

Reuben finally met her gaze. His cold facade slipped as he leaned towards her, a touch of the old, familiar zeal flashing in his narrowed eyes.

"The evil one can use many deceptions. You and Peter need to distance yourselves from this false rabbi, or it will mean trouble for you later. Turn him out of your house."

Beth opened her mouth to protest, but Reuben reached out a hand and gripped her arm just above the elbow. He said the words that he knew would drive fear farthest into her heart.

"Remember what happened to other false prophets? To other revolutionaries and their followers, even your own family?" His tone lowered, and his eyes bored into her, making her throat dry. "You need to protect them, Beth. Do you want your family slaughtered or sold as slaves? Peter nailed to a cross?"

Beth jerked her arm free. Fear fluttered in her stomach as a fire burned in her heart. How dare he? When had Reuben become so heartless?

"Don't try to play my fears against me," her voice wavered despite herself. "Jesus will remain a guest in our house as long as wants." Reuben leaned away, taken aback by her anger. She stepped forward. "Have you actually listened to him at all? He isn't inciting the people to rebellion, like Judah ben Hezekiah did in Sepphoris."

She looked him up and down, from dark scribal robes to fringed shawl, and saw that he looked uncomfortable. Realization dawned on her, and she crossed her arms.

"You aren't worried about him leading the men into battle, are you? You're just insulted that he is confronting the Pharisees! Put aside your prejudice and listen to him, really listen to him." She thrust out a hand towards her rabbi.

Reuben's eyes remained fixed on her face, his expression stony once more. It nearly broke her heart to see him so closed off behind his wall of unbelief.

She pleaded, "The people are praising the Lord. This is what we have longed for, and I'm beginning to fear that you will miss it all."

Reuben scoffed. He twisted his head at her, his eyes narrowed as he said, "I have dedicated my life to the study of the scriptures, and *you* would try to teach me? You, a girl who can't even read?" His sharp words cut her. His nostrils flared as he hissed, "You used to heed my advice, Beth. Why won't you listen to me anymore?" She saw a twinge of pain in his eyes, but he quickly hid it and crossed his arms. "Stop echoing the beliefs of ignorant fishermen."

She felt like he had slapped her. Was that what he thought of her? Did he think her so weak that she would simply repeat whatever she was told without conviction of her own? "I'm not—"

Reuben sliced his hand through the air, chopping her words. "Turn back from this reckless path, before it's too late."

He spun on his heel, and without a backward glance, he returned to the Pharisees, straightening his shawl. He spoke a few words to them, and they looked up and cast disapproving glances her way.

She retreated to stand with Hannah. She believed she was right to support Jesus, but that didn't make standing in opposition to the local Pharisees easy.

Like the recoil of a taut bow, her boldness sent shock waves through her as her temper cooled. Despite her brave words, fear of retribution from those in power did hang over her. In the too-recent past, entire towns had burned and families had been utterly destroyed, all for trying to restore Israel to God.

She dared to hope with Jesus it would be different. He didn't seem anything like the revolutionaries who screamed for Roman blood and Jewish freedom. Jesus was kind and gentle. He taught wisdom, not warfare. Surely Jesus would not lead her husband to the cross.

She held her lower lip between her teeth. She closed her eyes and could see the raven with its glinting eye, waiting to feast on the dying man as he struggled for each agonizing breath. She quailed at the image, forcing her eyes open.

She reached out an arm and encircled her sister in a tight, protective hug. Hannah looked upwards with questioning brows but allowed her older sister to take comfort in the closeness.

"Beth?" Peter hastened up with a wide smile.

Beth felt her worries shift to the background as she looked on his eager face. Her husband was healthy, safe, and here with her. There was nothing to worry about. The contrast between his open spirit and Reuben's bitter attitude was stark.

Peter beamed as he said, "Jesus just announced that he wants to leave this afternoon."

Beth had known for several days that the rabbi planned to do another preaching journey, but she still felt her heart sink at the prospect of saying goodbye to her husband. She understood why Peter longed to go with Jesus. When had such a man walked the earth? She, too, was stirred by his mighty power and inspired by his words. Jesus taught all who wished to listen, and she was not the only woman who had sat with his disciples to learn from him. Yes, she understood why Peter wanted to go with the rabbi. Understanding did not stop the burning she felt in her throat.

Peter eyed her as if trying to read something in her face. His tone was subdued as he trailed a finger over her cheek. "I don't know how long we will be gone," he said. Beth squeezed Hannah a bit tighter, loneliness already sweeping over her. Peter hesitated, then added, "You know, you could come."

"Me?" Beth gasped, her heart leaping.

Peter nodded but held his hands out defensively. "This will be for more than a single night. It is a hard way to travel, and I know you prefer to stay near home."

Beth glanced at her sister and then at the house. Family and comfort. That was all she had ever wanted or needed before.

Her eyes shifted to Jesus. What else would the prophet say and do? Curiosity flickered within her. Peter's invitation made her want to throw open doors she used to hold tightly closed. Now she could not only stay with Peter, but she could also witness with her own eyes the kingdom being born.

She felt a thrill rush through her at the idea, but her next words were soft. "I would like to go."

"Really? You would?" Peter tilted back his head and laughed. "You keep surprising me. Not many women want to tramp all over the country. My little dove hides a brave soul."

He laughed again as he clasped her shoulders and dropped a kiss on her cheek. She tried to smile in return, but his praise of her courage made her stomach swoop. What was she getting herself into?

"Mama won't like it," Hannah said crossly, stamping her foot. "I don't like it! It isn't fair. Why can't we all go?"

Beth tried to placate her sister, but Hannah spun around, long hair whipping, and ran off.

"She'll calm down," Peter shrugged, brushing a hand down Beth's arm. "We'll be leaving within the hour. If you have anything you'd like to bring along, you'd better pack now."

"Anything I'd like to bring?" Beth raised an eyebrow. "You mean you'd go, just as you are?" Peter spread his arms and looked down at himself.

"What am I missing?"

"Bah!" Beth laughed, pushing him away. "I'll make sure we have what we need."

Peter pinched her chin with a playful scowl. "Women! Always making a fuss when none is needed." He laughed with affection before he rejoined the others.

Beth, with a knot of anxiousness in her stomach, went into the house. She needed to tell her mother. She knew it would be as Hannah had said; her mother would not be pleased. She puffed out a breath.

She found her mother in the courtyard taking down the washing. She told her mother the news in as few words as possible.

"How can you even *think* of such a thing?" Her mother threw up her hands. "Leaving me alone with the little ones. How is that fair to me?"

Beth felt a surge of guilt. "Hannah is eleven now. She can help you."

Tamar snorted. "Hannah is not like you were at that age. She is a child yet, an unruly child who would rather play than help." She sucked in her breath and let it out with a puff. "No, no! You've had your excitement. I've been more than understanding as you've skipped all over town following Jesus. It's time to return to your duties." Tamar snapped the cloth she was holding.

Beth clutched her skirts in her hands and chewed her lower lip. She felt her will splitting two ways. She wanted to be with her husband as he followed Jesus, and she also wanted to stay at home and please her mother.

"Was this Peter's idea?" Tamar narrowed her brows, then sniffed at Beth's expression. "You know it's only so you can do the cooking and the laundry." She yanked another cloth off the line. "Women do not follow rabbis."

"They follow this rabbi," the words fell from Beth's lips.

Tamar raised an eyebrow as she met resistance from her pliable, obedient daughter. Tamar set her hands on her hips, stubbornness on every curve of her body.

Beth drew a deep breath. "There are other women who are disciples now. Some wealthy women are supporting him financially. Even Aunt Naomi is going to follow him." James and John weren't too happy about that, but Naomi was determined.

"I heard that too." Tamar shook her head and clicked her tongue. "I can't believe Zebedee is allowing it. She's leaving that poor man to care for himself. Or rather, he will be here every day for his supper."

Tamar huffed angrily, but Beth knew that Tamar loved to cook for others and would enjoy her brother-in-law's company.

Tamar gestured to the house. "This is your domain, Beth. This is where we women do our work for the Lord. Our cooking and cleaning, keeping the purity laws, teaching the children, that is all service to Him."

"I know that." Beth went forward and took one end of the blanket, helping her mother fold it. "And I enjoy being at home. But we can't deny something is happening out there in the world, and for once, I am invited to be a part of it."

"Why do you need to be a part of it?" Tamar made an angry noise deep in her throat. "I wish you had a child, so you would stop being one yourself."

Beth reeled as if her mother had struck her. Though she and Peter had managed to find intimate moments over the summer, her womb was empty. Every disappointing month had made her longing for a baby grow until it was an ache that throbbed in quiet moments.

Tamar saw her daughter's face and softened, coming forward to cup Beth's cheeks. "Forgive me, my daughter. I didn't mean it."

She drew Beth into a tight embrace. Beth felt hot tears dripping onto her mother's shoulder. Her mother was right. If she had a baby of her own, she would be more than happy to stay at home. As it was, being busy helped her forget her empty womb.

Tamar stroked her hair. "I'm only worried about you. I cannot bear to lose another child."

Beth squeezed her mother tighter, guilt racking her. Twice, before the birth of Hannah, her mother had to bury an infant son and see their tiny bones and her hopes gathered up and sealed away.

Beth loved her husband, but she loved her mother too. Perhaps this was all a mistake. She could change her mind, right now, and stay in Capernaum. She was surprised when the idea of staying safely at home didn't satisfy.

Tamar stepped back and Beth wiped her eyes on her sleeve. Tamar became brisk once more, though her tone was calmer as she said, "The garden is ready for harvest. Will you leave that all to me?"

"Hannah can help you," Beth's said again, and her voice was calm.

Despite every reason to stay, despite the nervousness she felt in her gut, she still desired to go. Tamar looked her up and down and pursed her lips like she was considering the quality of an item at the market. She shrugged and turned away.

"I see you've made up your mind. Very well, do what you want if you care nothing for my wisdom."

Beth reached out and caught her mother's hand. "I do care for your wisdom," she spoke, emotion thickening her throat as she looked down at the calloused hand, burned by cook fires, pricked by needles, yet soft and gentle for her children. "I shall be like Sarah, who went with her husband Abraham when God called him to leave his home."

Tamar's face softened. Beth was encouraged and rushed on. "I want to be with Peter, and I freely confess that I have a hunger to learn more about what Jesus is teaching. I couldn't go to school like Reuben—" she felt a pang as she said his name, remembering the icy coldness in his eyes "—but Jesus is willing to teach all who will listen. He moves on. If I wish to learn, I have to go with him." She caught her mother's resistant eye and smiled. "I may only be cooking and scrubbing laundry, but if so, I am still doing the Lord's work, aren't I?"

Tamar was silent for a long moment. Finally, she smiled, shaking a scolding finger. "You have too much of your father in you. That man could talk me into anything!" She laughed and her eyes relaxed. "He would have liked Jesus, I think." She patted her daughter's hand. "I'll help you get ready."

Beth felt a strange sense of unreality as she packed for Peter and herself, bringing only what they could carry: some food, a blanket, water skins, a flint for making fire, and a valuable iron knife, all stuffed into a clay cooking pot and a traveling bag.

When she came out of the house, she saw Jesus and his disciples were already waiting. Naomi was there, holding a heavy bag bulging with supplies. It was clear she was not about to let these young men go hungry.

Beth's heart pounded as she embraced her mother, already missing her. She tried to get a hug out of angry Hannah. David gave his sister a rough, boyish kiss, wiping his eyes on the back of his hand.

Jesus turned towards his disciples with eagerness and vitality in his face. "Come," Jesus said. "Let's go and proclaim the kingdom!"

13

FATHER'S FAULT

"**D**efinitely not!" Reuben held up both hands in protest, alarm coursing through him.

He stood in the doorway of Philemon's house, wishing that he could duck back inside and slam the door on his father's unreasonable request. For once, he wished his father was still ignoring him.

Ebenezer set his jaw and glared as his eldest son dared to refuse him. "I know you think you're better than the rest of us." Reuben opened his mouth to retort, but he snapped it shut as his father crossed his muscled arms over his broad chest. "And I'm well aware you don't want to help in the family business," Ebenezer said. "I've let you have your way, no matter the hardship to the rest of the family. I haven't interfered with your new—" Ebenezer worked his mouth as if struggling around the word "—trade." He sniffed, making his opinions clear. "I wouldn't ask for your help if I had any other choice. All the other hired men are taken. James and John are off lolly-gagging with that rabbi again. Why Zebedee let them go, I'll never know. How much profit has he lost by having to pay hired men to take their place?"

Well, at least Reuben and his father could agree on something.

Jesus was no good for the family. However, Reuben pressed his lips together and didn't add his thoughts.

His father cleared his throat. "I've already agreed to fish with Zebedee's crew this afternoon with the dragnet. We'll be casting while out at sea." He jabbed a thumb over his shoulder, pointing to the Sea of Galilee. "We need a full crew on each boat. Your brother is feeling sick, so I need you."

Reuben knew that the method the men had planned was an effective, yet difficult way to fish, even for a seasoned fisherman. It was far harder than the usual method of simply dragging the massive net to shore. Reuben slumped against the door frame and groaned.

"I haven't fished in over four years. I will be no good to you."

Ebenezer looked his eldest son up and down, taking in Reuben's dark, scribal robes and ink-stained fingers, and sighed. "I don't doubt it. But you're my only option—unless I want Zebedee to fish with someone else today. I need the money, Reuben. Surely you can swallow that headstrong pride of yours long enough to help your flesh and blood?"

Reuben flushed. *He* was headstrong? It was his father's stubbornness that was driving the family apart, not his. Reuben realized that this was the longest conversation they had shared since he had told his father he was leaving for Jerusalem. Bitterness rose up and wrapped its hands around his throat, making it burn.

He blurted, "For the past few years you've treated me like a stranger. Now you come to me, begging for my help?" Reuben wished the impulsive words unsaid as Ebenezer pulled himself up to full height, seeming to swell with anger.

Ebenezer spoke through gritted teeth, "*Begging?* Though you're doing your best to forget it, I am still your father. I will act and speak to you as I see fit. So you'd better keep a civil tongue in that head of yours."

"Yes, Father," Reuben dropped his eyes, and Ebenezer deflated.

Reuben glanced towards the Sea of Galilee that shimmered in the early afternoon sun. The idea of being trapped on the small fishing vessel with his bitter father made Reuben quail. Yet, no matter their differences, this was his family asking for help.

"All right then," Reuben sighed, turning from the doorway. "I'll meet you down at the boat."

Philemon looked surprised when Reuben told him he was going

down to the nets. "You're going fishing? Truly? Today?"

Reuben nodded with a sigh. "I'm leaving now, if you can spare me." Reuben clung to the hope that Philemon would have an important task for him, something to prevent his being able to fish.

"No, of course, you should help your father," Philemon said, his eyebrows still sky-high. "I'll handle things here."

Reuben smothered a disappointed sigh and went down to the center pier. The narrow, wooden structure was packed with noisy men preparing their boats. Zebedee was there, with his thick curls lashed with a leather thong.

"Come on, pick up your feet!" Ebenezer bellowed from his rented boat, waving his arm.

Reuben gritted his teeth. His father's booming voice helped communication between the fishing boats, but he didn't relish having it near his ear for the next long hours. He sighed and picked his way carefully towards the boat.

"Well, well, look who it is," one of the fishermen said, noticing Reuben and elbowing his neighbor. "Come back to sling nets with the real men again?"

"Come on now, it'll be good to have him," the other man chortled. "He looks about the right size for bait."

Reuben's felt the blood rush to his face as all the fishermen roared with laughter. It was always this way among them. They were a rough and tumble bunch, and Reuben hadn't missed them at all.

Reuben hastened forward and clambered aboard his father's rented boat, tripping a little on his way in. His clumsiness earned him another peal of laughter.

"Welcome, brother!" Ben said, slapping Reuben's shoulder with a large, calloused hand. A wide smile split his sun-browned face.

Reuben saw with surprise that his brother was now several inches taller than him. He felt a squirm of conscience that he was neglecting the relationship. His little brother felt almost like a stranger to him. Of course, if Ebenezer hadn't seen fit to scorn Reuben, things would be different. So it wasn't really his fault.

"Not fishing in that, are you?" Ebenezer asked, gesturing to Reuben's attire. Both his father and brother had already stripped down to their short, sleeveless tunics.

Reuben gritted his teeth and removed his prayer shawl, folding the striped, fringed garment. He removed his long overcoat and shivered as a cool autumn breeze blew over his bare arms. It was easier to work in the short, sleeveless tunics, but he felt uncomfortably naked.

He tucked the garments in with the others.

"Cast us off, Ben," Ebenezer called out, and Ben untied the thick rope from the iron loop on the pier. With a huge heave, the burly youth pushed the prow of the boat towards the open water. Reuben felt butterflies swooping in his gut.

"Well, don't just stand around," Ebenezer bellowed from the rudder. "Reuben, get the sail down!"

Reuben jumped to action, his fingers fumbling on the coarse ropes. He could feel his father's simmering frustration and tried to work faster. Finally the sailcloth was free, and it snapped and caught the breeze.

Zebedee had his sail set already and was sailing smoothly away from the pier. Ebenezer brought his boat alongside his. They navigated along the shoreline until one man spotted a school of tilapia.

Reuben's stomach swooped. It was time to begin.

"Take hold, boy!" Zebedee tossed Reuben the head-line of the weighted net.

Reuben rankled at being called a boy, and the twinkle in his uncle's eye was lost on him. The net spilled out of Zebedee's boat into the water, the weighted end sinking out of sight. The net was wide enough to reach to the bottom of this portion of the inland sea. Reuben wrapped the rope around the horn cleat and held the end with taut, determined fingers.

Ebenezer and Zebedee increased the distance between each other as the net was let out between the boats. The weights on the foot-line held the twenty-six-foot wide net straight up and down in the water.

"That's all of it," Zebedee's voice rumbled across the expanse.

The dragnet was massive, almost a thousand feet long. Reuben gritted his teeth and gripped the rope so hard his knuckles were white. He didn't dare release his end and embarrass himself in front of everyone again. Ben grabbed hold of the line as well. Soon Reuben's forearms twitched with weariness as the two boats sailed parallel to one another, chasing the fish before the swooping net. Usually, they would bring the net to shore and haul the fish up onto the pebbled beach. The method they were using today was trickier, but it often yielded a better catch.

Ebenezer shouted over to Zebedee, and they began to maneuver towards each other until the net was encircling the fish like a mesh barrel. The shallow-keeled boats were cumbersome, but Zebedee and Ebenezer had decades of practice. As the net was overlapped and the fish trapped, Zebedee went around the circle again, releasing a floating Veranda net around the circumference to stop any fish from jumping over the net and escaping.

Reuben's stomach churned. He knew what was coming. The men began to throw the cast nets into the trapped school of fish. These circular nets were weighted all around and fell over the fish, the weights coming together and trapping the fish as it sunk.

Ebenezer's voice was brassy as ever. "Go on, Reuben, bring up the nets."

He had no choice but to rise, take a huge breath, and dive into the deep water. It washed over his head as he dove down to the bottom of the lake. All sound was smothered, and he felt his skin pimple with the cold.

He gathered up the weighted bottom of the cast nets like he had when he was a boy, catching the pinned fish inside the net like a bag. Other hired men were diving as well. He could feel the current of their swimming nearby, and the slippery fish swimming around his legs.

The thrashing net in his hand, Reuben pushed off from the sea bed and kicked his feet. He broke the surface and sputtered, gasping for breath. He hadn't swum like this in years.

Ebenezer emptied the cast net as Ben tossed another with a flick of his wrist, the net swooping out and landing in a perfect circle before disappearing beneath the surface.

The men in the boats crowed with delight as they heaved net after net onto the boat. The silvery fish flapped as the men dumped them into baskets.

Reuben miserably dove again and again to the depths. He didn't dare ask to trade places with Ben. His younger brother had far outstripped him in throwing skill, and Reuben refused to look like an idiot.

"Let's go again," Ebenezer called with a grin to Zebedee when the last net was brought up.

Zebedee agreed. Reuben panted as he tried to haul himself out of the water. His trembling arms couldn't lift him, and Ben laughingly hauled him aboard.

"You've got more fish," Ben called to their uncle, "but I've caught the biggest!"

Zebedee's laughter boomed across the water. Reuben shivered as the breeze blew over him, his tunic plastered against his chest. He was too wet and weary to think of a suitable retort.

Another school of tilapia was spotted, and once more the net was stretched out as they sailed forward and corralled the fish.

"In you go, Reuben."

Still exhausted from his last dive, Reuben's knees wobbled as he stood to dive in. It wasn't any better the second time. He was grateful this fishing style wasn't attempted at night when the temperatures dropped and the water became as welcoming as a shroud.

By the time he brought up the last net of fish for his father, his legs were cramping and his numb fingers were almost useless.

Ebenezer called down to Reuben, who was still in the water, clutching the side of the boat with white knuckles. "Quit playing around and get in."

With a groan, Reuben hauled himself into the boat. His teeth chattered so hard he feared he would knock them right out of his head.

They had a good catch between the two boats. Ebenezer and Zebedee agreed it was time to head home. Reuben sank to the bottom of the boat with relief, soaked through and shivering.

Ebenezer rummaged where they kept their dry clothes. He roughly dried his face, neck, and arms before throwing a garment to Reuben. It caught the wind and flew past Reuben's fingers, falling into a basket of feebly flopping fish.

Reuben snatched it up. He sighed heavily as he held up his wet and scaly shawl. The symbol of his membership to the Pharisee party now reeked of fish.

"Whoops," Ebenezer said, not looking sorry at all.

Reuben gritted his teeth and refused to dry off with his shawl like it was a common piece of cloth. He held it in front of him, sitting silent, cold, and stiff on the wet bottom of the boat.

The boats arrived back at the pier and Reuben had to help unload the catch and sort it on the rocky shore. He wiped the back of his hand over his brow and all he smelled was fish.

"Reuben?" a voice called incredulously, and Reuben lifted his face.

His stomach dropped with horror.

"Simeon!" he cried out. He looked down at his wet clothes and naked, spindly limbs. Blood rushed to his face.

Simeon's gaze was more chilling than the deep depths of the sea. "I had no idea you had returned to your old trade."

"No! Never!" Reuben cried out.

He glanced to his side. Ben had overheard and was looking hurt. Reuben didn't pause to think of his brother. Ben might not understand, but it was important that Simeon did.

Reuben hastened to his rabbi but drew up short when Simeon's nose twitched. Here was his Jerusalem rabbi at last, and Reuben was a smelly, foolish-looking mess. Reuben could have run back into the sea and drowned himself.

"Has Philemon cast you off?" Simeon asked. His eyes bored into Reuben so hard it hurt.

"No, Rabbi Simeon, this is was the first time that I have fished in years, I swear," Reuben insisted, fighting down panic.

If he lost Simeon's good opinion, Jerusalem would be lost to him forever. He cast his eyes to his father who was watching the exchange with folded arms.

Simeon eyed Ebenezer with cold curiosity. "Your father?" Simeon asked.

Reuben was forced to introduce the two men, his stomach clenched the entire time. Ebenezer, though he was but a simple fisherman, dared to frown at Simeon. The two men scarcely nodded to one another, both seeming to regard the other as unworthy of their attention.

"Well," Simeon said, his eyes sweeping the beach. "I shall go and see your teacher Philemon and wait for you there."

"Of course, Rabbi, I shall be with you as soon as I can."

With weak knees, he went to wash his hands in the lapping water. This was a disaster. Why was Simeon in Capernaum? Why now, of all times, did he appear without notice?

As soon as Simeon disappeared from view, the fishermen began their coarse jokes again, most of them thinly veiled and directed at Reuben. He sniffed and ignored them.

"Running off before the job is done?" Ebenezer stomped up in a skittle of pebbles.

"I think you've got it handled," Reuben flicked his hands dry, his voice hitched with anger.

He retrieved his outer tunic and damp, smelly shawl. His father stood with folded arms, his expression hard and disappointed. Zebedee noticed that trouble was brewing and came over.

"We're grateful for your help today, Reuben," Zebedee said in his low, rumbling voice, glancing at Ebenezer.

Ebenezer didn't say anything. Reuben pulled his long outer tunic over his damp hair, feeling warm for the first time in hours.

"Well, I don't plan on helping again," Reuben snapped, lifting his chin. Ebenezer lifted his as well.

"I'd hardly call what you did today help," Ebenezer sneered. "You've chosen your trade well. You would never make it as a fisherman." Zebedee put a hand on Ebenezer's shoulder, but the man jerked away, his jaw working. "I could have done better without you."

Reuben's hands shook with anger, so he buried them in his damp shawl to hide them. He glared at his father. Why was the man so hard-headed? The man was so obsessed with earning enough money to buy a boat that he was willing to alienate his son.

"I do better without you in my life!" Reuben yelled.

Was that a flick of pain in his father's eyes? Reuben felt a momentary stab of remorse, but he shoved it aside. His father had started this mess. Why should Reuben feel sorry? His father was ignorant and crude, unable to understand anything beyond himself.

Reuben turned his back on his family and marched into town with as much dignity he could muster. His father might have cost him everything. He needed to make things right with Simeon. He had to.

He ducked into the house and heard Philemon and Simeon talking around the table in the inner room. He didn't join them right away. He fetched a basin of water and took it to his partitioned sleeping area. He stripped down and washed as best he could, trying to rid himself of the fishy smell. He sniffed his hands hopefully and sighed.

He donned his second set of clothes, drawing the soft linen undershirt over his head, then a warm, clean, long-sleeved tunic. It was woven of dark wool to hide errant droplets of ink. He belted it at his waist, feeling more like himself. He smoothed his hair and beard and felt the lack of shawl around his neck. He had only the one. He pressed his lips together. He disliked going before the other men without it, but he had no choice.

He took his clothing to Philemon's wife and asked that she wash it for him. She accepted the damp, smelly bundle with a grimace.

As he approached Philemon and Simeon, he felt naked without his shawl. He swallowed hard when their eyes flicked to his neck, noting its absence.

He ceremonially washed before going to the table. On the table were a hearty stew, fresh bread, and dried figs. The men were already halfway through their meal. Reuben whispered a hasty blessing and dug in without hesitation. The spiced lentil stew lit a cozy fire within his belly, the warmth spreading to his fingertips as he ate ravenously. Simeon and Philemon chatted about news in Jerusalem.

Simeon's tone sharpened. "I was surprised to arrive and see a former student of *mine* among the local fishermen." He let that hang for a second, Reuben's ears burning as Simeon asked Philemon, "Is that usual?"

Reuben habitually raised a hand as if to smooth his shawl, but dropped it at once, hoping no one had noticed.

"Not at all," Philemon smiled. "He's been busy in his apprenticeship to me. That's the first time he's been back at the nets in years."

Reuben relaxed a little.

Simeon turned his gaze on Reuben. "I hope it is the last." Reuben nodded vigorously. Simeon granted him the hint of a smile. "We will say no more on the matter. I am here for more than a simple visit." He turned to Philemon. "Reuben's letters about this Jesus of Nazareth have been helpful to me. I have presented them to the Jerusalem Pharisees and the Sanhedrin. Everyone is pleased that I can keep them up-to-date on what this so-called prophet is up to."

Simeon nodded at Reuben, and Reuben swelled with pride. The praise made it almost worthwhile to be forced to remain in Capernaum.

"Your most recent letter, Reuben, where you wrote that Jesus had left Capernaum and was going on another preaching circuit, has us all concerned. We cannot sit idly by, letting this Jesus of Nazareth sow confusion and conflagration among the common people. We, with our deep understanding of the law, are not so easily swayed by a false prophet. It is our duty to lead the people, and we *will* lead them— back to the traditions of the elders."

Philemon's eyebrows twitched at Simeon's urban, showy way of speaking, but Reuben had to bite his tongue to hide a smile of pride. His rabbi spoke better than any man he had ever heard.

Philemon clasped his hands on the table. "So, what do you plan to do?"

Simeon tented his fingers under his chin in the way Reuben remembered so well. "I shall go out myself, and warn the people in person."

Philemon's eyebrows shot high, and Reuben was equally taken aback. He looked at his wealthy Jerusalem rabbi, trying to picture the polished man traveling for weeks on bad roads, sleeping in questionable beds in rural inns, and eating rough meals seated by a fire. It taxed his imagination severely.

"It's a bold move," Philemon said, considering. He began to nod, and then he smiled. "I think it's just the thing."

Simeon smiled a little and nodded. "I am glad you agree. I would like Reuben to travel with me."

"Me?" Reuben sat taller, his pulse jumping. He felt a surge of relief that Simeon still thought well enough of him to ask for his assistance.

"Yes, you," Simeon said with a hint of sarcasm. "You are Galilean, are you not? And, obviously, you understand the ways of the common countryman." Reuben flinched under the barb. "You know the area, and can be a guide for me. Not to mention, you have heard this Nazarene speak many times. You can help me craft the best arguments to counteract Jesus." He shrugged his slender shoulders and turned to Philemon. "Furthermore, Reuben has spent three years under my roof in my tutelage. He knows my ways well, saving me the trouble of having to explain myself."

Though Reuben was flattered that Simeon wanted his help, he felt a stab of frustration. He wanted to go back to Jerusalem, not wander the countryside chasing Jesus. On top of his other offenses, the false prophet had dragged away his cousin, Beth. She had left her house in imitation of Jesus' disciples, abandoning her duties, her mother, and her siblings. How was that right?

Despite his frustration with her, he missed her gentle companionship and the way she would smile at him with pride. She had always listened with sympathy when he needed to unburden his heart. Ever since Jesus had come to Capernaum, the false prophet had stolen away all her admiration and loyalty.

Reuben clutched his hands under the table as he remembered their recent argument. Beth had sided with Jesus, over him.

Philemon stroked his beard. "Very well then. You seem to have given this careful thought. I'm disappointed to lose Reuben, I'll admit. He's a fine apprentice."

Simeon nodded. "I am pleased to hear that. I will return him to you when I have finished my tour so he can complete his apprenticeship with you. A man needs a trade after all."

Reuben jerked back as if someone had thrown cold water in his face. "Why can't I go back to Jerusalem with you?" He was frustrated at the petulance in his tone. He cleared his throat as Simeon and Philemon stared at him. He drew a breath. "What I mean to say is, what reason is there for me to stay? I'm copying the scriptures for the mezuzah and phylacteries now. What more can you teach me, Philemon?"

Philemon's expression hardened, and he crossed his arms. Simeon's eyebrows shot up to his scar, and Reuben shifted in his seat. He regretted his impulsive words, yet wasn't he right? His sharp memory and steady hand made transcribing a natural trade for him. Perhaps it was too prideful to mention his skills aloud, but he wouldn't let a sense of humbleness keep him from returning to Jerusalem as soon as possible.

"Apparently, there's more you need to learn." Philemon shook his head, a sharp crease between his brows. "I'll excuse your rudeness this once, understanding your youthful zeal and ambition."

Reuben had to bite his tongue. What did Philemon know of ambition? The man would be completely content to stay in little Capernaum for all his life. Reuben needed to be at the heart of the Pharisees, discussing the most current interpretations and filling his mind with the law and traditions if he was to be a prestigious teacher someday. Being a scribe was only a stepping stone to his true destiny. His mind chafed like a tethered colt. Philemon should tell Simeon that he had learned enough. He was holding him back purposefully.

Simeon shared an amused look with Philemon as he said, "Impatience belongs to the young."

The men both chuckled with a sort of fatherly patience for a wayward child. Reuben ducked his head with angry embarrassment, trying to hide his emotions from the older men as he berated himself. He should have slowed down and crafted his arguments better.

That evening, Reuben cleared his throat as he showed his rabbi the comfortable place he had prepared. He had thought of every detail, trying to compensate for what Philemon's small home lacked. He had swept and dusted a partitioned area of the upper floor. He had found the best blanket and bolster for the guest to use. He had filled an oil lamp and left a few scrolls for his teacher to peruse. In a fit of generosity, he had even added his padded sleeping mat atop the guest pallet to double the comfort. He fidgeted with his belt, waiting for Simeon's approval.

Simeon hardly noticed any of it, giving the space only a cursory glance before turning to his disciple. The two of them were alone. The sounds of Philemon and his wife with their children were soft in the other room. Simeon raised a hand and set it, a little stiffly, on Reuben's shoulder. Reuben appreciated the friendly gesture, one that Simeon didn't often make.

"Do not be hasty in wanting to come back to Jerusalem," Simeon counseled. When Reuben opened his mouth to protest, Simeon cut him off, his tone insistent. "Look about you. Think. Realize!" The rabbi gave him a little shake. "God has dealt favorably with you, placing you in the middle of this troublesome situation."

"What do you mean?" Reuben furrowed his brow, still lost.

"Who are you in Jerusalem? Just another student." Simeon held up a finger. "A brilliant student, perhaps, but one without a name or fortune to make others take notice of him." Reuben had to admit the truth of what Simeon said. He was nobody. He stared down at his feet, frustrated with his insignificance. "But now, your name is mentioned favorably before the Sanhedrin in Jerusalem, all because of your clear and informative letters about this Jesus. You are talked of now. When you have traveled with me and assisted me with this task, once more will you be discussed by the greatest Pharisaic minds of our time."

Reuben began to understand, and he looked up, feeling a tingling warmth spreading through him. Marvel for Simeon's keen political understanding rolled over his mind. Yet, his fear of being left in obscurity and forgotten in Capernaum niggled at him.

"So, you *do* want me in Jerusalem, someday?"

Simeon clicked his tongue. "Why are you so wrapped up in that question? Of course, I do. I have seen your keen reasoning, your sharp debating skills, and your unparalleled memory. But you are raw clay. Give your career into my hands and I will shape you into a powerful force, a man whose judgment is sought, whose opinions are weighty, and one who will make men sit up and take notice."

Reuben felt a thrill of eagerness. It was exactly what he wanted, and the idea that he might actually attain his goals pulsed through him. He bowed his head to his rabbi in deference, using the gesture to cover a delighted smile.

"All right, Rabbi," he said, schooling his features to match his rabbi's calm expression before lifting his chin. "I give myself to your guidance. Tell me what to do and I'll do it."

"Good!" Simeon said. Closing the subject, Simeon turned and inspected the sleeping arrangements his student had made for him. Reuben searched his face for a sign of approval. Simeon twisted his mouth then smiled ruefully at his student. Unaware that Reuben would be sleeping on the floor he said, "Well, it will have to do. I must harden myself for rough living."

"Yes, Rabbi," Reuben said. As he turned away he raised his eyebrows. If Simeon considered this rough sleeping, he was in for a rude awakening on the journey ahead.

The next morning Simeon woke Reuben as the sun began to rise. The Jerusalem rabbi was eager to begin his mission.

Reuben stifled a yawn as he joined Simeon and Philemon in the quiet workroom. His muscles ached from fishing the day before, but he kept his discomfort to himself. The men gathered around a simple map of Galilee, deciding on the route Simeon and Reuben would take. Word had trickled into Capernaum from the towns Jesus had visited, and Simeon was determined to follow hot on his heels.

Daniel hobbled into the room where they hunched over the map. Philemon had already apprised him of the plan. Daniel readily, and unsolicited, gave his approval and advice. Simeon had a fixed smile throughout, impatience in his eyes.

There was a tense moment where Daniel considered journeying with Simeon and Reuben, which would have slowed them considerably. Reuben's eyes flicked back and forth between Daniel and Simeon. He listened as Daniel talked himself out of such taxing travel, and gave a quiet sigh of relief.

A donkey was purchased for the journey. As Reuben led the

donkey home, the soft brown beast twitched his long, dark ears and batted his absurdly long eyelashes in a mellow way, making Reuben hopeful that the donkey would be an agreeable helper.

Reuben loaded the animal with the supplies Philemon's wife packed for them: packets of lentils, bread, salted fish, dried dates, sloshing water skins, and a bulging wineskin. A small camp pot and blankets were stowed away as well. Reuben could make a basic traveling soup, and he hoped Simeon would not turn his nose up at his simple cookery. With any luck, they would find adequate lodgings and hot meals in every town they passed through, but he felt better being prepared.

Once the donkey was loaded, Reuben awkwardly saddled Simeon's horse. Horses were only for the wealthy, and Reuben had little equestrian experience. The tall, dappled gray beast shook his mane and swung his long face to eye Reuben doubtfully as he adjusted the girth.

Simeon came out of the house, bidding Philemon farewell. He noticed the loaded donkey with surprise. "Surely we will not need all that? Are there not inns and markets in the towns of Galilee?"

"Better to be safe," Philemon said, with a nod of approval at Reuben.

Simeon did not look convinced, but he allowed Reuben to hold his foot so he could smoothly mount his horse. Reuben took up the donkey's lead, patting the beast to soothe some of his growing trepidation.

As they took the main road through town, they passed Ebenezer, Ben, and Zeb on the beach. The two young brothers looked like double reflections of their thick-chested, broad-shouldered father. Reuben sniffed. Apparently, Zeb was recovered from his illness. All three sets of eyes swiveled towards Simeon. A mounted, wealthy Jew was a matter of interest.

When Ebenezer recognized Simeon, his mouth hardened into a thin line and his eyes flicked to Reuben.

Reuben averted his gaze and lifted his chin. Now his brothers could see what sort of a man had become his patron. Reuben's mouth twitched as he suppressed a smirk. He felt a growing sense of scorn for his simple, coarse father, and condescending pity for his brothers. Their only ambition was to scrape enough money for a boat. A boat!

Reuben looked at Simeon's back. The man was leading him to greatness. Reuben would far outstrip them all.

14

THE WORK OF BEELZEBUB

Simeon rode beside Reuben, picking over his memories like a carrion bird intent on cleaning every strip of meat from the bones. Reuben led the donkey, reciting every word that he recalled Jesus saying and every miracle he had seen Jesus perform. Simeon's questions were relentless as he asked for minute details about Jesus' style of speaking, his mode of recruitment, and his disciples. Reuben's tongue thickened, his feet stumbled in his distraction, and still, Simeon persisted. Reuben was anxious to please and didn't dare to ask for a reprieve.

"So, you are resolved then?" Simeon peered down on him, his gaze sharp. "You have no doubts that Jesus is a false prophet?"

"None at all," Reuben was vehement. "He has openly aligned himself against the Pharisees, determined that his teachings, and *only* his teachings, are the way to live. He seems to think he's a new Moses, come to tell us how to please God."

He glanced up as Simeon adjusted his reins and listened with his head tipped to the side. The rabbi's attention was flattering, and Reuben felt a sense of relief as he vented his frustrations about Jesus. His tone became bitter as he said, "You can tell what kind of man he is by his followers." Reuben thought of Matthew and frowned. "He has tax collectors, women, fishermen, and other common men following him around, calling *him* Rabbi."

"What of his miracles?"

"The work of Beelzebub!" Reuben cried out. "His power is unholy, and he uses it to convince the people that he is righteous. I'm not fooled."

Simeon nodded, satisfied. "Very good. I think we have our beginning. We need to remind the people of our sacred traditions. It is our traditions that have bound us together in unity as foreigners have sought to scatter us. It is the traditions of the elders that have kept us true to the law that Moses gave us, a true law that teaches us how to please the Lord."

Reuben's heart swelled with pride as he looked on his wise, poised rabbi, feeling the power in his words. He couldn't have asked for a better man to emulate. He was confident that if anyone could set the people back on the proper path, Simeon would.

The first town they made it to was Chorazin. It was placed atop a hill, only about two and a half miles from Capernaum—an easy walk. Simeon was energetic at the beginning of his mission. Reuben found his rabbi's mood infectious, and he smiled. It did feel good to be actively working for the people.

Reuben couldn't help a twinge of trepidation as he noticed Chorazin was still pulsing with gossip about the miracle worker. Jesus had only left a few days before—after dazzling the entire populace with his powers. Reuben glanced upwards with worry but saw Simeon was undeterred.

The wealthy Pharisee rode down the main street greeting all that he met with a noble nod, and soon everyone was wondering who this new, obviously important Pharisee was. After securing the best room in the inn—which was little more than an enclosed space with a mat and a chamber pot—and stabling the horse and donkey, Simeon smiled at Reuben, rubbing his palms together with eagerness.

"Shall we get to work?" Simeon asked, a gleam in his dark eyes.

Reuben nodded and followed his rabbi, nervously smoothing his shawl.

Simeon perched on the steps of the local synagogue, where many of the more affluent village men were gathered for discussion. Reuben and Simeon waited and listened for a moment.

"I saw him heal my neighbor Nahum from blindness."

"The man is astonishing, simply astonishing!"

"I've heard that some people are calling him the Son of David."

"He's the one we've been waiting for, I just know it."

Simeon cleared his throat, and the small crowd of men looked his way. Simeon smiled. "Forgive me for interjecting myself, but I know the man of whom you speak. It is Jesus of Nazareth, correct?"

"It is," one of the better-dressed men said with a bob of his head, his eyes taking in the prayer shawls around Simeon and Reuben's necks. "I think most people around here have heard of him by now."

"Indeed, I am sure you are correct," Simeon said as he nodded. "I was just wondering if you have all *actually* accepted him as a prophet?" He didn't give them time to answer. "Perhaps you do not know what is being said in Jerusalem?"

Another man leaned forward. "You're from the Holy City?"

"Of course," Simeon said with a smile. "I have been sent here from Jerusalem by the foremost Pharisee scholars. I have come to make sure that everyone has the most recent, troubling information about this Nazarene." The men looked worried, and Reuben hid a smile at Simeon's shrewd understanding.

A white-bearded man cleared his gravelly throat. "I'm one of the leaders of the synagogue here in Chorazin. Tell me what is being said about the Nazarene."

"I am sure *you* were able to discern that there is something not right about Jesus." Simeon bowed his head in polite deference to the man's age and position. "I am sure you saw how he tramples on the traditions. How he flouts the purity laws. The Pharisees in Jerusalem have also witnessed his words and his actions. We know what he truly is. Jesus of Nazareth is trying to deceive the people, and attempting to replace Moses."

Several eyebrows shot up at this comment, and the men muttered to one another. Simeon continued with a sad shake of his head, "The common people are so vulnerable. We men, the leaders of our communities, must not be led astray. We must hold true to the law and traditions."

"But his miracles!" a man protested.

"Bah!" Simeon scoffed. "What are his miracles to us? We do not need signs and miracles, we have the Torah to guide us. Are we pagans, to be drawn away from the truth by a man with a few tricks?

We do not chase after fancy showmen, and we certainly do not follow sorcerers. We have the law and the traditions of the elders to be our guide. They light our way, and no one shall sway us from the truth."

"What are you saying?" a man asked, his brow furrowed. "He isn't a prophet at all?"

Simeon leaned towards the men as if to share a secret, and they automatically leaned forward. Simeon's voice was low but passionate as he said, "We have listened and observed for many long months and have come to the conclusion that Jesus has an evil demon. He is working under the power of Beelzebub!" The men all gasped.

"It can't be true!" a man cried out.

"But it is," Simeon said. His dark eyes were bold. "His own miracles give him away. Did you hear that he healed the servant of a Roman *centurion*?" The men all looked discomfited. "Our future Messiah will rid our country of foreign oppressors, not heal them. It is more proof that Jesus is in league with the Romans and their false gods." The men glanced at one another in concern.

Simeon gestured to Reuben. "My disciple here has spent many months living near Jesus. Tell these good men what you have observed."

Reuben's mouth was as dry as the dusty road. He glanced at Simeon for encouragement, but his teacher only raised his eyebrows, tapping his fingers on his knees. Reuben cleared his throat and hoped he wouldn't stammer.

"He has touched lepers." Several of the men flinched. "He breaks bread with tax collectors and sinners." More murmurs of dismay. Reuben paused as he thought of Beth, and he added, "He's drawing women from their proper sphere, enticing them away from their hearths." The men looked at each other. Reuben knew they were thinking of their wives and daughters. Reuben glanced at Simeon. He looked pleased, and Reuben grew more confident.

He looked these Chorazin men in the eye, and spoke faster, "He tries to sway the people by talking of a coming kingdom, but does he have an actual plan to bring it to be? No! He just talks riddles and parables, using nonsense to sound wise. There's not one learned man among his close disciples. He surrounds himself with commoners because they are easily puffed up and not shrewd enough to see that he is deceiving them." Reuben was flushed with passion.

Simeon nodded, smoothly taking control again. "They are not like *you*," he said to the men, who shifted a little under his praise. "You are educated, aware, and I can see that you are all true Jews, through and through." Simeon allowed them to digest his words. He looked back to the white-bearded man. "I shall be here for the week. May I speak in the synagogue on the Sabbath?"

"Of course. We'd be honored," the man said with a nod of his white head. "In the meantime, you must be my guests this evening."

Simeon accepted graciously.

On the Sabbath, Simeon stood before the citizens of Chorazin and gave a rousing sermon of hope for a coming Messiah. One of royal blood, from King David's lineage. One placed by God Himself to rule in the name and might of the Lord. He painted a picture of a warrior on a fine warhorse with a drawn sword in his hand and given all authority. Simeon explained that the Messiah will rout the Romans and send those dogs to Hades. A true Messiah will usher in an era of everlasting peace, and the children of a united Israel would bask in a country of freedom and abundance. The Messiah would restore both Jerusalem and the Temple.

Then the Temple would be graced by God's presence, the Shekinah, which would come down and fill the Temple. The whole world would know that Israel's God was the one true God.

Reuben was moved. All around him men and women nodded their heads. Reuben had to smile. Jesus, with his ragtag following, did not look anything like the true Messiah.

They left Chorazin in good spirits and traveled over dusty roads to the next town. And the next and the next. Simeon was welcomed everywhere. His message was universally appreciated. Jesus asked the people to repent and change their ways. Simeon told them to stay as they were and to trust the traditions and the teachings of the Pharisees.

Jesus' miracles were revealed to the people as nothing more than the tricks of an evil demon. Simeon warned them not to be deceived by Jesus, but to wait and pray for the true Messiah.

Naturally suspicious of strangers and with a generational wariness of anything that pushed against tradition, the people forgot Jesus and slipped back into their old lives, back under the wise influence of the Pharisee teachers. Reuben felt a peaceful satisfaction that he and

Simeon were doing good work for the Lord.

Despite their success in town after town, Simeon's patience grew razor thin. Though he was gracious in public, Reuben bore the brunt of his rabbi's frustrations in private. Simeon lamented unceasingly about the beds, the food, the roads, and the rough lifestyle of the country in general.

Reuben tried to be understanding. After all, this was not the comfortable life Simeon had been raised to expect. Still, the constant complaining grated on Reuben's nerves until his patience frayed almost to the breaking point.

Autumn was nearly spent and the winter rainy season was threatening when Simeon finally had all he could take. He turned his sleek horse for Capernaum, and Reuben followed behind him, leading the humble donkey. Reuben scratched the simple beast behind its ears, and it closed its eyes and leaned its head towards him. He had grown fond of the quiet animal these past weeks. The simple beast was so easy to please.

Reuben had never dreamed he would be eager to return to little Capernaum, but as they arrived on the outskirts of town, footsore and exhausted, he felt a rush of relief. They had done good work but he was glad it was over.

Philemon was happy to see them return, and his wife fed them a delicious, savory meal. This time, Simeon looked with gratefulness at the clean and soft bed that Reuben was able to prepare for him.

"Well, my disciple," Simeon said as he sat on the padded mat with a satisfied sigh. "We are finished. I will go back to Jerusalem in the morning. Continue to write of any news you hear about Jesus. In particular, I want to hear of the towns that do not accept him." He knuckled his back and groaned. "I am eager to go home." He eyed Reuben up and down, and then he granted him a small smile. "You did well. When I tell our Jerusalem brethren of our trip, I will mention you often."

It was the first hint of praise that the Jerusalem rabbi had given him in weeks. Reuben's heart warmed. He humbly returned the praise onto Simeon, and he was more generous than Simeon had been to him.

To have such a great man overseeing his career was more than he could have ever hoped.

15

LOVE ME ABOVE ALL

Autumn was losing its grip, allowing low, cloudy skies and frigid nights to push their way over Galilee. The fields they passed were seeded with barley and wheat in anticipation of the winter rains. They spent the Day of Atonement fasting in a small village. They rested in the wilderness for the Festival of Booths.

Beth felt frustrated during the festivals. This was hardly better than last year. She had Peter, but now she was missing the rest of her family. Her heart yearned for things to go back to normal.

Jesus led them away from the village. This one had been much like every other Jewish town—steeped in tradition with rustic people in simple homes living much the same as they had for generations, eschewing the modern world and its corruption, distrustful of foreigners.

The road beneath Beth's feet was little more than a winding path linking farming villages. The day was dreary, and it matched her mood.

She knuckled her lower back. She was always sore these days. Worse, on the road, she felt like a tag-along. What good was she doing with her presence? Perhaps her mother was right after all.

She looked up the line of disciples. Her eyes rested on Peter's broad back. He strode ahead of her talking cheerfully with James. She was with her husband and able to care for him as she desired, yet each mile further from home felt longer than the last.

All the other disciples followed Jesus eagerly, pleased for the opportunity. The number of followers was always shifting, but around Jesus a heart of steady and true disciples had formed—men who had been with him since the first days, Peter among them.

Jesus dedicated a lot of his time to teaching these faithful disciples. He filled them with his message of the kingdom and showed them how to interpret the law as he did—with love for the Lord and love for one another as the center of every commandment. Jesus did not absolve any of the responsibility of following God. If anything, he demanded more! He asked for their whole heart, not just their outward deeds. She had learned so much that she was sure Jesus' message was engraved deep in her mind.

At every village he healed and taught. The down-trodden rejoiced as their sicknesses were carried away. Their eyes shone with eager anticipation as he prophesied a coming kingdom. Many believed in him. Some did not, their toil-hardened eyes doubtful as they scowled at the young rabbi.

She had lost count of the towns and villages had they been through. Was Jesus planning to visit them all? She felt a growing sense of weariness. She rolled her ankle on a loose stone and grimaced. If she was at home right now, she would be sitting at her loom. She missed the feel of the threads and watching the colorful patterns grow beneath her nimble fingers. At the end of the day, she could see just how much she had accomplished.

Now, her days consisted of walking, miles and miles of walking, before helping make camp and cooking plain food over an open fire with Naomi or one of the other women.

She was the youngest of the female disciples. Two brothers named Joseph and James had their mother with them, a quiet woman named Mary. Mary generally kept close by her sons, her long braid swinging over her shoulder as she served. Other women were wealthy supporters, and Beth felt she had little in common with them. Naomi was family, but the no-nonsense woman didn't invite heartfelt conversation.

With no close friends among the women, and Peter so often busy with the men, she often found herself feeling lonely and left out.

As she trudged, a nagging thought returned to prick her, like a sliver too deep to remove. Why did Peter have to follow Jesus? Hadn't he heard and seen enough? If Peter would go home then she could too. Perhaps, if they were at home, they could find the private moments they needed to conceive a child.

She blushed as the intimate thoughts warmed her mind. Though she was with Peter every day, they were always with the others, sleeping in the open with no privacy at all. The yearning for quiet moments with her husband made her heart hurt. If only Peter would return to Capernaum!

As if he felt her thoughts dwelling on him, Peter glanced over his shoulder to smile at her.

She returned it halfheartedly before dropping her eyes, shame filling her. He believed in Jesus and his kingdom with his whole heart. Believed enough to sacrifice his desires and comforts. Did she? When challenged by Reuben those long weeks ago in Capernaum she had staunchly defended Jesus. Had personal difficulty already worn down her faith in Jesus, exposing the self-doubt and fear that made up her core?

She gazed ahead and saw Jesus at the forefront, Peter following a few paces behind him. She had an unsettling moment of clarity. She wasn't following Jesus quite like the others. She was following her husband. If Peter hadn't come, she would have had few qualms watching Jesus leave Capernaum.

She hitched the bag higher up on her shoulder, feeling uncomfortable. Did it matter that she had only left her home because of Peter? She believed Jesus was a prophet and a miracle worker. She and Peter both believed. Wasn't that enough? Couldn't she and Peter go home now, back to their quiet lives?

Weighed down by her thoughts, she helped make camp a little before the next village in a brown, grassy area. There were a few low trees to break the wind and a muddy stream that waited anxiously for the rain to replenish its low bed. The women began to build cook fires and lay out the supplies.

Their rabbi wandered off on his own. Jesus seemed to need time for solitary prayer before joining the crowds to heal and teach. Was it for courage? Reassurance he was doing what was right? Beth wasn't sure, but every time Jesus returned he was a man renewed, an emotion she coveted.

"This is the last of it," Naomi said and tipped the dried beans into the clay pot Beth had filled with water. "Thank goodness tomorrow is Monday. We'll need to replenish our stores in the market."

Beth measured in cumin and salt and stirred the beans. She nestled the pot close to the heat but did not allow the coals or flames to touch the clay. Feeding seventy or so people on a small budget was a difficult task, but Naomi was as shrewd as she was commanding and had taken over the organizing of the camp with a firm hand.

The next morning the dew was sharp and cold on the faded grass. Jesus' followers rubbed their palms together for warmth as they walked into town. Jesus taught and healed. Peter hung on Jesus' every word and action. Beth found herself drawing back, languid and uneasy, unwilling to watch Jesus today. Self-doubt and homesickness took their turns in her mind.

As the afternoon waned, Jesus took the others back to camp, but Naomi called Beth and Judas Iscariot away to the town market.

Beth glanced sideways at Judas as he stomped up behind them with a grim face and hunched shoulders.

"Enjoy your shopping, Judas," John teased him. Judas made a face over his shoulder and John laughed.

Beth had noticed Judas Iscariot was popular among the others. He was eager and had a fierce desire for a restored Israel. Beth often overheard him and Simon discussing how the Romans might be pushed out of the land. Judas' ideas were complex, and he put a lot of thought into battle lines and high places. It was plain that Judas took pride in his keen mind. He obviously had grand ideas for his future. Perhaps that was why he was less than eager to be summoned for a tedious chore. Yet, someone had to manage the group's funds.

On this busy market day, the city center was full. The air was pungent with spices. The fragrance mingled with the scent of chickens in small pens, the sharp tang of dyes, and the yeasty scent of baked goods.

Naomi took it all in with a glance, searching for what they may need. Fresh fruits and greens were out of season, but merchants had mounds of beans and lentils, grains and dried dates, figs, honey, and raisins.

Naomi marched up to a booth and scooped up a handful of

beans, testing their weight and sniffing them. She dove into bargaining with barbed enthusiasm.

They visited several stalls and soon had three heavy baskets full of food. Judas handed over the coins whenever Naomi asked for them, boredom all over his face. Beth saw him toying absentmindedly with the moneybag, weighing its contents.

She raised her eyebrows when she noticed a small dagger also hanging at his belt, almost hidden. None of the other men carried weapons, did they?

Naomi pursed her lips as they passed a booth displaying all sizes and styles of footwear. "John needs new sandals," she said. Judas rolled his eyes as the eager seller began to show his wares.

A few minutes later, Naomi was still haggling eagerly when Beth glanced over and Judas was gone. She turned her head up and down the wide street, her alarm rising when she did not see the disciple anywhere in the market.

Naomi finished her transaction by purchasing the sandals with her own coins, and she turned with a satisfied look on her face. She noticed the missing man. Naomi frowned at Beth.

"Where's Judas?" she accused as if Beth had misplaced him. Beth had no answer. They waited and waited, Naomi's impatience growing with every passing minute.

"We can't carry all this ourselves." Naomi gestured to the three large baskets. She crossed her arms and scowled up the street. "Where on earth could he have gone?"

"Perhaps he ran into trouble?" Beth said, gripping her basket with white knuckles.

As if on cue, a pair of Roman soldiers strolled by. One was munching on a wheat cake, licking honey off the back of his hand. There had to be a garrison nearby.

Naomi sniffed and said, "If he'd stayed put, he wouldn't have had any trouble to find."

More time passed, and the leatherworker began to close up his booth. The afternoon was paling; soon it would be twilight. They needed to leave soon or they would not be back before dark, and still, Judas did not appear.

The market emptied, and the few people that remained were strangers. Beth brushed her damp palms on her dress. This would never have happened in Capernaum, where people knew them and she could ask for help.

The women tried to manage the three baskets between them, but Naomi winced in pain and rubbed her back.

Naomi blew a strand of hair out her eyes. "There's nothing for it. One of us will need to go find him." Her gaze told Beth just who Naomi thought should go. Beth squirmed as her aunt continued, "If you can't find him, you must go back to camp and get the others for help."

"Alone?" Beth shrank.

Two women without escort was bad enough, a single woman wandering around in a strange town would be taken for a lady of loose morals.

Naomi put her hands on her hips. "We can't leave a basket. If we do, it'll be stolen before we return."

Beth pulled on her lip. She knew Naomi's plan was their best option, but she was hesitant to walk away from the only person she knew. With her gaze cast to the ground, Beth slowly set off down the market street.

Where would Judas have gone? She turned the corner. Perhaps there was an inn or a tavern where Judas had stopped for a bite to eat. They were all getting tired of eating the same camp food day after day.

She went down the dirt street, lifting her eyes periodically as she looked for a likely place. At the end of the next street was a two-story building, and a group of men in traveling clothes went inside. That had to be the inn.

Steeling herself to go inside a public building, unaccompanied, and without knowing if Judas was even inside, she crept forward. She was almost to the door when a rowdy bunch stumbled out. She jerked back when she realized they were Romans.

Two of the men still clutched sloshing cups, and all five were drunk. She felt cold as bleary eyes raked her over in open appraisal.

"What's this?" a man said, pointing her way with his drink in hand.

Her stomach plummeted.

They moved towards her, and she spun around to hurry away. One of the men lunged forward and seized the pink shawl she wore wrapped around her hair and shoulders. It caught around her neck, and a gasp escaped her. Her heart racing, she freed the long cloth and it slipped from her hair. Without her head covering, she felt exposed and vulnerable.

She began to run, but despite the wine, the Romans were still faster than her. Within seconds they had cornered her a little way from the tavern. Forced to stop, she turned and eyed them with her heart in her throat.

A passerby noticed what was going on and paused, looking concerned, but then hastened away.

"An unveiled woman, all alone?" one of the men jeered, his breath foul with cheap wine. "Well, well."

Beth felt sick, and she wondered if she should cry for help. It would do her little good. Who would dare fight the Romans for a woman they didn't even know?

"What's going on here?" a familiar voice said, and Beth sagged with relief. Judas pushed one of the men aside. He saw Beth's wide shawl and snatched it from the man's hands and handed it to her. She tossed it over her head with shaky hands.

"Oh, it's you," one of the Roman men slurred at Judas. "First you ruin us in dice, and now you want to ruin this sport too?"

Beth bit her lip hard, fearing Judas would do something rash. How often had she heard him speak of his hatred for Rome? These were the worst sort of Roman soldiers! She glanced at him and was surprised to see Judas was completely at ease. He even smiled.

"This woman is married to a friend of mine. There are eager women back inside. Go and find your pleasure with one of them."

Beth was taken aback at his charm, but then she noticed the clenched fist at his side, sinews popping on the back of his hand.

The men shifted their feet but looked loathe to walk away. Judas flicked a coin to the leader, and it glimmered as it spun through the air. "Here, go have another round on me."

The man fumbled but caught the coin. He examined it, then shrugged and led the way back inside. The others stumbled after him, beginning to laugh again.

As soon as their backs were turned, Judas' lip curled in disdain, and he fingered the dagger in his belt with fire flashing in his eyes.

"Dogs, all of them." Judas spat on the ground. He turned on Beth, snapping, "What are you doing wandering around like this? Where's Naomi?"

Beth trembled with mingled fear and anger. She felt hot tears welling up but pushed them back. She would not cry like a guilty child.

"I was looking for you," she said. "We've been waiting and waiting. We didn't even know where you were."

Judas looked at the sky with obvious surprise, the twilight fast descending. He noticed her expression, and his scowl morphed into an understanding smile. Beth was disturbed by how easily he slid from one mood to another. She glanced back to the tavern, then to Judas again.

His tone was apologetic. "Of course. I was gone longer than I planned, but I had business. I thought you heard me when I told you I was leaving for a few moments."

Beth turned her face away and searched her memories. She was positive Judas hadn't said anything before he disappeared. And what business would a disciple of Jesus have in a tavern?

She glanced back at the moneybag. Despite their purchases, it was fuller than before.

It clicked in her mind. The Roman had mentioned dice. Judas had been gambling with the community money.

Judas followed her gaze, and his fist closed around the leather pouch. "What better way to fund Jesus' revolution than with the money of his enemies?" Judas gave her a crooked grin.

Beth didn't smile back. She wasn't sure how she felt about gambling, and now she was feeling confused about Judas.

"Let's go find Naomi," Beth said, turning back. She wanted to get out of this town and back to Peter as soon as possible.

Judas stepped in front of her. "Don't tell tales on me when we get back," Judas said with an easy chuckle. "I didn't mean any harm to anyone, and we are coming back with more money than we left with. If you had waited in the market nothing would have happened with those Romans. Nothing did happen to you; I was here to protect you." His words were insistent.

Beth rubbed her temples, feeling stress pounding in her head. Without thinking, she spoke aloud, "I never should have left Capernaum."

Judas looked sympathetic. "Perhaps it's time for you to return home. I don't think this is the life you desire, is it? You're one of the believers. That's enough to have a place in the coming kingdom. There's no need for you tramp around the countryside."

Beth lifted her eyes to his face, her chest swelling with longing as he spoke the exact words on her heart. He understood her.

"Shall we?" he said with a charming smile, stepping aside and gesturing to the street.

Beth nodded with a small smile, and they strode back to Naomi. Her heart still fluttered from her run-in with the Romans, and she pulled her shawl up higher on her head, making a deep cowl that hid her face.

Naomi scolded Judas like a fury all the way back to camp, and he bore it without a word. Naomi didn't know about the Romans or the gambling, and Beth didn't tell her. Naomi must have thought her scolding was punishment enough for his laggard behavior for she let the matter drop when they arrived back in camp.

"I was getting worried," Peter said, coming up to Beth.

Ignoring the eyes of others around her, she threw herself into his arms. She pressed her face into his chest. He held her close, rubbing her back.

"Is something wrong?" he asked, pulling her back with his hands on her upper arms, studying her face in the dim light.

Her eyes slid past him. Judas was smiling and talking to Simon, but his eyes flicked to meet hers. His gaze was friendly. Should she tell Peter how Judas was raising money for Jesus' cause by gambling with Roman soldiers?

Judas came up, putting his hand on Peter's shoulder in a brotherly way. "Some off-duty soldiers tried to cause some trouble. I took care of her though; don't worry, my friend."

Peter looked at Beth with sympathetic concern, and he wrapped one arm around her. Drawing her to his side, he thanked Judas.

Beth realized the opportunity she needed had presented itself. This would be the perfect time to tell Peter that she felt unsafe on the road and that he should take her home to Capernaum. How could he refuse after what had happened? They would both be safe at home and could go back to their old lives. Judas was right. Both she and her husband believed in the kingdom. Surely that was enough.

Yet, as she looked at Peter and saw his inner joy at being one of Jesus' disciples, the words stuck in her throat. She sighed as Peter kissed the top of her head, and she leaned against his side.

Unable to explain to her husband how she truly felt, Beth went to help the other women. She glanced at Judas Iscariot from time to time, pondering both his actions and his words.

She stared into her cook pot, her mind going round and round like the beans she stirred.

When Naomi announced that the meal was cooked to her satisfaction, the disciples gathered around the pots.

Jesus returned from solitary prayer to eat with them. Taking a loaf, their leader said the blessing, broke the bread and began to pass it around. They all ate right from the hot pots, carefully using their bread to scoop the hearty stew.

From the moment Jesus entered the camp, the mood shifted. They clustered together like a band of brothers with Jesus as their leader. They asked him questions and he answered with wisdom. They joked with him, and Jesus laughed as loud as the rest, his head tipping back. Jesus didn't forget the women but stopped and talked to them too.

Beth slipped around the group, hovering on the outskirts. Usually, she would have laughed with the others. Tonight she ate silently, unable to shake her homesickness.

Her chin jerked up as Jesus rose and stood before them, back straight and his eyes gleaming with purpose. Within a heartbeat, silence fell and all eyes turned to him. Beth felt her skin tingle. Something was happening.

His voice rang out with power as he called, "Simon Peter. Andrew."

Beth's jumped as if pinched, hearing her husband's name. Peter and Andrew rose to stand before Jesus. Jesus grasped Peter's shoulders and kissed his cheeks as he said, "I give you the authority to cast out unclean spirits. I give you the authority to heal every kind of disease and sickness."

"Truly, Jesus?" Peter's voice was awed, and he glanced over his shoulder to Beth. His eyes were wide, and his mouth hung open. She swallowed hard, pride for her husband welling up within her. Was it true? Would her husband be able to cure people the way Jesus did?

Her pride was followed by a painful realization. If Peter was given this gift, how could he ever return to a simple life at his nets? Tears burned as Peter stood near Jesus, and she tried her best to smile for him.

Jesus said the same words to Andrew and then called again, "James and John, sons of Zebedee."

James and John scrambled over each other in eagerness to stand before Jesus. He spoke the same words over them, kissing their cheeks. Both of the men stood beside Peter and Andrew with their stances wide, chins up, faces beaming. Naomi sat with her chin raised, fiercely proud.

"Philip and Bartholomew." Beth saw them jump up with pleased, red faces and join the others for the blessing.

"Thomas and Matthew."

Thomas went forward at once, but Matthew still sat, his eyebrows high.

"Me, Jesus?" Matthew looked around himself with self-doubt evident in his face, and the other men were smiling encouragement at him. "But I was—I am ..."

"Come, Matthew," Jesus commanded, and he smiled.

Matthew walked in a daze to Jesus and stood with the other men. After Jesus kissed his cheeks, Beth saw tears were streaming into his beard.

"James ben Alphaeus and Thaddaeus."

"Simon the Zealot, and Judas Iscariot."

Beth watched as Judas stood up and went forward with an easy grin. She resolved to tuck away her concerns about Judas. She couldn't fault his faithfulness to Jesus.

After Jesus had kissed Judas' cheeks, he stepped back and looked at the men. Beth counted. Twelve men stood before them, and she recognized the significance of the number that represented the twelve tribes of Israel.

Jesus' voice rang through the secluded area, "Go to the lost sheep of Israel. Preach to them, 'the kingdom of heaven is at hand!' Heal the sick, raise the dead, cleanse the lepers, cast out demons!"

Beth was startled. Go? She sensed a shift in Jesus' ministry, and worry for the future flooded into her heart once more.

Jesus beckoned the twelve he had chosen, and they made a tight circle around one of the small, crackling fires. The other disciples drew closer until they were a huddled gathering of men and women, a united group.

Beth glanced right and left from her place in the circle and saw all eyes were fixed on Jesus as he spoke. She saw no fear, only excitement that something was happening at last. The kingdom was taking another step forward. She tried to share in their eagerness, but her worries rose up and choked her.

Their rabbi put his hands on the shoulders of the men beside him, and his tone became earnest. "Freely you received, so give freely as well. Do not gather copper, silver, or gold."

Beth glanced at Judas and thought she discerned the slightest shadow pass over his eyes.

Jesus continued, "The authority I give you is real. The cities that do not receive you or heed your words will be judged harsher than Sodom and Gomorrah."

The twelve men glanced at each other. Many looked nervous to have such a responsibility.

"I'm sending you out like sheep among wolves. You need to be shrewd as snakes, but innocent as doves. I want you to be aware that what I ask of you is dangerous. You will be handed over to the courts, scourged in the synagogues, called the sons of the devil. Don't fear men, they can only kill the body. Fear the One who can destroy your body and soul in hell."

Beth felt her heart pounding, and she wove her fingers together to hide the trembling. Unable to sit, she rose to her feet, hovering in the background of the disciples where the air was cool and the night was dark.

Looking through the little crowd, Beth noticed Peter and Andrew sitting with backs straight, their arms around each other's shoulders in brotherly fashion as they heard this grim prophecy of their future. Her cousins, James and John, looked *eager* for the coming trials, their minds buzzing with adventure.

Jesus' warning continued, "You will be brought before governors and kings for my sake, your words and deeds a testimony to them."

Matthew hugged his precious bag of scrolls, his face heavy. "Jesus, I'm not like you. My strength is in the written word, not in speaking. How can I speak before powerful men?"

"Don't worry about what you'll say, or how to say it." Jesus leaned towards him with a small smile. "The Spirit of your Father will speak in you at that hour."

Jesus looked solemnly around at them all. "The kingdom of heaven does not come without resistance. I do not bring peace, but a sword. Brother will betray brother, even to death. A father will betray his child, children their parents. A person's enemies will be those of his household."

Beth saw Reuben's face before her. The last time she had seen him, he had been full of jealous anger. She trembled as she remembered him speaking to the other Pharisees and how their cold eyes had turned her way. She pushed the memory away.

Jesus' words did little to comfort her as he said, "You will be hated by all because of my name. You must endure to the end to be saved." Jesus' tone quickened. "When they persecute you in one city, flee to the next."

Jesus paused, and they could hear a sparrow chirping on a branch. It was innocent and carefree, and Beth was jealous of the simple creature. Why must Jesus tell them this foreboding future? Would the little bird chirp so cheerfully if it knew the hawk circled?

"Don't forget my love for you; I care about what happens to you." Jesus' voice was low and earnest. His eyes swept over them all, and Beth could see the truth in his words as his eyes met hers for a brief moment.

He motioned to the sparrow in the tree. "That bird, what's he worth? You can buy two of him for almost nothing. Yet, not a single bird falls to the ground without the notice of your Father. You're worth much more than sparrows. If anyone gives one of my children even a cup of cold water to drink, I say to you that he will not lose his reward. If a man receives you, he receives me. He who receives me receives Him who sent me. Don't underestimate your worth and your duty."

Jesus rose to his feet and began to move among them, grasping shoulders, meeting eyes face to face, his voice ringing with authority.

"I ask you to be faithful to me. Stand with me! Deny me before men, and I will deny you before my Father in heaven. Confess me before men, and I will confess your name before my Father in heaven. What I tell you in the darkness, speak in the light; what you hear whispered in your ear, proclaim it from the housetops.

"You must love me above all, more than your father or mother, your son or daughter." When Jesus saw the Twelve did not quail, he added, "You must take up your cross, and follow after me."

The Twelve nodded.

Beth took an involuntary step back. No. Not a cross. Not for Peter.

Jesus' voice rose in pitch until he cried out, "He who has found his life will lose it, and he who has lost his life for my sake will find it."

Beth took another step back, even as everyone else leaned towards Jesus, eyes shining. She bit her tongue to keep from crying aloud and pressed her hand to her heart. Peter was asking Jesus a question, but Beth's ears were full of a sound like rushing wind.

She turned and fled from the group, putting a tree at her back and separating herself from the others, those who were almost too willing to suffer. Her breath came in rough gasps.

She should have asked Peter to take her home when she had the chance. Now he was officially one of Jesus' chosen apostles, men who were sent out to do his purposes. She had been worried about Peter's safety when Jesus was doing all the healing and talking. Now all eyes would be on her husband. He would be drawing admiration, but also hatred.

She hadn't forgotten her heritage. She still ached for a restored Israel, with God once more the head of her people, leading them, perhaps through Jesus as His chosen King. Surely though, there must be other men to do what Jesus needed, military men, scribes, or elders. Why Peter?

Scourging in the synagogue. Persecution. Brought before governors and kings. Fleeing from city to city. Taking up a cross.

She felt nauseous and doubled over, groaning. She was only a woman, her husband was only a fisherman. Who was she that she should suffer in the revolution? Who was her husband that Jesus would pull him out from other men, set him up with authority, and send him out to be hated and persecuted?

Too late, she was too late. Jesus had already chosen her husband, and Peter might lose his life—and then what would she do? She had already lost her father. She couldn't lose Peter too.

She knew her flaws. The fears that gnawed her heart were as well known to her as the faces of her family. James had often teased her by calling her a mouse, and she had to admit to herself that he was right. She crouched on the ground, curling in on herself.

How did the women of her past do it? How did Sarah, Rebekah, and Rachel leave their homes for a foreign land? How did the prophetess Deborah lead the men to war? How did Ruth leave her home for the sake of her mother-in-law? How did Esther stand up to a king? How did her mother run through the night to escape the Roman armies?

Clutching these examples of brave women, Beth fought against her fears and her desires, wrestling with them until she had them locked in a corner of her mind.

She straightened and rose to stand. Though she trembled, she knew her duty. It had been ingrained in her since she sat at her mother's knee, hearing all the stories of her forefathers. Beth knew that she, like her ancestors, had to give the Lord what she loved most. It was the way of God's people.

She prayed to God now, begging him not to take Peter from this earth. Prayer did not renew her like it did Jesus, but she felt a little calmer.

Beth paced back and forth, drawing in the scent of damp grass and trying to gather herself before she spoke to Peter. She puffed out a breath. Her husband would be eager and proud and have no thought for his safety. Impulsive man!

The stars were sharp in the sky, and when she glanced back to the camp she could see the men were adding more wood to the fires.

After several long minutes, Beth felt collected enough to return to the other disciples. They were speaking to each other, planning.

She felt alone as she slipped through the crowd until she could see Peter. He was speaking to Andrew. When they noticed her, they fell silent. Her brother-in-law rose and walked away, setting a hand on her shoulder for just a moment.

She sat beside Peter. She was calmer now. Resolved, but her soul still felt heavy.

"So?" he said, raising his brows.

"So?" she echoed, trying not to crease her brows.

Peter furrowed his forehead. "What do you think?" He waved his hand around at the camp. Everyone was chattering and busy. "About what Jesus said?"

"Does it matter?" she said lowly. Peter didn't reply, and Beth sighed. She looked in his eyes and saw his resolution to go with Jesus, no matter how she felt. Her calmness fled and her temper sparked. "Would you stay if I asked you to?"

Peter pressed his lips together. "Don't do that, Beth. We both know the answer, and I don't want to argue. Not when I'm leaving."

Leaving. She nodded once, her neck feeling tight. Jesus had warned them that they had to love him above all. Her heart sunk. "What will you do, Beth?" Peter asked, leaning towards her as voices and movement shifted all around them. They would all break camp at first light, their close-knit group scattering. "Will you go with Jesus?"

He told her Jesus and the remaining disciples would be continuing on their way while the newly created Twelve went on their first mission. Homesickness rolled over her again.

"I think I should go home. My mother would appreciate the help. I could use some rest."

Peter nodded, his eyes searching her face. He knew what she wanted, yet he couldn't give it to her. Her heart hurt. She reached up and touched the shadowy side of Peter's face, the other half ruddy in the fire glow. He looked at her with a touch of worry. Her words were tremulous as she said, "To be honest, I don't have the heart to go about the country if I can't go with you."

She had given her heart and body to her husband. She would follow him anywhere, even if she suffered long miles far from home. Could she follow Jesus like that? She needed time to decide.

"If you think that's best," Peter said, and his Adam's apple bobbed. "Maybe I was selfish to ask you to come along. It's been too much for you."

"No!" Beth cried out, reaching out to grip his forearm. She lowered her tone, but her voice was insistent. "I wanted to be with you, Peter. I always want to be with you."

He smiled. He leaned forward and kissed her, his lips tender. He drew back and traced her jawline with a finger. Unspoken words hung heavy between them. She reached up and held his hand to her cheek, leaning against it.

She knew with all her heart that he loved her. Yet, she had to share his heart with Jesus. If she were to ask Peter to leave Jesus and return home with her now, she would be asking him to deny his heart. If he agreed, it would break him. If he refused, it would crush her. She closed her eyes. It was better to say nothing at all. So instead, she smiled with trembling lips as she prepared to say goodbye to him once more.

Peter, Andrew, James, and John escorted Beth and Naomi safely back to Capernaum. They stopped at the northern edge of town.

Beth had felt far from home while she was on the road. As she prepared to say goodbye to Peter, she felt the pull of homesickness change direction.

Without Peter, how could she be truly home?

Naomi hugged each of her sons, speaking a blessing over them. Kissing her boys on their cheeks, she sent them forward with dry eyes, a brave and wise mother.

Beth found herself twisting Peter's tunic in her hands, her feeble self-control failing, unwilling to let him go. Would he suffer as Jesus had said?

Finally, Peter took her hands, held them to his heart, and kissed her tearful face goodbye. He turned and walked away, eager to begin the mission Jesus had given them.

"We will be back in a few weeks, Beth," Peter called back over his shoulder with a grin, eager to try his new power, fearless to go and proclaim Jesus' message. "Rest and enjoy your time with the family. And don't worry!"

Beth watched him march down the road with his brother until he was lost from sight. She felt a stone fall into her stomach. It became difficult to draw a full breath as the bands of anxiety coiled themselves around her chest.

Again she was left behind, wondering when her husband would return. And after Jesus' prophecy of what would befall those who followed him, she felt even more concern for Peter and Andrew's safety than before.

She shook her head. How could they do it? How did they cheerfully forsake comfort and safety for uncertainty and danger? She turned back to Capernaum, knowing she had much to consider.

It was good to see her house. Just the sight of it, with its image of security, raised her spirits. The bracing breeze off the Sea of Galilee, the bobbing fishing boats, everything and everyone familiar to her, beat upon her heart like sunshine after a storm. She ran to her front door.

"Mama! I'm home."

16

A WOMAN SENT

Beth rolled over and stretched on her soft bed, drawing deep the familiar scent of home. She saw Hannah's tangled hair and her mouth hanging open as she snored. It was dawn. Light and birdsong seeped through the cracks of the shuttered window. Beth smiled. It did feel good to be home.

As the days flew by, she slipped back into her old rhythms, yet she didn't feel fully satisfied. She carried an ever-present ache within her as she did her chores or met with friends and neighbors.

While she had been on the road with Peter, her thoughts had always turned for home with its comfort and familiarity. Now that she was home, her mind followed Peter as he traversed the land without her. She twisted her mouth ruefully. She was like a wayward sheep always wanting the grass it couldn't reach. If only Peter would stay home with her, then she wouldn't need to choose.

Her mind was so full of Peter that her memories often returned to all she had learned sitting with him at Jesus' feet. She shared those memories with Tamar, Hannah, and David, and all three were eager to listen as she shared what Jesus had taught her.

At synagogue she chanted the prayers, heard the scripture paraphrases, and listened to one of the men give a sermon. It was all familiar—the words and themes she had grown up hearing.

Though she sat with friends and neighbors, she felt uncomfortably like an outsider and tried to figure out why. She glanced around the room. Everyone looked the same. Perhaps it was she who had changed.

Her eyes turned to Reuben. Her cousin sat upright, his phylactery on his left arm. The leather thong wrapped around and around, binding him. He thought Jesus had a demon. She thought Jesus was a righteous prophet. As she looked on Reuben's averted face and remembered all they had shared, she had to swallow hard.

She missed him. Why did she have to choose between Jesus and Reuben?

Jesus' words rose up and haunted her. *"You must love me above all, more than your father or mother, your son or daughter. You must take up your cross, and follow after me."*

The words were difficult, and she pulled back from them. Peter loved Jesus like that. He was willing to leave it all for Jesus, leave everything. Was she?

Beth sat at the loom one afternoon, the dreary winter rains pounding on the roof. Her hands were clumsy and she found herself sitting motionless, lost in gloomy reverie.

Tamar found her there and sat beside her, putting her arm around Beth's shoulder. Beth leaned against her mother.

"You've been troubled since you returned," Tamar said. "I know you miss your husband, but this feels like something more. What's bothering you?"

Beth sighed. "I don't know if I can explain myself." She gathered her thoughts and tried to lay them out in some semblance of order. "I believe Jesus is a prophet, and I believe in his message. He's a righteous rabbi as well as a prophet, teaching those who follow him to go out and do as he does." Tamar waited for more, but Beth was silent.

"Why does this trouble you?" Tamar prompted.

Beth rubbed her cheek against her mother's shoulder. "I just wonder, what do I *do* with my belief? What place do we women have in this kingdom of heaven? The men may preach, or fight for him when the time comes." She swallowed hard. She hoped the time for battles was still far away. "What is my purpose?"

Tamar squeezed her. "Do not underestimate yourself, or the worth of women. Don't forget the women of our past." Her mother turned Beth's face and looked deep into her eyes. "We have great heroes, Deborah and Esther, who saved many men's lives. More quietly perhaps, we have the women who both supported and raised great men. There have even been foreign women in our scriptures who have shown great faith: Rahab, Tamar, and Ruth, brave women in the lineage of our great King David. The stories of women are often untold, but every woman who gives her heart to the Lord matters."

Beth smiled a little. These great women had been on her own heart a lot lately.

"But ..." Beth whispered, "... what if Jesus asks more of me than I can give?" Beth was ashamed of her cowardice and turned her face away. It was one thing to admire great women, another to be one.

Tamar sat quietly for a long moment, then turned Beth's chin back to her own. Beth gazed on her mother's familiar face, and it made her throat burn.

"Why do you ask that?"

Brushing away tears, Beth told her mother all that Jesus had said when he prepared the disciples to go out without him: persecution, scourging in the synagogues, even crucifixion.

Tamar's face paled and sharp creases cut between her wide brows. She asked, "So you think Peter is in immediate danger?"

"Yes! No. I don't know." Beth threw her hands into the air. "Even if he comes back safe this time, will he always?"

"Only the Lord knows," Tamar said. "Peter knew the danger, yet he went where Jesus sent him."

"And what about me? What do I do?"

Tamar had no answer.

The next morning Beth rose earlier than usual, unable to sleep. Wrapped in a blanket against the winter chill, she knelt and tried to pray. No words would come, only a painful longing that she could not express.

She rose to her feet, frustrated, and padded barefoot through the house. This home was the symbol of the dream she had treasured—a quiet and happy life with Peter and her family.

Her hand traveled over her flat abdomen and she felt the lack of life inside her. Her thoughts tumbled. Was her empty womb a precursor to an empty life? Was Peter's obedience to Jesus the end of all her dreams? Did she have to give up her husband, hand him over to Jesus to serve and to suffer?

What if—the thought made a shiver run down her spine—what if she was called to suffer physically for Jesus because of her belief? Women were not immune from whipping or stoning by the synagogue, or torture and crucifixion under Rome.

A brief image of looking up and seeing ravens circling overhead flitted across her mind before she forced it away.

She turned back to the stories of her people for guidance. Abraham had been asked by God to take his son Isaac, the one that he loved, and slay him upon the altar. Had Abraham wondered as he led his son on the road, 'Of all the fathers and sons, why did God choose me and mine?'

"You must love me above all."

She knew she had to be faithful, as Abraham had been, to give to God without holding back. Abraham had obeyed, and because of his obedience, God had established a covenant with him: his children would be as numerous as the stars in the sky or the sand on the seashore.

But it was so hard. She fell to her knees, groaning as if in pain.

"You must love me above all."

Perhaps this is what God demanded of her. This was her role. He wanted her to give Peter to His work. Even if that meant they would never have a quiet life at home.

Her hands fluttered over her empty womb. Though her heart rebelled, how could she refuse the Lord? She clasped her hands over her heart, knowing what she had to do.

She would stop wishing Peter would leave Jesus and come home. She would never ask him to abandon Jesus for her own sake. She would free him in her own heart, and let Jesus use him as he saw fit.

A sense of calmness descended over her as she relinquished control. Holding fast to that calmness within, Beth squeezed her eyes shut and a prayer rose from deep within her soul. She prayed for courage to do what needed to be done. She prayed that God would use her husband for His good purposes, and spare Peter as He had spared Isaac.

After giving Peter into God's hands, she felt peace greater than she had enjoyed in years. Kneeling, wrapped in a blanket, warm and safe in her home, she reflected on her past journey with Jesus and felt shameful embarrassment. She had been too focused on herself and only concerned with her own needs. It was no wonder she had been filled with doubt.

Beth rose in her peace and began her morning chores as the pale winter sun rose, humming to herself.

It was mid-morning when she heard a call from without the house. "Beth, my girl!" Zebedee's voice boomed.

Beth rose from where she was kneading bread dough with Hannah and walked to the door, wiping her hands on her apron.

"Hello," she said, smiling at her uncle as she stepped outside, drawing her hand up to shield her eyes from the sun. The winter air was fresh on her face.

"We've had a great catch," Zebedee said, leaning back and hooking his thumbs in his belt. "I'm taking the fish to Magdala to sell for salting. Would you like to come with me? Naomi turned her ankle last night, so she's sent me a list for her shopping." He leaned towards her and lowered his tone. "Truth be told, I could use a woman's help." His eyes implored her beneath his graying brows.

"Of course," Beth grinned, ducking back inside.

Tamar requested a few items of her own. Hannah sat with her hands motionless in the bread dough, crestfallen at being left behind.

Zebedee, his usual kind self, noticed and said in his rumbling voice, "Hannah may come too—if her mother can spare her."

Hannah rose to her feet as if pulled by strings, her eyes gleaming. Tamar laughed and gave her permission.

Beth and Hannah rushed around, washing up and dusting off their woolen dresses. Beth tossed a shawl over her hair, and the sisters strode with their burly uncle down to the pier.

Beth remembered going to Magdala with her father as a girl, and she felt a pang that Hannah did not share that memory. This would be Hannah's first time to see the busy market.

They clambered aboard the boat, stepping around several baskets laden with glistening, silvery fish. The girls found places to sit and Zebedee and one of his hired men sailed the boat towards the port of Magdala.

Hannah went to the bow and leaned far over to trail her fingers in the water. Beth smiled at her adventurous sister, so unlike herself. Beth knew, if only given the chance, Hannah would grab at the chance to travel with Jesus with both hands, declaring every hardship an adventure, excited to be a part of something big.

Beth lifted her face heavenward and breathed deeply the mix of fresh air and familiar odor of fish. She closed her eyes and grinned. She felt today was going to be a good day.

Magdala was about three miles away. Though it was close to Capernaum in distance, it was far apart in style. Magdala throbbed with the pulse of the world, and the people were occupied with turning a profit. It was set at an important crossroads, pressed together, and noisy. The town had several inns and taverns with separate lodgings for Jew or Gentile. Many men were employed in salting fish to send in barrels all over the country. The worldly Magdalenes were better dressed than their humble neighbors, and their houses were modern and large, giving the city a feeling of bustling wealth.

Yet, Magdala had something of a reputation. Beth had heard whispers of houses that kept plush beds for weary travelers, with willing women to warm them. Houses that good men never went near.

They docked at the large port. Zebedee had to pay a small coin for the privilege of tying his boat to one of the many piers. The head fishmonger was a balding man who made up for his lack of hair above with an excessively long beard. He inspected Zebedee's load. With a snap of his fingers, his hired workers unloaded the fine catch, and Zebedee accepted a short stack of coins.

He gave Beth Peter's share, which Beth tucked away in her little bag. Zebedee waved off her earnest thanks with a rumbling chuckle.

"Come on," Hannah said, taking her uncle's large hand and tugging him off the pier. "I want to see everything."

"I don't know." Zebedee frowned and pulled his beard as he glanced at the sun. "It's later than I thought. Perhaps we'd better head for home."

Beth saw the twinkle in his eye, but Hannah looked crushed. Zebedee boomed out a laugh and tousled his young niece's hair. She glared playfully.

"Oh, Uncle!" Hannah said as she laughed with him.

He jovially led his nieces to the market in the center of town.

On both sides of the market street was a narrow, stone colonnade, and under this protection from the elements were dozens and dozens of stalls with loud merchants plying their goods.

Hannah was excited, but for once, she stayed close to Beth. Together they admired pottery, hand knives, bolts of cloth, and fine silk scarves from exotic lands. There were fresh baked goods, glass dishes, fragrant spices, perfumes and oils, cooking utensils and other items beyond count. A pen of chickens squawked and fluttered. Goats and sheep bleated while men and women haggled with raised voices. Dogs sniffed around for scraps.

The girls' pace was slow, and Zebedee stopped every few feet to talk to yet another person he knew.

A lavish, fringed booth, draped with a yellow cloth, drew Hannah's attention with its beautiful jewelry. The woman inside the booth smiled, her teeth pearly white against her dark skin. She appeared to be a few years older than Beth, with thick and curly dark hair. Her garment was of expensive, scarlet material. Over her hair was a veil so delicate it was almost transparent. She wore a necklace and several bangles that rattled on her slender wrists. Despite her finery and her easy smile, her cheeks were ashy, and sunken shadows lurked under her hollow eyes.

"Looking for something special today?" she asked in a husky voice. She sounded as if she was ill.

Beth answered, feeling a little homely next to this wealthy woman. "No, we're just looking. They're very beautiful." She blushed at her awkwardness.

The woman continued to smile and said, "Well, you must show me your favorites."

Hannah was pointing out a little brooch shaped like a glittering beetle when the woman stiffened, her hands splaying on the counter-top. The sisters stared in alarm as the shopkeeper put a trembling hand over her eyes and slumped forward.

Beth cried out as the woman collapsed to the ground behind the booth. The woman's muscled guard lunged forward as Beth hastened behind the counter into the booth, but he paused when he saw Beth was only coming to help.

Beth gasped when she saw the woman was having a fit. She crouched and tried to restrain the woman as she thrashed on the dust, ruining her delicate veil. Froth was coming from her mouth, and her eyes were open and glassy.

Beth looked up at the guard and cried out, "What's happening?"

"She gets like this sometimes," he said with an uncomfortable shrug, glancing away and keeping a close eye for thieves who might use this chance to rob the booth. "Lately, it's been worse."

"Hannah, get help!" Beth commanded her sister.

Blood began to mix with the foam as the woman rigidly jerked her limbs and head. Hannah darted away, searching for Zebedee who they had left somewhere behind.

Beth's heart raced. She had no idea how to help this woman. She wished she had the power of Jesus; he could heal this woman with only a touch.

The woman began to gag and choke. Beth turned to her only hope. Prayer was her only weapon against whatever demon had taken hold of this woman.

"Lord, please!" Beth prayed aloud, the prayer coming from somewhere deep within. "I don't have the power of your servant Jesus, but I believe his healing power comes from You. I ask You, please heal this woman. Do what I cannot!"

At that moment, Beth felt someone near. She glanced up and was amazed to see Jesus himself crouching beside her. There had been no word that the prophet was in the area.

Jesus closed his eyes and put his hand on the woman's head. For a moment, her body became so rigid that the only part of her touching the ground was her head and the heels of her feet. Then, with a great sigh, the woman fell limp.

"Is she all right?" Beth gasped.

"Yes, she'll be fine." He looked at Beth, his brown eyes delving into her soul. Often in the past, she had turned from his piercing gaze. Now she gazed back at him, marveling in his power. Jesus seemed to like what he saw. He smiled at her with an expression that reminded her painfully of her father had been proud of her.

He nodded in approval as he said, "Your faith is great."

Beth's eyes moistened at both his praise and the memory.

Hannah came panting up with Zebedee. Beth stood to tell them what had happened as Jesus helped the woman rise to her feet. Her cheeks were lustrous with a healthy glow, and the shadows under her eyes were gone. She was beautiful. Her expression was dazed, like someone awakening from a dream. She used her ruined veil to wipe the blood from her cheek.

"I feel like … me," she said, her hoarse voice replaced by one rich and musical. Her eyes moved slowly. "It's been so long since I've felt whole."

She turned to Jesus, and her face spread into a beaming smile. She thanked him again and again. Then she turned, reached out, and took Beth's hands in her own.

"I heard your prayer over me like a beam of sunlight in a storm. I'm so grateful." Beth ducked her head, and the woman continued. "I'm Mary. Please, you and your friends must come and dine with me at my father's house. Just allow me to close up my shop."

The woman looked over to speak to the man who had healed her, but Jesus had disappeared. Beth looked up and down the street. It was like he had vanished into thin air.

"Who *is* that man?" Mary leaned towards Beth and whispered in an awed tone. "He radiated with power. How did he heal me like that? For years I've seen the most famous physicians, and none of them could do a hundredth of what he did for me in a second."

Beth smiled, energy flowing into her soul like life-giving water in a desert. Filled by her rabbi's praise of her faith, she softly began to tell Mary all about Jesus. She told her about the kingdom Jesus proclaimed and the miracles she had seen him perform. The words tumbled out one after the other in a stream.

Mary hung on every word as Beth's soft voice proclaimed Jesus to her. Somewhere in a corner of her mind, Beth could hardly believe how easily the words came. She had never spoken openly like this to a stranger, and she had certainly never tried to share Jesus with one.

Mary led them to her expansive, tastefully-furnished home, and they reclined on soft pillows as they ate foods brought by servants. Hannah looked around the luxurious room in awe as Beth continued to speak and answer Mary's many questions.

The conversation paused only for a moment when Mary's elderly father shuffled into the room to see why she was home early.

Mary's voice was thick with emotion as she told him that she had been healed. Tears came into his yellowed eyes. He held her smooth face in his wrinkled hands and shakily kissed her forehead. She led him to a soft couch to rest, and he listened for a while before falling asleep.

Beth's voice was feather-soft, but Mary didn't seem put off by her shyness or by the way Beth often looked at her hands when she spoke. Mary only cared about the words that fell from Beth's lips as she shared the Jesus she knew, and his message of the kingdom of heaven.

Twice, Beth hesitated and turned to Zebedee, sure he could explain better than she. Zebedee just grinned and gestured that she should continue.

After sharing it all, Beth reached out a hand and set it on Mary's arm. She was surprised at her boldness, but she didn't pull back. She searched Mary's face and saw her openness to Jesus' message.

"We must understand," Beth said, her low voice urgent. "The kingdom Jesus preaches is near. He has invited many men, including my husband, to work with him and spread the news. They've given up everything to follow him. He tells us to repent of our sins and set our hearts right with the Lord and with each other. If we are faithful, Jesus is going to lead us into the kingdom of heaven."

Mary clasped her free hand over her heart. "I didn't think I would ever see anything like this. This is amazing, simply amazing! I have to be a part of it." Her eyes sparkled with enthusiasm. "How can I stand behind a booth all day selling trinkets when this is happening out in the world?"

"The men are returning two weeks before Purim," Zebedee said. "Why don't you come to Capernaum and meet them? Jesus will be there."

"You can stay with us," Beth invited. Mary agreed at once.

As Beth stood up with Zebedee and Hannah to go home, Mary rose and hugged her. Beth was surprised, and she stiffened for an instant before relaxing and hugging the other woman back. She felt a bond to the wealthy shopkeeper already.

"Thank you," Mary said, squeezing. She broke the embrace to look Beth in the face. "You say Jesus sent out men to share his message. It seems he sent a woman as well."

Beth left Magdala with her heart light, excited to share what had happened with Peter. Shy as she was, uneducated, full of weaknesses, she had been able to speak of Jesus with confidence.

It had been Jesus who had healed Mary, and she was sure Jesus could have told Mary all about the kingdom, but for some reason, he had left the task to Beth. The mighty prophet seemed eager to have others work alongside him—even her, a lowly fisherman's wife.

Her heart pounded at the idea that she too could speak of what she had witnessed.

She had felt a great sense of calm this morning. Now, as the boat swept over the waves, she felt that if she spread her arms, she could soar on the breeze.

She was eager to return to Jesus, not just as the wife of one of his disciples, but as a true disciple herself. She had not forgotten the trials Jesus had foretold, but she knew that she, like Mary, could not stand by and live her old life when such amazing things were happening in the world.

If Jesus was willing to have her, she would leave everything and follow him.

Spring chased away the winter chill and brought her husband back to her waiting arms. Peter ducked under the doorway late one afternoon and caught her up in a hug, exhausted but full of happiness, brimming with stories about the people he had met and overflowing with wonder at the miracles that he and Andrew had been able to perform in Jesus' name.

The rest of the Twelve trickled back into Capernaum, taking up residence in Peter's home, and waiting impatiently for Jesus to return from his travels.

When Jesus arrived home it was a joyous and noisy reunion. Everyone was eager to share what had happened to them, and the house reverberated with laughter.

Beth's cheeks ached from a smile that would not dim as she served the men supper, listening as the disciples told about their adventures.

Jesus lifted his face towards her, laughter still dancing in his eyes as James and John finished their tale. He beckoned to her. She flushed and came forward at once, holding out the platter of bread, thinking he wanted another loaf.

"Why don't you introduce your new friend?" Jesus asked, glancing at Mary Magdalene.

Mary Magdalene glowed with a pretty awareness as Jesus turned to her.

"Of course," Beth gulped, setting the bread down on the table.

She stood upright and cleared her throat, her palms dampening as eyes flicked her way. Beth felt her cheeks flame as she said, "Uh … This is Mary of Magdala. She was healed by Jesus and wishes to devote herself to being a disciple."

The disciples looked taken aback.

"Magdala?" some of them whispered to each other with raised brows.

"What about your husband?" Judas asked with a small frown.

"I'm unmarried," Mary replied, and several of the young men shifted at that news. Mary continued, "My father passed away just over a week ago."

Her lips trembled, and she dropped her chin and looked at the floor for a moment. When she lifted her face a moment later, her eyes were liquid.

"What about your year of mourning?" Andrew raised his brows. "Don't you have relations to answer to?"

Mary's eyes skipped around the room. She twisted her finger as everyone stared at her, questioning and doubting. Beth wished she dared to vouch for Mary, but the words stuck in her throat.

Mary took a deep breath. "My uncle came for me, but I told him that my father had arranged with an agent to sell the house. It was much too big for me to live there alone. The money was given to me as my inheritance. My uncle wasn't happy." She twisted her mouth. "He insisted that I hand over the money to him and come under his roof until a husband could be found for me. I refused."

"You refused?" Simon sounded shocked.

Mary's independent actions were a serious breach of womanly honor. Mary blushed but didn't recant the words.

"I guess it won't surprise you that my family has cast me off." Mary lifted her damp face, a glint of pride in her face. "I accept that, and I stand firm in my decision. Before he died, I told my father my plan to follow Jesus. He gave me his blessing."

Her eyes moved around the room again, her expression pleading with them to understand. "I know our traditions say I'm supposed to wait at home in mourning, but how can I do that?" She held out her hands, imploring them. She cried out, "I do mourn. I loved my father. I was his only child, laid in his arms when he was already full of years. He loved me and cherished me, and I grieve for his loss." A few tears slipped unchecked down her cheeks. "But I can't wait for a year. There's a kingdom coming, and I wish to be a part of it. I need to be a part of it." Mary looked at Jesus, clasping her hands under her chin. "I will give all that I have, and all that I am, to your service. I only wish to sit at your feet and learn from you, Rabbi."

Beth knew how it ached to lose a father. She felt pangs of sympathy as the woman laid bare her heart to strangers, not knowing how they would react. She also felt a prick of conscience. Mary had fully given herself to Jesus without holding back. How did she walk away from her family and her old life so easily?

Some of the men were doubtful at Mary's desire to follow Jesus without a brother, son, or husband to accompany her., but Jesus rose and went to her, putting a brotherly hand on her shoulder.

Mary calmed under his gentle smile and wiped away her tears with the back of her hand.

"I welcome you," Jesus said sincerely. Mary gave him a wavering smile, the joy on her face illuminating her beauty.

Peter jumped to his feet and went to stand with Jesus. With his usual impulsiveness, his words tumbled as he welcomed Mary and invited her to stay in his home for as long as she wished.

"Think of us as your family!" he said grinning. Mary glanced at Beth with uncertainty at this grand gesture.

Beth chuckled to herself. Peter was surely a man led by his emotions. At least this time, his impulse was in line with her desires. Beth smiled and nodded, and Mary's shoulder's relaxed as she accepted.

Beth was glad Mary was joining them. Perhaps she would feel less lonely with another woman disciple near her own age.

In the days that followed, they all witnessed Capernaum turn cold shoulders towards Jesus. Women ducked away when he and his disciples passed. Men who had been friendly before now averted their gaze.

Beth witnessed with her own eyes Reuben and Philemon purposefully crossing the street to avoid Jesus—and her. Philemon remained aloof, but Reuben glared at Jesus, his expression seething with animosity. Reuben's bitterness troubled Beth, but she didn't know what to do about it.

While the other Pharisees shunned Jesus, Jairus supported the traveling rabbi, refusing to cast off the man who had raised his daughter from the dead. Beth did not doubt that his faith in Jesus was causing him and his family a great deal of strife.

In the face of so much bitterness, Jesus didn't speak in the synagogue any longer, but he taught the willing and openhearted in Peter's house.

17

LORD OF THE SABBATH

Friday waned. The sun would soon set and the day of rest would begin. Reuben loved the Sabbath. It was good to be still and meditate upon the Lord, remember all His goodness and trust in His providential hand. The ignorant Gentiles mocked the Sabbath and called the Jews sluggards for refusing to work on the seventh day. The Jews, however, knew that the Sabbath is a gift, and accepted the day of rest with joy.

Reuben was feeling particularly at ease this Sabbath. Like the local farmers surveying their crops with satisfaction, the spring was showing the success of his and Simeon's efforts for the pharisaic cause. Three of the larger Galilean cities that Jesus had visited had turned against him, even though Jesus had performed the bulk of his miracles among their townspeople. As victories, Reuben could count Chorazin, Bethsaida, and, best of all, Capernaum.

The corners of Reuben's lips curled upwards as he recalled when Jesus had returned to Capernaum at the end of winter. If he had expected a warm welcome, he was sorely disappointed. Most of the people now eyed him with distrust. Jesus had not been asked to speak in the synagogue again.

The only barb that niggled was that Jairus still proclaimed Jesus was a prophet. Still, one elder's opinion was easily swept aside.

Reuben looked forward to telling Simeon of their success in person. He had been invited to come after the feast of Purim to celebrate the Passover Feast and Week of Unleavened Bread with his rabbi, and he would stay in Jerusalem for two whole months. Each time he reread the letter he felt a warmth course through him. The invitation was a comfortable reminder that Simeon had not forgotten his eager, though distant, disciple.

They arrived at Daniel's home where Reuben was invited to spend the Sabbath this week. Reuben had spent most of his Sabbaths with Philemon. Reuben had not spoken to his father since that disastrous day of fishing which could have cost Reuben his entire career. Before, he had been hurt when his father had ignored him; now it was he who crossed the street.

Daniel's household was in a flurry. Daniel was a widower with four children and many grandchildren, but his daughters lived with their husband's families in other towns, and his son had the great honor of working in the Temple Courts. Daniel shared his home with his widowed and aged sister, and they had two servant girls and a steward who lived with them.

All Sabbath preparations had to be completed before sundown, so the servants were scrambling as Leah shouted out last-minute orders. The spotless house smelled fresh and clean. In the courtyard the wash was being flicked off the lines. From the delicious smells wafting to his nose, Reuben knew supper was prepared. The food for tomorrow was ready and set aside.

Reuben and Daniel waded through the chaos serenely. Going upstairs they changed into their best clothing. Reuben loved the peacefulness of his Sabbath routine. When he came back downstairs, he saw Leah had lit the oil lamps. The table was prepared, and so the men sat. The servants rushed in at the last second with their freshly washed faces dripping onto their good sets of clothes.

The sun dipped beneath the horizon. Leah and Daniel led them as matriarch and patriarch of the household as they recited the ritual prayers and blessings. They all took their turns washing, purifying themselves before they ate the bread. The whole household ate the meal together with easy conversation and laughter.

After the closing prayer, they all rose and strolled down to the service in the synagogue, greeting friends and neighbors.

Philemon arrived in the synagogue, scanned the crowd, and came and sat by Reuben. He leaned over, his tone bitter as he said, "I see Jesus is still here. Why did he bother to come back? We don't want him."

"I think we've made that abundantly clear. He'd be thick not to notice," Reuben scoffed.

He glowered at Jesus, though the man did not glance his way. If Jesus would only remove himself from Beth and Peter's home for good, Reuben could start to repair his friendship with Beth and guide her back in line with the elders.

The meeting was opened by Daniel who rose and called out to the congregation in his wavering voice, "Bless the Lord!"

Daniel led them in the chanting of the Shema. The usual scripture readings followed in both Hebrew and Aramaic. Reuben loved the sound of his native tongue—it was like music to his heart.

The next morning, after a cold breakfast, Daniel and Reuben walked to the synagogue again.

Daniel gestured away from the main road to the little track on the outskirts of town. "Let's take the back road. I'd like to see the ripening fields."

Reuben was happy to comply. The whispering fields were a pleasant sight, swaying golden in the spring breeze. Reuben walked with his hands behind his back, imitating the wise scribes he studied under.

"I'm looking forward to the discussion today," Reuben said. "I hope we go back to where we left off last week, debating the resurrection. It's so frustrating when we jump from one subject to another without closing it properly."

Daniel chuckled and winked. "Ah, but you see, a subject from the Torah is never closed. I'm pretty sure the scriptures were written so that we would always have something to debate; it is a gift from God who knows our nature."

Reuben smiled. Every Sabbath it was the same. The men would argue as they dissected and analyzed even the tiniest law, and each man would grow louder and louder as both their ire and their enjoyment increased.

Looking ahead, Reuben saw Philemon engaged in an angry discussion with a man Reuben recognized as none other than Jesus.

Daniel squinted. "What's happened now?"

Philemon's angry tones carried to Reuben's ears as the scribe shook his finger in Jesus' face. "Why don't you teach your disciples to obey the Sabbath? I saw them picking the heads of ripened barley, threshing them in their hands, and eating the kernels. This is forbidden on the Sabbath!"

Reuben and Daniel hurried forward and were in time to hear Jesus' reply, "Haven't you read what David did, when he became hungry and entered the house of God? Didn't he eat the consecrated bread, which none but the priests may eat, and even gave it to his companions?"

Philemon drew up to his full height, his face darkening as Jesus questioned his understanding of scripture.

Reuben bristled as he strode forward. Jesus was speaking to Reuben's teacher, a scribe. Who knew the law better than a man who copied it out perfectly, over and over? What was Jesus' trade? Carpentry, it was said. Where had Jesus been educated? In some little, rural synagogue.

Reuben and Daniel flanked Philemon in support. The three Pharisees stood facing Jesus with his band of young men behind him. Reuben scanned them with a scowl, making note of those he recognized. He saw Beth hovering near Peter as Philemon and Jesus stood toe-to-toe on Sabbath law.

Beth knew as well as anyone that a Jew could be whipped for breaking Sabbath rules. Her thick brows were drawn together and she was biting her lower lip. Reuben was glad she was fearful. It was her common sense trying to lead her back to wisdom. If only she would yield to her well-placed worries.

While Philemon vibrated with suppressed rage, Jesus stood with his hands grasped behind his back and his stance wide and frustratingly confident. Jesus said, "Or haven't you read in the law, that on the Sabbath the priests in the Temple break the Sabbath and are innocent?"

That was true, Reuben had to admit. The priests were allowed to tend to their duties on the Sabbath. It was their busiest day of the week.

Jesus spread his arms. "But I say to you, something greater than the Temple is here."

Reuben furrowed his brow, suspicious.

Jesus leaned closer to Philemon, his eyes unwavering. "If you had known what this means, 'I desire compassion and not sacrifice', you would not have condemned the innocent. The Son of Man is Lord of the Sabbath."

Philemon sputtered, and Reuben's eyebrows shot up. Not waiting for Philemon to reply, Jesus turned and continued his way into town, his followers giving the Pharisees measured glances as they passed.

Philemon turned his back on Jesus, yanking his beard, his eyes flashing. "His time is coming, mark my words. He cannot speak such blasphemy and not have God's hand come against him."

Philemon continued his bitter tirade until Daniel laid a wrinkled hand on his arm, and motioned they should continue into town. Philemon continued to mutter as they walked.

Reuben, despite himself, found Philemon's diatribe fading to a dull hum as he dwelt on what Jesus had called himself. He knew the title 'Son of Man' was taken from the prophecies of Daniel.

"I kept looking in the night visions,
And behold, with the clouds of heaven One like a Son of Man was coming,
And He came up to the Ancient of Days and was presented before Him.
And to Him was given dominion, glory, and a kingdom,
That all the peoples, nations and men of every language might serve Him.
His dominion is an everlasting dominion which will not pass away;
And His kingdom is one which will not be destroyed."

The scribes had interpreted this difficult text and understood that Israel itself was the Son of Man, the chosen nation who would triumph over the beastly kingdoms of the world. That Jesus would take this title for himself, take on the entire role of Israel, was a sign of his deluded self-grandeur. Reuben shook his head. The man was dangerous to them all.

Throughout the Sabbath service, Reuben glared at Jesus and his disciples. Their serenity grated on his nerves. Beth glanced at him in concern, but he glared at her too. If she insisted on believing in this false prophet who trounced on the Sabbath traditions and called himself the Son of Man, she deserved his scorn.

After the service, when women were lingering in conversation and the men were settling in to debate the finer points of the law, Philemon drew Reuben aside.

"Question Jesus," he said. "Let's display his disregard for the

Sabbath for everyone to see. We'll use his weakness for theatrics against him." He whispered instructions, and Reuben's mouth twisted up into a crooked grin of approval.

His eyes fell on the unsuspecting man in the corner of the synagogue. Jared was private and withdrawn. Due to his deformed hand, he had never married. He lived alone on his paltry farm, barely making ends meet. Even simple tasks were difficult for him. Jared's eyes widened in surprise when Reuben approached, smiling. Reuben took his arm and led the confused man to Jesus.

"Rabbi Jesus," Reuben called aloud. His tongue stumbled a little over the title, but he knew a flattered man is easier led. "I would like to ask you, is it lawful to heal on the Sabbath? Here is a man whose hand is withered, and I wish to know if it is permissible to heal on the holy day of rest?"

Reuben tried not to smirk and reveal Philemon's shrewdly laid trap. Jesus would show everyone that he cared more about his power than honoring the Sabbath.

Jesus didn't answer at once. He stroked his beard, his eyes probing until Reuben's smile faltered. Jared tried to walk away, but Reuben reached out and pulled him back. By this time, the entire congregation had stopped to listen.

Jesus looked around the room and called out, "Who is among you, that if they saw a sheep fallen into a pit would hesitate to lift him out, even on the Sabbath?"

A long silence followed, then muttered discussion. Reuben sighed. He knew the men liked to debate abstract questions—they were easier than trying to sort out the real problem before their eyes.

A man said to his neighbor, "Lifting a sheep takes effort. It is work. We mustn't work on the Sabbath. Then again, we mustn't be cruel, no matter the day of the week. So what to do?" And the other man nodded.

"It is the old question," Jairus piped up, fearless under Philemon's weighty glare. "Can the right thing to do be the thing that allows evil to happen?"

Around the room, heads nodded with thoughtful expressions, and Reuben shifted his feet as he listened. Most of the men began saying they would rescue a sheep in distress, even on the Sabbath.

Jesus tilted his head as he asked Reuben, "Are you saying that you value a sheep more than a man?"

Reuben flushed with angry embarrassment as eyes turned on him. He dropped Jared's arm like a dirty rag and stepped away from the crippled man. How was he supposed to answer without sounding like a fool? Unable to look at Jesus, he glared at Jared instead.

Jared stared at the floor, his shoulders hunched. He held his deformed hand close to his chest, looking like he wished he had stayed home this morning. The rest of the people waited with bated breath. Would Jesus heal on the Sabbath?

Jesus came forward and touched Jared on his arm, and Jared slowly lifted his eyes to Jesus' face.

Jesus spoke, "Stretch out your hand."

Jared stared and gave a little tremble. Reuben watched as the quiet farmer lifted his hand before his eyes, and slowly spread the fingers wide. As he did so, the twisted bones straightened, the tendons and muscles relaxed, and it was healed. Jared turned his hand this way and that in wonder, opening and closing the fingers for the very first time. He beamed at Jesus.

Then Jared saw the Pharisees observing him with stony, cold faces, and the mixed reactions from the crowd. The smile slid off his face. His nervous gaze flicked to Reuben. Reuben scowled even deeper, wishing he had never brought the man to Jesus. Jared seemed to shrink, and he drew back to his quiet corner.

Jesus turned to his disciples and led them out. No one made a move to stop him. No one cried out that he should be punished for breaking the Sabbath. Even Philemon was wise enough to see the synagogue was divided. He wouldn't risk making the people chose between the Pharisees and Jesus—not until he was sure the people would choose properly.

Reuben gritted his teeth. The man had profaned the Sabbath, yet he would walk away unpunished. It wasn't right.

"Well done, Reuben," Philemon spoke in his ear. "We'll meet later and find other ways to expose Jesus for the blasphemer he is. Soon we will be well rid of the man."

Reuben glanced over his shoulder to where Jared was quietly showing his healed hand to all who would look, his face lit up in bashful joy. Reuben wasn't sure that Philemon's plan had the success he was trying to claim. Sure, they had exposed Jesus using his power on the Sabbath, but he had realized too late that it would have been better not to remind the people of Jesus' miracles. It would be best if both the miracles and the man were forgotten.

The next day, a messenger boy came to ask if the Capernaum elders would come to Magdala for an emergency meeting with the local synagogues. A massive crowd was gathering near Magdala, growing larger and larger as Jesus healed the people. The elders were anxious to be get rid of this false prophet as quickly as possible.

"Already another opportunity to expose Jesus has fallen into our lap." Philemon clapped his hands and rubbed them with glee.

Reuben felt less optimistic. Daniel, Philemon, Reuben, and the teacher Ezra all gathered to go together.

"Jairus?" Daniel spoke as the other man hung back. "Aren't you coming?"

Jairus raised his chin. "I refuse to go to a meeting that interferes with the man who raised my daughter from the dead. I'll stay and mind the school while Ezra is gone."

Daniel nodded sympathetically. The return of a child was something a man could not forget, no matter the source. Philemon wasn't so understanding. He pressed his lips together and strode to the pier in a snap of robes.

Together, the Pharisees were given a ride in a borrowed boat to the nearby town. They marched down the street to the Magdala synagogue. As they entered, Reuben saw that more elders had been summoned from several of the nearby towns. They were all tired of this pretentious rabbi who was careless of tradition. Soon an angry discussion shook the stone building, everyone debating what should be done about the Nazarene.

"Enough!" Philemon leaped to his feet, gesturing in the air to silence everyone. "While we sit here bickering, Jesus is out among *our* people." Reuben saw some elders were offended, but none could disagree with Philemon's words. "We must follow the model the Jerusalem rabbis have set for us. Our brother Simeon made sure the people were reminded of the truth. It is due to him that so many towns rejected Jesus' teaching."

Reuben was hurt that he was left out of the praise but did his best to shrug it off. After all, it was still his rabbi that was honored, and that honor must reflect on Simeon's disciples.

Philemon continued, "We mustn't let Jesus speak without challenge. We must confront him at every turn. Let's go right now and open the people's eyes to his blasphemy."

Philemon's counsel was accepted. The men all rose and filed out of the building to find Jesus. Soon Reuben found himself on the heels of the elders as they pushed their way through a milling, noisy swarm to where Jesus stood.

Just as they arrived, Reuben saw a man being brought to Jesus, led by the hands of his aging parents.

The gray-haired father pleaded, "Our son is possessed by a demon. He has been since he was a young child. He is both mute and blind. Please, Rabbi, will you heal him?"

The crowds were transfixed, and their wide-eyed adulation reminded Reuben of a time when he had seen a pagan sorcerer performing on a street corner. Jesus didn't seem to be trying to lure an audience to pay him for a show, yet the Nazarene was drawing a crowd that would make any street sorcerer green with envy. Instead of coins, he was paid in attention for his speeches.

"We should stop Jesus before he can touch him," Philemon muttered through gritted teeth, taking a step forward.

"Careful," Daniel cautioned, resting his wrinkled hand on his former apprentice. "We can't stop him by force or we will incite the crowds. We can't allow a riot." Daniel's eyes flicked back to Magdala, no doubt thinking of the Roman soldiers stationed there.

"Surely he can't actually heal the man," another Pharisee scoffed.

Unable to stop Jesus, they all watched to see what would happen. Reuben pressed his lips together with a gnawing sense of helplessness.

Jesus went forward and laid his hands on the demon-possessed man, who jumped a little at the sudden contact. Jesus bowed his head and his lips moved silently. The startled man rubbed his eyes with his palms. He turned his round eyes to his parents and they stared at him in wonder. It was like watching a reunion of long-lost relatives. The man brushed his hands upon his mother's face, feeling the familiar contours.

"Mama?" he gasped, his voice almost childlike. He turned to the old man, running his hands over his father's features. His fingers came away damp with his parents' tears. "Papa? What happened?"

His mother threw her arms around her son and wept.

"Surely this is the Son of David!" a man exclaimed in the crowd.

The Pharisees' heads snapped towards the speaker. Reuben

clenched his fists. Not this again. His eyes were dragged to Beth. It had been after such a misplaced phrase that he and Beth had argued. They hadn't spoken since. Her eyes met his, and he could tell that she remembered too. Reuben jerked his gaze away.

Philemon's nostrils flared. He shouted over the people. "Do not be fooled. This man casts out demons by the power of Beelzebub! His power is from the devil himself."

The crowd was alarmed. The Pharisees were respected leaders, and now a whole group of them stood glaring at Jesus. The people looked to Jesus with a measure of doubt. Reuben's fists loosened.

Jesus replied just as loudly, "Any kingdom divided against itself is brought to ruin. If Satan casts out Satan, he is divided against himself and his kingdom will collapse."

The crowds turned to the Pharisees to see how they would answer. Reuben was sure Philemon would have a good rebuttal, but he saw with frustration that the scribe was stumped.

Jesus didn't wait for Philemon to gather himself but lunged towards the Pharisees. His face was darkened by the sun, the wind had tousled his hair into disarray, and his clothing was worn from travel, but most noticeable were his eyes. They blazed.

Reuben swallowed hard at the fire in Jesus' gaze, but he tried to hide his disquiet by raising his chin.

Jesus put a fist on his hip as he looked on the Pharisees' proud faces. He waved his free hand at them. His tone was mocking as he said, "Your disciples cast out demons; by whom do they get their power?"

Reuben was stymied, for Jesus spoke the truth. Reuben himself had witnessed a demon cast out by one of Simeon's colleagues. The exorcism had required a dozen men to fast for three days, a sacrifice, and a night of prayer. Clearly, having the power of a demon gave Jesus greater ease to cast them out.

The Pharisees looked at each other. Reuben willed one of them to answer Jesus. Couldn't even one elder make Jesus eat his own words for once? They were all silent.

Jesus continued, "So if I cast out demons by the Spirit of God, what then? The kingdom of God has come upon you!"

Daniel's brows sank low over his eyes. Philemon's face mottled as Jesus turned his backs on the Pharisees as if they were not worth his attention. Jesus faced the shifting crowd, where the people looked like sheep waiting to know who was to be their shepherd.

Jesus' voice carried over them all. "He who is not with me is against me! He who does not gather with me, scatters." He turned his blazing gaze back to the Pharisees. His tone was authoritative, low, and dangerous. "You should be careful with your words. Speak against me, and it will be forgiven you. Speak against the Holy Spirit, and it shall not be forgiven—not in this age, or the age to come."

His ominous words hung in the air.

The Pharisees huddled together, trying to find some way to put Jesus in his place. Reuben peeked over his shoulder at Jesus' face and saw he was shaking his head, swelling with frustration as they conspired against him.

Jesus lunged forward. "You brood of vipers!" he yelled. The words fell like a whiplash, and the elders scattered and recoiled from him. Reuben was struck with the similarities to the prophet John. "Your hearts are so full of evil, it's no wonder the words that pour forth from your lips are dripping with poison."

Jesus returned his attention to the uneasy crowd. Reuben heard him speaking to them, but his words for them were gentle. Jesus saved his wrath for the Pharisees.

"The man is impossible," Philemon hissed, yanking on his beard. Reuben thought to himself that if Philemon spent too much time around the Nazarene, he wouldn't have a beard left.

Daniel leaned on his walking stick with his gnarled hands. "The man has a tongue like a double-edged sword and he's not afraid to use it. We're not doing any good here. I think we'd better withdraw for now."

Philemon looked ready to protest, but the Capernaum teacher, Ezra, stood by Daniel. "If we leave now, we show our disdain for him."

The large party of Pharisees gathered up what was left of their dignity and strode away, chins high. They would not consider themselves beaten.

Reuben straightened his prayer shawl and, out of habit, glanced at Beth. He waited for her to look back at him and catch his eye like she usually did. She didn't. She forgot him and kept following Jesus like just another brainless sheep.

Reuben felt like a lump of hot coal was dropped within his chest. Jesus would not be the only one who suffered for his words;

innocent, naive Beth would be dragged down beside him. He must be stopped.

18

KINGDOM OF HEAVEN

B eth sat outside the house with her face turned to the sun. She felt a shifting movement beside her, peeked open one eye, and saw Mary settling in.

Mary was wearing the simple clothes that Beth and Tamar had provided her. The white under-tunic was sleeveless and woven of linen, made from flax grown in Galilee. The long-sleeved overdress was patterned with vertical stripes of brown and pink and gathered at the waist with a wide belt. Mary had wrapped a band of yellow cloth over her thick, unruly curls and tied it behind her, pulling her hair back from her face.

"I thought you were listening to Jesus in the house?" Beth asked, smiling at her before closing her eyes and turning back to the sun.

Mary laughed. "I was, but I went out the back door to get a drink of water. When I came back, two more had entered the house and I couldn't squeeze my way back in."

Beth chuckled with her. The press of people had been more than she could handle. The two women sat in quiet companionship. Beth dozed a little, lulled by the muffled drone of Jesus' voice.

Beth dragged open her heavy lids when she heard a multitude of voices drawing nearer. She saw a snaking line of people walking down the road from the north. Beth wasn't surprised. Jesus drew people like flies to honey. Just not those in Capernaum.

The man at the front walked up and stopped before the house. "Is this the house of Peter the fisherman?" he demanded.

Beth and Mary rose to their feet. Beth glanced at Mary, and Mary caught the hint and spoke for them.

"It is," Mary said. The man moved towards the open front door. Mary asked, "Are you here to see the rabbi? I'm afraid the house is packed full."

"I am," the man said, puffing out his chest, seeming disgruntled that a woman was questioning him. He glanced over his shoulder at the crowd of expectant faces that pooled before the house. "We all want to hear him speak."

He went to the door and saw the house was indeed too crowded for him to enter. He fell back, frustrated. After a moment, he went to talk with his friends, and they cast shifting glances at the packed house.

A middle-aged woman, bordered by two men in their late twenties, broke away from the crowd and came forward. Beth and Mary gave the trio a polite greeting.

"Peace be on you," the woman said with a sweet smile. "I've come to see my son, Jesus. I'm Mary, and these are two of Jesus' younger brothers, Joseph and James."

Beth was tongue-tied. How should she act towards the woman who had borne a prophet? She tried to speak, but when she opened her mouth no sound came out.

Mary Magdalene leaped forward and greeted Jesus' mother with joy, kissing her hand. Jesus' mother was taken aback as Mary Magdalene said, "How blessed you are to have borne such a son!" Her eyes turned to the dusty and tired brothers. "You're so blessed to call Jesus your brother!"

Beth thought she saw a tinge of bitterness brush across Joseph's face.

Jesus' mother was gracious and kind to Mary Magdalene. She answered her many questions with patience and good humor before setting her hand on Mary Magdalene's arm, "We shall talk more another time. Where's my son? I need to speak to him. We've come a long way."

Jesus' brother crossed his arms. His tone brooked no opposition as he said, "Let him know we're here, will you?"

Beth knew from Jesus' that his father had died some years past. He had a large family, but before this day, none of them had left Nazareth to travel with him. She glanced at the grim brothers with uneasy curiosity.

"Of course." Mary Magdalene was eager to help. She hastened to the front door and called inside, "Behold, Rabbi! Your mother and your brothers are here and they want to speak to you."

Beth could hear Jesus' response from inside the house, "Who is my mother, and who are my brothers?"

Mary Magdalene darted a glance back at Jesus' family, her face flushing. Jesus' brother's expressions darkened. Joseph glared at Beth as if it was her fault. Beth, embarrassed, looked at her hands and wished she could slip away without notice.

Jesus spoke again, his voice wafting out the open door. "These men and women here, they are my mother and my brothers. For whoever does the will of my Father who is heaven, he is my brother, and sister, and mother." And he went back to teaching.

Mary Magdalene turned from the door and took the few steps back to Jesus' family with her hands palm up. She stammered, "I-I don't know what to say."

Jesus' mother looked hurt. She lifted her eyes to Beth's face, and the lines in her brow smoothed away at Beth and Mary Magdalene's obvious discomfort.

"It's all right," she gave a weak smile. "I don't pretend to understand everything my son does or says. He seems to know my mind better than I know his."

Jesus' mother shared a look with her other sons. The brothers looked about to speak, but Mary gave a subtle shake of her head, and they clamped their jaws shut.

Mary stepped forward and caught Beth and Mary Magdalene's chins with gentle fingers, looking into their eyes. She smiled, the expression making her motherly face lovely. "The important thing for you to hear is that he has welcomed you, women who do the will of the Lord, as his sisters. In his eyes, you are as much his family as we are."

Beth was sure Jesus' mother felt the bitterness that rose off her sons like steam from a pot. Beth suspected that she had needed to be the bridge between Jesus and his brothers before.

Jesus' mother said, "He has always had a great heart for love, even as a small child. It seems his love has brought you all into his family. So don't be embarrassed for me. We shall simply sit and wait for him." She sat before the house and gestured for her reluctant sons to do likewise.

Beth remembered her hostess duties as with sudden anxiety. How could she fetch food and drink when she couldn't even get through the door? She stammered an explanation and apologized profusely. Jesus' mother was understanding, but James and Joseph were disgruntled.

Beth leaned against the house again, feeling her embarrassment fade away with an inner warmth more powerful than the sun. Jesus had extended the bonds of family to all who believed, including her. Why such a powerful and righteous man would want to claim someone so fearful and doubting as herself was a mystery, but she felt profound gratefulness.

Jesus came out of the house. His audience poured out the doorway after him and the crowds outside surged forward when they saw he had emerged. Jesus was immediately swamped. Beth and the others scrambled to their feet to keep from being stepped on.

Jesus' eyes swept the crowd and landed on his mother and brothers. He moved forward and caught up his mother with a warm embrace, lifting her right off the ground. She laughed and patted his back for him to set her down. She stepped back, hands on his arms, and her eyes glowed with love. With heads together, they whispered private words, and Mary nodded at something he said. Jesus kissed her on her forehead.

"Have you been well?" Jesus' mother asked, eyeing him up and down with pursed lips. "You look as if you haven't been eating enough. That, or you've been walking too much."

Jesus bore her motherly concern with cheerful patience, but the sons of Zebedee chortled at their rabbi being fussed over by his mother. Naomi's eyes narrowed, and she reached out and smacked both her sons simultaneously on the back of their heads. They ducked away from her, still grinning with boyish glee.

Jesus shook his head with a look of mock consternation for the rowdy pair, and turned to his brothers and greeted them with a warm smile. His brothers were frigid by comparison and glared at the crowds.

"This is ridiculous," Joseph snapped. "We'll be trampled or crushed by this mob. What are they hanging around for? Send them away."

Jesus frowned at his younger brother, setting a hand on his shoulder. "Peace, Joseph. You are too quick to anger." Jesus looked at what his brother had called a mob, and his gaze softened. "They only seek a shepherd to lead them."

Jesus' brothers scowled deeper and flanked their mother as if to guard her against the milling masses that surrounded them, jostling and clamoring for Jesus to speak. More and more people pushed forward, and Beth grabbed Mary Magdalene's arm as she was shoved a step forward. Despite her time traveling with Jesus in the autumn, anxiety wrapped around her chest as she felt the press of the crowd.

Jesus called over the clamor, "I will go into a boat and speak to you from there."

He pressed forward into the throng, the people reaching out to touch him as he passed. Beth and Mary Magdalene gripped hands and slipped in the wake of the Twelve before the crowd pressed back in. They made their way down to the pebbly shoreline where the breeze was fresh.

With the sight of open water before her, Beth began to relax. The crowd watched as Jesus went down the pier and clambered aboard Peter and Andrew's boat. The brothers rowed the boat until Jesus was bobbing just off the shoreline. Behind the kind-eyed rabbi was a background of gleaming water dotted with white-sailed boats, rising green hills, and an endless sky.

The people near the water's edge sat or crouched, and like a wave, those behind sat as well so all could see and hear.

Beth saw Jesus' mother having quiet words with her sons. They looked reluctant to stay and listen. With lowered brows they plunked themselves down and glowered over the rippling water at their brother. What did they see when they looked at Jesus? They had eaten and played with him, gone to school and done chores with him. She tried to imagine how they were feeling. Perhaps they thought he had risen too high. Perhaps they assumed he thought too well of himself.

Jesus waited until the people grew quiet.

"A sower went out to sow," Jesus called, his rich voice full of feeling and expression. "As he sowed, some seeds fell beside the road, and the birds came and ate them up. Others fell on rocky places where the soil was thin. Immediately they sprang up, but when the sun had risen they were scorched, and because they had no root they withered away. Others fell among the thorns, and the thorns came and choked them out. And others fell on the good soil and yielded a crop—some a hundredfold, some sixty, and some thirty. Who has ears to hear, let him hear."

Beth tried to puzzle out the parable. While Jesus knew the barley and wheat crops were ripening for the spring harvest, surely he was speaking of more than simple farming? And such yields! No farmer had ever enjoyed such a successful harvest. Jesus began another story, and she did her best to listen and understand.

"The kingdom of heaven may be compared to a man who sowed good seed in his field. But when his men were sleeping, his enemy came and sowed tares—weeds that look like wheat—among the wheat, and went away. But when the wheat sprouted and bore grain, the slaves could also see the tares.

"His slaves came and said to him, 'Sir, did you not sow good seed in your field? How then does it have tares?'

"And he said to them, 'An enemy has done this!'

"The slaves said to him, 'Do you want us to go and gather up the tares?'

"But he said to them, 'No, for while you are pulling them up you may uproot the wheat with them. Allow both to grow together until the harvest, and in the harvest time the weeds will be burned up, and the wheat will be gathered into my barn.'"

The crowd was silent as they puzzled over Jesus' words.

"Tell us more about this kingdom," a man yelled out to the boat.

"When will it come?" Many voices in the crowd called out in agreement, and heads were nodding.

Beth watched Jesus. She often wondered the same thing, admittedly with a stew of emotions—joy for the future of her people muddled with fear for the coming battles that would be fought to ensure that future. When would Jesus lead his followers over the land to clear out the evil that plagued her people? As she looked on Jesus' face it was hard to imagine him leading a military campaign like the great King David of years past.

As she thought of the coming battles, she chewed the inside of her cheek. If Jesus went to war, Peter would be right at his side. Peter would insist on being first into the fray—she just knew it. She pictured him in armor and with a sword in his hand, yelling a war cry as he charged into the countless Roman armies.

Feeling the familiar waves of anxiety rising higher and higher, she floundered for self-control. Her promise to never pull Peter away from Jesus ached like a sore tooth, but she gritted her teeth anyway. She must be brave. She turned her eyes back to Jesus, swallowing her fear in a painful lump.

The crowd waited with bated breath. Would Jesus reveal when it would be time to take the kingdom?

Jesus called over the crowd, "The kingdom of heaven is like a mustard seed planted in the ground. So tiny, and yet within a single season, it will outgrow all the other herbs and be large enough to shelter the birds." As he spoke, Jesus held his arms out as if to shelter the birds himself. He smiled. "The kingdom of heaven is like leaven, which a woman took and hid in three pecks of flour until it was all leavened."

Then Jesus directed Peter and Andrew to turn the boat back to the dock, his teaching finished for the day. Beth furrowed her brow. She hadn't understood a word of what he said.

A man nearby grumbled, "Mustard seed and leaven? This is what we came so far to hear? I want to hear a prophet, not a sage."

Mary Magdalene leaned over and whispered in Beth's ear. "Has he always spoken in parables?"

Beth chuckled. "Pretty much. Though he'll answer our questions in private. Usually." The crowd was humming as they questioned one another.

That evening, as the moon began to rise, Beth was back inside her own house. The crowds were dispersed, but Peter's house was full of the faithful. Everywhere she looked, Beth saw another disciple of Jesus crowded into the house for the evening meal. The oil lamps were lit, casting the room with a wavering light. Jesus' mother was given a comfortable place near her firstborn son. Jesus' brothers took themselves to a corner, where they sat and looked at the devoted disciples with puckered brows. Beth, Tamar, Naomi, and Mary Magdalene slipped among the men, serving.

Peter called out to Jesus, "Why do you speak to the people in parables? How will they understand?"

Jesus took a piece of bread from Tamar, blessed it, and looked over at Peter. "To you it has been granted to know the mysteries of the kingdom of heaven, but to them it has not been granted. For whoever has a true desire for the kingdom, more shall be given, but whoever has shut themselves off, even the little bit they have will be taken away." Jesus accepted the fish Mary Magdalene held out. He wrapped a steaming white morsel in his bread as he continued, "It's the prophecy of Isaiah being fulfilled.

'You will keep on hearing, but will not understand;
You will keep on seeing, but will not perceive;
For the heart of these people has become dull,
With their ears they scarcely hear, and they have closed their eyes.
Otherwise, they would see with their eyes
And hear with their ears, and understand with their heart
And return, and I would heal them.'"

Beth held the dish low so her brother and sister could help themselves, and felt Jesus' words prick her. Was her heart dull? Did she close her eyes? Why else would the kingdom be such a mystery to her? She looked back to Jesus and he met her gaze, smiling with understanding.

Jesus took a sip of watered wine and looked around at his disciples. "Blessed are your eyes because they see, and your ears because they hear. Many prophets and righteous men would love to see and hear what you do.

"When anyone hears the word of the kingdom and does not understand it, the evil one comes and snatches away what has been sown in his heart. This is the one on whom seed was sown beside the road.

"The one on whom seed was sown on the rocky places, this is the man who hears the word and receives it with joy. But, his faith is shallow. When affliction or persecution arises because of the word, he immediately falls away.

"The seed sown among the thorns is the man who hears the word, but the worry of the world and the deceitfulness of wealth choke the word, and it becomes unfruitful.

"And when I spoke of seed being sown on good soil," Jesus smiled as he said, "this is the man who hears the word and understands it; men like this bring forth fruit, some a hundredfold, some sixty, and some thirty."

The men were all served, so Beth took a loaf and fish for herself and found a place to sit. Now that Jesus had explained the parable, she wondered at her obtuseness. But with understanding, came a new worry. What soil was in her heart? She knew her anxiety well, it had been her unwanted companion for many years. Would her constant worries choke out her ability to work in the kingdom?

She glanced at the others sitting in the room, men and women both. Every one of them looked eager and confident, and yet Beth felt wholly inadequate.

She shifted as the remembrance of the words Jesus had prophesied months before returned to haunt her. *Persecution. Flogging in the Synagogues. Crucifixion.* His words had nearly undone her faith and made her want to pull Peter away from him too. When strife fell on them like a hailstorm, would she be able to stand firm? Was her faith deep enough?

Peter was speaking again, and Beth shoved away this heavy introspection and turned her mind back to the present.

"What about the tares in the wheat, what did that mean?" Peter asked, leaning forward. Beth felt a modicum of relief that she was not the only one who needed further explanation.

Jesus brushed crumbs off his hands and replied, "The one who sows the good seed is the Son of Man, and the field is the world. The good seed is the sons of the kingdom. The tares are the sons of evil, and the one who sowed them is the devil. The harvest is the end of the age, and the reapers are angels. At the end of the age, the Son of Man will send for his angels, and they will gather out of his kingdom all that do wrong, along with those who commit lawlessness, and will cast them out. But the righteous, they will shine forth as the sun in the kingdom of their Father. He who has ears, let him hear."

Beth was relieved that she did understand. Perhaps her ears were not too dull after all. The other disciples were nodding as well.

Mary Magdalene spoke up, her eyes shining as she begged, "I've missed so much of what you've taught the others. Please, tell me more about this kingdom of heaven."

Jesus looked pleased with her desire to know more and drew a hand over his beard. Everyone settled in, feeling comfortably full and cozy in the house. David crept over and snuggled on Beth's lap, and Hannah leaned against her mother. Beth saw that Naomi and

Zebedee were discretely holding hands. Jesus' mother leaned forward, her lined expression content as she gazed at her firstborn.

As Jesus gathered his thoughts, Beth studied the twelve disciples Jesus had chosen specially, men who had followed their rabbi for almost two years. Four were of her own family. Matthew, she had known as a child. From her quiet observances, she felt as if she was getting to know the other seven. They were men of varied trades and backgrounds, and they had all left their homes and livelihoods to follow Jesus. Some had been followers of John the Baptist, brought by Andrew to Jesus. Others had been found in various cities where Jesus had traveled. Simon and Judas were from Jericho. The dangerous, winding road to Jericho was plagued by a violent zealot, Barabbas. As eager as the two men were for a restored Israel, Beth thought it was to their credit that they had chosen to follow Jesus and not the highwayman.

Beth looked back at the two she knew best. When Peter and Andrew had first left to go with Jesus, she had thought they would be back in their boat within a month or two. Beth had no idea when, or even if, her husband would return to his nets. At least for now, everyone was back home, together and safe.

She enjoyed the cloistered, family feeling that saturated the air like a fine incense. She had not forgotten how Jesus had called them all his brothers and sisters, and tonight she reveled in the feeling.

Wisdom and enthusiasm were merged in his expression as Jesus said, "The kingdom of heaven is like a treasure hidden in a field, which a man found and hid again. From joy over it, he goes and sells everything he has and buys that field. Again, the kingdom of heaven is like a merchant seeking fine pearls, and when he found one of great value, he sold all that he had and bought it.

"The kingdom of heaven is like a dragnet cast into the sea and gathering fish of every kind." Jesus paused and chuckled as the fishermen all nodded and elbowed each other with grins. They liked this comparison to their trade. "When the net was filled, they drew it up on the beach and sat down and gathered the good fish into containers, and the bad they threw away. So it will be at the end of the age. The angels will come forth and take out the wicked from among the righteous." Jesus looked at his disciples in the eyes, "Have you understood all these things?"

Beth looked around the room. Everyone, even young David,

nodded their heads and answered, "We understand."

Jesus nodded with a smile. "Everyone who becomes a scribe of the kingdom of heaven is like the head of a household who brings out of his treasure things old and new."

His words hung in the air for a long moment, like a gull soaring over the sea.

Jesus stretched and rose to go outside. The cloistered feeling was broken. The women stood and began gathering up scraps of bread and dirty dishes. Many of the men left to go out with Jesus, and those who remained talked of everyday, simple things. Andrew sat with Jesus' brothers, engaging them in polite conversation. Tamar shooed away a reluctant Hannah and a yawning David, telling them to prepare for bed.

Life was ordinary again, but it felt as if a sweet dream had been shared among them all. Beth wanted to hold that feeling tight. Beth understood that these words of the kingdom were precious, a treasure to be held alongside the teachings of Moses She was awed that she had heard them firsthand.

Beth thought of Jesus' description of a scribe of the kingdom of heaven and gave a little sigh. Reuben was training to be a scribe of the law, immersing himself in the teachings of Moses and the words of the Prophets. Yet, he had set himself against Jesus.

She furrowed her brow as she worked. How could something as wonderful as Jesus' teachings divide her family? For the first time, Ebenezer had sided with Reuben and the elders and scorned his brother, his sisters-in-law, and their children for their belief in Jesus.

Jesus had warned them it would be this way, but it did not comfort her when she thought of her divided family. Reuben had been her favorite cousin, her childhood best friend. She still thought of him as he was before, full of eagerness and enthusiasm, rich with hopes and dreams for the good he might do when he was a trained Pharisee. She remembered his coldness the last time she saw him and shivered. Feeling her mood spiraling downwards, she drew a deep breath and looked around the room with a little shake of her head. It didn't do any good to dwell on what she could not change.

Mary Magdalene swept the floor with more enthusiasm than skill and spontaneously broke out into a joyful song. The song cut through Beth's melancholy for Reuben.

Emboldened by the kingdom talk, Beth sang along. Naomi, Jesus' mother, and Tamar joined in, and the five women lifted their voices in praise to God.

19

PRICE OF REVOLUTION

The closer they drew to Nazareth, the heavier each footstep fell. Beth was uneasy. Her mother's family had been from Sepphoris, mere miles from Jesus' hometown. If history had been different, she could have dropped in to see her cousins, aunts, and uncles. As it was, she was only nearing their graves.

Her mother's family were all gone. The men were killed in battle or crucified, their corpses left to rot until they fell free from the spikes that restrained them. Their wives and children were put to the sword at their feet or dragged away to Rome to be sold as slaves. As she neared the home of her forefathers, it was like their spirits cried out their warnings to her, 'Go back! The price of rising up is suffering and death.'

"Take courage, Beth."

She jumped and whipped her face towards the voice. It was Jesus, and his expression was sympathetic. She tried to nod and smile at the rabbi, but she felt the feebleness of the attempt. He turned his face forward and walked companionably by her side.

Jesus' steps were confident. He had more reason than she to fear for the future—he was the spearhead, the leader, the target. Yet, he strode with his arms swinging. Courage spread outward from him like perfume. She took a deep breath and felt the tension drain out of her neck and shoulders. Jesus nodded at her with a grin. He moved to talk to one of the others. She smiled to herself and shook her head. How did he always know when someone needed a bit of encouragement?

Jesus' mother and brothers were traveling with them as they walked the journey from Capernaum southwest to Nazareth. They were striding on what was little more than a trail instead of taking the circuitous route of paved roads. This lonely path was more dangerous than the busy trade routes; they could be set upon by bandits or attacked by wild animals, but it was faster.

Beth had traveled so little in her girlhood that she had never even heard of Nazareth until she met Jesus. Now she was journeying to his hometown. She would see the synagogue where he had studied, the places he had played as a child, and meet the rest of his brothers and sisters. Despite the looming specter of Sepphoris, she was curious to see Nazareth.

Their trail led them upwards into mountainous territory. As the red sun dipped low, they found a suitable spot to make camp in a quiet place. The women began to prepare supper.

Mary Magdalene tossed a few more sticks into the fire and gazed thoughtfully to Jesus' mother. "When did you know?"

"Know what?" Jesus' mother asked.

"That your son would be a prophet?" Mary Magdalene said. Beth glanced up from measuring the spices into the clay pot.

Jesus' mother chuckled. "Sooner than you might expect."

Beth looked inquisitively at her, and Jesus' mother beckoned the two younger women closer. Her eyes were illuminated by the flickering light from the flames as she whispered, "His very conception was a miracle. He is no ordinary man. He was conceived of the Holy Spirit."

"The Holy Spirit?" the two women exclaimed at once. Jesus' mother shushed them as others looked their way.

"Is this a secret?" Mary Magdalene whispered.

"Yes and no. There are a few others who know the story, and some who were witness to the history that surrounded Jesus' birth."

Beth glanced over to the men. "But you don't want everyone to know?"

Jesus' mother looked at her two sons that sat apart from the disciples. Her expression was sad. "Not all are ready."

Beth nodded once.

Mary Magdalene grinned, looking pleased to be let in on the secret. "What do you mean, Jesus was conceived through the Holy Spirit?"

Jesus' mother smiled. "Just what it sounds like. You see, Jesus' papa didn't father him. Though I was betrothed, I was a virgin when I became pregnant."

Beth's stared blankly. "What?"

Jesus' mother chuckled again. "Yes, it sounds incredible. Joseph thought so too when I told him. His face looked something like yours." Beth quickly wiped the disbelief from her expression.

"Yet, he still married you?" Mary Magdalene raised her eyebrows. "Even though you were pregnant with . . . a son that wasn't his?"

Jesus' mother smiled. "He wasn't going to. He planned to discreetly divorce me, but before he did, an angel told him the truth. I was pregnant through the Holy Spirit. The angel told Joseph to name the child Jesus." Jesus' mother gazed across the camp to where her eldest son spoke to his disciples. Her face was soft. "Don't you see? My son is Immanuel, God with us."

Beth's heart turned over at the title. Jesus was unlike any prophet who had ever walked the earth. Was he truly God's presence walking among his people once more? She and Mary Magdalene shared a glance.

Beth nestled the pot of lentils close to the fire. "What did your family and your hometown think?"

"Nothing," Jesus' mother shrugged. "Joseph never breathed a word against me. He was a good and righteous man, my husband." She was silent a long moment, lost in her memories. "Jesus was born in Bethlehem, which is the city of David you know. After he was born, we were visited there by Magi from the east. They brought gifts and bowed down before my little son. When Joseph questioned them, they said they had followed a star. They declared with certainty that the star proclaimed the birth of a king."

"Really?" Mary Magdalene gasped. "The star led them straight to you?"

"Well, not quite. Bethlehem is only a few miles outside of Jerusalem. When they saw the star hovering so near the Holy City, they assumed a royal child would be born there. So they went into the city and began asking around, 'Where is the he who was born King of the Jews? We have come to worship him.' Herod caught wind of it and summoned them to his palace."

Beth put a hand to her mouth. King Herod had a bloodthirsty reputation. His jealousy had led him to slaughter his own wife and sons for fear they were plotting to usurp him. Jesus' mother saw her expression and nodded solemnly.

"Yes, we were in grave danger. Joseph was visited by another angel who told him not to wait but to take us and flee to Egypt. We left in the middle of the night. We settled in Egypt, and it was much later that we heard what had happened to Bethlehem." Jesus' mother swallowed several times and Beth felt fear creep down her neck. She fought the urge to flee the conversation.

Mary Magdalene hesitated a moment before she whispered, "What happened?"

Jesus' mother dropped her chin and spoke to her hands. "Soldiers killed every boy child under the age of two." The younger women gasped and Jesus' mother held out her hands as if to plead with them. "It broke my heart when I heard. For days, I wept. At first I felt guilty, but then I was angry. So angry! Jesus' birth should have been a time of great rejoicing, but Herod turned it into a time of mourning. This is why we need my son to be king, for he will be kind and merciful. Have you ever seen him cruel or selfish? Have you ever seen him think of himself first? No. He is the king we need. The king who will rule justly and in the name of the Lord."

"Oh, yes Lord!" Mary Magdalene cried out, swept away by passion.

Beth was silent. She couldn't bring herself to rejoice—her mind was trapped in Bethlehem with all the wailing mothers. The two Mary's voices faded, and all she could hear were screams of mothers being thrown aside and the sound of fathers dying to save their sons. She clamped her hands over her ears, but the sound of death only became louder.

For the first time, she was relieved she had no children of her own. She felt sick to her stomach at her shameful cowardice, yet she was relieved for her empty womb. The world was hard and cruel, how could anyone bring a child into it?

She rose and stumbled away from the other two women, stammering that she needed a private moment. She walked away from the camp into the brush, ignoring the branches that hooked her dress and snagged her hair. When she was alone, she fell to her knees as the last light receded from the slopes.

"Your will be done," she whispered a snippet of the prayer Jesus had taught them. She felt hot tears run down her cheeks as she echoed the phrase over and over again. "Your will, Lord! Not the will of corruption and evil. Oh, Lord, those babies, those mothers! How does Jesus bear it? Moses was rescued from the massacre of infants thrown into the Nile, but Jesus … oh! His birth was the *cause* of Herod's wrath. This world is so broken, Lord. Please Lord, if Jesus is Your son, help him restore Israel to You."

She stayed on her knees until her tears were spent as she mourned babies she had never known and shared the grief of mothers she had never met.

When she was calmer, she returned to the camp. Mary Magdalene squeezed her arm as she walked past, and Beth tried to smile.

Jesus came to the fire and sat near his mother, chatting with her. Beth tugged on her lower lip and stared at him, wondering and silent. It was difficult to talk with the others when her mind was so full. She was relieved when it was time for bed.

Beth curled on her side in her blanket, her back resting against Peter. She slowed her breathing, but she couldn't slow her mind. If what Jesus' mother said was true, then even before his birth Jesus had been marked out for something special. For two years now, he had taught and healed, proclaiming a coming kingdom of heaven. What would his destiny be? How would he be God With Us? It was a long time before she fell asleep.

When the sun dawned, her heavy mood dissipated like a morning mist. Jesus' mother's story seemed like a bad dream now that Beth stood in the light of day with bird song and fluffy clouds overhead. She and Mary Magdalene didn't talk about what Jesus' mother had told them, but Beth tucked it away in a corner of her mind until she could find the right time to tell Peter.

By mid-morning they had climbed the rough trail to its summit. They stopped atop the narrow ridge. Beth panted as she gazed down the steep slope at Jesus' home. She saw a village tidily tucked in a narrow valley, with handsome houses of stone and mortar. Because of the lack of space, some of the houses were ingeniously cut right into the hillside, their fronts jutting out from the rock face. The two-story houses each had small courtyards and pens for animals. The town being so snug allowed room for crops and grazing up the slopes around the outskirts.

Beth thought the view was cozy and pleasant, but it wasn't the sort of town a king would call home. She had to remind herself that King David had been a mere shepherd before he rose to the throne.

"Look, you can see Sepphoris from here," Matthew called out, looking the opposite way.

Beth stiffened but dragged her eyes north to the large, walled city perched atop the hills. Sepphoris. Her mother's hometown. Her stomach dropped with a lurch as she pictured the beautiful city as a smoking ruin and the paved road leading out of the city lined with rough crosses. Judah ben Hezekiah had tried to lead the people to freedom from Rome. He had only led them to slaughter.

Mary's son, Joseph, came and stood beside Matthew. He gazed proudly across the distance. "Nazareth men helped build that city. You should see the Sepphoris synagogue, the mosaic floor is second to none. The city is ten times more beautiful than before."

Beth shuddered, wrapped her arms around her middle, and turned her back on Sepphoris.

Mary and her sons led the way as they picked their way down the steep road into the valley. The locals raised hands in greeting, and many came forward to talk.

They paused before a natural spring, and the disciples quenched their thirst with the fresh, cool water. Beth felt the curious eyes of the townsfolk and stepped closer to Peter.

A gray-haired man came up and slapped Jesus on the shoulder in a rough but familiar way. "What's all this, Jesus?" His hand swept the disciples. His voice was teasing, but with an edge to his tone. "You leave us to make your own home, and now you return . . . a rabbi?"

"Ah, Enoch, nothing gets past you," Jesus teased with a chuckle. "Yes, these are my disciples."

Enoch scuffed the back of his hand over his nose and shot a look over his shoulder at some of the other Nazarene men. They all wore simple tunics, sturdy sandals, and the look of working men used to a difficult life. Some held farming tools in their hands. Beth saw that they didn't gaze on Jesus with any particular favor.

Enoch looked like he might have said more, but Jesus' sisters arrived with their children, and all conversation was lost in a noisy, family reunion. Jesus kissed his sisters, then picked up a toddling boy and cradled him in the crook of his arm as everyone talked at once.

Jesus' mother herded them all to her home. The daughters had moved in with their husband's families, but Jesus' brothers all worked in their father's trade and lived in the family home.

As Beth entered Jesus' childhood home, she saw the ground floor was part stable, part workroom. On one side were stalls for animals, and on the other were chisels, hammers, planers and other tools for woodworking. She saw newly crafted farming tools created from wood by the hands of these skilled carpenters. In sturdy baskets were other tools for working with stone, ready to be carried to a worksite. Jesus' brothers were married, and the house had been expanded to hold their wives and children. It was crowded, but full of love. The noisy chatter rose in volume as stories were swapped of what had happened while the family had been apart.

There wasn't enough room for all of Jesus' disciples to stay in the patriarchal home, so Jesus' sisters invited the rest to sleep and eat in their homes.

The women threw together a reunion feast and everyone crammed into the house. Children tumbled everywhere and made themselves comfortable in any available lap. Food was plentiful, and wine flowed. Jesus' brothers relaxed now that they were at home in familiar territory, and became good hosts. Late into the night, the disciples and Jesus' family talked and laughed, the sons of Zebedee loudest of all.

Beth fought sleep as long as she could, enjoying the bustle and love she felt all around her. She felt a pang of sympathy for Jesus. How hard had it been to walk away from this comfortable life to become a traveling rabbi?

The next morning, Jesus went down to the synagogue with his disciples. He began to teach the men who were there. The synagogue in Nazareth was small. It followed the same design as the one in Capernaum with its high windows, pillars, tiered seats, and a storage closet to keep the scrolls.

The Nazarenes grumbled as Jesus taught them about the kingdom. They shook their heads and muttered. Beth heard one elderly man say to his neighbor, "Who does he think he is? Suddenly he thinks he's something special, that *he's* worthy to teach us? We've known him since he was a small child."

On the Sabbath, Jesus was politely invited to speak, but his message was coldly received. The disciples had grown used to Jesus' message of the kingdom meeting resistance, but here in Nazareth his old friends and neighbors dismissed Jesus out of hand. Even his siblings looked uncomfortable, and Beth saw how their grumbling hurt their mother.

The next day, Jesus healed a few people, but the people muttered with doubt. Enoch, who appeared to be a leader in the community, stood before Jesus and challenged, "Where did you get this power?" His words were an accusation. Jesus only sighed and shook his head at them.

That night, Matthew simmered with anger as the disciples broke bread together with Jesus. "What right do they have to treat you this way?" He ripped his bread over and over until it was little more than crumbs. "I deserve such treatment from people, but you've done nothing wrong. You healed that woman, yet they look at you as if you are an impostor.

Jesus put his hand on Matthew's shoulder. "A prophet is not without honor, except in his own household and hometown."

Peter tilted his chin and said, "They can't see you as anything but the carpenter boy who grew up in their midst."

"And from the sounds of it," James chuckled, "you're one big disappointment to them."

John's eyes were teasing. "Yes Jesus, you were supposed to be married and have six sons by now. What were you thinking?"

The sons of Zebedee roared with laughter, but Beth thought the boisterous young men were probably near the truth. In such a small, close-knit community, perhaps the locals saw Jesus leaving Nazareth for Capernaum as abandonment. When he returned as something more than they expected, they balked, like a sheep asked to go through the north gate when it had passed through the east gate every day since it was a lamb.

During their time in Nazareth, Beth kept reflecting back to the time of revolt in Sepphoris. If Jesus was indeed born for greatness like his mother believed, would he remember the massacre that had wiped out an entire generation of men in the area? Was that why he didn't speak of battles yet—because he knew the heartbreak they brought?

Jesus was nothing like those men who tried to wrest power for themselves, men full of pride, hatred, and eagerness to shed blood. She had to believe, somehow, Jesus would do things differently. It comforted her. Though she wanted to give her best to God, she didn't want to relinquish her husband to a bloody death on a battlefield. She knew it was selfish, yet she couldn't help it.

20

JERUSALEM AT LAST

Reuben joined the throng that bustled outside the fortified city gate. His pulse quickened as he waited his turn to enter Israel's most precious city. In his time away, his longing to live in the Holy City had only grown. Jerusalem was home to the Temple that served as the heart of the Jewish people, and today its veins throbbed with life.

Ahead of him, heads began turning with furrowed brows. Reuben glanced back to see what drew their attention. It was a Roman procession, with slaves in the front carrying the banner of a proud Gentile house. Behind the slaves marched several armored soldiers with their short, scarlet capes slung over one shoulder. Next came a closed carriage where a young woman in jewels peeked from behind a curtain. Behind the carriage were two men on tall warhorses, their age and appearance showed them to be father and son. With their haughty air, they were obviously men of standing and wealth. The horses were well-fed and groomed, lifting their oiled hooves high and tossing their proud heads.

Glaring, the Jews hastened to the side to allow this Gentile procession into the Holy City. People grumbled as they had to give precedence to foreigners. It was only a week past Purim. The festival celebrated the story of Esther, the Jewish queen who had saved her people from massacre. Their history was filled with stories of deliverance, which made it hard to be patient when the oppressor's yoke sat heavy.

Reuben waited until the Roman procession disappeared from sight, and then he fell in among the crowd and entered through the Northern Gate. Putting the Romans from his mind, he directed his steps towards the house where he had spent the happiest years of his life. He enjoyed pleasant memories as he walked past familiar buildings in the crowded Large Market. He passed a respectable tavern he had visited many times with his old school friends, and a tall inn that served excellent pastries.

He followed the main road through an archway in a multipurpose wall. The wall divided the new, northern section from the older portion of the city. The dividing wall had a roadway on its top, connecting the wealthy Upper City directly to the Temple Mount, rising over the shabby Lower City. The wealthy could avoid the Lower City entirely if they wanted. Encased within the arched wall itself was an aqueduct. This marvel of engineering brought much-needed water from outside the city walls.

Emerging from the arched gateway, Reuben glanced towards the Hippodrome. He secretly hoped he might catch a chariot race this visit. Though it was yet more proof of foreign influences, he couldn't deny it was exciting. The massive oval track was encircled by tiered seating, enough for thousands of eager spectators.

Reuben turned to the west, away from the Lower City with its nondescript, yellowish stone buildings that hugged a warren of twisting, narrow roads. There lived the olive farmers, the potters, the tanners and dyers, and all the other commoners. Instead, his path took him up the slope and through another wall that separated the lower and upper sections of Jerusalem. The road in the Upper City was wide and clean.

His pace quickened with anticipation as he strode past the large Theater, a half-circle, open-air structure where plays, recitations, and speeches were read. He had never attended. While the theater was growing in popularity among Jerusalem's elite, Simeon didn't approve of plays based on Greek literature. Still, the landmark was familiar, and he felt the warmth of returning home.

He saw a well-dressed family strolling together, laden with

purchases. A handful of Sadducees swept past him, and he inclined his head to the rival party. The wealthy scholars nodded only slightly in return, eyes touching on his Pharisee shawl. Most of those who lived in the Upper City were of the Sadducee party, the cream of Jerusalem.

Reuben continued uphill. The large houses were constructed with gleaming white stone and tiled roofs, boasting covered porches and expansive courtyards. The largest and most elegant of these homes was occupied by Caiaphas, the current High Priest. Caiaphas had, of course, been raised from the Sadducee Party. Reuben, as a mere Pharisee's disciple, had never enjoyed the pleasure of seeing the inside of the High Priest's palace for himself.

At the highest point of the Upper City were the fortified walls that surrounded Herod's Palace. Enclosed within that bulky barrier a beautiful, modern building that was just shy of being the same height as the sacred Temple Mount.

At last, Reuben could see Simeon's house. Despite his eagerness to return, his throat dried as he walked up to the entrance. It would take only one foolish mistake to lose Simeon's good opinion and all this would be out of his grasp forever. Reuben pressed his lips together. He would never let that happen. Determined to surpass all Simeon's expectations, he rapped his knuckles on the tall double doors.

A moment later a familiar servant pulled back a door to admit him. Reuben stepped forward with a grin, pausing to touch the mezuzah. "Hello, Jacob."

Jacob was in his mid-twenties. The steward's son was short but athletically built, broad at the shoulder and narrow at the hip. He wore a tidy, calf-length tunic in a practical dark brown. Reuben had often chatted with Jacob during his lengthy stay with Simeon. The young man had been a friend to him when most of his fellow students, envious of Simeon's partiality, had begun to purposely leave him out. He had found Jacob possessed a quick mind and an eager vitality.

With genuine interest, Reuben asked, "How have you been?"

"Busy," Jacob laughed, leading the way into the house. "Father's giving me more and more responsibility. He's still determined that I learn how to be Simeon's steward when he's gone. A competent one, if he can manage it."

Jacob motioned to a bench. Reuben sat and removed his sandals. A basin of water was handy, and Reuben gave a comfortable sigh as he allowed the servant to wash his tired and dusty feet.

Reuben whispered, "Are you still going to those meetings?"

Jacob glanced to make sure no one was nearby. "I am. Though it remains a secret." Reuben nodded to show he would keep his friend's confidence. Jacob grinned. "You should come sometime."

Reuben shook his head, but he smiled with understanding. "The Zealot cause may be noble, but I have my own path to follow."

He knew the young man needed a vent for his nationalistic frustrations, but Reuben would rather meet in public to teach the law than gather in secret to plan for war.

His feet clean, Reuben rose. He left his sandals by the door with several other pairs and moved further into the room.

"Wait here. I'll tell Simeon you've arrived." Jacob dried his hands on an old cloth and hastened towards the staircase.

Reuben was left to look around. With a happy sigh, he saw the room was exactly as he remembered. The striped mats were colorful upon the cool, tile floor, but lined up with precision. Set in a perfect semi-circle, the newest fashion in chairs were stained a deep hue and polished with beeswax until they gleamed. A small table held a few functional items. To the side of the room was a low table for meals. It was spotless, with fringed cushions spaced with care. Reuben himself had seen Tabitha, silent as a ghost, fussing around this room, shifting items an inch this way or that until they were perfect. With such standards to uphold, it was no wonder the woman always had a twitchy, nervous look.

Reuben lowered his bag to the floor. Hands clasped behind his back, he stood by the wall that was painted with the traditional inscription of the pharisaic teachers. He read aloud the inspiring words, "Be deliberate in judgment, raise up many disciples, and make a fence around the law."

Reuben knew, deep within his core, the importance of the traditions of the elders. They clarified the finer points of the Torah Law. These interpretations put a fence around the law, for if one does not break through the fence, one will not be able to break the law itself.

He glanced up the stairs. He could hear the low hum of voices coming from the classroom. He sniffed the familiar incense Simeon liked to burn, and he felt as if he had never left. How many countless hours had he spent sitting before Simeon, his faith being sharpened and honed? Simeon was outfitting him for service—to teach the people how to live righteous lives and how to please God. His people needed to show God that they were repentant, for that was when God would move back into Israel as He had in their past, sweeping away their enemies and restoring Israel to its true glory.

The noise upstairs changed. Reuben heard easy chatter and footsteps. Simeon appeared at the top of the stairs, followed by four unfamiliar young men in their late teens.

Simeon walked towards Reuben, his arms opened wide in welcome and a smile showing from within his trimmed beard. He embraced Reuben gracefully, his hands barely touching him. Reuben warmed under the embrace. When he raised his head, he saw the four youths eyeing him with curiosity as they slipped on their sandals and went out the front door.

"We'll be back before dark," one of them called, and Simeon waved them away without a glance.

"Welcome, Reuben," Simeon said in his measured way as the door shut behind his students. "Please, use your old room to refresh yourself after your journey, and then we'll share the news."

Reuben felt a lift of satisfaction hearing Simeon had kept his room for him. Reuben hurried up the familiar staircase to the second floor where Simeon and his students slept and studied. The rooms for the students were only large enough for a narrow bed, a washstand, a utilitarian chest for personal belongings and a small, colorful mat for a bit of a homey touch. Each room had an oil lamp fixed to the wall for evening readings. Reuben set his bag on the chest and sighed happily as he recalled the many hours of memorization, reflection, and prayer he had spent in this cozy room.

A gasp made him turn to see a young woman staring at him with wide eyes.

"Reuben?" she whispered. She had a towel over her arm and held a pitcher of water with both hands.

"Hello, Michal," he said with a polite smile for Jacob's younger sister.

She was petite, with pink cheeks and a long, black braid falling over her shoulder. He was surprised to see a smile breaking on her face. Why was she was looking so pleased? He had rarely spoken with her before. She was just a quiet serving girl in the background while he was a scholar focused on his studies.

He cleared his throat and asked, "How are you?"

"Fine, of course," she said, still staring. Reuben noticed for the first time the dimple in her left cheek when she smiled.

Reuben waited for her to say something more, but she just stood there and grinned. It was unnerving. He licked his lips. "Uh ... Can I help you with something?"

"Oh!" she said, shaking her head with a light laugh. She held up the large earthen jug she was holding. "I was told to bring this upstairs. It's so nice to have you back again."

She smiled once more, and Reuben felt a tinge of warmth in his face as he accepted the jug and towel. She took a step back and Reuben awkwardly shut the door. He poured the water into the basin and washed his face and hands and shook the traveling dust from his clothes.

Returning downstairs, he saw Simeon was waiting for him near the basin. Already filled was the two-handled *netilat yadayim* cup which the Jerusalem rabbis preferred, and nearby was a length of cloth. Simeon took the cup in his left hand and poured it over his right hand twice. Then he did the same on the other side, holding the handle in his purified hand and being careful not to touch his unclean hand to his clean one. Holding up his wet hands, he chanted the usual blessing.

"Blessed are you God, King of the Universe, who made us holy with His commandments and commanded us in the washing of the hands."

The washing complete, Simeon dried his hands on the towel and Reuben took his turn. Even though he had already washed his hands, this was a ceremonial cleansing, a careful time to purify oneself. He said the blessing for the washing and then was silent. In stricter Pharisee households, speaking was not permitted until the bread had been broken.

Simeon knelt at the table, Tabitha and Michal setting dishes of food before him. Simeon waved the women away as Reuben came and found his place. Reuben's gaze followed Michal as she left the room.

Simeon took a loaf of bread and held it. He said the next blessing, "Blessed are you, Lord, our God, King of the universe, who brings bread from the land."

Simeon tore the loaf in two and passed Reuben half. They each took a bite, and the ritual was complete.

"So, Reuben, tell me of Capernaum. Tell me about Jesus of Nazareth." Simeon poured them each a cup of wine.

Reuben took the scroll he had brought and passed it to Simeon. "Daniel has written you a careful account."

Simeon accepted the rolled papyrus but tossed it aside. "I'd rather hear it from you." Simeon eyed him, his fingers pressed together under his chin.

Reuben was flattered. He told all that he knew about Jesus' more recent activities. "So," Reuben summarized, "While I feel our—I mean *your*—efforts had success, particularly in some of the larger cities, the crowds still flock to him."

"So, his fame continues to grow." Simeon looked thoughtful, his eyes narrowing as he drew a hand down his fringed shawl.

Reuben took a long drink from his cup to soothe his tired throat.

Simeon tilted his head, a gleam in his eye. "But, with fame will come the eyes of men of power. We will not wait too long, I think, before justice is dealt. Look at that so-called Elijah from the wilderness. He has been languishing in prison for over two years now. Perhaps Jesus will join him and they can preach this kingdom to each other."

Reuben laughed halfheartedly at Simeon's dry wit, but he was surprised to hear that news. "John is still in prison?"

"Herodias does not have a reputation of forgiveness," Simeon said, dipping his bread and raising an eyebrow. "Herod Antipas cannot release John and keep favor with his wife."

"Then why let him live at all?" Reuben asked, and then shifted his seat when he realized how callous he sounded. Simeon chuckled, unoffended.

"Apparently he finds having a resident prophet diverting. I hear he goes down to the prison to listen to John rant and rave and finds it quite amusing. When he traveled to the Jerusalem palace for Purim, he even had the man brought with him." Simeon shook his head at the absurdity, but then tapped his bearded chin with tented fingers. "In all seriousness, I think part of Herod Antipas believes John truly is a prophet, and that is enough to make him cautious."

Herod Antipas liked to parade about like a king, but he was only granted the titles of tetrarch of Galilee and Perea, and he kept that power only by the whim of Rome. When he came to Jerusalem for the festivals, his father's palace was opened up once more.

Reuben's countrymen grudgingly accepted Herod's Antipas' rule because he at least had a little Jewish blood. Though he claimed to follow the true God, the people knew him to be fickle, unreliable, and fond of the Greek lifestyle. Still, he was a veil between them and Rome. He was also more bearable than his father, King Herod, had been. Even though King Herod had rebuilt the Temple—returning it to its true glory—his legacy was blood and cruelty. Thankfully, Herod Antipas had more restraint.

To some, he was a perfectly acceptable ruler. The Sadducees and Herodians had seen the way the wind was blowing and had welcomed Herodian rule. Their reward had been leadership positions in the Temple and permission to run the Temple Courts, a lucrative business. Some days, it felt to Reuben that only the Pharisees held fast to traditions and truth.

There came a sharp rap at the door, and Jacob hastened from the back room to answer it. He brought Simeon a rolled scroll from the messenger.

Simeon broke the seal with his thumbnail and read the brief note.

"Speaking of Herod Antipas," Simeon said. "He is having a birthday party in three days at the Jerusalem palace. It appears that I am invited to attend." He twisted his lips. "The invitation coming so late is a subtle slight to the Pharisees, of course." He cast the scroll on the table for Reuben to read for himself.

Reuben picked it up and scanned it. "Will you go?"

Simon raised an eyebrow. "We cannot refuse the invitation of a ruler to a feast. It would be better to spit in his eye." Simeon pursed his lips and looked his student up and down. Reuben shifted in his seat under the scrutiny. Finally Simeon said, "I think you should attend with me. You need to meet the men of power in Jerusalem, and an event like this would be a good opportunity for some introductions."

"Me?" Reuben asked, surprised and pleased. Beyond what this royal feast might do to prepare him for his future career, he had to admit he was curious to see Herod's Palace for himself. He accepted Simeon's offer at once.

The next morning, Reuben was up early. He joined the other students for scripture readings, prayer, and breakfast with Simeon. It was easy to see that Simeon had a low opinion of his new batch of students, young men whose fathers had paid large fees so they could study and live with the esteemed scholar. Simeon was often curt and sarcastic with the young men, and his deference for Reuben was soon apparent. The four young students scowled at Reuben over breakfast, but he ignored them. If Simeon thought them second-rate, then he didn't need their friendship.

After he had eaten, Reuben prepared to go to the shops. None of his clothing was suitable for a royal occasion.

"Reuben?" Michal called, hastening into the room. "You're going out, right? May I go with you?" Reuben saw she had a basket on her arm. She explained with a dimpling smile, "Papa doesn't like me to go alone, and Jacob can't go until later. The best fruit will be gone by then."

"Of course," Reuben said, surprised by the warmth that crept up his neck at the sight of that dimple.

They walked together to the northern side of the city that housed the shops and the market. The Large Market was open every day except the Sabbath.

As they walked, Michal shifted closer to Reuben to prevent being separated from him in the jostling crowd. She glanced up at him through her lashes, and Reuben found he didn't mind the closeness. They made their way down the rows of booths and she asked his opinions on everything. She held up a plump fruit for him to smell, and as he bent his head Reuben realized with surprise that he was enjoying her company. Once her basket was full, she accompanied him to a well-known tailor that Simeon had suggested.

Michal teased him playfully in the shop. Though he usually hated to be laughed at, her tone was always light, and he found himself laughing too.

The shopkeeper and his wife were eager to please, and they draped many brightly hued and embroidered garments before his eyes. Soon Reuben had a completely new outfit picked out, though it needed to be fitted to his height. The clothing would be delivered to Simeon's house on the morning of the birthday feast. The rush cost extra, and Reuben was grateful for the small money bag Simeon had passed him that morning.

They went out of the tailors, and Michal pointed at a shop across the way. "Come on, you need to see this shop. It's owned by a Pharisee with a strange history." She leaned towards Reuben, her eyes pulling him closer. "Everyone was talking about him years ago, whispering that he had caught leprosy. Well, we knew it had to be true, because just like that—" she snapped her fingers "—he disappeared. No one knew where he went. Then one day, he came back, cured. He tells everyone he meets that he was healed by that famous rabbi, Jesus." she grinned. "I don't believe Simeon thinks much of Simon the leper, because he frowns whenever he's mentioned."

Reuben had taken a few willing steps towards the shop, but now he froze in his tracks. His second glance jolted his memory. He recognized the shop because Simon was his father's cousin. He knew full well that Simon had indeed been healed by Jesus, and he felt uncomfortably sure Simon was still loyal to the Nazarene rabbi. It was no wonder Simeon disapproved of him.

Did Simeon know Reuben and Simon were related? He shifted at the thought. He couldn't do anything that might displease his rabbi. It would be better to sever the family connection than risk another embarrassment like the fishing fiasco.

"I don't think we have time," Reuben said, squinting up at the sun. "We've been gone too long already."

Michal's face fell, but she swiftly hid her displeasure.

"You're probably right," Michal said. She twirled the end of her braid and smiled up at him. "I guess I lost track of time. Next time, then."

His cheeks warmed. It sounded very much like she wanted to walk out with him again. As he hastened her away from the shop, he resolved to make sure future walks avoided this particular street.

Reuben wrestled with his feelings all the walk home. He was glad that his cousin had been healed. He didn't wish leprosy on anyone, and Simon being healed was a fitting reward for his kindness to Beth's family after the death of Benjamin. Yet, Jesus was a false prophet. Reuben didn't trust Jesus or his motives—not one bit.

They walked back to the Upper City, and the grateful and the distrustful feelings rubbed against each other until his mind felt raw.

As they entered Simeon's home, he left his uncomfortable musings at the door. Michal gave him one, last, warm smile, and hastened away to her chores. Reuben went to the lecture room and immersed himself in the eloquent lecture that Simeon was presenting to the other students, putting Jesus far from his mind.

21

Her Desire

The day of Herod Antipas' birthday feast arrived. The tetrarch declared a holiday for the city in his own honor. Determined to be admired, he hired jugglers and acrobats to perform throughout the city. Bakers handed out sweetbreads freely and musicians played on street corners. As a great fan of Greek athletics, he also had young men performing feats of endurance and strength for a public show at the gymnasium. As the Greek style was to exercise in the nude, pious and reserved Jews did not attend. Perhaps the most anticipated entertainment for the eager crowds were the chariot races scheduled in the Hippodrome.

Reuben worked up the courage and asked Michal to walk around the town with him. So he didn't appear too forward, he invited her brother as well. Their father, Alexander, gave his approval for the trio to leave for the day. Jacob left the house with them willingly enough, but they were barely at the end of the street when the young man stammered his excuses and darted away.

"Do you know these friends he is going to meet?" Michal asked Reuben as they watched Jacob disappear around the corner. "He never tells me anything about them."

Reuben did not doubt that Jacob was going to a meeting with

fellow Zealots, but he didn't want to give away Jacob's secret. Instead, he cleared his throat and said, "I guess it's just you and me today."

Michal looked up at him with a smile. "Then I shall rely on you to keep me safe." It took all his self-possession to not puff out his chest as they walked side-by-side down the street and joined the festivities.

The city was in revel. At least for today, everyone gave begrudging praise to Herod Antipas. They went to the Hippodrome and watched a thrilling chariot race. When the chariot Michal cheered for won, she reached out and grabbed Reuben's arm in excitement. When he glanced down on her touch with surprise, she blushed and hastily removed her hand.

Reuben and Michal nibbled on sweetbreads and chatted like old friends as they strolled the streets aimlessly. He was surprised at how much they had to say to one another. To speak openly with an admiring young woman was like a ray of sunshine after a long, rainy season. It was the way it had been with Beth—before Jesus had ruined everything.

Late in the afternoon, Reuben and Michal returned to Simeon's house. Reuben felt completely happy and satisfied. As they parted, she peeked up through thick eyelashes.

"I'm happy you asked me to go out with you today." Her voice was a little breathless, and it made him swallow hard. She walked away, glancing over her shoulder at him. Reuben pulled his eyes from her as Jacob darted through the front door, panting hard but grinning.

"I've been trying to find you for hours. What a mob out there." Jacob bent double, his hands on his knees. Reuben suspected that Jacob didn't want his father to know he had spent the day on his own.

"Did you have a good day then?" Reuben raised a brow.

"The best," Jacob said. He looked like he wanted to say more, but Alexander strode into the room. The small man had a short, gray beard and wild brows over keen eyes. He eyed the two young men up and down and Reuben shifted his feet.

Alexander spoke to his son, "Take up some heated water for Simeon. He would like to wash before he dresses." He turned to Reuben. "I recommend you get ready as well. Simeon will want to be punctual."

"Of course," Reuben agreed, hurrying to the steps. With Simeon, it was always best to be the first one ready. He tossed Jacob a friendly grin over his shoulder, then ascended the stairs of the house with a light, bouncy step.

He washed in the basin in his room. He trimmed his beard, humming a little to himself. Setting aside his dark, scribal robes, he dressed in his new clothes. He brushed his hand over the soft, blue fabric of his embroidered linen robe, marveling at its luxury. He arranged his prayer shawl over his shoulders and smoothed the fringe. As he waited downstairs for Simeon, Michal passed by.

"Look at you." Michal clasped her hands and smiled. Reuben stood a little taller and warmed under the open admiration.

Jacob came into the room and gave him a low whistle. "You don't look like a country boy today!"

Reuben raised his nose, putting on his most snobbish expression. Jacob and Michal laughed and Reuben flushed and grinned. Had he ever laughed like this back in Capernaum? Laughing with Michal and Jacob, he knew he never wanted to go back.

A rap sounded on the front door and the trio shifted into seriousness. Jacob ushered in a small group of men as Michal slipped away. Reuben went forward and greeted the others from their party.

Simeon came down the stairs wearing a fine, scarlet robe. He had a thick sash in white and yellow stripes around his trim waist. After the pleasantries were exchanged, the Pharisees left for the feast. Reuben felt his excitement rising.

Reuben had seen Herod's fortified palace every day for three years, but always from a distance. It was hard to miss with its soaring walls and triple towers. The most beautifully ornamented tower was named after Mariamne, the beloved wife of King Herod, but that was before she had lost the king's favor and was executed by her jealous husband. The palace stones were practically mortared with royal intrigue and political excitement.

Reuben was determined to see and remember everything. He smiled to himself as he pictured Michal's fascination as he recounted every detail.

Simeon showed their invitation to the armed guard at the gate, who waved them in. Reuben followed his rabbi as he gracefully ascended the stairs to the raised courtyard which enclosed the palace. Reuben saw that the huge palace was divided in two, with a lush garden in the middle.

"There are two wings, you see," Simeon explained to Reuben. "Named after Augustus and Marcus Agrippa, unfortunately. Each wing has banquet halls and room to sleep hundreds."

They entered the man-made grove, and Reuben drew in the scent of fragrant blooms and greenery, a scent one did not often find in the bustling, stone city. An artificial stream gurgled, and marble fountains splashed water. A winding, cobblestone path led them past the staggering array of flowers, shrubs, and full-grown trees, all carefully tended. He looked into one of the fountains as they passed and saw exotic fish brought from some far-away sea. Above his head the sky was darkening, but bronze braziers had been placed along the paths, casting the courtyard in perpetual twilight.

Hundreds of guests milled about the gardens, laughing and displaying their finery. Reuben recognized a few of the faces, high-ranking Jewish men he knew only by reputation. Several of the wealthy men had brought their fashionable wives.

A woman around Reuben's age passed by on her husband's arm, her spicy perfume causing his nose twitch. He glanced her up and down. These women were unlike any he knew. Dressed in silk and with their hair elaborately braided, they wore heavy, jeweled earrings that danced as they moved. He privately felt he preferred Michal's simple dress and her honest laughter.

Simeon leaned towards him, his voice low. "All of Jerusalem's leading families will be here, as well as many from the surrounding cities and estates. And there will be many Roman dignitaries as well." Simeon pointed out many people to Reuben, wealthy or influential, and he introduced Reuben to those they passed.

The Jews and the Romans stayed in separate parts of the grove, the differences in their ways a difficult barrier to overcome.

From a distance, Reuben observed the Roman men with their close-cropped hair and beardless faces, some in burnished dress armor, others in flowing togas with elaborate embroidery. The Gentile women's gowns left their arms and shoulders bare. They wore bracelets on their pale arms, and jewels and flowers in their curled and braided hair. Unlike the Jewish women, most had their lips painted red, and their eyes and brows were lined with cosmetics.

He raised his eyebrows when he recognized the Roman father and son he had seen at the gate when he had first arrived in Jerusalem. It appeared his supposition had been correct.

Simeon noted his gaze and said, "That man is from Rome. Herodias' daughter has been staying in his household for the past year. For a little *culture*, apparently." Simeon sniffed in disapproval.

Eventually, after they had made a slow circuit of the gardens, the Pharisees moved towards the palace itself. They passed through an enormous doorway and followed other guests down a broad hall until they arrived at the banquet room.

Reuben had to restrain a gasp at the opulence. Valuable tapestries depicted flowers, sheaves of wheat, vines, grapes, and animals. Bronze figurines were set in recesses in the walls, reflecting the light from the dozens and dozens of raised braziers and hanging lamps. The room was filled with low tables laden with gold platters of delicate cakes and pastries, and pitchers of ruby-colored wine. Reuben glanced downwards and noticed the mosaic beneath his feet. It was an elaborate display of leaping fish and arching waves set in multiple blue hues. Musicians sat on one side of the hall playing gentle music that wove among the constant conversation.

As he absorbed the grandeur and saw powerful men taking their ease, Reuben felt painfully out of place. Someone laughed, and he flinched. Were they laughing at him? Could they see through his fine clothes and recognize his rustic upbringing? His eyes flicked to see if any heads turned to him. He saw with relief that no one frowned his way.

He drew a slow breath through his nose and let it puff out his lips. He vowed to himself that he would not let any shadow of his humble past show.

Reuben looked ahead in the room to see Herod Antipas greeting those lined up to pay their respects. He was seated on an ornate throne, his posture one of ease and comfortable wealth. He tilted his head a fraction of an inch as the influential men and women of the land bowed their heads to him. The middle-aged ruler had the appearance of a powerful man gone to seed. He wore an expensive, brilliant white robe with a wide purple band at its hem and several thick rings on his soft hands. His wife, Herodias, glittered with jewels and was dressed more elegantly than all the other women. She smirked and lifted her pointy chin as the people bowed.

The Pharisees joined the long queue. It was a half-hour before they reached the ruler. Reuben bowed his head with the rest of his party, and their group presented a small chest of intricately carved cedar. Herod Antipas smiled and indicated with a lazy wave of his hand that they could pass the tribute to a servant, who set it with a growing pile of gifts.

As they found their seats, Reuben asked Simeon in a whisper if they would be eating this evening. Jews, of course, could not eat communally with foreigners, or eat food prepared by their hands. It would be unclean to dine with those who ate forbidden foods and meat sacrificed to idols.

"Why, of course," Simeon said, as he stopped at a washbasin. "Herod Antipas is well aware of the cultural differences and has two kitchens. The Jews will be served food that has been prepared separately." Simeon ceremoniously washed his hands, and Reuben followed suit, murmuring the blessing.

He went to the table where the bread had already been laid out. He broke off a piece and ate it, then whispered the rest of the blessing. It felt a little strange to be eating in this way, and Reuben's conscience twinged as he looked over at the foreigners who didn't bother to wash. They just dove into their meals without proper consideration of where the blessings of nourishment came from.

He glanced at his rabbi who reclined on his cushion. Surely if Simeon thought it was all right to eat here, it was. He sniffed appreciatively at the platter of pastries and reached out to take a small, star-shaped one filled with cooked fruit. He murmured in appreciation as it melted on his tongue.

Herod Antipas and his wife rose from their thrones near the entrance and moved to the head table. Reclining at the long table with the royal family were several Roman dignitaries on one side, and on the other were Caiaphas the High Priest, his father-in-law Annas, and a few other men of great Jewish families. The royal couple lay on their sides on couches and their guests were provided with comfortable cushions.

Once he had shifted into a comfortable position and the servant had helped array his finery, Herod Antipas gave a wave of his hand. A gong sounded. Immediately, servants carried in trays and trays of food. Reuben's eyes widened and his mouth watered. He had never seen such a display of delicious and elaborate foods in one place. He tried everything.

As the wine flowed and the evening wore on, the banquet hall became louder and louder. Herod Antipas clutched his large goblet, his thick fingers glittering with jewels and his belly shaking with laughter as his guests worked hard to entertain and please him.

When the guests had sated much of their hunger, Herodias summoned the entertainment she had arranged for her husband's pleasure.

First came several youths, completely nude to better show their fine muscle tone. The Jewish women averted their eyes, modesty well-ingrained in them. The Roman and Greek women present felt no bashfulness and cheered the young men as they wrestled and showed feats of strength. Herod Antipas was entertained, and he clapped his jeweled fingers in pleasure. The youths paraded out the door and the guests leaned forward in anticipation of the next performance.

The Pharisees shifted as seven women rushed into the room, prancing and tumbling. Reuben felt his face redden and looked away. The women were hardly wearing anything at all. He had never seen so much of a woman's form before. He glanced at Simeon who coolly observed the entertainment. Reuben assumed he would be permitted to watch as well and took a peek.

The women's hair hung in long braids to their waist, tied with bells that tinkled with every step. They danced and twisted into fantastic, impossible shapes, even contorting until their feet touched their heads. They tumbled, and threw each other in the air to flip around, and walked on their hands with dainty feet pointing at the ceiling, their oiled bodies glinting in the flickering light. The guests cheered and applauded the spectacle. As the acrobatic women danced from the room, many of the men stood up and yelled for their return, promising money and some even proposing marriage—to the raucous laughter of their fellow guests.

Herod Antipas thumped his cup on the table, sloshing wine, his face red from drink. Reuben noticed Herodias watching her husband. Her lips curled into a smile, but her eyes were narrowed.

Two musicians entered the room and sat with their instruments. One held a drum and the other a lyre. The music thrummed slow and intense. Everyone's attention was fixed on the door, waiting to see what was coming next.

Setting each dainty foot precisely and with hips undulating, a young woman entered the room. Her measured pace was deliberate.

She caught the attention of all. She was dressed in a sheer garment that covered her neck to ankle, yet showed every curve of her figure. As she moved to the center of the room, people began to whisper.

"It's Salome! It's the daughter of Herodias!"

Reuben was shocked that Herodias would allow her daughter to dress and perform in such a way. Yet, when he glanced at the mother, he saw Herodias was fiercely proud as she gazed at her beautiful daughter. Reuben shook his head.

The music began to speed up and Salome's movements matched the pace, her darkly lined eyes brazenly gazing around the room, bare arms twisting, with hips rolling to the music. Faster and faster the music went and her nimble feet flew as she danced. No cat-calls or loud cheers disturbed this performance. The audience was spellbound, holding their breath as she tossed her hair.

When she finished, the guests roared and clapped, many hitting the table with their hands or cups. Reuben and the other Pharisees gave a few claps, not wanting to show approval for such a display, yet not wanting to offend their host.

Herod Antipas heaved himself to his feet and spread his arms wide. The guests quieted. "A fine dance. Superb! You have delighted us all. Please, dear girl, ask for anything you wish. Up to half my kingdom, ask, and it shall be yours."

The words were an echo from Purim, the festival not long past that recalled when the Persian king had promised the same to Esther. Simeon looked to Reuben and raised an eyebrow. The guests murmured at this extreme generosity. The panting girl glanced at her mother, who nodded.

"All I desire," the girl said, clear and strong, "is the head of John the Baptist, given to me on a platter."

An audible gasp rippled through the room. Several young men cheered drunkenly in approval of her request. The tetrarch slumped back onto his couch, the blood draining from his face. His eyes cast about as if looking for an escape. Herodias looked like a cat with a mouse. Salome still stood before him, chin high, shifting from one foot to another, every movement sensual in her filmy dress.

Simeon whispered near Reuben's ear, "What a foolish oath to give, and for such a reason. If John is beheaded the people may revolt. He has gotten himself into a fine mess."

Herod Antipas stood again, a smile on his sickly face. His voice wobbled as he called out to guards standing near the exit, "Send word to the prison. I order John the Baptizer beheaded, and his head brought here as a gift to Salome."

The applause was loud, and Reuben was surprised when many of his people clapped at the order to behead one of their countrymen.

One of the guardsmen hastened away as Salome sat at the head table. Many men, young and old, rushed over to speak with her. She appeared to flirt with them all.

Herod Antipas, his face a horrible, ashy shade, fluttered a weak wrist and music began. Servants bustled around the room refilling wine pitchers. The revels regained their momentum, but the tetrarch set down his goblet and brooded.

Reuben had lost his appetite. He clearly remembered the wild man at the River Jordan who had called the Pharisees a brood of vipers. He was no friend to the failed prophet, but neither did Reuben wish the man such a violent end, despite his callous words to Simeon a few days past.

Another of the Pharisees leaned over and whispered to Simeon, "John should have been more careful in his words. He brought this on himself by speaking against Herod Antipas."

Reuben raised his brows at his fellow Pharisee. Reuben knew full well that the Pharisees didn't approve of Herodias any more than John did. Only John dared to say something about it. Though Reuben wasn't a follower of the Baptizer, he felt a flicker of admiration for the man's bravery.

"Indeed he did," Simeon said and nodded at his friend. "Uncouth men will suffer for their words. These times require subtlety in politics, not brash bluster."

In what seemed like a short time, the guard reappeared. Reuben felt his stomach drop. John had been given little time to prepare for his fate.

The guests turned in their seats, some standing for a better view. The guard grimly held a tray with two hands as his heavy sandals rang on the stone floor. Reuben recognized the long hair at once. The head's eyes were open, his expression slack, the fire and vitality gone. Reuben looked away as his stomach rolled. A woman fainted, adding to the general excitement.

Salome rose and accepted the platter from the guard. For the first time that evening, her face was not winking or seductive. She carried the platter to her mother and set it down with a little thud. The head tipped over, revealing a gory neck as the room gasped.

Many of the Romans thought it was a good joke and jeered. The crowd buzzed. Herodias twisted her lips into a cruel smile and made a quip to the man sitting next to her. Herod Antipas sipped from his goblet, staring at the unseeing face of the prophet. He splattered ruby droplets on his pure white robe without care.

"I think we can go now," Simeon said smoothly as the noisy crowd picked up where it had left off.

The other Pharisees were also ready to call it a night. As one, the Pharisees rose and wound their way out of the room. As he walked, Simeon smiled and nodded at certain Jews.

Reuben took a relieved breath as he exited the hot room for the cool evening air. The grove was quiet now and Reuben tried to purge his mind with the lush greenery, but the dismembered head was all he could see.

22

HEALED BY A TOUCH

Beth lifted the lid, unhooked the rope, and drew up the heavy jug from the well. The rope was coarse and wet in her hands. She poured water into her water jar, careful not to spill any. She was the first at the well this morning, the usual meeting place for the local women as they began their day. The last stars had just set in the pale sky.

Closing the well to keep it clean, Beth took her heavy jar and heaved it over her head with a practiced motion. She walked for home, balancing it with one hand. She splashed the water over the garden, and as she turned to go back to the well, Mary Magdalene came from the house carrying a jar of her own.

"Here you are," Mary Magdalene said and smiled. "I tried to help your mother prepare breakfast. After my last attempt, she seems a little hesitant to accept my help." Mary Magdalene made a comical face.

"Well, I won't send help away," Beth said with a laugh, and the women walked side by side.

By the time they arrived back at the well, the other Capernaum women had gathered with their tall jars. Their chatter and laughter died as eyes swiveled to Beth and Mary Magdalene. Beth felt a clench in her gut and swallowed hard. Many of the Capernaum women had taken it into their heads to shun her. Women she had known her whole life glared and whispered to one another.

One of them, a darkly beautiful young woman named Rachel, smoothed a hand over her swollen belly. The move was innocent enough, but the woman's sneering gaze directed at Beth made the motion into one of disdain. Beth shifted her feet as she and Mary waited for their turn.

Rachel spoke to her friend, but her eyes kept flicking back to Beth, taunting her. "Malachi is eager for his firstborn. I've been praying that I shall provide him with a son." Again she brushed her palm over her rounded middle. "Of course, if this one is a daughter, I'm sure a son will soon follow. We were only wed last year, and already I am with child." Her eyes dragged over Beth like gravel.

Beth's throat burned with pain and embarrassment. Mary moved closer, and Beth could feel her friend's simmering anger.

Rachel's full lips twisted with satisfaction as she looked at Beth. Beth bit her tongue hard to stop the tears from spilling out. The small jug of water was lifted from the well, and Rachel held her tall jar steady as another woman poured the water in. "But then again, my husband is always near home. He is dedicated to us. He works so hard to provide, so I know he loves me dearly. I'm sure we shall have a houseful of happy children."

Mary Magdalene made a noise deep in her throat and stepped forward. Her tone was dripping honey as she spoke, "Rachel, don't you fear the evil eye as you stand here bragging of your good fortune?"

Rachel's expression darkened at once. Rachel's family was very superstitious. Many people believed that accepting praise or speaking aloud of one's good fortune incited envy in neighbors or demons, and envy brought bad fortune. Rachel murmured a rote prayer and turned to spit on the ground to ward off demons.

Rachel's eyes shot back to Beth and Mary. "Of course, that is no fear of yours, *Magdalene.*" She hurled the name like a rock. "You have nothing worth envying. You have no family, no husband, and have no honor to lose."

The other women at the well stood shocked at this exchange, staring between Rachel and Mary. Beth tried to pull Mary away, but the woman was rooted to the ground, staring down the heavily pregnant Rachel.

Mary's chin came up. "I have a family."

"Ha!" Rachel mocked. "Of course, I forgot. Jesus calls any fool who follows him his *family*," she sneered. "I'd rather be an orphan."

Mary opened her mouth again, but Beth spoke in her ear. "Come on, just leave her be. We're only giving her what she wants."

Rachel overheard the soft words. "Ah yes, little Beth. Run along home. Goodness knows you aren't there often enough. Leaving your mother to run your household. Tramping around the countryside when you should be tending to your hearth. But of course—" Rachel said as she opened her eyes wide "—perhaps you were worried that your husband's eyes would wander if you weren't near. Goodness, it would be so easy for Peter to forget the barren little wife back at home." She looked around at the other women and laughed, inviting them to join her in her cruelty. Only a few did, and some of the older women were flushed with anger at Rachel's sharp tongue.

Sophia, Beth's neighbor, charged to the well with her oldest daughter, a girl about seven-years-old. The woman looked livid as she snapped, "Hold your tongue, Rachel."

Beth tried to smile at Sophia, but her lips only wobbled.

Rachel opened her mouth to retort, but one of the other women, Agatha, spoke up as well. "Beth has done nothing to you, leave her be." Beth knew that Agatha had been healed by Jesus and that the woman believed too, in her quiet way.

Rachel was momentarily taken aback, but almost at once she regained her sneering expression. "I had almost forgotten, you touched the false prophet and were healed. Or so you say." The dark-eyed woman smeared Agatha with open disdain. "So, what? Are you going to leave your home and start following the false prophet too? Do you think that is the proper role for a woman?"

Agatha was silenced and stared at the ground.

"Leave her be, Rachel," Beth found her voice at last.

Rachel's jug was finally filled, and she heaved it atop her head. Balancing it with one hand, the other resting on her round middle, she sniffed as she walked away with as much grace as a heavily pregnant woman could muster. "I've wasted enough time. I wouldn't have it said that *I* shirk my womanly duties."

It was awkward and quiet at the well as the other women filled their jars and hastened for their homes. Few would look at Beth or

Mary. Agatha left with her head bowed. Soon only Sophia, Mary, and Beth were left.

Puffing a slow breath out of her cheeks, Beth began to draw up the water. She offered it to Sophia first.

"No, you go ahead," Sophia declined with a smile. Her gaze flicked between Mary Magdalene and Beth. "I hope you know that not all of us think poorly of you." Sophia reached out and touched Beth's arm. "I think you're brave."

Beth ducked her head. She wasn't brave. She was just trying to do what she felt was right, even though fear and doubt plagued her at every turn. She and Mary filled their jars and walked back towards the house. They began to sprinkle the water over the garden.

Beth looked at Mary who worked beside her, the wealthy woman now doing common labor. Mary would have been respected and waited upon back in Magdala. How things had changed.

Beth asked, "Do you miss your old life?"

"Sometimes," Mary said, then grinned. "I miss my comfortable bed the most. A single bolster is just not the same." She chuckled, but Beth couldn't join her. Mary emptied her jar and set it down. Her expression grew serious. "I know what you're really asking. Sometimes I miss the simplicity of how it used to be. I always knew what to expect. I would manage the household and servants, gossip over trivial matters with my friends, care for my father, and work in my stall at the market. There was a comfortable routine to my days."

"Now everything's uncertain," Beth whispered.

Mary nodded. "It's uncertain, yes," she admitted. "Yet there is great hope, isn't there? I feel like before I was going through the motions of faith. I believed in the Lord, I performed all the proper rituals and traditions, but it didn't affect me personally. Scripture study and discipleship were only for the men. Now I feel a part of something, and I like it."

Beth nodded. It was the boys who went to school to learn the Torah and Hebrew so they could read the Holy Scripture. Beth had been taught portions of the law at home by her mother, but it wasn't the same. Having Mary here to understand some of what she felt soothed her raw emotions.

"I also feel like I am a part of something bigger than myself," Beth said with a shy smile. "Though I am a woman, Jesus has never made me feel inferior. He seems to appreciate the things we women do in our quiet service. Personally, I'm happy to stay hidden in the background. That is my nature." She grinned at her friend, cocking a brow. "It may not, perhaps, be yours?"

Mary looked innocent. "Who, me?" She laughed at herself. "I'm not a background kind of woman, I'm afraid. I never have been. I liked being busy in my stall in Magdala. To be honest, I wasn't eager to be married. I didn't want to be stuck at home with babies and overseeing the cooking and cleaning."

Beth furrowed her brow. She couldn't understand her friend's casual feelings towards marriage and raising children. What better gift was there than a child of one's own?

Rachel's cruel word at the well rose up again and filled her mind— *barren*. She pressed both hands to her flat abdomen and had to fight back sudden tears. Surely she wasn't barren?

Mary saw her expression and came forward to wrap an arm around her shoulder. They stood for a long moment, each lost in her thoughts.

Mary cleared her throat. "Do you think something is preventing you from becoming pregnant, Beth?"

Beth flushed at the personal question. "I don't know," she admitted. "Peter and I have been married for four years. Four years!" she said again, shaking her head in wonder. The time had flown by.

Mary tilted her head. "But Beth, these past few years Peter has been so busy with Jesus, has there been time to . . ."

Beth's cheeks burned. She whispered, "The times are few and far between, but when we are home we do live as husband and wife." Mary pursed her lips, and Beth sighed. She swallowed hard. "Perhaps I *am* barren."

"If you might be, why don't you ask Jesus to heal you?" Mary asked holding out her hands in question. Beth's eyes opened wide as she recoiled from the idea.

"I would be far too embarrassed," Beth cried out.

Mary raised an eyebrow. "More embarrassed than if you had been possessed by demons?"

Beth turned and touched Mary's arm, afraid her insensitivity had hurt her friend. "Of course not, I didn't mean—"

"I know you didn't," Mary said, patting Beth's hand. "I just wanted you to remember that Jesus doesn't judge the way the world does. He wants a full life for everyone."

Beth nodded, but still pulled back from the idea of asking Jesus to heal her from something so personal. Anyway, she reasoned, maybe nothing was the matter with her. Perhaps it just wasn't her time. Surely when things were calmer, quieter, and more settled, she would conceive. She heard the hum of many voices inside the house and ruefully wondered when such a time would come.

Mary went back into the house, but Beth lingered outside to pull a few weeds in the garden. She glanced back towards the well. It had been kind of Agatha to stand up for her.

Agatha had been healed by Jesus many months ago. Beth had witnessed it with her own eyes. She had seen the radiant expression on the woman's face when she realized she had been cured. Agatha also had been too embarrassed to ask Jesus for healing. She had suffered from a slow hemorrhage for years and the condition left her unclean. She couldn't go to synagogue or the Temple, and she couldn't conceive. So, in desperation, Agatha had pushed through the crowd that pressed close around Jesus. In faith, she had reached out and touched the fringe of Jesus' cloak. Beth remembered how Jesus had stopped and spoken to Agatha and had praised her faith.

Beth felt a tremor move through her. Couldn't she do the same? Just reach out her hand and touch Jesus one day? She was often near him, it would be easy to do. Excitement bubbled up inside of her.

Just as quickly, fear drove into her like a spear and her happy eagerness was struck down. She remembered the story that haunted her at night when the house grew quiet and her mind was free to wander. For weeks she had tossed and turned in her bed thinking of the Bethlehem tragedy and the powerlessness of the common people.

If Jesus' birth had brought a massacre, what upheaval would the coming kingdom bring? She felt uncertain in her desire for a baby, and it unsettled her. Perhaps it was not the best time to bring a child into the world. Perhaps she shouldn't meddle with fate.

"Beth?" Hannah said, snapping Beth alert. "What are you doing? It's time to eat."

"I'm coming," Beth tried to smile for her sister. She followed the young girl inside. Hannah had dutifully swept and tidied the house while her mother had prepared bread and hot barley porridge. Beth felt a surge of pride for her sister. The child was turning into a young woman.

The men were in the courtyard near the cook fire. Jesus sat cross-legged. The disciples were seated around him, men and women both. Beth sat near Peter, taking some food for herself.

Tamar, with a look of motherly concern, came into the courtyard with a disheveled young man. He appeared exhausted and he had puffy red eyes.

"Jesus of Nazareth?" the young man asked, eyes searching the room. Jesus rose. Everyone fell silent and Beth felt a sense of foreboding.

"I've met you before. Nathaniel, isn't it?" Jesus said. "You're one of John's disciples."

"Yes, I am." Nathaniel sagged under those words. His voice rose a little in pitch. "Or I was. John is dead. He was beheaded by Herod Antipas at his birthday feast."

Beth froze in horror as tears begin to leak down Nathaniel's face. John had been in prison so long that some had started to think that eventually he might be released. Now he was dead. It had been John who had first started the message of the kingdom. It had been John who had heralded Jesus. The loss of John felt like a mighty blow against the kingdom that he and Jesus professed.

Her pulse hammered like the hobnailed sandals of Roman soldiers marching to the door. Was Jesus in danger? Was Peter in danger because he followed him? Was she?

The disciples sat in silent shock as Jesus pulled Nathaniel into a hug. The man sobbed on his shoulder like a son with his father. Jesus murmured words to Nathaniel and the young man drew strength. He stepped back with a nod and left them. Jesus turned to his disciples with red eyes.

"I need some time alone to grieve my cousin," he said. Before anyone could say anything, Jesus turned and left the house. The disciples stared after him, still reeling from the news of John the Baptist's sudden death.

The morning, then noonday passed. The disciples grew restless. Beth shared her fears for Jesus' safety with Peter.

"I understand how you feel, but we don't even know which way he went." Peter frowned, lines between his brows. A heavy silence hung over the disciples as they sat in the courtyard.

"We could have freed John, couldn't we?" Simon the Zealot jumped to his feet, his voice loud and accusatory. "Jesus has done harder things than that."

"Perhaps," Andrew said, rubbing the back of his neck. "Or perhaps this is the way it had to be."

"Why?" Simon said, his raised voice catching the attention of others. "Do we need another martyr? I've had my fill of them. I want heroes, men who change the world." Simon's voice was bitter. Beth sensed a deep turmoil inside him and wondered what had happened in his past that made his eyes burn with such intensity. Simon held out his fist, shaking it at the open sky of the courtyard. "How long? How long do we need to wait for a true Israelite king? A true heir of David who will bring the people together and lead us into the glorious kingdom Jesus has been talking about? I would take up my sword and follow him anywhere."

Judas Iscariot nodded in eager agreement. His handsome face glowed with passion as he said, "Wouldn't we all."

Hannah flew into the courtyard, her hair in disarray but her face split with a wide smile. She cried out, "I've heard where Jesus is! He's in the wilderness near the shore, healing a huge crowd of people." The men looked at each other. As if one body, the men and women rose and hastened out of the house.

They needed three boats to hold all the disciples, and the fishermen guided the boats northwards around the shore, everyone sweeping the shoreline for any sign of Jesus or a large crowd. A good distance from any of the cities, Peter pointed from the stern of his boat.

"Is that ... ?" Peter trailed off with wide eyes. "Could that be ... *people?*"

Beth saw a mottled mosaic of color spreading up a hillside. Her mouth fell open when she realized the entire hill was full of people, a vast crowd of thousands.

They drew nearer, and the disciples marveled at the sheer numbers who had sought out Jesus.

Jesus, though he was grieving his cousin, was walking through the crowd alone, healing. The disciples anchored the boats, splashed to the shore, and wove their way through men, women, and children to join their rabbi. Jesus saw them and greeted them. His shoulders were sloped but his eyes were full of love for the swarms of people.

The loss of John the Baptizer was great, but here was powerful proof of the success of Jesus' mission. Beth spun a slow circle and stared at the droves of eager people. She realized how faith in this kingdom Jesus was preaching could transform her entire nation.

Jesus spoke a few words to his disciples then continued among the people. Their hands reached out to brush his clothes and to touch his outstretched hand as he passed. Beth saw their eager faces, their longing, and their joy. Jesus healed all who needed it.

Beth shifted her feet as she watched him work. He would heal her if she asked, she knew it. Fear and embarrassment held her back.

The sun tipped towards the horizon, and Beth's stomach rumbled. They hadn't eaten since the morning. Jesus came up to his disciples.

Philip spoke to him, "It's getting late. Shouldn't you send the people away so that they can go into the villages and buy food?"

Jesus shook his head, surveying the vast crowd. He spoke to his disciples, "They don't need to go away. You give them something to eat."

Philip's eyebrows shot up, and he looked at the other disciples in alarm as they, in turn, looked to one another. Where would they gather the money? Even if they had enough coins, where could they find so much bread? A meal to feed all those gathered here would take weeks of planning.

Philip leaned towards Jesus. "This is all we have." He held forward a basket.

John looked into the basket and laughed. "Ah, of course. Look at his bounty! We have here five loaves and two fish."

"Hardly enough for me," James said, and the brothers laughed again.

Jesus grinned at their banter but sat on the grass. "Bring them here to me."

Beth watched with curiosity as Jesus motioned to the crowd. "Sit! Sit!" he called. James and John took over the instruction. With the strength of voice given by their father, they galloped through the crowd, calling out to people to seat themselves. Beth watched as the crowd moved like wind through tall grass, rippling as the thousands were seated. Men, women, and children sat and looked towards Jesus.

Jesus took the five loaves and two fish and tipped his face toward heaven. Beth heard him blessing the food. Then, setting the food back into the basket, he tore a loaf in half, then another, then another, over and over again. How was this possible? She had seen the five loaves with her own eyes. How was he finding all this bread?

"Bring baskets," Jesus called, and the disciples spread out until more than a dozen baskets were found.

Jesus dumped the bread into a basket Matthew was holding, and Beth gasped as she saw the basket filled to the brim.

"Go," Jesus said. "Feed the people."

Beth realized her mouth was hanging open and snapped it shut. Basket after basket was handed out. Beth brushed sweaty palms on her skirt and took a full basket from Jesus. She met his eyes, and he grinned at her as she heaved up the overflowing basket. His smile stayed with her and gave her courage.

Beth wove among the people as they reached out hands and took what they needed from the basket.

"Where did this come from?" they asked over and over.

"From Jesus," was Beth's shy response.

The people murmured with appreciation. She went back and took another basket, and again went among the people. Glancing around, she saw the other disciples all doing the same. Her heart swelled. No matter what the Capernaum women said about her, there was no other place she would rather be than right here, working with Jesus.

The sun dipped below the horizon and twilight cast its veil over the world as Beth handed out the last of her basket. She was tired after hours of serving. She groaned, knuckled her back, and went up to Jesus. Judas and Simon had their heads together, adding figures and gesturing. Beth took a loaf for herself and began to eat as she watched them.

"That's just over five thousand men!" Simon exclaimed, "Five thousand men who left everything to be here with Jesus." His voice was awed as he looked back over the vast multitude. The shadows were descending, but Beth could see a fanatical grin in Simon's eye. "This is just from a day. Imagine how many more will come now that Jesus can feed them."

"What are you saying?" Peter returned with his basket. Simon cast his arm over the crowd.

"This could be it," Simon's voice was awed. "This might be the time Jesus finally reveals himself to the world. We have the start of an army, right here. And what an army it would be. Jesus can heal and feed them all! We would be unstoppable, Peter," his voice dropped and he clasped Peter's shoulder with a little shake. "Unstoppable."

Peter raised his brows as he contemplated Simon's words, and

Beth felt her stomach flip. Would Jesus use these people here and raise an army to chase the foreigners out of the fractured land of Israel?

John's voice carried over to them, "See, look. They have all eaten their fill and there are twelve baskets left over."

Simon's eyes were wild as he exclaimed, "It is a sign! Twelve baskets, twelve tribes of Israel. This is it. It's time for Jesus to make his claim as king!"

23

GOD'S SON

Beth scanned the crowds of people, the bread turning to sand in her mouth. Was this the moment when everything changed?

Jesus came up, his steps lagging with exhaustion. "Go down to the sea and take a boat to the other side," he commanded wearily. Simon's face fell. "I would like to be alone. I haven't had time for prayer."

"Please, Jesus. Let us stay with you," Simon pleaded.

It seemed to Beth that Jesus did not intend to take an army this night. Instead, he wished to be alone to share his grief with God.

The other disciples didn't want to leave Jesus either, their protests clamoring together.

Jesus replied firmly, "Go. I need time to talk with my Father." Burdened with his loss and working tirelessly to help the vast multitudes, Jesus looked sore in need of quiet contemplation and prayer. Beth felt sympathy, but Simon lunged forward, his face stopping mere inches from Jesus'.

"This is your chance, Jesus. Seize it!" he begged, quivering with anticipation.

Jesus shook his head, his eyes probing. "Do you understand the timing of my Father, Simon? Do you make that claim? Go to the other side with the others. Go."

One by one, the disciples turned and dragged their feet back down the far side of the slope towards the lake. Andrew took Simon's arm and pulled him along. Beth glanced back and saw Jesus standing alone on the hilltop as the darkness fell around him.

She heard him calling out to the crowd, sending them back to their homes. She stumbled on a loose stone and brought her attention to picking her way in the dimness. The only light came from the rising moon peeking behind thick clouds. The disciples made it to the shoreline, and Beth cringed with cold as she sloshed into the sea with the others. John and James took charge of one boat, Andrew another, and Peter the third.

"Are we really just going to leave him behind?" Simon bemoaned to the others. He lagged behind on the shore, clinging to the hope that Jesus was ready to reveal himself.

"Enough, Simon," Judas' tone was impatient.

With a deep, audible sigh, Simon untied the last boat and waded out to the others. James and John leaned over the edge and hauled him aboard. Peter swung his boat around and pointed the bow for home. The wind blew in their faces, and the boat shuddered, clumsily slapping against the waves. The wide fishing boats did not tack into the wind well, and the fishermen struggled with their unwieldy crafts.

"The wind is against us," Peter called out from the rudder. "If we are going to make it home, I'm afraid we're going to have to row."

The men groaned.

The shoreline melted into the night behind them as the men bent their backs and pulled against the wind and waves. The moon and stars were obscured by clouds scuttling through the sky. The wind continued to blow hard and straight, and Beth gave up trying to keep her shawl in place and allowed the wind to whip through her hair. Mary's curls danced with a life of their own, a strange creature in the shadows. Her face was turned back to where they had left Jesus.

"I wish there was some way I could comfort him," Mary said as she leaned towards Beth. "He does so much for others, and this he chooses to bear on his own."

Beth felt the same way, but Thaddeus overheard and said, "He isn't alone. He told you, he's speaking with the Lord. God will give him comfort, of that I'm sure."

The men changed positions often, taking turns at the oar. The wind stung Beth's eyes and filled her ears until they throbbed, and still they rowed on and on. The waves pushed and jerked the little boats. It felt as if the sea was alive, and it was mocking them.

As the daughter of a fisherman, Beth knew that large bodies of water were famous in pagan stories as the realm of fickle gods with little concern for men. The superstitions of the sea were rampant among those who lived near the shore, even among good Jewish fishermen. It wasn't easy to shake the feeling that the deep and dark water was fighting them, clawing at the little boats with foaming fingers, yearning to pull them all into its greedy, swirling mouth.

Beth tried not to think of the stormy sea but fixed her gaze to the black shore where they had left Jesus. She hoped he was finding solace as he prayed and reflected on the life of John.

On and on they rowed, the three boats keeping each other in sight as best they could.

"This is taking forever!" Andrew complained in a shout above the wind as he sailed near his brother. "Have we been pushed off course?"

"Look for yourself. The stars say Capernaum is that way!" Peter's weary voice was cross.

Beth looked up. It was hard to get her bearings when the clouds kept obscuring the stars with their dark shadows. Peter was confident though, and she trusted him.

The night wore on until they reached the darkest, coldest part of the night that preceded the dawn. The men were exhausted. Beth's eyes were gritty and her bottom ached from the hard seat. The wind had beaten her down and she squinted trying to see the lights of home, dreaming of her still, soft bed.

"What is that?" Mary shouted, pointing over Beth's shoulder behind them. Beth whipped her head around as the men in all three boats dropped their oars and cried out in alarm.

Beth's heart grew cold as ice as she saw a billowy apparition moving on the water towards them.

"It's a ghost!" Matthew cried out in terror.

Beth gasped and jerked back. She wished she could turn and flee, but she was trapped on the boat. The waves seemed to be holding them back so that the spirit could overtake them. The men fumbled for the oars and began to row disjointedly. They didn't make any headway.

The spirit was almost upon them, its garments and hair billowing. Beth choked down a scream as Mary clutched her arm.

"Take courage!" a familiar voice cut through the wind. "It's me. Don't be afraid."

Beth strained to see in the darkness. Was it truly Jesus, walking on the water?

Peter, at the stern of the boat, let go of the rudder and leaned out. "If it's really you, Lord, command me to come out to you on the water."

"No!" Beth cried and grabbed the back of Peter's robe. His impulsive nature was going to send him to the bottom of the sea.

Peter turned his face to her, but it was shadowy in the night. "If it is Jesus, I'll be all right." He turned back to the spirit.

Beth refused to let go, and shouted, "What if it isn't?"

Jesus—if it was truly him—called out, "Come!"

Peter tried to step out of the boat, but Beth jerked him back. He looked back, and his tone was serious. "Let go."

Beth had to force her fingers to open and let her husband go. She felt his tunic slip from her fingertips and the wind whip through her empty grasp. Her hand hung in the air. The other disciples murmured and shifted behind her, but Beth only had eyes for her husband. He swung his leg over the side of the boat. Beth held her breath as his second leg followed, and then let it escape in a gasp as he stood beside the boat as firmly as if he was standing on solid ground.

Jesus came forward. She now knew for certain that Jesus had walked across the waters to find his disciples. She marveled at Jesus' power and stared with wide eyes as Peter's silhouette was supported above the surging depths.

Peter turned and looked at Beth. As the clouds scuttled out of the way, the moon shone on them all. Peter's illuminated face was full of excitement and joy. He turned and took several slow steps towards Jesus.

"If I didn't see it with my own eyes, I would never believe it," Thomas shouted.

The disciples lunged forward to see better, and the boat lurched. Mary screamed as the boat tipped to the side, threatening to throw them all into the water. Peter glanced back and saw their fear. Beth's stomach dropped as she saw her husband look away from Jesus. With wide eyes, he saw the whipping wind and the surging waves.

Beth cried out and stretched out her arm to him as he began to sink.

"Lord!" Peter cried, reaching his arms out to Jesus. "Save me!" Jesus was there in an instant, grasping Peter's hand and drawing him up. He kept his arm around Peter as they walked back to the boat.

Jesus shook his head and looked at Peter with affectionate disapproval, like a father chastising his son. "You of little faith, why did you doubt?"

Peter tumbled into the boat, wet to his waist. Beth caught him in a fierce embrace. Her mind was flooded with relief at his safety and astonishment at the fact that, for a few moments, her husband had walked on the water with Jesus.

Jesus stepped into the boat and the wind died.

The three boats were near one another, and all eyes were fixed on Jesus. Beth's ears rung in the stillness. Beth watched Andrew disappear as he threw himself prostrate on the floor of the boat, bowing with his face to the rough planks. Peter also bowed low in his boat, and then one by one the other disciples all bowed or bent their heads, many murmuring words of astonishment and praise to God and acknowledging Jesus' power and authority.

Beth shifted until she too could bend forward at her waist, prostrating herself in a way that she had never done before, except in worship at the Temple. Yet, somehow, it felt right to bow to Jesus. Her heart hammered as she felt the boat bob beneath her.

When she sat upright again, the sky in the east was paling. The sun would soon rise.

"You are truly God's Son!" a disciple cried out, and Beth felt the hair on her arms and the back of her neck rise. The messianic title shattered the still air like lightning, both bright and terrifying. The other disciples echoed the astonishing, earth-shaking proclamation.

God's Son. The phrase felt as shocking as a plunge in icy water. Yet, who else could he be? This was the second time Jesus had controlled the wind and the sea. It reminded her of a proverb.

"Who has gone up to heaven and come down?
Whose hands have gathered up the wind?
Who has wrapped up the waters in a cloak?
Who has established all the ends of the earth?
What is his name, and what is the name of his son. Surely you know!"

Her heart leaped. Did she know?

She remembered a time when she had heard such words spoken in the recent past. It had been when Andrew returned from his time with John the Prophet, and he recounted to them what he had seen when Jesus had been washed in the Jordan.

"It sounds crazy, but when John's cousin came out of the water, a light came out of heaven and landed on him, gentle as a dove. The cloudless sky rumbled like thunder, and I heard, 'This is My beloved son'."

After John had plunged him into the Jordan, Jesus had received words of affirmation from his heavenly Father. Now, as he returned from grieving the same man, Jesus had once more been given words of affirmation. This time from the lips of his disciples.

As the wood of the boat pressed into her knees, Beth's mind raced. *Who* was Jesus, truly? He was far beyond what she had expected the Messiah to be.

Jesus did not try to stop their worship, but as the sky lightened he looked on those he loved and smiled.

One by one, the disciples rose up and found their seats, expressions distant as if they were coming awake after a powerful dream. Jesus too found a seat.

The men, their weariness forgotten in the wake of their astonishment, returned to their oars. The sails were lowered. Without the wind fighting against them, the three boats sped toward Capernaum. The rising sun cast beams across the water, turning the murky depths into shimmering beauty. Jesus called over his shoulder, directing the disciples to stop at the Gennesaret Valley. They anchored the boats and went ashore.

The men clambered around Jesus, their excited voices a muddled mix of exclamations. Mary paused beside Beth and drew her hand around Beth's waist.

Mary said, "He may have grieved for the loss of the Elijah, but it certainly hasn't caused him to falter, has it?"

"It makes you wonder what will happen next, doesn't it?" Beth murmured. "What more can he possibly do to show his great power and authority?"

"What indeed?"

Word of Jesus' arrival spread like wildfire, and soon crowds gathered, bringing their sick. Despite being up all night, Jesus was moved with compassion for the people and he healed them all. Beth saw terrible illnesses cured by a single touch of the fringe on Jesus' cloak.

She brushed a hand down her middle and blushed at the thought of speaking to Jesus about her empty womb. She shook back her hair. There wasn't any need to give this problem to Jesus—none whatsoever.

24

SACRIFICE

Reuben's visit with Simeon was planned to last for several weeks. He was pleased that he didn't have to go home until after the festivals of Passover and Pentecost. He was eager to enjoy every moment back in Jerusalem. He joined Simeon's other disciples in their studies, ignoring their envious stares and immersing himself into Simeon's sharp, brilliant lectures. He visited the tomb of David and spent time praying and hearing men speak in the magnificent Temple Courtyard.

The only mar on this perfect visit was that he rarely saw the steward's son, his friend Jacob. When the young man was not rushing through his chores he was disappearing into the city. Alexander's unruly brows knit together whenever he watched his son rush out the door. Reuben wondered how much the steward knew about his son's zealot activities. However, it was not Reuben's secret to tell.

As the happy days slipped by, Reuben found himself spending more and more of his free time with Michal. He whiled away many hours talking with her while she did her mending and chores and walking with her to the market. Her cheerful way of looking at life was like a breath of fresh air in his life.

He realized he had become lonely in Capernaum. Though he had

Daniel and Philemon to speak with, one couldn't be a friend of equals with a teacher.

Michal's eyes danced when she looked at him. She laughed and talked with him. She was easily pleased—a particular blessing when he felt constant pressure to live up to the expectations of others. As he lay awake in his bed at night, he began to dream about what it would be like to take Michal as his wife.

Reuben knew shrewd Simeon must have noticed his marked attention to Michal, and so he felt a rush of nerves when his mentor drew him aside one afternoon to a quiet chamber.

"So," Simeon spoke, and then looked at Reuben with a lengthy, pregnant pause. "What is your interest in my servant, Michal?" Simeon's stony eyes pinned Reuben down.

Reuben flushed with pleased embarrassment. He was about to smile and extol Michal's many virtues, but then he looked more carefully at his rabbi.

Simeon didn't look pleased. He looked just the opposite. Simeon's cold expression startled him.

"In-in-interest?" Reuben stammered, his mouth bone-dry. He stalled, trying to get a hold of himself. "What do you mean?"

Simeon's eyes continued to bore. "You have been paying her uncommon attention this visit."

Reuben fumbled. He knew what his heart desired, but his tongue curled under Simeon's cutting gaze. He remembered his vow to himself when he had returned to Simeon's house. He wouldn't do anything, anything at all, that might jeopardize his standing in Simeon's eyes.

Reuben replied while drawing a hand down his shawl and pulling his fingers through the fringe. "We have only been friends. Nothing serious has been said."

Simeon sniffed. "Of course not. I would expect any suitor of hers to consult me first. Just because she is in a low situation in life does not make it permissible to toy with her affections or ruin her virtue. It would cost her position in my home, to the great shame of her family."

Reuben's face burned, and he had to clasp his hands behind his back to keep them from gesturing wildly. "I would never do anything to dishonor her. You should know me well enough to know that I reserve myself for the marriage bed. I-I enjoy her company."

Simeon's lip curled as he sneered, "So you *are* interested in her, a lowly servant? A woman whose father has sold himself into my service? She is my property."

Reuben opened and shut his mouth as Simeon kept him pinned. The heavy realization that Simeon definitely did *not* approve of the budding relationship scattered his thoughts.

Reuben had not thought less of Michal for being a servant. She was kind, open, and admiring, and that had been enough for him. Yet, Simeon had never steered him wrong before. Perhaps Simeon's derision was well placed. He felt his stomach clench. He had tried for years to rise above the fishing nets and obscurity of Capernaum.

Reuben was chilled by Simeon's dark eyes and felt a tremble of fear move through him. He needed Simeon's favor. Would Simeon cast off his patronage and send him back to Capernaum and anonymity forever? That could never happen. He wouldn't let it.

He tried to retreat. "She-she is pleasant to talk with during my idle hours, Simeon," he paced his words carefully as his mind scrambled to pluck out the right ones from his muddled mind. "But I have no plans to marry soon, and ... I'm not sure she is the proper choice for me."

The words cut his throat as he said them, for on his mind was written the image of Michal's hand placed in his by her father. He snatched that thought, rolled it up, and shoved it far away to the recesses of his mind.

Simeon sniffed and turned away to look out the window. Reuben sagged at the release from those piercing, dark eyes.

"Why would Michal not be a good choice for you, Reuben?" Simeon's voice was soft, probing, as he looked out his window that faced the Temple. His tone was the same as when he quizzed Reuben after a lesson.

Reuben searched for words that would make Simeon happy. "She is as you said, only a servant. Her family is likewise employed, and she has nothing to offer, except herself. She's a pleasant person to talk with when there is none better, that's all." He felt the lies burning his mouth like coals, but what else could he say?

"But you do plan to marry someday?"

"Yes, that's my hope," Reuben was relieved to speak truth again. "Once I am done my apprenticeship with Philemon and can take a house of my own."

"What kind of a woman would you choose, Reuben? To walk with you in your life as a Pharisee? As a man of understanding and learning who could do much good in the world?"

Reuben was flattered, yet in his mind was a warning to veil the full truth. He thought of Michal's happy manner, and how nice it would be to have a woman like that by his side. Yet, would such a description please Simeon? He didn't think so.

He answered in a measured, cautious tone, "A woman of unquestionable virtue and morals, of course. A good homemaker, quiet, hardworking, obedient. One with a well-placed family that I would be proud to introduce to my friends and that can help further the good work of the Lord."

Simeon turned from the window and smiled at last, a true, wide smile, one Reuben rarely saw. Reuben felt like a ray of warm sunshine warmed him from within.

Simeon came forward to grasp Reuben by the shoulders. "A worthy woman, worth far more than rubies!" he exclaimed. "I am sure we can find my prized student such a wife someday." He raised a finger like a stern but loving father. "But for now, Reuben, you must focus on your studies."

"Of course, Simeon," Reuben bobbed his head.

Simeon had actually said the words—Reuben was Simeon's prized student! Simeon nodded and tapped him affectionately on the cheek twice. Reuben swallowed proud emotions with difficulty, clearing his throat. Simeon turned and glided from the room, hands clasped behind his back, chin high.

Reuben puffed out his breath, feeling exhausted and yet strangely uplifted. He turned to go when a small movement behind a screen caught his eye. With a feeling of foreboding, Reuben stepped forward.

Michal stood frozen with her broom, her large brown eyes liquid with accusatory tears. Reuben's heart sunk as he felt his face burn with embarrassed shame. He didn't know what to say.

An errant thought flicked through his mind. Had Simeon known she was here? Reuben shut that thought away.

Reuben opened and closed his mouth, hating how foolish he felt as he floundered for words. He had done the right thing—of course he had. Pleasing his rabbi was essential to his happiness. Yet, he knew he had spoken shamefully of a friend, of a kind and generous woman, one that he had encouraged with his attention. One that he was beginning to love. He had cast her aside to further his career, and the realization of what he had done hit him like a punch to the gut.

His eyes tracked a tear that slid down her smooth cheek, and he longed to reach out a hand and brush it away and apologize for the lies he had spoken. Yet, his loyalty to Simeon bound him. He did nothing.

Michal stifled a sob and rushed past him out of the room.

Reuben let her go. It was better this way. He must live up to the words he had spoken to please Simeon. Still, he wished with all his heart that she had not been hurt by them.

The day of Pentecost felt flat to Reuben. Even as he stood among the great assembly at the Temple, he felt utterly alone. Pentecost celebrated the wheat harvest and gave thanks for another year of the bounty that the Lord gave His people. Reuben stood in the Temple Courts but didn't see the smoking altar. His gaze was turned inwards as he looked at his life.

He had sown bushels of hard work in his efforts to be a fully-fledged scholar, a Pharisee, and a scribe, but had yet to harvest the benefit from his labors. He needed Simeon to forward him in his career, so he must bow to Simeon's will if he was to have the full future he desired. He swallowed hard, chaffing against the yoke that he had put around his own neck.

The last few days of his visit were the loneliest he had ever experienced. Michal avoided him. He didn't see her at all, except as a shadow escaping from the room when he entered. Reuben had to fight the urge to go to her, apologize, and renew the friendship if he could. The idea made him sigh with longing, but he didn't dare displease Simeon.

He felt relieved when it was time for him to return to Capernaum. He reasoned that several months apart would do both Michal and him good. When he returned, he halfheartedly hoped there could be a renewed, though cooler friendship between them.

As he left Simeon's house for the journey home to Capernaum, he walked with a feeling of determination. He reminded himself that he had known he would have to make sacrifices in his pursuit of the law. His feet were set on the path of becoming a renowned teacher like

Simeon, and Michal was only the first of many self-sacrifices in his future. He knew how it had to be. Yet, as he thought of her for the hundredth time that day, he felt deep regret.

Reuben left through the Northern Gate. Once he was out in the open, he set a steady pace away from Jerusalem, traveling the familiar road that he had walked many times since childhood. Another familiar sight greeted him like a slap; not far from the gate were four men on crosses. Reuben avoided looking at them, but he couldn't block out their husky voices pleading for water.

The city was soon far behind him. Reuben fell in with a traveling group. Travelers found protection from bandits in numbers. As they came up to a clump of trees, Reuben saw a trio of young Roman soldiers standing in the shade, eyeing Reuben's group with arms crossed and smirking expressions. Reuben prepared to walk by them without comment.

A soldier called out, "You there! You with the shawl." Reuben slowed, and the man said, "Yes, you." Reuben stopped but kept his eyes averted from the pagan. The Roman came up to him carrying his heavy pack. He dropped it at Reuben's feet. "You look hale," he mocked, eyeing Reuben's slight frame. "You may carry my pack for the next mile." Reuben felt indignation rise in him, his cheeks flaming. The Roman soldier laughed at him, and his friends came up and laughed as well. Reuben's gritted his teeth. The group he had been traveling with hastened their steps and pulled ahead.

Reuben glowered up at the tall, broad soldier. He wasn't much older than Reuben, but his chin was beardless and his hair cropped close around his head. His nose was crooked, as if it had been broken and not set properly. The three Romans wore the short robes the foreigners favored, which ended well above the knee. Their sturdy, hobnailed sandals laced up the shins. From their expensive belts and tilt of their chins, these were not only soldiers but wealthy ones too.

Reuben's throat burned with his refusal, but he swallowed back the retort. He knew this soldier was well within his rights to ask Reuben to carry his load for a mile. It was Roman law and all subjected peoples were forced to obey.

His face hot, he struggled to lift the heavy leather bag. It felt as if it was filled with stones. He added its weight to his satchel, and with his jaw clenched, began to walk his mile, counting the steps. The soldiers marched on, teasing and making crude jokes, many of them mocking the Jews. Sweat beaded on Reuben's brow as he staggered under the heavy load and the unrelenting sun. At the end of the mile, to the very step, Reuben stopped and lowered the bag to the ground.

He took two steps and heard one of the other soldier's call, "Oi! Where are you going? I need you to carry my bag for a mile." The three laughed all the harder.

Reuben swallowed, bitter resentment churning in his heart as he took the second soldier's pack. Again he walked, counting the steps until his mile was up. As he set the bag down, he knew what was coming.

"Jew! Carry my bag for a mile," the last soldier said with a mocking, falsely regal tone.

Reuben, his shoulder screaming, took up the bag, sweat trickling between his shoulder blades. He stumbled on a loose rock. His throat was parched with thirst, but he had resolved not to rest until he had parted ways from these arrogant youths.

Finally, his third mile was complete.

"There's a good man," the soldier slapped him on the back as he took his bag. Reuben jerked away from his impure touch, glaring. The soldier shouldered his bag—making it look much too easy—and the three young men marched on, leaving Reuben standing in the center of the road alone with his simmering rage. He let them get ahead of him. After a few minutes, he took a drink of water, roughly wiping an errant drop with the back of his hand. He rolled his shoulders to ease the stiffness and started walking again.

Reuben was three full days on the road. He spent the nights at inns along the way, paying a coin for a hard mat in a communal room for Jewish men and a simple breakfast. He walked sunrise to sunset, traveling with others when he could. He kept a sharp lookout for Roman soldiers, but he didn't see the three that had troubled him again.

Capernaum, simple fishing city that it was, looked good to him at the end of his journey. Reuben went straight to Philemon's home. He was eager to wash the journey from his skin.

Philemon rose to greet him with a smile and an embrace. The children ran up and hung on Reuben's arms and wrapped themselves around his legs. He laughed and teased them before their mother called them away.

"I'm going to wash in the lake," Reuben informed Philemon. "I feel ... unclean." He gathered up fresh clothing, a flask of olive oil to loosen the dirt, and a curved wooden paddle for scraping the oil from his skin. He walked far away from the fishing town to a sheltered bend with trees crowded close to the shore. Reuben peered around before disrobing and wading into the water. As the cool water rose above his shoulders, he drew a deep breath and sank beneath the surface. He wished he could wash his thoughts of Michal away as easily as he did the dirt on his skin.

Reuben plunged back into his usual routine. Thoughts of Michal plagued him day and night, but his sore heart pushed him to work harder. His happiness lay in the future, and he needed to get there as fast as possible. Philemon was impressed by the increase in his student's dedication.

For two weeks Reuben immersed himself into his work, drawing up contracts, crafting letters of business for local tradesmen, and translating documents from one language to another. He copied scriptures for the phylacteries and mezuzah without making a single error.

He and Philemon were deep in work, kneeling at their small writing tables, when Daniel came through the doorway leaning on his staff.

"I have guests for you to meet," Daniel called out with a grin that crinkled his whole face into wrinkles. Behind Daniel were several Jerusalem Pharisees. Reuben was surprised to see them, and he rose to his feet with Philemon. Reuben knew these scholars as friends of Simeon, and Simeon hadn't made any mentioned of a delegation coming out from Jerusalem. He frowned, pricked by worry. Why had Simeon neglected to tell him? Was his rabbi still cross about Michal? He pushed his concerns to the background as the Jerusalem Pharisees all nodded at him.

Daniel continued in his wavering voice, "They arrived last night and are eager to hear Jesus for themselves. Have you heard where he is today?"

Reuben looked at his teacher. Philemon's eyebrows raised as he replied, "I believe he's in the open field near Peter the fisherman's house." The Pharisees nodded as one. Philemon glanced at his student. "Why don't we go along, Reuben? Then you'll have some new information to write to Simeon."

Reuben smiled and discreetly rubbed his hands together, already picturing Simeon's approval of his detailed letter. It would be a good idea to remind Simeon of his usefulness.

They found Jesus among a small crowd of men and women sitting on the grass. They looked very common, Reuben thought with a sniff as he recalled the cool and polished lecture room at Simeon's.

Tamar and another woman with thick, curly hair, were carrying baskets covered with white cloths. As they uncovered them, Reuben saw the baskets were full of bread. Beth came forward with several wineskins slung over her shoulder. She paled when she saw the Pharisees arraying themselves in a confrontational line before Jesus and his followers. Her eyes flicked to Reuben, and he saw with satisfaction that she looked worried. Good. As long as she was anxious, it showed that she wavered in her allegiances. There was hope for her yet.

Without pausing to ceremonially wash his hands, Jesus reached into the basket and took a loaf. He said a blessing and began to eat. Reuben watched with surprise as the basket was passed among the group, everyone reaching in and taking a piece without stopping to purify their hands. He curled his upper lip. The people in this rabble were a mishmash group from many walks of life. No doubt many of them bumped elbows daily with Gentile pagans.

He thought of the soldiers from the road and bile rose up in his throat. Polluted pagans! Reuben had to fight off a crawling feeling on his skin. Glancing over the crowd with a shake of his head, Reuben knew he wouldn't have felt comfortable dining with several of them, even if they had purified properly beforehand.

The Jerusalem Pharisees muttered among themselves as they watched this flagrant breach of tradition.

Daniel spoke up, his quavering voice stern, "Why do your disciples break the tradition of the elders? They eat bread, but do not wash their hands."

Jesus raised his eyebrows. "Why do you put your tradition in a greater place than the word of God?" Daniel's chin jerked, and he opened his mouth to retort, but Jesus was continuing, "For God said, 'Honor your father and mother', and 'He who speaks evil of father or mother is to be put to death.'" Jesus rose to his feet. His next words rang out sharp and clear. "But, despite the word of God, your precious traditions teach: 'Whoever says to his father or mother, "Whatever I have that would help you has been given to the Temple for God's use" is exempt.' How does that make any sense? A man gives to the Temple, and suddenly he doesn't need to honor his father or mother by caring for them? This is a prime example of how you invalidate the Word of God for the sake of your man-made tradition. You hypocrites!"

The Jerusalem rabbis were shocked at Jesus' tone and words, but Philemon jeered. "Ah, that again," he scorned. "I wondered when we'd hear his pet name for us."

A few others took Philemon's cue and relaxed a little, laughing at Jesus. Reuben joined in their mockery. It felt good.

Jesus saw their laughter and shook his head at them. "Rightly did Isaiah prophesy of you,

"This people honors me with their lips,
But their heart is far away from Me.
In vain do they worship Me,
Teaching as doctrines the ideas of men.'"

The Pharisee's laughter died on their lips, and as one their eyes blazed as this scripture was used to disparage them.

Jesus called around to the crowd, "Hear and understand. It isn't what enters the mouth that defiles the man, but what proceeds out of the mouth that defiles the man."

Reuben could feel the Pharisees around him seething at Jesus' belligerent lack of respect for their traditions.

"We will not listen to this," one said, and the rest nodded. As one, they turned and walked away, whispering to one another. Only a moment in Jesus' presence had been sufficient to insult them and solidify their doubt of him being a true prophet.

Reuben hung back as the others left. He needed more for his letter to Simeon. Hovering on the outskirts of the rabble, he heard Jesus answering a concerned disciple, "Leave them alone; they are blind guides trying to be leaders. We all know if a blind man guides a blind man, both will fall into a pit."

Beth's husband called out, "Explain the parable to us."

Jesus replied with a chiding tone, "Are you still lacking in understanding, too?" Peter ducked his head, then lifted his chin sheepishly as Jesus continued, "Don't you understand that what goes into the mouth passes into the stomach and is eliminated? But what comes out of the mouth—evil thoughts, murders, adulteries, fornication, thefts, false witness, slanders—these are the things that come out of the mouth and defile the man. To eat with unwashed hands—" Jesus took a bite of bread "—this does not defile a man."

Jesus looked up, and his eyes shot straight to Reuben. The steady, self-righteous gaze made the young Pharisee uncomfortable. Drawing up to his full height, Reuben turned and left, his hands smoothing the fringe on his prayer shawl. Yet, as he strode away with his chin high, he realized that his pain about Michal had been pushed to the background in the distraction of the Pharisees doing battle with Jesus. He twisted up his mouth. Perhaps something good came from false prophet after all. He walked away, already crafting his detailed letter to Simeon in his mind.

25

FAITH OF AN OUTSIDER

Beth stood with her face to the Mediterranean. The bracing wind felt good on her damp forehead. She gripped the wooden rail, breathed deeply the briny breeze, and marveled that she was so far from home.

She had never laid eyes on the vast Mediterranean Sea before, and now she found herself visiting one of the principal port cities, the opulent city of Tyre. It was an ancient city, rich in history. Tyre had once been an island, but a Greek named Alexander the Great had done the unthinkable. He cast stones, dirt, and sand into the sea until he had made a bridge across the water and taken the island for himself. Many Jews heard the echoes of the prophet Ezekiel in the city's downfall.

Tyre was now forever linked to the mainland. It boasted large twin ports on the north and south sides of the coastal city. Beth stared as a vast ship with towering sails and rows of oars sailed past her. The wooden deck was full of passengers and its hull was surely packed full of merchandise. It would berth at a distant port in some exotic land beyond her knowledge. As the world expanded before her, she realized how little of it she had seen and felt her corner of the world shrink.

She turned a slow, full circle and saw elaborate stone architecture and houses several stories high. The city was full of massive, ornate arches and vast columns supporting gateways, walls, and colonnades in unfamiliar designs. Equally foreign people milled about everywhere. She heard a dizzying array of languages and saw a plethora of hairstyles and garments from all over the world.

Jesus the healer-prophet and his closest, most ardent disciples had come to Tyre, but the metropolis ignored him. No one realized or cared who he was, and he didn't inform them.

So why had Jesus come to this pagan place full of false gods and impurity? They had entered the city through a necropolis, a massive stone graveyard with marble tombs. Beth had seen with her own eyes people sitting among the tombs, lounging and enjoying a picnic. On the marble sarcophagi there had been flowers and food and wine laid out—as if the dead could possibly enjoy them.

Beth shook her head as she mulled over the cultural differences between these people and her own. She felt the miles between Tyre and her home yawning wide, and she understood more than ever why her people pulled back from mingling with the pagans. She felt like an outsider for the first time in her life—a foreigner who wasn't pleased with what she saw. She chewed on her lip.

Tyre had once been part of the land promised to Israel, land given to the tribe of Asher. Perhaps Jesus had come to visit this severed portion of David's inheritance in the same way a person liked to walk past a house they had once owned—to see how it had changed and to reminisce over days gone by.

Beth furrowed her brow and peered at her rabbi. Jesus stood staring over the Mediterranean and his posture was relaxed. His cheeks and eyes were brightened by the salty air and he looked invigorated again. Maybe he had simply brought them here for a break—a respite from the needy crowds and the bitter jealousy of the Pharisees.

Beth glanced at her husband. Peter and Andrew were watching the small boats with sunburned fishermen bobbing on the water. Beth smiled as the two Galilean fishermen sized up their coastal counterparts.

"Look at those traps. They're pretty clever. Those floats must be so the fishermen can find them and pull them back up." Andrew pointed a long arm over the water. "I wonder what they bait them with?"

"It's too bad we don't have any of these murex shellfish back home," Peter chuckled. "We'd be rich!"

Beth leaned her elbows against the rail and joined her husband in watching the Tyrian fishermen at work. The shellfish would be taken north of the city, salted, and a tiny amount of glandular fluid extracted to make the world's most coveted purple dye. Garments woven of Tyrian purple were the most expensive in the world. The dye itself was worth more than its weight in gold.

As the light shifted towards late afternoon, Jesus turned away from the sea and walked past the men back towards town. Peter fell in behind the rabbi. The others gathered up as well, and Beth and Mary Magdalene walked arm-in-arm as the rabbi and his most faithful followers strolled down the paved street.

Jesus led them past the newly constructed temple dedicated to the Roman god, Apollo. The magnificent marble structure was swarming with visitors. Beth frowned at the massive building as she saw people purchasing animals for sacrifice to a god made of stone. How could they not see that their faith was in a man-made divinity? The priests accepting meat and coin were growing fat off a cruel deception. It soured her stomach.

Judas whispered to Simon, "Someday, this whole place will be rubble. Every shrine to Apollo will lie in ruins. I just hope I get to see this one burn with my own eyes. This should be Israel's land!" Beth heard Simon agree.

In the quest to hold Israel for the true God, prophets, judges, and kings had pulled down idols and smashed their altars. Would Jesus do the same? How long could God let the smoke from these pagan altars pollute His sky?

Jesus led them through the busy streets to the agora, the large public space near the heart of town, now filled with a bustling market.

Beth realized they should use this chance to buy supplies. With Naomi absent this trip, she had somehow ended up in charge of organizing the day-to-day needs—a duty Beth took on with strong feelings of inadequacy. She whispered to Peter, who motioned to Judas to bring the moneybag. Beth haggled over simple ingredients for their supper, sure Naomi would have gotten better prices.

Though the aroma of freshly baked bread at a nearby booth made her mouth water, Beth knew they couldn't buy it. It hadn't been prepared under the purity requirements of the Jews.

Jesus led them to the outskirts of Tyre. They had rented a small house for a few days, and Jesus took them inside.

"Tell me what I should do," Mary said, looking over the small bag of produce.

Beth murmured instructions as the two women washed the herbs and fruits and prepared a quick unleavened bread. The women worked quietly so they could listen as Jesus taught the disciples again. Jesus was careful to include the busy women in his discourse. His attention to them caused the women to smile at each other.

Their rabbi had taken full advantage of the quiet days away from the bustle and crowds and had filled the hours with private instruction. Beth did her best to commit everything he said to memory so she could share it all with her family when she returned home.

The next day Jesus announced they would be going back to Galilee.

"Sounds good to me," Peter grinned at Beth. "I'll be happy to shake this pagan dirt off my sandals."

Beth agreed. She hurried to gather up her and Peter's few belongings and enough food to last several days.

Jesus and his disciples just reached the outskirts of Tyre when Beth heard the slap of sandals chasing them.

A voice called, "Jesus of Nazareth! Jesus! I need your help!"

Beth and the disciples looked back in surprise. They saw a woman racing through the necropolis after them, dressed in the clothing of the Phoenicians with glittering gold armbands and swinging earrings.

"What does she want?" Matthew furrowed his brow.

"She's just a pagan, ignore her," Judas said. He shrugged and turned his back to her.

Beth looked at Jesus and saw him striding ahead. She cast one more glance at the running woman, then followed Jesus.

The woman came closer, shouting, "Jesus, please I need your help!" Jesus still walked on. "Please! I know who you are. Word of your power has spread, even to us. I need you to heal my daughter."

Beth bit her lip and wondered how Jesus would respond. The woman wasn't one of them. She was a descendant of the Canaanites, living on land that rightfully belonged to Israel.

The woman was right on their heels, wailing as the disciples kept on walking. "Son of David!" the woman cried, startling Beth with the appellation. "I know you are the Son of David. Please, heal my daughter!"

Peter looked at Andrew. "How does this pagan know who the Son of David is?" he asked, frowning.

Andrew pursed his lips and shook his head. "She doesn't understand what she's saying."

Jesus kept walking along the road, and the woman kept crying out to him, over and over again. People passing by stared at her and gave her a wider berth. Beth tried to ignore the woman, but the pleading tones struck a sympathetic chord in her heart even though the woman was a Gentile. Surely Jesus, compassionate as he was, felt it too. Yet, he refused to stop and talk to this woman.

The disciples began to mutter to each other as the woman persisted, chasing them down the road, calling out again and again.

Beth saw James turn and look at the woman as something like sympathy swept over his features. Beth saw him work his mouth, then call ahead to Jesus with an exaggerated, annoyed tone, "Jesus, this woman is driving us mad. Heal her daughter so she will leave us in peace."

The other disciples nodded and agreed. Beth saw Jesus stop, glancing at James with a smile. The Phoenician woman's eyes widened with hope and she rushed forward. She fell at Jesus' feet.

Jesus' expression was unreadable as he said, "I was sent only to the lost sheep of Israel." James looked awkward but said nothing.

The woman heard and yet was undeterred. She bowed low as she said, "Lord, please help me."

Jesus swept his gaze over his disciples as if waiting for them to say something. They silently shuffled their feet and adjusted their bags on their shoulders.

Jesus' tone challenged his followers as he said, "It isn't proper to take the children's food from them and feed it to the dogs." He turned to look down on the woman, his face inscrutable. Beth was puzzled. Why had Jesus stopped if he didn't want to help her?

The woman did not give up but lifted her trembling chin to look Jesus in the face. Beth saw faith shining in her damp eyes. She appeared sincere. Somehow, Jesus' ministry had taken hold of this Gentile woman.

The woman spoke with a hitch in her tremulous voice, "Yes, Lord, but the children often drop food for our little dog to eat under the table."

Jesus smiled at her words and crouched so his face was level with hers. He took her hands in his own as he praised her, "You have great faith." He pulled her to her feet. "Your daughter is healed."

The woman burst into tears and kissed Jesus' hands.

Matthew whispered, "And he shall proclaim justice to the Gentiles, and in his name, the Gentiles will hope."

Beth felt a prick of conscience. Did *she* want hope for the Gentiles? Since she was a child, she had known the weight of Rome on the shoulders of her countrymen. All her people wanted was freedom, a restored Israel to shine forth in glory. Yet, if Israel did regain her glory, it would affect the neighboring countries—for good or ill. She had never given the other nations serious thought, thinking only of her people.

She remembered feeling small on the port of Tyre, watching the ship sail off into the wide world. A beam of light was breaking into her mind, but she pulled back, uncertain if she was ready to see what was revealed.

The Phoenician woman left them and hurried back to the city. Beth glanced after her. She could picture her running all the way home and embracing her daughter with many happy tears.

Jesus turned the opposite way, away from Tyre, and led his disciples back into Galilee. They camped along the roadside, keeping away from the crowds, yet word began to trickle over the land—Jesus had returned.

Beth was surprised when Jesus didn't stay in Galilee, but once again led them into Gentile populated territory. Jesus led them around the Sea of Galilee to the eastern side of the inland sea to the Decapolis. Here was another area that, like Tyre, had been promised to the descendants of Abraham yet was instead held by Gentiles with foreign gods.

"Why are we among pagans again?" Judas growled at Peter as they walked along the road. He glanced at Beth and lowered his tone as if trying to exclude the woman from the conversation. "Shouldn't we be in one of our cities, among our own people? How else will we begin the revolution?"

Peter stroked his beard. "I know what you're saying, yet I think

Jesus is more focused on a spiritual revolution right now. I don't think he's ready for battles."

Judas snorted, looking up the road where Jesus was a little way ahead. "What is he waiting for? The people would crown him king today—if he'd only let them." A long pause followed. "Unless he isn't the one we're waiting for after all."

Peter jerked away. "After everything we've seen, how can you even think that?"

Judas lifted his hands in defense. "I don't deny that God's hand is with him. But maybe he's only the forerunner. Maybe *he's* the Elijah, not John the Baptist. If what you say is true and he's only interested in spiritual matters, then we might need to wait for another to lead us into true battle. After all, Jesus hasn't actually said he's the Messiah, has he?"

"Not outright," Peter admitted.

Beth felt a flutter in her stomach as Judas' words pushed a sliver of doubt into her mind. What if Jesus wasn't the anointed one? She shook her head. Who else could he be? She had seen his power for herself. She had heard him proclaimed the Son of David and the Son of God, and he hadn't denied either. He called himself the Son of Man. Those were messianic titles.

"Something's happening up ahead," John's loud voice called back, and everyone's eyes turned up the road. When she saw what it was, Beth's throat dried as her palms dampened.

A vast, incredible multitude was gathered on the road as if waiting for Jesus to arrive. Jesus didn't break stride as he moved towards them, and the multitude surged forward like a tidal wave.

At the sudden advance of so many blurred faces, Beth froze on the road as the rest hastened after Jesus. She stood as if turned to stone, staring at the churning sea of people. There were thousands, literally thousands.

Jesus turned off the road and headed into the hills. The disciples and the crowd followed after him.

Beth rose on the balls of her feet to run after them, but it was as if her sandals were rooted to the ground. The unexpected mass of people milled and trampled, a stampede of voices and faces that blurred together into a roiling wave, threatening to sweep away anyone that dared cross its path.

Her husband and her friends all disappeared into the hills, the crowd pooling behind them. Beth stood alone in the center of the road, her skirts clutched in her palms, her breath short and rapid. She had been so proud of herself earlier, thinking that her childish fear of crowds had diminished. She shook her head.

The river of people dwindled to a trickle. Beth took a tentative step forward. When they were far ahead, she strode after the crowd, the last of them all, hot with embarrassment at her fears. How could she even consider herself a disciple of Jesus if she couldn't handle the crowds? Her stomach soured and she pressed her hands to her abdomen.

As she left the road and walked over the grassy slopes, she saw a fellow straggler. A Greek woman walked ahead of her. She cradled a baby in one arm, and her little boy's hand was clasped in the other. The toddler's stubby legs slowed their progress, and the distance between the woman and the crowd was growing. The little toddler stumbled and fell, and the mother leaned over to help raise the little boy to his feet.

"Come, Severus," the mother said eagerly. "We don't want to miss the prophet."

Beth felt strange as she witnessed the scene. This Greek woman saw Jesus as a prophet. She had left her house to follow him into the wilderness. A Greek believed when so many of Beth's people did not.

Beth moved a little closer. Everything from her upbringing told her to avoid this woman; she was a stranger, a foreigner, and her people were living on land that rightfully belonged to Abraham's descendants. Yet, as the distance between the woman and the surging crowd grew and the mother did her best to hurry her little one, Beth felt an unexpected bond with the woman.

Beth went up to her, surprising herself as she said, "May I carry your little boy for you?"

The Greek woman stared uncertainly at Beth, noting her Jewish clothing. Beth smiled, her cheeks warming. If Jesus could heal a Gentile, she could give a little kindness to this one.

The woman's expression softened to gratefulness. "Thank you, I would appreciate it."

Beth reached down and picked up the little boy. He was heavier than he looked, and his eyes were framed by long lashes. He popped a finger in his mouth and stared at her as she settled him on her hip.

Beth walked forward with the woman, both of them following

after Jesus. A Jew and a Gentile. Beth thought it was a strange picture.

"My name is Selene," the woman smiled. "My husband is up there … somewhere." She gestured up the hill. "He's helping carry his brother to Jesus for healing. I'm afraid we fell behind."

"As did I," Beth said with a rueful chuckle.

Selene glanced Beth up and down. "Do you come for healing?"

"No, I'm a disciple of Jesus."

"You?" Selene's brows shot up to her hairline. "A woman?"

Beth laughed. "I'm just as surprised as you are."

Selene hesitated a moment before laughing too.

As they walked, Beth told her why she had begun following Jesus, how he had healed members of her family, and that he taught the people to prepare themselves for the kingdom of heaven.

The Greek woman looked wistful as Beth told her of the coming kingdom. She said, "I'm envious of you. You have much to hope for."

Beth was surprised to be envied by a Greek with their modern culture and high-minded philosophy. She studied Selene's profile and wavered a moment before telling her how Jesus treated foreigners. As Beth spoke about the Phoenician woman's daughter being healed, Selene's eyes widened. She hitched her baby up higher on her hip.

Selene looked ahead at the crowd, her expression distant. "Perhaps I have something to hope for as well."

Jesus led the multitudes deep into the wilderness. Beth and Selene were far back, and their progress was slow. By the time they approached the crowd, it was clear that Jesus had already set to work. Beth could hear rejoicing voices, snatches of song, and loud praises to God.

Beth quailed as she neared the enormous, noisy crowd. She chided herself. She thought she had moved past this. Why was she so afraid today? As she hitched up little Severus on her hip and strode forward, she realized she never would have spoken to Selene if she *hadn't* fallen behind. Selene would still be struggling on, alone. She chewed on her lip, thoughtful.

They stepped into the outskirts of the crowd. Selene looked around for her husband, and Beth's anxiety faded into wonderment. Who would have thought to seek willing people in the area around the Decapolis? What rabbi would have come here and ministered to the lost people? Beth was sure that Jesus was the first.

They came to the inner circle of Jesus' disciples. Jesus was healing all who were brought to him as the disciples watched and helped as necessary. Strewn around the area were abandoned crutches, kicked aside by the celebrating masses.

Peter waved an arm at Beth, looking relieved.

As she walked forward with Selene, Beth saw two men sitting near Jesus. It took her a moment to recognize them as the demon-possessed men from the tombs. Had they prepared the crowds for Jesus' arrival, their lives a living testament to his power?

"There's my husband." Selene's shoulders relaxed. She pointed to a man who stood near Jesus, helping hold another man on a stretcher. "My brother-in-law," Selene explained. "We hope Jesus can help him, though he is very sick." The barest hint of doubt was in her voice.

Beth saw Jesus turn towards Selene's family and speak to them. Impulsively, Beth reached out to clutch Selene's arm, whispering, "Remember all that Jesus has done. Have faith. Believe he can do it."

Selene shot Beth a furtive glance, then looked back at Jesus as he spoke to her husband. She stared at her brother-in-law, and her lips pressed together as her nostrils flared. Beth saw her drawing every drop of faith she had into her heart. Jesus laid his hands on the crippled man and he was instantly healed, moving his legs and sitting up.

Selene gasped out in joy, gathered her skirts in one hand, and ran to her husband. Beth followed quickly on her heels, still holding little Severus. Selene threw herself into her husband's chest in a one-armed hug, crying out praises to God as she gazed at her healed brother-in-law.

Beth felt the familiar rise of hope for the future. She passed the little boy to his father and turned to join her friends.

"Thank you," Selene called with a tremor in her voice, the simple words heavy with meaning.

Beth looked back over her shoulder, smiled and nodded.

Jesus stayed in the wilderness for three days, and the crowds stayed with them. Beth didn't see Selene again. If the woman remained in the crowds, they were not destined to meet again. Beth felt a strange pang of loss. There had been a connection between her and the Greek woman, one she couldn't explain. It seemed, however, that it was to be a brief one.

Beth sifted through their dwindling supplies. The food she had packed for the disciples was almost used up. Beth pursed her lips and surveyed the crowds, sure they must be running short as well.

Jesus came up to her, and said, "I feel compassion for the people. They've been with me for three days and have nothing to eat. I don't want to send them away hungry and have them faint on the way."

Jesus looked at Beth expectantly and she widened her eyes. Did he honestly expect her to produce bread for all of those here? She held out her hands as she said, "Where would we get so many loaves? We are miles from town."

Jesus folded his hands and asked, "Well, how much bread do you have?"

"Uh …" Beth stammered and looked in her satchel. A shiver ran down her spine. It was like an echo of the words Jesus had spoken weeks ago when he had fed five thousand people on the hillside.

Beth's voice wavered as she looked up. "Seven loaves. And a few small fish." She glanced at Peter. His eyes lit up with excitement as he watched. Would Jesus do it again? Would Jesus feed these people like he had fed the children of Israel?

Jesus grinned and spread his arms. "Have the people sit down."

It took a bit of time to spread the word and seat the people. Thousands of faces turned to Jesus as he sat on a hilltop, the few loaves and fish before him in Beth's satchel. He bowed his head and prayed, then he broke the bread. Like before, Beth saw the food multiply and multiply. The disciples carried food throughout the crowd until everyone had eaten their fill.

When they had fed the people, the disciples came back together, carrying the leftover food in baskets. Judas had undertaken to count the crowds again and he came back last of all.

"Four thousand men," Judas said, shaking his head with wonder.

He and Simon put their heads together and whispered as Beth scanned the multitudes. Five thousand before. Four thousand now. That was indeed an army. She glanced at Jesus. He did not look like a general surveying his troops but like a shepherd overseeing his flock.

Matthew glanced down at the baskets, and his eyes widened. "Look, there are seven baskets left." The other disciples looked at

Matthew in confusion, and he gestured with his hands as he continued, "Remember before, there were twelve baskets like the twelve tribes of Israel. Now, there are seven baskets, just like the seven nations of Canaan that Joshua drove out. Do you think Jesus made it that way purposefully?"

The disciples murmured, but no one knew for certain.

Peter spoke to the Twelve, his tone low and serious. "One thing I do know, with the miracles Jesus has been performing and the crowds that are being drawn to him, I think he's reaching a point of no return."

The disciples glanced at each other, nodding. Beth's fears awoke and wrapped themselves around her throat and she swallowed painfully. She knew Herod Antipas' eye had to be on this healing prophet who could draw thousands of men to himself with ease. Surely the Roman governor in Jerusalem was also keeping a close watch on Jesus' movements. How much longer could Jesus move freely in the crowds before soldiers came to arrest him like they had the Baptizer?

"He doesn't seem like he wants to fight," Mary protested.

Judas looked grave. "If Rome's eyes turn his way, he might have no choice." His eyes gleamed and Beth's brow furrowed.

Mary was silent.

"Well," said James, looking at his younger brother who nodded at him. "We'll stand with him. Come what may."

The other men were solemn, and they all echoed the phrase like a pledge, "Come what may."

Beth felt the hair on her arms stand up and her stomach swooped. A heavy silence followed.

Simon chuckled, dispelling some of the seriousness of the moment. "Let's hope it comes sooner than later. I feel it in my bones. We're getting close to the moment."

Beth felt it too, though she did not share Simon's eagerness. Herod Antipas would not walk away from the throne for the Messiah, nor would the Roman Governor. Not without a fight.

26

MESSIAH

Jesus remained in Capernaum briefly after his time in the Decapolis. Beth had private, intimate hopes for Peter and herself during this respite at home. When she was on the road, her mind was constantly filled with dreams of the kingdom of heaven. Now that she was home, she looked around their lovely home and dusted off her dreams for the future. She folded her hands under her chin. She warmly imagined herself and Peter sitting at this table, children all around them. The cruel words Rachel had spoken pushed themselves forward but she shook her head. She refused to believe she was barren. All she needed was some time with her husband.

As the days went by, she grew frustrated when Peter did not seem to share the same longings. Peter came to bed late and rose early, always busy with the other men. Beth wrestled with feelings of jealousy and tried to be patient. Surely, it wouldn't always be like this.

Tamar drew Beth aside one afternoon. "Stop your brooding, daughter," she chided, and Beth flushed, wondering who else had noticed. "Come, I have something to show you." Tamar showed her a new garment on the loom, part of a set of clothing for Jesus.

Beth admired the finished outer robe. It was creamy white wool with black and brown vertical stripes. She trailed her fingers down the half-completed tunic that was stretched within the wooden frame. It would be woven in one piece, a fine, quality garment.

Tamar fingered the soft linen with a motherly smile. "Jesus' old set is getting worn and shabby. I thought he might like a new set of clothes for Passover this year."

Beth agreed, and she was happy for the distraction.

She and her mother divided their time at the loom, their fingers flying as they wove the shuttle back and forth. When Peter sat with the men late into the night, Beth wove by lamplight. Even Hannah came and helped, and Beth praised her sister's growing skill. She felt a pang in her throat as she watched her sister's nimble fingers.

Hannah was growing up, and Beth was missing it. She ran her hand down Hannah's smooth hair and smiled when Hannah looked up to her in question.

Watching the clothing grow on the loom was satisfying. Beth took special pleasure in making the pattern on the shawl, doing her best work for Jesus. She wove blue through the tassels, one on each corner of the cloth.

When the weaving was completed, Beth spread the clothing on the bed. The mother and daughters stood with their arms around each other and admired the new garments.

"It's nice to have you home," Tamar whispered, and she squeezed Beth closer.

Beth leaned against her mother. It was nice to be home, peaceful and relaxed, with no breaking and setting up of camps or uncertainty around every bend of the road. Even so, she couldn't allow herself to get too settled. She knew Jesus was going on another journey, and soon. He'd mentioned it at breakfast.

"Now," Tamar said, her tone brisk again. "Beth, you go and give the clothes to Jesus."

"Me?" Beth protested.

"I'll do it!" Hannah said, bouncing on her toes.

"Well, do it together then," Tamar said and laughed at her daughters.

Beth and Hannah carefully folded up the garments, Hannah humming. The women went downstairs. Beth's pulse quickened as she neared Jesus with Hannah skipping at her side. Jesus was seated and surrounded by the other men. Beth's face flushed as curious eyes turned her way.

Beth cleared her throat. "These clothes are for you, Rabbi. My mother and I made them for you." Hannah jabbed her in the side, and Beth flinched as she tacked on, "Hannah helped too."

"For me?" Jesus asked in surprise as he accepted the bundle. He ran his hand over the cloth.

"Do you like them?" Hannah asked with a wide grin.

"Of course I do!" he said, reaching out and pinching her chin with a wink. His gaze encompassed all three women as he said, "Thank you, my good friends, for this thoughtful gift."

Beth blushed and spun away, happy that Jesus was pleased.

Only a few days later, Jesus gathered up his closest disciples and set out on the road again, slipping away from the crowds and the bitterness of the Capernaum elders. Without hesitation, Beth took up her traveling bag and joined the disciples. Her steps were light as she strode with her husband, following Jesus and leaving her home behind. Mary Magdalene glanced over, her thick curls bounced with each step. The friends shared a smile.

This time Jesus led them northwards to the district of Caesarea Philippi. The area was lush and green, nestled at the southern foot of Mount Hermon, and Beth found it beautiful. The district would be idyllic, except for the ancient pagan shrines chiseled into the rock centuries ago, and the new, more prominent Roman temples.

Caesarea Philippi was in the region of Herod Antipas' brother, Philip. Philip was nothing like his hot-blooded father. He was even-tempered, ruled wisely, and managed to keep the peace between his Jewish and Gentile subjects.

Jesus and his disciples strolled about the outskirts of Caesarea Philippi enjoying the green freshness. They had arrived in the area quietly and were left to themselves. Once again, Jesus desired separation from the crowds.

Beth saw many Gentiles of various nationalities visiting temples with tributes of food, coins, or trinkets. The Gentiles paid Jesus no mind. Beth pursed her lips trying to understand how they could be so devoted to their lifeless idols when a true prophet walked among them.

Jesus and the disciples ambled towards one of the popular sites for visitors. Frothing water gushed out of the mountain beneath the mouth of a large cavern. As they filed into the shadowy coolness of the cave, the sound of rushing water filled Beth's ears. Ahead of them was the strange feature that drew people to this place.

Beth and Peter peered down a sharp precipice into a dark pool of water, ink-black with unfathomable depths. This was the source of the water gushing from the face of the mountain, flowing from the rock itself and cascading down to join the rivers that flowed into the Sea of Galilee. The unending quantity of fresh water was mysterious and astounding.

"What's this?" John pointed to an immense coil of rope tied through a metal loop and fastened to the stone wall. There was a weight on the other end.

A man standing near a grotto for the god Pan heard John. With a knowing smile, he said, "Set the weight into the water and measure its depth."

John and James' eyes lit up, and they began to uncoil the rope. They lowered it into the pool while counting the length.

"That's all of it and we haven't even found the bottom!" John exclaimed, laughing with his brother.

As they pulled up the dripping cord, the men marveled over the pool. John leaned far over the edge for a better look until Andrew reached out and pulled him back.

Beth peeked once more at the black water, felt her stomach swoop, and took a hasty step back. The idea of falling in and drowning in the unending pool was disconcerting. She could see why the place had earned the name The Gates of Hades. Something about this imagined gateway to the land of the dead had driven the pagans to worship here for a millennium.

When they had satisfied their curiosity, the group left the cave and sat in a pleasant grove near the tumbling river. The birds were singing and the grass near the water was lush and soft. Beth thought it was such a shame that the picturesque view was so polluted by the worship of false gods. She sat beside Mary Magdalene who was lying on her back soaking in the warm, autumn sunlight. A butterfly drifted by and insects buzzed. The mood was peaceful—until Jesus' voice broke the stillness.

"Who do people say that the Son of Man is?"

The sleepy mood shattered. Mary jerked bolt upright and all the other disciples shifted and stared at each other. Jesus hadn't declared himself as the Messiah, not yet. Beth's pulse quickened as she glanced around at the others. She felt their burning desire to have Jesus confirm all their hopes. Yet, eyes flicked to one another, and Beth knew none of them wanted to be the one to say it.

Andrew licked his lips. "Some say John the Baptist."

"Some have said Jeremiah or one of the prophets," Philip offered, his voice a little higher-pitched than normal.

Bartholomew said, "I have heard some say you are Elijah." Heads bobbed all around.

Jesus heard it all and asked, "But who do *you* say that I am?"

Beth sucked in her breath and glanced around at the other disciples. Kneeling in boats only a few months ago, they had bowed low before Jesus, worshiping him and calling him the 'Son of God'. Yet, now they hesitated. It was one thing to cry out in passion after the moment of a miracle, another to declare boldly in the bright sunshine.

In a loud and clear voice, Beth heard her husband proclaim, "You are the Messiah, the Son of the living God."

Beth's breath escaped in a puff. She stared at Jesus, waiting to see what he would say. Jesus didn't reply at once, but rose to his feet and came towards Peter. A thrill shot down her spine.

Here, where evil resided and false gods were worshiped, would Jesus raise his battle standard, revealing himself? Would he stand before the Gates of Hades and declare that he was indeed the Messiah and that he had come to do battle with the powers of evil, death, and corruption?

Jesus crouched before Peter and smiled. "Blessed are you, Simon Peter son of Jonah, because flesh and blood did not reveal this to you, but my Father in Heaven."

Excited whispering broke out around her as Beth felt her stomach swoop. They had hoped, they had followed Jesus believing he was worth dedicating their lives to, but to hear the confirmation from his own lips was like the sun finally breaking over the horizon after a long, cold night.

Judas nodded at Simon, relief plain on his handsome face as he clapped his friend on the back.

Jesus put his hand on Peter's shoulder, and Peter stared as Jesus said, "I say to you that you are a rock, and on this bedrock, I will build my church and the gates of Hades will not overpower it. I will give you the keys of the kingdom of heaven, and whatever you bind on earth shall have been bound in heaven, and whatever you loose on earth shall have been loosed in heaven."

Peter bowed his head, overcome at Jesus' words. Beth felt a surge of pride for her husband.

Beth heard Simon whisper to Judas, "Things will move forward quickly now."

Jesus overheard. He rose to his feet, his face serious as he examined each face. "Don't tell anyone that I am the Christ."

Simon's mouth fell open.

Judas leaned forward, crying out, "Why not, Lord? Shouldn't we tell everyone the Messiah has arrived? They'll flock to you in droves."

Jesus shook his head, and said, "It's not the time."

Judas flinched as if he had been struck. Simon's eyes pleaded with Jesus and Beth felt a pulse of sympathy.

Jesus was resolute, calm. He didn't seem to be pulling back from the role of Messiah, but he was determined to continue on the path he had chosen. Beth was confident Jesus would do it his way, in his own time. He had thrust his banner into the ground but he wasn't marching just yet. In her heart, Beth secretly was relieved the time for battles was not upon them.

As the sunlight faded they made a simple camp away from the city. Beth sat near the fire warming her hands as the cold night pressed against her back. By the flickering light, she studied the faces of the others and saw excitement, eagerness, and deep longing.

Judas leaned towards Jesus. His tone was pleading as he said, "Rabbi, I understand that this isn't the time you will show yourself to the world. Can you tell us when that time will come?"

Everyone stared expectantly at Jesus. He looked around the fire before he spoke, his voice serious and low, "The day is coming when I will go up to Jerusalem—" the disciples shifted eagerly "—and I will suffer many things." Beth felt the mood change to confusion and alarm as Jesus continued, "I will suffer at the hands of the elders, chief priests, and scribes. I will be killed, and raised up on the third day."

Jesus' prophecy of his death fell like a hammer to her head, leaving Beth staggered. She wanted to cry out that he couldn't die. He was their friend, their rabbi, and he needed to lead the people to the kingdom.

Peter jumped to his feet and beckoned Jesus away from the fire. He hissed near his ear, "God forbid it, Lord! This shall never happen to you."

"Get behind me, Satan!" Jesus' voice was like a whip-crack, and Peter quailed. "You are a stumbling block to me; for you aren't setting your mind on God's interests, but man's." Jesus strode away into the night. Peter stared after him, his shoulders slumping.

Beth winced at Jesus' passionate rebuke. She clutched her hands in her lap, squeezing until her nails bit into her palms. Guilt washed over her. Peter had said the words, but she had agreed with him in her heart.

Sympathetic tears burned as Peter came back to the fire and threw himself down beside her. She leaned against him wanting to comfort him, but he shook his head and dropped his face into his palms.

She could barely hear his words as he mumbled, "How can *I* be a rock in the church? Unless he means I have rocks in my head. I don't understand, I just don't understand."

The fire snapped and crackled, the sparks flying up into the night sky as if they wanted to join their twins, the stars. The disciples brooded on Jesus' ominous prophecy. They sat as if they had been carved from the same trees that surrounded them. Confusion covered every face, but one. Beth saw Judas' eyes burning as he snapped a twig and tossed the little pieces one by one into the flames.

Judas muttered, "So which is it to be? Messiah, or martyr? He can't be both. He hasn't *done* anything yet." He hurled what was left of the twig into the hungry flames. "What good is a Messiah if he dies and we're all still under the yoke of Rome? What good is healing everyone if they're going to die subject to pagans?"

Simon gazed at Judas with pained sympathy. "Perhaps," Simon weighed out each word as he spoke. "Perhaps he is speaking in parable again." He looked up at the other disciples, and his tone became more confident. "It must just be a parable, for he speaks of dying and rising in three days. He can't mean, really, truly killed. Just suffering a great deal and then rising from his tribulation on the third day." His confusion fell away, and his eyes shone. "It's simply a parable so that we know that his rise to power will not be unchallenged. Even his own people will doubt and get in the way."

There was a long minute of silence.

Judas' expression smoothed. "Yes, I think you're right."

Jesus' rebuke still sitting heavy on his shoulders, Peter only shrugged and said, "Perhaps."

Jesus returned to the fireside, his movements jerky with suppressed zeal. He started speaking even before he sat, his tone earnest. "You need to understand." He paused, making sure everyone was focused on him. "If anyone wishes to come after me, he must deny himself, take up his cross, and follow me."

Beth swallowed hard, remembering how those words had nearly broken her faith before. She shuddered as the briefest picture of Peter on a cross swept through her mind before she slammed shut the door on that nightmare.

Jesus' tone was passionate as he continued, "For whoever wishes to save his life will lose it, but whoever loses his life for my sake will find it. For what will it profit a man if he gains the whole world and forfeits his soul? What will a man give in exchange for his soul?" Jesus let that hang in the night air for a moment. "For the Son of Man is going to come in the glory of his Father with His angels. He will then repay every man according to his deeds."

Several of the disciples shifted with interest, and Beth wondered if Simon the Zealot had been right, for how could Jesus come in glory if he died at the hands of his own people?

Jesus looked around at them and said, "Truly I say to you, there are some of those who are sitting here who will not taste death until they see the Son of Man coming in his kingdom."

Beth's emotions washed first one way, then another. Fear and excitement. Eagerness and reluctance. The desire for freedom and honor for her people churned against the repulsion of pain and suffering for those she loved.

For once, no one asked any questions. They all just sat, overcome by their emotions, lost in their thoughts.

After a long moment, Jesus threw more fuel on the fire, wrapped himself in his cloak, and prepared to sleep. One by one the others did the same.

Beth lay down with the fire on her face and the cold air on her back. This was it, the moment they had waited for. Jesus had declared himself. Even so, her and Peter's future felt just as uncertain.

They stayed in the area for several days. The people discovered where Jesus was and flocked to him once more. Jesus avoided the large cities and drew away to the mountains. He chose a place near a large, craggy mount whose top reached up to the clouds. Jesus moved through the crowds speaking and healing but keeping his true identity hidden.

Beth could see the secret practically bursting out of the others. James and John kept winking at each other. Mary often watched Jesus and sighed happily.

Not all were happy, though. Judas continued to brood over Jesus' reluctance to reveal himself. Peter still sagged under the rebuke Jesus had given him.

In the afternoon, Jesus came up to the disciples. "I'm going up the mountain to pray. James, John, and Peter, I want you to come with me." Jesus clapped a hand on Peter's shoulder and smiled at him like a brother.

Peter's eyes brightened for the first time in days, and he turned his face to Beth. She smiled and gratefully nodded at Jesus. Peter's happiness hung so much on Jesus' approval.

Matthew glanced at the large crowd, worried. "But what about the people?"

Jesus raised his brows. Holding out his hands to all his disciples, he said, "You tend to them."

He turned and began to pick his way up the stony path, the rocks crunching beneath his sandals. The Zebedee brothers and Peter were right on his heels.

Beth turned back to the crowds, sweeping her eyes over hundreds of people. They all needed something—healing or hope. In the face of so great a need, she felt insignificant.

Once, after dealing with the Pharisees, Jesus had told the disciples to take on his burdens for they were light, and his yoke for it was easy. Beth did not feel either light or easy at that moment.

Beth saw Andrew nearby, and she whispered, "What can we do, without Jesus?"

Andrew chuckled. "I thought the same thing when Jesus sent us out to work without him. It was just Peter and I. I felt so anxious, I almost didn't walk into that first town." He rubbed his bearded chin as he remembered. Mary Magdalene looked up and came over to listen as Beth's brother-in-law continued, "Jesus had laid his hands on us, but we were untested. We gathered our courage and began to tell the people what Jesus had told us—'Repent, the kingdom of heaven is near.' As we preached, I saw a little boy who was blind. My heart pounded so hard that I was sure everyone would hear. I walked towards the boy and knelt before him. My hand shook as I reached out and laid it on his head. I had to push away my doubt and remember everything Jesus had done. A peace came over me and I was able to speak with confidence, 'In the name of Jesus, be healed!' And he was. Just like that, he blinked and the milky color was gone from his eyes." Andrew shook his head, grinning. "I had never felt anything like it before, I felt so—"

"Powerful?" Mary Magdalene breathed.

"Whole," Andrew said with a secret smile.

Beth was moved by Andrew's experience, yet how could his story apply to her? Jesus hadn't laid his hands on her. He hadn't given her any special gifts. She hung back as the others began to move through the crowds.

Instead of going out with the disciples, she built a fire. She wasn't useless, she told herself feebly as the rest of them set out to help the people. She could prepare a meal for them.

The afternoon waned, the winter sun sinking low in the sky. The disciples ate the food Beth had cooked for them. They were grateful, but she still felt embarrassed that she alone had refused to go out and help. The crowd grew peaceful, many preparing themselves an evening meal while waiting for Jesus to return.

The weather shifted. A sudden wind snapped at Beth's shawl and she felt the hair on her arms stand up. Worried for her absent husband, she scrambled to her feet and peered up the mountain. A swirling, thick fog descended and covered the summit, but it wasn't shadowy or gray—it was dazzling.

All the people stood and stared, their faces tipped upwards as they watched the cloud. Men spoke in hushed tones. The fog didn't feel natural; it was almost hypnotic in its movements. Beth imagined it might look something like the Shekinah—the presence of God— when He had descended on Mount Sinai or upon the Temple in the days of old. The thought made her nervous. Her husband was up there.

Then, as quickly as it had appeared, the fog dissipated. It melted away just as the last rays of sunlight disappeared and dusky twilight took over. The people murmured and went back to their campfires.

The stars began to rise and Jesus still didn't return with her husband. Beth began to worry, pulling on her lip and shooting glances at the mountain. Its looming, shadowy presence felt ominous. She wrapped herself in a blanket and sat staring at the embers of their fire.

Beth jerked as frightened shouts rang through the night. She scrambled to her feet, her blanket dropping at her feet. She saw torches waving at the edge of the crowd. The disciples scrambled up from their fire and ran to see what was wrong. Beth shifted her feet, then sucked in a breath and fell in behind them.

The shouts grew louder as she approached the edge of the crowd, and her legs felt heavy with fear. It was probably nothing. Maybe Jesus had come down the mountain another way. Maybe the crowd was just eager to see him. She reached the edge of the crowd and saw Andrew standing in a pool of light cast by a torch. She went to stand with him, panting.

"More people have arrived," Andrew said as he glanced at her. "But something seems wrong."

Several men held torches aloft, and in the flickering light, she saw the newcomers retreating from a young man who lay before them. He thrashed on the ground, foaming at the mouth.

Mary Magdalene stumbled up beside Beth, panting and pushing her curls out of her face. "What's wrong with him?" she gasped.

Beth looked at Mary with surprise and wondered that she didn't recognize the symptoms. "You looked the same before Jesus healed you." Mary's eyes widened, and she stared at the young man with fearful pity.

A short man stepped forward from among the newcomers. He wrung his hands, sweat glistening on his forehead despite the chilly air. "Please," he begged. "We came to the rabbi for healing. That is my boy! He's often like this. He's injured himself untold times. Can you help him?"

At the sound of the pleading father, the demon became even more violent. The boy's body went rigid and an unearthly scream ripped from between his clenched jaw. It was terrifying to behold. People scrambled away from him. His eyes rolled back in his head until only the whites showed.

Andrew hesitated, then rushed forward with Thomas. The two men tried to restrain the young man, but the boy was unnaturally strong.

"Be careful!" Beth cried out. Could Andrew and Thomas manage a demon this powerful?

Thomas heard her. He spoke to Andrew through gritted teeth, "This looks beyond our abilities."

Andrew set his mouth and prayed aloud with a tremulous voice, "In the name of Jesus, I pray that this demon would go out of this boy."

The boy began to cackle as he twisted out of their hands. Beth felt nauseated as the demon began to mock their weakness. If only Jesus were here. What could they do without him?

The people beside her stirred, and a whisper of excitement rushed through the valley. She turned and felt unbridled relief as Jesus broke through the crowd, his powerful eyes blazing in the torchlight. Peter, James, and John were at his heels, all bearing the look of awe-filled shock. Beth wondered what had happened on the mountain top, but Jesus was taking in the scene in the valley.

The boy's father saw Jesus and threw himself at his feet. "Lord, have mercy on my son, for he's a lunatic and very ill. He often throws himself into the fire or the water. Your disciples couldn't heal him."

Jesus looked at his disciples and the crowds behind them, shaking his head. "You unbelieving and perverted generation."

His eyes met hers, and Beth squirmed. Had her doubts stopped the disciples from healing? Her cheeks burned.

Jesus gave the disciples a frustrated sigh. "How long shall I be with you?" Jesus spoke like a man running out of time, and the disciples glanced at each other with worry. He shook his head and said, "How long shall I put up with you? Bring him here to me."

Thomas and Andrew went to the boy, each taking an arm. They carried him with difficulty, the boy thrashing between them.

Jesus rebuked him and the demon came out. The boy was cured, though limp with exhaustion. His father rushed forward and embraced his son, thanking Jesus.

Andrew and Thomas looked abashed at their failure to do what Jesus did so simply. Beth swallowed hard.

"Come," Jesus said, and led the disciples back to their camp, a little ways from the crowd.

Beth, still hot with embarrassment, served Jesus, James, John, and Peter the supper she had kept warm for them.

Jesus hadn't taken more than a mouthful when Andrew leaned forward, his expression frustrated. "Why couldn't we drive it out?"

Jesus dipped his flatbread into his stew and took another large, hungry bite. After he swallowed, he looked at the disciples in the eyes. Beth felt like his eyes lingered on her the longest. She bit the inside of her cheek.

"Because of the littleness of your faith! You don't seem to realize that if you have faith, even just a mite as tiny as a mustard seed, you will say to this mountain, 'Move from here to there,' and it will move. Nothing will be impossible for you."

Beth glanced at the craggy heights of the mountain and tried to imagine having that kind of faith. It felt impossible for someone like her. Jesus was the powerful one. She ducked her head as Jesus ate his supper.

Beth hadn't forgotten the strange cloud on the mountain. Jesus and the others made no mention of it, though James, John, and Peter often looked at each other with eager expressions as if they were sharing a wondrous secret. As they prepared to bed down, Beth asked her husband what had happened on the mountain.

Peter gripped her hand as his face glowed. "I want to tell you so badly, but—" his face fell a little, "Jesus told us to keep what we saw a secret, until a specific time. I will tell you that it was glorious."

Now she was even more curious. She stuck out her lower lip. "You can't tell me anything?" she wheedled. It felt strange for Peter to withhold something from her. "Not even a hint?"

Peter laughed and shook his head. "You'll have to wait."

Wait. Sometimes it felt as she ever did was wait. She sighed and lay beside Peter. In the dark shadows of the night, Peter pulled her close.

Beth tugged her shawl up a little higher on her head and selected the figs as quickly as she could. She could feel the disdain from the shopkeeper roiling over her. She felt a sudden longing for the obscurity of Caesarea Philippi or Tyre. No one had noticed her there.

They were back in Capernaum, but Beth didn't feel like she was at home. The animosity for Jesus and his followers had only grown. Her fingers were clumsy as she counted out the coins. Setting them down without a word, she turned away from the booth.

Peter fell into step beside her. "What's wrong?"

Beth raised brows at him and answered, "They hate us here."

Peter glanced over his shoulder, back at the market. "Why do you think that?"

"I don't think it," Beth shook her head. "I *feel* it. I don't know how you can't."

Two well-dressed men stopped in front of them, blocking the street and glaring. Beth and Peter drew up short.

One of the men lifted his chin and asked, "Does your rabbi pay the Temple tax?"

"Of course, why wouldn't he?" Peter said, indignant. "I'll fetch money for you."

The man pursed his lips but nodded once as he stepped to the side. Beth blew out her breath as she and Peter continued to the house. Even the Temple workers were set on edge by Jesus' presence. She shook her head and looked up at her husband.

"Peter, Jesus isn't quite what I expected."

Peter's laughter rolled. "I don't think he's what anyone expected."

Beth stopped and put out a hand to hold her husband. "I'm serious. I thought the Messiah would fight Rome. It seems like Jesus is fighting everyone *but* the foreigners. He's made enemies of the Pharisees. We aren't welcome in the synagogue." She rubbed a hand roughly over her forehead. She felt a headache coming. "How will we worship the Lord properly if we don't have our synagogue? Where will you read the Torah? How do we belong to our community?"

Peter folded his arms as he looked back towards town. He shrugged. "Well, we'll continue to meet at our house."

"You mean, we will make a new synagogue?" Beth was doubtful.

"Maybe," Peter said.

Beth was frustrated. "This is our life, Peter. You need to care a little more."

He shook his head. "You need to worry a lot less."

She pressed her lips together to smother a useless retort and followed him as he strode back to the house. As they ducked under the low doorway they saw the other disciples were gathered. David and Hannah were sitting beside Jesus, laughing at a story he was telling them. Jesus noticed the shadow move across the open doorway and glanced up. He saw Peter and called out, "What do you think, Simon Peter? From whom do the kings of the earth collect tolls or taxes—from their sons, or from foreigners?"

Peter darted a sideways glance to Beth and she felt odd. Did Jesus know what had happened on the street?

Peter replied, "From foreigners."

Jesus smiled and held out his hands, encompassing the room. "Then the sons are free."

Peter scratched his beard as his forehead furrowed with concern. "Do I not pay the Temple tax, then?"

He had paid the tax every year. Every Jewish male of age did. The funds helped pay for the sacrifices in the Temple Courts.

Jesus' smiled and pinched David's chin, and the boy grinned. "We don't want to make a stumbling block for others who don't understand." Jesus looked back at Peter. "Go out to the sea, cast a hook, and take the first fish that comes up. When you open its mouth, you will find a four-drachma coin. Take that and give it to them for both of us."

Peter looked surprised at Jesus' directions, but he ducked back outside.

"Wait for me!" David called, scrambling to his feet. He raced out the door after Peter.

Beth smiled after her brother. He was growing in height and confidence. Hitching up her basket, she went to help her mother prepare the supper. David came back with Peter and eagerly told everyone how it happened just as Jesus had said. The disciples smiled and nodded, all were kind to the young boy.

Tamar leaned towards her daughter, worry lines between her brows as she looked on her only son. "It's been difficult for him lately. He's lost a few friends."

"Because of Jesus?" Beth asked, her heart sinking as she studied her brother's face. His soft cheeks were slimming and his legs and arms were lengthening. He would soon be a young man. Tamar nodded and Beth sighed. "It isn't fair! Why should Peter being a disciple make things difficult for David? He's only a child."

"David believes in Jesus too, you know. Just like you do. Just like Hannah and I do. He remembers all the stories you've told him from your travels. He recites the parables to his friends, but they laugh at him."

Beth looked at her mother in surprise. "He does?"

She hadn't thought how she might be affecting her family when she shared what she had learned at Jesus' feet.

"Oh yes," Tamar chuckled at her daughter's expression. "We are all believers here."

Beth looked around the room at the men and women who filled Peter's house. They were relaxed now, resting after their journey. The mood had been much different the night before, a tension so tight it felt as if the air would snap like a frayed fishing line. She swallowed hard as her eyes rested on Jesus.

Last night he had said it again. He had said he would be betrayed by the leaders of his own people. He said he would be killed and raised on the third day. It had been hard to hear it again, and they hadn't understood him any better. Emotions had been high—anger, disbelief, pain.

Beth leaned her head towards her mother. "If he is prophesying his death, what will happen to us who follow him?"

Tamar pursed her lips and had no answer.

Beth heard raised voices from the corner of the room. James and John were standing toe to toe, their necks flushed.

Naomi snapped, "Enough, you two! I raised you better than this."

John and James quieted at once, but they glowered at one another as they slunk to opposite sides of the house.

John sat down in a tangle of long limbs and looked at Jesus. His voice was petulant as he asked, "Who is the greatest in the kingdom of heaven?"

Jesus raised his eyebrows as he looked between the two brothers. James glared at his younger sibling, and Beth half-expected John to stick out his tongue.

Jesus gestured for David to stand up, and he said, "Truly I say to you, unless you turn around and become like little children, you will never enter into the kingdom of heaven." James and John looked abashed, and the rest of the disciples were listening in surprise. Jesus looked around the room. "If one of you humble yourselves like this child, they are the greatest in the kingdom of heaven. If you welcome one such as these in my name, you welcome me."

Jesus gestured to those around the room, and his tone turned grave. "Whoever causes one of these little ones who believe in me to sin, it would be better for him to have a large millstone hung around his neck and be drowned in the depths of the sea. See that you do not despise one of mine." His tone deepened. "Their angels in heaven are always watching."

Jesus looked at David and his expression softened into a smile. He drew the boy to sit beside him and put his arm around his shoulders. "What do you think?" Jesus asked kindly. "If a shepherd loses a sheep, doesn't he leave the rest of the herd to go find it?" David bobbed his head. Jesus squeezed the young boy. "I tell you the truth, when the shepherd finds his lost sheep, he rejoices more over that one than all the rest."

David beamed at Jesus, his expression full of love. Jesus smiled at him like a father with his favorite son, and it made tears prickle in Beth's eyes. David would have learned so much about God at her father's knee. She felt grateful to Jesus for his kindness and attention to the fatherless boy.

Jesus looked around the room. "If your brother sins against you, go talk to him one on one. If he listens to you, you have gained your brother. But if he doesn't listen, take with you one or two others to try to persuade him. If he still won't listen, bring it to the body of believers. If he refuses to listen, he must be like an outsider among you. You must treat him like a Gentile or a tax collector."

Eyes fell on Matthew, who ducked his head. Thomas set his hand on Matthew's shoulder and shook him with brotherly affection. Matthew smiled with appreciation.

Jesus' gaze swept the room as he said, "Whatever you bind on earth will be bound in heaven. Whatever you loose on earth will be loosed in heaven. If two or three of you agree on anything you ask, it will be done for them by my Father in heaven. For where two or three are gathered in my name there I am, in the midst of them."

"So how many times should I forgive a brother?" Peter asked, stroking his beard. "Seven times?"

Jesus shook his head. "Seventy times seven!"

David mumbled, "That's a lot of forgiveness," and blushed when everyone laughed.

"Yes," Jesus chuckled. "For this reason, the kingdom of heaven may be compared to a king who wanted to settle accounts with his slaves. One was brought to him that owed an enormous sum, ten thousand talents. The servant didn't have the money so the master ordered him to be sold, along with his wife and children and everything he had, so the debt could be repaid. The servant fell on his face and begged him, 'Be patient with me, and I will repay it all!' The master had compassion on him and forgave the debt.

"But the slave went out and found one of his fellow slaves who owed him a hundred denarii. He began to choke him, saying, 'Pay me what you owe!' The fellow servant fell on the ground and begged him, 'Be patient with me, and I will repay you.' But he didn't want to, and he had him thrown in prison until he could pay back what was owed.

"When the fellow slaves saw what had happened, they reported everything to the master. The master summoned the slave and said to him, 'Wicked and ungrateful slave. I forgave you a huge debt because you begged me. You should have shown mercy, as I showed mercy to you.' And the master threw the slave to the jailers until he could repay everything that was owed." Jesus looked around at them and the room was silent. "So also my heavenly Father will do to you if you do not forgive your brother from your heart."

The men fell into conversation and discussion. It wasn't long before Beth saw James and John shuffle up to one another and whisper with their heads together. They walked away with relaxed expressions, and Naomi nodded in approval.

Perhaps they could be a little synagogue all of their own. It almost felt like Jesus was trying to teach them Deuteronomy all over again—how to live as the people of God.

She remembered what Jesus had said last night about his death, and her smile faltered. She remembered back at the mountain when Jesus had been exasperated with them and had said, *"How long shall I be with you?"*

If Jesus did die, how could they continue without him? How would they keep from slipping back into the old ways of outward piety, of tradition over mercy? Her heart turned over as she looked at Jesus.

He couldn't leave them!

27

A RABBI'S CALL

With trembling fingers, Reuben broke the seal and unfurled the scroll. He had slept fitfully for weeks while waiting for Simeon to reply to his letter. He shook his head. His fate was reduced to a single sheet of papyrus. His pulse quickened as his eyes flitted over the tidy letters.

"I am gratified to hear of your quick progress through your apprenticeship with Philemon. I would have expected no less of one with your aptitude, for did not I ascertain your sharp mind before anyone else? My judgment has never erred. I am sure that we can get you business in Jerusalem. There is always scribal work to be done for our brethren here, and you shall have no lack of income with me to give you recommendations.

It is fortuitous that your apprenticeship to Philemon is completed at the same time Jesus of Nazareth has released Capernaum. If he is spending as little time in the area as you have written, it is pointless for you to remain in that little village any longer. Come join me in Jerusalem as soon as you have made preparations. You shall have your old room and a place at my table. We shall complete your education on the law and traditions together."

Reuben had to pause and blink hard to dispel the tears from his eyes. At last! He was going back to stay in Jerusalem. His period in the wilderness was ending, and his promised land had come. He cleared the lump from his throat and returned to the letter.

"I take up my pen again after receiving some correspondence from a former student of mine, Eliab ben Jezreel. He has requested that I join him at his country estate in Perea. He seeks my advice on an important matter. I remember that the two of you were friends during the year your education overlapped. It would be good for you to cultivate that friendship further, for his father's passing has made him wealthy, and therefore, influential. Plan to meet me on the road, and we shall journey to see him together."

The letter continued with the particulars of when and where to meet, and Reuben saw with alarm that he would need to leave the very next morning if he didn't want Simeon to wait for him at the inn. He leaped to his feet and stared around the room. His mind flit through all the tasks he would need to complete, but he was unable to settle on a reasonable plan of action. Philemon entered the room at that moment.

"What's happened?" he asked, noticing Reuben's expression with alarm. Reuben told him about the letter. Philemon raised his brows. "You leave so soon? Well, you must go and say goodbye to your family, then. I would go now if you want to catch your father and brothers before they head down to the boats."

"Of course," Reuben said, seizing upon the practical advice.

He tucked Simeon's scroll with his personal possessions and then trotted to his father's house. His pace slowed as the humble dwelling came into view. For years now, he had intended to leave Capernaum behind, and he had made no secret of that to his father. Reuben's chosen path had strained their already fragile relationship. He had always been different from the rest of his family—a branch grafted on the wrong tree.

Reuben ducked under the doorway and called out a greeting. His voice wobbled, showing his nerves, and he felt a surge of self-conscious annoyance.

"What are you doing here?" Ebenezer's brash voice nettled

Reuben as his father's face appeared above him, looking down on his firstborn in both attitude and manner.

Reuben refused to let his father cow him. He clambered up the ladder so he could speak to his father face-to-face. He glanced to the side and saw his mother. Her expression was akin to pained hunger. Reuben didn't understand it, and he put thoughts of her aside for the moment.

Zeb and Ben were matching stone pillars, their expressions flat and revealing nothing of their feelings. He wished for their self-possession as he turned to face his father.

Ebenezer's arms were crossed over his burly chest, and Reuben saw the streaks of gray in his temples and beard with surprise. The idea that his father was growing old unsettled him, but only for a moment. He remembered that he was heading to Jerusalem, and if his father couldn't see the talent of his firstborn son and be proud of the future that awaited Reuben, then the broken family was not Reuben's fault.

"I came to say goodbye," Reuben said, smoothing his shawl and lifting his chin. "I leave for Jerusalem in the morning. I don't know when, or even if, I shall return."

Ebenezer's eyes blazed, and he worked his jaw. "*That's* how you take your leave of us? You don't even *pretend* to care what I think? If you feel so little respect for your family, then get. Go! Leave my house and don't trouble yourself to return."

Reuben's mother stepped forward with her hands clutched in supplication. She cried out, "Ebenezer, no!"

Ebenezer didn't even glance at his wife as her face dissolved into tears. He snapped, "Enough woman. The boy has made his disdain for us more than clear." Reuben's mother shrank back.

Reuben opened his eyes wide, and then anger flooded into his veins. "I am the one who humbled myself to come and say goodbye. It's *your* insufferable pride that has driven this family apart. It's your arrogance and stubbornness to reclaim some paltry honor you lost that blinds you to the fact that my future is in the law, not in fishing boats. I am destined for more!"

"Then why are you here? Have you just come to crow over us with your good fortune?" Ebenezer's eyes were two burning coals. "You think you know what is most important in life? Go and claim it then. See if it gives you all you desire."

Reuben gritted his teeth, and with an effort, he pulled his gaze off his father's face to look at his brothers. Both had hunched shoulders and their eyes cast to the floor. "Goodbye, Zeb. Goodbye, Ben."

Neither answered him. How could they, with their father poisoning them against him?

Reuben's mother gasped out a sob. Ignoring her husband, she ran and threw her arms around Reuben, weeping. Reuben breathed her familiar scent and his heart wobbled. He realized how little he had seen his mother these past years, and his conscience pricked him. He felt his mother's soft embrace wind around his frame and his mind. It brought an impulsive desire to apologize to his father and to try to repair the breach between them.

The idea lasted only a moment, just until lifted his gaze to his father's bitter face. His resolve hardened within him. The disease in the family tree was entirely his father's doing. Why should he humble himself when he wasn't the one at fault? If he needed to prune himself to thrive, then so be it.

He pulled back from his mother and turned and left his childhood home without a word or backward glance. As he smoothed his hand over his shawl he realized it was damp with his mother's tears.

Reuben made a quick round of the town. He mumbled an awkward goodbye to Uncle Zebedee and Aunt Naomi, both of them looking at him with pity. Reuben left them as soon as politeness allowed. He didn't want pity for his estrangement from his father; he wanted happy congratulations as he stood on the threshold of greatness!

His farewell to Ezra, his boyhood teacher, was more satisfactory. Ezra was both happy and proud of him, and Reuben felt a warmth of gratefulness to his old rabbi.

Reuben then spent long minutes with Daniel, and he was careful to thank the aged Pharisee for his attention over the years. Without Daniel, none of this would have come to be.

As twilight descended, Reuben wavered outside Tamar's house, uncertain if he wanted to go inside. He knew Beth wasn't there. There would be no farewell from the best friend of his youth. He remembered her happy pride for him all those years ago when they had sat before her house and talked of the future. Was she still proud of him, or did she think he was an enemy?

He drew his courage and went inside. Tamar had always been kind to him. He couldn't slight her now.

Tamar was surprised to see him, but she bustled around the room bringing him refreshments and refusing to let him go until he had eaten. Reuben knelt at the low table and took some of the wheat cakes she pressed on him and sipped a cup of wine.

"I'm sad to see you go," Tamar said, her motherly face soft. "I wish your leaving wasn't so sudden. Beth would have wanted to say goodbye."

Reuben swallowed the wheat cake with difficulty. His throat suddenly felt too small.

Tamar continued gently, "I know this distance between the two of you has been hard on her. She misses your friendship."

Reuben cleared his throat, and his voice in his own ears was sullen, "It seems she has found a new friend. Jesus."

Tamar chuckled, unperturbed by his bitterness. "She has, yes. But there is something about the friends of our childhood, isn't there? They remind us of who we were—before we grew up and found the world grew too."

Unbidden, Reuben's memories flew back through time, remembering the simple pleasures of boyhood. His mind was flooded with the recollections of his mother smoothing his brow as he drifted to sleep. He remembered chasing Beth through the grassy fields, the sun glinting off her hair. He could almost hear the easy laughter and feel the comfortable feeling of love and acceptance.

For the first time in his life, he felt the pang of longing for a simpler time, when the future was a distant worry and his pleasures were firmly fastened in the present moment. He jerked back from the memories, finding they brought as much pain as sweetness. Reuben slammed down his cup harder than he intended, sloshing a little wine on the table. He leaped to his feet.

"I should go. I will pray for your continued good health and happiness."

He fled from the room and didn't look back. He rushed to Philemon's house. He packed with feverish speed, stuffing his few belongings into a single bag. He ate supper with Philemon's family as the sun set, speaking a little too brightly of the future, his laugh a little too loud.

He rose with the sun the next morning, and Philemon and his wife said farewell to him in the doorway.

Philemon took a step forward. He put an ink-stained hand on Reuben's shoulder and smiled encouragingly. "It's okay, you know, to be a little afraid of the future. It's natural to be sad to leave your family and home."

Reuben swallowed back a bitter retort. He was not sad to leave Capernaum, not one bit. This was the moment he had waited for, for a long, long time. Instead, he said a polite goodbye to Philemon. He had no strong affection for the scribe, but he would always be grateful to him for giving him a trade.

Reuben's mood lightened the further he got from home. He was able to laugh at his foolish sentimentality and return once more to anticipations of the happy future that he would have in Jerusalem.

By the time he met up with Simeon in Jericho, he was feeling buoyant and eager. Together they traveled east into the province of Perea, Simeon riding his dappled gray horse and Reuben on foot as usual. Reuben had never visited the territory past the opulent and green center of Jericho before, and he looked about himself with interest. The area was mountainous, often arid and coarse, but had valleys of lush fertility with flowing streams and plentiful palm and date trees.

They turned off the main road and bent their steps down a smooth, straight lane spread with crushed limestone and bordered by fig trees. Soon they could see an expansive, modern villa surrounded by fields of grapevines. The grapes had been picked in the late summer and crushed on the wine press on the hill, yielding their rich juices. Now, as spring returned to the land, dozens of workers moved down the rows caring for the tender plants as the cycle began again.

"It is clear why the scriptures refer to Israel as a vineyard," Simeon looked down from his horse and smiled at his pupil. "It is a noble and rich profession."

"With a wonderful product as well," Reuben dared to make a feeble joke, and Simeon granted him a small smile.

Reuben's eyes swept over the rich land, his mind on its owner. He was eager to see Eliab again. Eliab's final year of schooling had been Reuben's first year, and the open young man had eased Reuben's transition to urban life. He had felt adrift when Eliab returned home to Perea, leaving Reuben with only envious fellow students and the servant, Jacob, for companionship.

When they came to the large double doors of the villa, a servant greeted them with a bow. They were ushered at once into a cool hall. Rabbi and disciple were seated on a bench and offered refreshing cups of watered wine from a silver pitcher. They had their sandals removed and their dusty feet washed.

As the cool water soothed his tired feet, Reuben wondered what answers Eliab sought from his previous teacher. Simeon had informed him that Eliab's father had died a year ago. Eliab had inherited the bulk of the fortune. Now that his year of mourning had ended, the wealthy young man wondered what his scholarly and political goals should be for the future.

"Rabbi Simeon," a cheerful voice called out.

Reuben stood in his damp, bare feet. He saw his friend approaching, richly dressed and with arms outstretched in welcome. Eliab noticed Reuben with a surprised expression that gave way to pleasure.

"And you've brought Reuben. Excellent! Excellent!" Eliab embraced Simeon, the former disciple dressed in fine, scarlet robes and the teacher in simple linen.

Reuben looked his old friend up and down with growing unease. Reuben had only seen him in plain student's garb with a tasseled prayer shawl over his shoulders. The simple attire had disguised the vast difference in upbringing and rank between him and his friend. This blatant reminder of Eliab's wealth introduced a sudden, personal smallness Reuben disliked. He began to withdraw into himself.

Eliab, however, came over and wrapped Reuben in a firm embrace. Eliab's open manner melted the years and barriers of rank away, and he was Reuben's old friend once more.

Reuben felt foolish for his jealousy. He laughed and pulled back to examine his friend up and down in an obvious way. "You do know you look like an exotic bird, don't you?" Reuben teased.

Eliab clapped him on the shoulder. "Well, I won't say what you look like in those black robes, my friend."

As they shared another laugh and a second, more exuberant hug, Simeon watched with aloof approval. Eliab led his two guests from the entranceway into a pillared room.

As Reuben accepted a plump, cushioned seat, he took in Eliab's home. Soft drapes and tapestries were on the walls. Cushions were heaped on plush couches and a lyre lay on a small table, as did a collection of scrolls. A half-eaten plate of fruit sat nearby and a woman's shawl was draped on a chair. Pretty ornaments and unusual curios crowded every open space, adding a feel of happy clutter.

Eliab told the men that his mother and sisters were home with him, but they didn't appear, giving the men privacy for this first interview. Eliab's younger brother, along with his wife and children, were staying in the family's Jerusalem house, so the three men had the large room entirely to themselves. After Simeon and Reuben had dined on choice meats and fruits with more wine from Eliab's vineyard, it was time for Eliab to speak with Simeon.

"I am glad you could come, Simeon," Eliab leaned forward. "I'll admit I have been struggling to know what the right thing is to do, now that my circumstances have changed."

Simeon tented his fingers under a small smile. "I am always available to help my gifted disciples, even when they leave to study under others. But, surely you asked Mordecai's advice. What counsel did he give you?"

"Is Mordecai one of the elder's here?" Reuben asked as he reached for another date.

Simeon frowned at Reuben's interruption, and Reuben flushed. He had grown too used to Philemon and Daniel's easier ways. He chastised himself.

"Yes, Mordecai is an elder," Simeon answered with a tiny flash in his dark eyes. "I know him well. He's a little . . . country."

Eliab pulled on his ear and drew a deep breath before speaking, a habit that brought back many memories to Reuben. "My father's death was unexpected. When I entered my discipleship I had thought it would be years—decades perhaps—before I was asked to step in and take my father's place. The running of the estate is time-consuming and requires vigilant attention, even with a good steward. Where does that leave my studies of law and tradition? With the constraints on my time, should I still work towards becoming a lawyer or teacher?"

Simeon nodded and tapped his slender fingers against his lips. He was a man well acquainted with the difficulties of the real world and the responsibilities of wealth. His mind was not clouded with fluffy thoughts of unnecessary, self-righteous sacrifice. "I understand your problem. And what, may I ask, does Mordecai advise?"

Eliab sighed and toyed with his silver goblet. "He's frustrated at my new, busier schedule. He wants more of my attention, *more* studying even as I struggle to carry the current load." He pursed his lips and shook his head. "He—and I, if truth be told—are worried that I won't be able to do both—become a Pharisee and retain my property. " He looked away and mumbled, "My mother thinks I might do better as a Sadducee."

Reuben burned to ask questions, but he bit his tongue. Simeon furrowed his brow as he pondered Eliab's conundrum. His head did not move, but his eyes swept over the luxurious room, the proof of the valuable property.

"Do not be too hasty to abandon your calling to join the Pharisees," Simeon said. "We may not have the power of the Sadducees, but our party is a pure one, and we need—" he paused delicately "—*noble* participants to forward our teachings. There are many ways to serve."

Reuben thought he caught Simeon's veiled meaning. To have political sway and the clout to petition before kings and rulers, the Pharisees relied on well-standing families. Eliab, as a wealthy land-owner, had a voice in the world. He would be an asset to the Pharisees. Of course, not all Pharisees saw the blessing of wealth in quite the same way. From the advice he had given, Reuben suspected Mordecai to be one of those who saw wealth as a burden, an obstacle to devoted faith.

Eliab was still troubled. "But my studies require so much time, and I feel so divided—"

"I will speak with Mordecai. I'm sure we can arrange things so that you can still study and participate in our party. Perhaps you will not be a lawyer or a great teacher, but you can still be useful." Simeon raised his eyebrow. "Surely you still hold strong to the beliefs that made you choose the life of a disciple? Surely you still wish to do good work for the Lord?"

Eliab was quick to say, "Of course I do."

Reuben hid a little smile and wondered if Eliab could have said anything else.

Simeon clapped his hands on his lap. "Very well then. I will speak with Mordecai tomorrow. Do not forget, wealth is a gift from God, given to the righteous. Think of our forefathers, Abraham, Isaac, and Jacob. They were wealthy and powerful because of their faithfulness. While grasping after wealth and trying to rise above the place we have been given by God may be shameful, you were born into your position of wealth and power. Do not scorn the favor that God has shown you. He is obviously pleased with you."

Reuben flushed with embarrassment. His family was almost penniless. Ebenezer was a hard worker, but backward and stubborn. Was Reuben trying to grasp at wealth and honor that he did not deserve? His hand rose to his shawl and he took comfort in the soft linen. No! He just wanted to serve God in the best way he could. If that meant he needed to rise above the position he had been born into, surely no one would fault him.

Simeon waved away offers of more wine and rose to his feet, "If you will forgive me, I am wearied from our journey. Would you have a servant show me where I may retire?"

"Yes, of course," Eliab said.

He summoned a serving boy with a lamp to lead Simeon to the guest quarters. Reuben was not ready for bed yet, and so he remained behind. After Simeon left the room, the young men lost some of their reserve and fell into talking of old times, friends, and past fun.

The hour grew late, and in the safety of the night, Eliab leaned a little closer to Reuben and whispered, "So, this Jesus of Nazareth that everyone is talking about, I've heard that you know him?"

Reuben nodded, then thought better and shook his head, "I don't know him, but I have observed him a lot over the past years. He has spent many months in Capernaum. Too many months."

"Is he like the people say? Are his miracles as fantastic as the rumors profess?"

Reuben pursed his lips, unsure how best to reply. "I've seen him heal, and even raise the dead." Eliab's eyebrows shot up, but Reuben held up a hand in caution as he continued, "But his teachings are adverse. He has no regard for tradition. He's careless of Sabbath observances, and he befriends people of low character. His chosen circle of closest disciples are drawn from common men, including those with questionable histories, like a tax collector. The elders in Capernaum, Bethsaida, and Chorazin are openly opposed to him. The Pharisees from Jerusalem are the same. They don't think he is of God, but a deceiver with power from the devil using sweet words to trick the people."

Eliab pondered Reuben's words for a long minute, but then he shook his head. "I don't think I can agree. I know you have witnessed

Jesus for yourself and my accounts are all second hand, but I can't see how such a powerful man can be of the devil. Why would Satan heal?"

Reuben was knocked off balance at hearing his friend disagree with him so casually. It was unexpected, and truthfully, unwelcome. It reminded him too much of his arguments with Beth. Why did Jesus have to keep interfering in his personal relationships?

Jesus' nature was a matter of great concern and bitterness in Jerusalem, and a topic that Reuben had reflected much upon the past three years. Reuben was offended that Eliab didn't give more credence to his firsthand observations.

Eliab, oblivious to Reuben's mood, poured another drink for each of them. "I think he must be a prophet. Mordecai thinks he may even be Elijah, making the people ready for the coming Messiah."

Reuben's voice was cross as he said, "Then Mordecai and Simeon are going to be hammering at each other tomorrow. Simeon is sure that Jesus means nothing but trouble for our people."

Eliab paused at Reuben's tone, but then grinned conspiratorially and leaned towards his friend. "It would almost be fun to watch my old and my current masters going at each other. Maybe we should go along, just to see."

Eliab had always been fun, slow to anger, and not easily flustered. Reuben found himself chuckling despite himself. It was hard to be angry with the easy-going man.

As the room grew quiet again, Reuben leaned forward. "You don't *really* believe Jesus could be a prophet, do you? The common people follow him because they enjoy a spectacle. They are anxious for a stand against Rome and hope he is it. You're educated. How can you believe?"

Eliab chuckled and answered with a wink. "And I would ask you, how can you not?"

Reuben put his cup aside and shifted to the edge of his seat. "I'm telling you, Eliab, the man is going to bring Rome itself down on our heads. The elders are just waiting for the right time to stop him, for the sake of the people."

Eliab rested his hand on Reuben's shoulder and met Reuben's gaze with equanimity. "The prophets were never popular in their time either. If he was universally accepted I actually might have greater doubts. But as it is . . ." he trailed off.

Reuben could not refute the past, but the people had advanced past the foolishness and hardheartedness of their forefathers.

Eliab took a long drink and set his cup on the low table. The wealthy landowner darted his eyes around the room and then whispered, "Don't tell Simeon, but there are some of our sect who have become disciples of Jesus' teachings."

Reuben sat back, surprised. Besides his cousin, Simon the leper, all he had ever heard from the Pharisees was malice towards Jesus. What did this mean, that those who loved the law and its traditions could also accept Jesus? How could that be possible? The idea repulsed him.

Reuben tried again. "If you could only hear him, you'd understand. The man sets himself up as greater than Moses even as he lives and behaves like a humble commoner. The presumption is ridiculous."

"Well, I'll be able to judge for myself soon enough," Eliab grinned. "I hear that Jesus is traveling through Perea on his way to Jerusalem. Let's go together to hear him speak. I'm so eager to hear him. It is odd how strong the desire is, even though I've never laid eyes on him before."

Reuben shifted at that statement. He jerked to his feet, declaring he was tired. He needed Eliab to know the truth about Jesus. He couldn't lose another friend.

Simeon went to Mordecai the next morning after breakfast. When he returned he was thin-lipped and curt, but he told Eliab that his training would continue on a more relaxed schedule. Eliab could reduce his studies to keep up the maintenance of his prosperous property.

"Mordecai was adamant that you entrust it all to your steward," Simeon scoffed. "Mordecai is a simple man, with a simple life. He doesn't understand the responsibilities of wealth and property."

Eliab looked relieved. "I do want to ensure that the property stays productive. I have family members to care for. I wouldn't want to pass it to my heir in a lesser state than I received it from my father." He stroked his chin and added, almost as a hasty afterthought. "I'm sure God would be pleased that I'm being responsible with the wealth He has blessed me with."

A few days passed while Reuben and Simeon stayed as Eliab's guests. Eliab's mother and sisters joined them in the evenings. Reuben found the unmarried girls pleasant and attractive to look at, yet his mind continued to turn back to Michal. The last expression she had worn for him was of hurt—hurt that he had caused her. Reuben wondered how long it would be before he forgot his feelings for her.

Word trickled in that Jesus was indeed in the country. Eliab was excited, but he hid his eagerness from his former rabbi. Simeon complained that Jesus was still parading about with his flock of misfits, and he dedicated long minutes to cutting Jesus down to size. Reuben kept his thoughts to himself. He didn't want to talk about Jesus at all.

On the fourth day since Jesus came into the region, Simeon left early in the morning to speak with the elders of the synagogue of Amathus, the base of the Pharisee sect in the province of Perea. Simeon was barely out the door when Eliab rounded on Reuben and entreated him to join him in seeking out Jesus. Reuben was hesitant. He didn't want to hear Jesus. He also didn't want to displease Simeon, not when he was finally back with his rabbi to stay. However, he reasoned that seeing Jesus in the flesh might dispel some of Eliab's cloud of fancy. Reuben, being unbiased, could point out the flaws that Eliab's overwhelming desire for a prophet might obscure.

The friends walked side by side. Eliab was grinning but Reuben felt like a little boy shirking his father's orders. They found Jesus outside a nearby village, seated with a crowd around him, teaching them.

Reuben took mental notes with his arms crossed. The teachings of Jesus were old news to Reuben now. The same words about a kingdom of heaven, a call to repent, and Jesus exhorting the people to live good lives. Reuben had to grudgingly admit that some of what Jesus said was good advice, though his phrasing was too earthy and common. If Reuben sorted Jesus' words and just selected the bits of advice on how to live a good life, he thought he could appreciate Jesus as a moral teacher. But the man insisted on going several steps too far. Not content with being simply a rabbi, he persisted in calling himself the Son of Man. Reuben recalled how many times Jesus had trampled all over the traditions and shook his head. It was obvious.

Jesus was not a moral teacher but a dangerous man trying to lead the people away from the truth.

Not all could discern the lies and deception. Eliab's face lit up like a rising sun as he drank in Jesus' words. Reuben frowned. This could not end well.

Little voices began to punctuate the air, and soon everyone was looking down the road to where a stream of children and their mothers were coming in a noisy, ragtag bunch, giggling and playing as they walked. They completely disrupted Jesus' teaching, and Reuben grinned.

A few of Jesus' disciples stepped towards the little crowd of children, trying to shoo them away. "You've interrupted the rabbi," one snapped. The mothers' faces darkened and their pace slowed. The children were crestfallen as the disciples waved their arms at them.

Jesus leaped to his feet. "Don't send them away," he called. "The kingdom of heaven belongs to ones such as this!"

The disciples looked surprised, but the children rushed past them to Jesus, crowding around him as if he were a favorite brother or uncle. Jesus laughed and talked with them, setting his hands on their heads to bless them. The mothers came forward holding their infants and held them out so Jesus could bless them too.

Reuben rolled his eyes at the whole scene.

The mothers left and took the children with them, heading back to the village. Jesus rose, preparing to leave, his disciples with him. With the now familiar swoop in his gut, Reuben recognized Beth among the women. He remembered again the image of them playing in the fields of tall grass. He felt the same pang of loss for their carefree spirits. He sighed. How had their paths grown so far apart?

The easy chatter of Jesus' followers was a dull hum as Reuben stared at Beth, a new concern growing. It was well known that Jesus was heading towards Jerusalem. Only a fool would think Jesus could enter the Holy City without conflict. Jesus had stayed in the outskirts for months now, avoiding run-ins with those in power, aware he had drawn too much attention to himself. The time was coming when Jesus would have to answer for his words, and Reuben had no desire for Beth to suffer along with her rabbi. If only he could convince her of Jesus' falseness.

Reuben was so lost in his thoughts that he didn't even notice Eliab leave his side. With a jolt, Reuben glanced right and left as Eliab knelt before the Nazarene. He fervently hoped Simeon would not appear.

"Teacher?" Eliab said. "What good thing shall I do that I may obtain eternal life?"

Jesus studied Eliab with a knowing expression, his eyes seeming to take in everything at once. "Why are you asking me about what is good? There is One who is good." Jesus deferred humbly. Then he said, "But if you wish to enter into life, keep the commandments."

Eliab appeared frustrated, and Reuben was surprised at Jesus' basic, generic reply. He screwed up his mouth. Where were the pithy parables?

Eliab persisted and asked, "Which ones?"

Reuben, despite himself, was curious to learn what the Nazarene valued most out of the six hundred and thirteen commandments. Which was the most important was a matter of constant debate between Pharisee schools and their teachers.

But Jesus responded with a basic answer once more, listing several of the ten commandments. "You shall not commit murder; you shall not commit adultery; you shall not steal; you shall not bear false witness; honor your father and your mother, and you shall love your neighbor as yourself."

Reuben saw Eliab was even more frustrated and it showed in his tone when he cried out, "But I have done all of that. What am I still lacking?"

Jesus gave him a small, understanding smile. "If you wish to be complete, go and sell your possessions and give to the poor, and you will have treasure in heaven."

Reuben watched Eliab's face as Jesus spoke. It was like a dreary cloud moving in on what had been a delightful morning. Reuben was sure Eliab was dwelling on his spacious home, his fields, his fine clothes, and many possessions. Jesus wanted him to cast aside the work of his father and grandfather, his birthright. It would impoverish not only him but his mother and sisters too. Reuben shook his head.

Jesus rose to his feet, took a step closer to Eliab, and put his hand on his shoulder as he said, "Come, follow me."

Eliab opened his mouth, his face full of longing. For a long, tense moment Reuben thought Eliab was about to throw away his life. But the moment passed and Eliab stepped back with a bowed head, allowing Jesus' arm to drop. Eliab turned and began to shuffle home.

Reuben saw his friend's sorrowful expression as he passed. Reuben, though relieved, was angered that his friend had been brought so low by the Nazarene.

Reuben felt the weight of a gaze, and he turned to see Beth's large brown eyes were on him. For once, he couldn't read her expression. Full of nostalgia, he gave her what he hoped was the smile of an old friend before he hastened to catch up to Eliab.

Eliab was not himself for the rest of Reuben's visit. Though the rich young man tried his best to conceal it, Reuben could discern how dejected he was. He had never seen anything affect Eliab this way. It was not the man's nature to be downtrodden. Reuben entertained himself in quiet moments by picturing all the cutting things he would say to Jesus if given the chance.

Simeon, thankfully, was oblivious to Eliab's silent suffering and was in excellent spirits. Reuben could tell his rabbi was proud that he had secured a wealthy, politically influential landowner for the Pharisee party.

On the road back to Jerusalem, Reuben was sure to inform Simeon all that he had learned from Eliab about several Pharisees turning into disciples of Jesus of Nazareth. He wished he had more specific names to give, but Simeon was pleased enough with this hint of information.

"Well done, Reuben. This shows that our time has run short. We must do something to stop the man before he divides our party. I will speak to our loyal brethren when we get back to Jerusalem and we will decide what must be done."

28

A BROKEN SANDAL

They camped near the Jordan River where the grasses spread thick and green and the trees reached for the sky, proud of their place by the life-giving water. Dusky twilight began to descend. The air turned sweet as the insects sang out their thanks for the day, a peaceful, comforting melody.

Beth knelt on the shore washing out the cookpot. Mary came up beside her, another pot in her hand.

"Lentil stew again." Mary made a wry face and stooped to fill her dirty pot with water.

Beth chuckled. "Not to spoil the surprise, but it'll likely be lentil stew tomorrow too."

Mary tipped her head back and groaned. "I miss fresh curds. And roasted meat, and proper bread." She scrubbed forcefully, as if to punish the pot for always giving the same old meals.

"Cheer up. We'll be in Jericho soon," Beth said with a smile. "There will be lots to choose from in the market. I'm sure you can find something for a treat." She rinsed her pot, dumped out the water and stepped back from the water. She felt the strap on her sandal give out and sighed with annoyance. "That's the third time today," she complained as she slipped it off her foot and inspected where the leather strap had been knotted multiple times.

"While I'm shopping for my treat, you can get new sandals," Mary said.

Beth laughed. "You forget, we weren't all wealthy before following Jesus. Peter has no coins left. We are entirely dependent on the generosity of others."

"So get some from the community purse," Mary said and stood up, bouncing droplets out of the round, clay pot.

Beth shook her head and tugged on the strap. "It'll last a while yet."

Mary glanced at the thin leather and raised her brows. "If you say so."

As they walked back into the camp, Mary laughingly called to Peter, "You need to convince your wife to get some new sandals, she is practically barefoot."

Beth flushed as multiple eyes turned her way and tried to laugh as Peter looked over with a furrowed brow. She busied herself arranging the fire, which was beginning to die down. Peter came over and leaned close.

"Why didn't you tell me you need new sandals?"

"We haven't the coins," Beth whispered. "They will do."

Peter was silent for a long moment. When he spoke, his voice was sullen. "You must think I am a poor provider."

Beth was pained by his expression. "Of course not." She forced a chuckle. "Really, Peter, Mary was only teasing."

Peter did not laugh with her. With weighted shoulders, he threw himself down beside the other men. Beth hoped he soon would forget the reminder that they were currently penniless, but his expression showed otherwise. Was his pride hurt knowing he was unable to provide properly because he had left his fishing nets behind? On their wedding day Beth had been confident in Peter's ability to care for her. She was clothed and fed, but right now that was due to the generosity of others. It was a humble way to live, perhaps more so for an able-bodied man.

Yet, hadn't Jesus asked that well-dressed man with Reuben to give up everything to follow him? Hadn't Jesus told them that it was easier for a camel to go through the eye of a needle than for a rich man to enter the kingdom of heaven?

Thoughts of Reuben brought a tightness to her throat. He had smiled at her for the first time in many months. She had been happy to see it, but the reminder of how rarely he wore a contented expression was difficult. She missed the curious and enthusiastic friend of her childhood. Now, he took one look at Jesus and retreated behind a wall of coldness. How could he hear the same teachings, witness the same healing power, and still not believe?

Jesus, sitting nearby, noticed Peter's expression and asked, "What's troubling you, Peter?"

Peter's gaze flicked to Beth before he asked, "You see that we've left everything and followed you. What will there be for us?"

The others looked over and conversation died as they waited to hear what Jesus would reply.

Jesus answered at once, "Truly I say to you, that when the time of regeneration comes, you who have followed me will sit on twelve thrones and judge the twelve tribes of Israel. And you who have left brothers, or sisters, or parents, or children, or farms for my sake, will receive many times as much, and you will inherit eternal life." Beth saw Peter's eyes go wide. This was far beyond coins for sandals.

Beth gazed at her husband, a simple fisherman, and tried to picture him upon a throne. The idea was so incredible that she couldn't manage it, yet pride rose up within her. Her husband a judge, like the heroes of old!

The other disciples began to talk all at once, but Jesus held up his hands. His grave expression and sober tone tempered them. "But many who are first will be last, and the last will be first."

Beth furrowed her brow. The conversation picked up around her while she was lost in introspection. How could the last be first? Jesus rarely gave them a message without building on some foundation he had laid before. She put her mind to work.

She thought of the Gentiles who believed in Jesus, even as the sons of Abraham rejected the Messiah who had been sent to them. She reflected on the tax collectors and sinners who had turned to Jesus with joy, while the Pharisees turned their back in scorn. She thought of Jesus telling them that the greatest in the kingdom of heaven were those who were like little children. She remembered the first time she had heard Jesus teach on the hill near her home. Blessed are the meek, the gentle, the peacemakers, the persecuted—not the proud, the brash, the war chiefs, the conquerors.

It was almost as if Jesus was telling them that the world was upside down, that the things he valued were not the things the world valued.

The stars began to show their bright faces, and the disciples rolled themselves in blankets, outer robes, and mantles. Beth slipped off her worn sandals and set them to the side before she laid down. She smiled at them—the knot would hold for a while yet. She could make-do for now. Her reward for faithfulness was ahead, somewhere.

Beth awoke late the next morning, a little stiff and sore from the miles they had walked. She noticed at once that Peter had disappeared. She rose to her feet, and a quick look around told her that all of the Twelve were gone, and so was Jesus.

She stretched, knuckling her back. She washed her face in the river, splashing the cool water over her neck and arms. When she came back to the cold bed of ashes, she saw the group returning with grim faces. They began to break camp at once.

She went up to Peter and asked, "What happened?"

"Just . . . just forget it."

She frowned at him but saw his expression was closed. She swallowed her questions and began to roll up her blanket.

It didn't take more than a few minutes to dismantle their simple camp, then Jesus led the way towards Jericho with his Twelve following close on his heels. The mood among them was strained and quiet.

The women glanced at each other wondering what had happened. Naomi pressed her lips together into a thin line and went to walk with her sons, questioning them. Beth sighed. Maybe her aunt would have better luck.

Judas Iscariot lagged behind, shaking his head. Beth and Mary Magdalene fell in behind him, hitching bags on their shoulders. Beth overheard Judas muttering to Simon the Zealot, "Why does he speak like that? Why does he dwell on crucifixion? Does he fear the people won't accept him as Messiah? Has he forgotten the vast multitudes who believe in him already?"

Beth's heart turned over with a sickening thump, and she drew closer so she could hear better. Jesus had once again spoken of his death?

Simon answered as they walked on, "You know my views on the

matter. He will meet opposition in Jerusalem. I have faith he will overcome it."

"But does he?" Judas tugged on his beard. "We have seen miracles. We've seen how Jesus bests every scribe or lawyer who tries to go up against him. Despite all of this proof, he still doubts himself. He speaks too often of this death and resurrection, and he's grown more quiet and serious. I don't like it. You may have faith he will overcome, but I fear he is second-guessing his abilities."

Simon was silent for a long moment. Beth felt uneasy at this picture Judas painted of Jesus. Simon replied with hesitation, "What should we do if he is?"

Judas hissed, "I won't let these years go to waste. I will not wait for another. We've seen too many so-called Messiahs come and die. Your own family has paid the cost of a revolutionary leader gone wrong. It's time for Jesus to take his stand. Jerusalem will be the place and Passover is the perfect time. Perhaps all he needs is some ... encouragement."

Beth empathized with Judas' doubts and struggles, for she had wondered the same thing. How could a man with Jesus' power die at the hands of his own people? How could a man claim to be their Messiah and then speak of his death? Even as she worried along with Judas, she felt her curiosity nudged by his comments about the cost Simon's family had paid. What had happened to them?

Passionate Simon, zealous though he was, placed his hand on Judas and for once spoke caution. "Jesus has never needed us to tell him what to do. Do not presume, Judas."

Judas's eyes flicked back, and he noticed how close Beth was following. She and Judas both flushed, and the men dropped the conversation.

Beth trudged silently. Jesus had enough power to cleanse the nation and restore Israel. It was what he wanted, wasn't it? She worried her bottom lip, wondering what this trip to Jerusalem would bring.

They camped just outside of Jericho in a quiet place away from the road. Beth was sure Jericho would swarm Jesus as soon as they learned he was near, and Jesus seemed to be preparing himself for the onslaught by drawing away by himself for prayer.

Beth had the more humble task of preparing a simple lentil stew over one of the campfires. She poured water into the cool pot and set it near the fire to slowly warm. If it heated too quickly the pot would crack. Mary Magdalene groaned when she saw the red grains sliding into the pot, and Beth had to laugh. She used a branch to gather the glowing coals and nestled the wide-mouthed clay pot right beside them. It would take almost an hour to cook the grains through, but then they would have a savory, filling stew to replenish them after the miles they had walked.

Peter brought her an armful of fuel for the fire. Mary Magdalene crouched on her heels, setting unleavened barley loaves on the coals, flipping the flatbread with nimble fingers as it cooked, the way Beth had taught her. On a second campfire other Galilean women worked to prepare food for their husbands and sons. Andrew and Matthew were reading from a scroll. Thaddeus was mending a tear in his coat.

Beth sighed with contentment. Everything was so simple today, so ordinary. It was moments like these when it was easy to forget where they were going—and what might happen when they got there.

As Beth's eyes landed on each faithful disciple, several dozen in number, she realized she could name every one of them. She smiled and shook her head. She marveled that she had come to know so many people beyond her hometown and that they knew and accepted the quiet fisherman's wife as one of them.

Beth turned her pot to cook the stew evenly, and saw Naomi rise. Her aunt moved away from her place by the fire with a look of determination. She called to her two sons and they came up and bent their tall, shaggy heads to her shorter, gray one. She turned on her heel and marched away to where Jesus had gone. Her sons followed, casting nervous glances back at the others.

They were gone a little while, and James and John appeared abashed as they returned with their mother. Naomi went back to her campfire, her face thoughtful, but Peter beckoned the brothers over.

"What was that all about?" Peter asked.

James and John shared a look, and James said sheepishly, "Well, remember when Jesus told us about our coming rewards? About sitting with him on twelve thrones?" James cleared his throat and continued, "Our mother asked that Jesus would give us places of honor, one at his right and one at his left."

"What?" Peter was indignant, and Beth paused in her stirring. Was Jesus at the point of deciding such things?

John held up his hands. "He said it wasn't for him to decide. He said his Father was taking care of that."

Peter jumped to his feet. "What a thing to ask! And secretly too, sneaking off like that."

His words and tone drew the attention of other disciples who came forward to hear what was going on. Soon many of them were arguing, trying to determine who was foremost among them. The women began to point to their men, and the noise grew until no one could hear what the other was saying. Beth stood frozen with wide eyes as she listened to the quarrel, her cook pot forgotten in the chaos. Though she didn't add her voice, she had her own ideas of who was great among the disciples. She was proud of her husband, the disciple who stepped out so often in bravery. He was older than many of the other disciples too. Didn't that count for something?

In the span of a heartbeat, everyone fell silent. Jesus was in their midst, his eyes flinty. They shrunk back, faces reddening, and Beth's cheeks heated at her unspoken words.

Jesus shook his head. "Listen to you," he chastised. "You've seen firsthand how the godless rulers throw their weight around, how quickly a little power goes to their heads." He let his words hang, allowing them long minutes to dwell on the selfish and brutal rulers of their day. Eyes began to sink to the ground, feet to shuffle. None of them wanted to be a judge like that. "It's *not* going to be that way with you." His tone was insistent, commanding. "Whoever wants to be great must become a servant. Whoever wants to be first among you must be your slave. The Son of Man did not come to be served, but to serve others—and then give away his life in exchange for the many who are held hostage."

Jesus looked from one to the other, making sure they had heard him. Everyone nodded and dispersed, embarrassed and quiet.

Peter sat near Beth plucking thoughtfully at a loose thread on his tunic. The camp felt hushed; the only noise was the rustle of wind through the trees.

Beth dragged her attention back to the simmering pot, turning it and giving it a good stir. She crouched on her heels and watched Jesus as he moved throughout the camp, talking with the others. She shook her head. She refused to believe Jesus was leading them to Jerusalem just so he could die.

29

HOSANNA!

It was pilgrimage time, when people began to lock up their homes and businesses to go to Jerusalem for the festival.

Beth, with the ominous prophecies of Jesus ringing in her ears, felt a little like a soldier going to battle. A soldier hoped for the best possible outcome—that God would be with them and victory would be theirs—but he also felt fear like a rock in his stomach as he worried that this would be the end of everything.

Perhaps the picture of a soldier rose to her mind on this cloudless dawn because this older district was near the site of the mighty Jericho of history, long ago conquered by the warrior Joshua. The once impenetrable walls had collapsed by the power of God as the priests blasted their horns. The divine sign was undeniable proof that God was with them.

Now, Jesus strode forth, leading a quiet procession as they prepared to cross the lengthy gap between the city districts of Old Jericho and New Jericho.

Just behind him were his Twelve. Beth and the other disciples who had followed the past three years came next. Then followed hundreds of other pilgrims. Some had followed Jesus for days or weeks, and many others had just joined in this morning as Jesus set out on the final leg to Jerusalem. People yawned and murmured to each other as they stretched their legs and breathed in the damp, dawn air.

They were a stone's throw before the gates of New Jericho when they walked by two ragged men sleeping by the road. As the crowds passed, the men awoke. Beth saw their necks craning as they positioned their ears to better hear what was happening. She realized the beggars were blind.

"What's going on?" one of them called.

"Jesus of Nazareth is on his way to Jerusalem," a voice from the procession answered.

"Jesus!" the man gasped and clutched the man next to him. Beth was startled at the shock and awe that filled their unseeing faces.

They scrambled to their feet, clutching each other for support as they stumbled forward, bony hands clawing outwards. "Master! Have mercy on us! Have mercy, Son of David!"

Beth's heart went out to them, and she looked ahead to see if Jesus had heard.

A man stepped out of the procession, and Beth frowned as he scolded, "Hush! He is on his way to Jerusalem." Others also hollered for the ragged, dirty men to be quiet.

The men ignored them and pleaded all the louder, "Mercy, Son of David!"

Beth saw with relief that Jesus was doubling back, and he stopped a few feet from the trembling, frantic men. He spoke kindly, "What do you want from me?"

"It's truly you!" the one gasped and dropped to his knees. "We've prayed that this day might come." He wept aloud.

His friend bowed to the ground, and with hands stretched before him in supplication he cried out, "Master, we want our eyes opened. We want to see!"

Beth saw Jesus' face, and he looked deeply moved. He crouched before the trembling men. He touched their eyes and their eyelids fluttered. Their eyes focused on Jesus. Their faces were illuminated with awe and joy.

"We are healed!" they exclaimed. They wept and kissed Jesus' hand. Jesus raised them to their feet and the two men stared in wonder at the huge crowd, which gaped back in amazement.

"Son of David!" was echoed among the crowd in awe as they

stared at Jesus with eagerness.

The two men followed the crowds into the city and caught the attention of many people who recognized them as the blind beggars. Beth's worry sank beneath a surge of hopeful anticipation. To Beth's mind, this was a new, divine sign given in Jericho. God was again with His people.

As soon as they left New Jericho behind, the road slanted steeply upwards. Beth eyed the trail with trepidation. The road from Jericho to Jerusalem was a hot, treacherous path that wound beside steep canyons and sheltered vicious bandits. She drew a deep breath, steeling herself.

The city fell away behind them as they climbed the Ascent of Adummin. Her calves burned and sweat beaded on her brow from exertion, despite the early hour. The cloudless sky portended the day would only grow hotter. Conversations died as the mass of people labored up the incline. Carrion birds wheeling in the sky overheard did not help lighten the mood.

The people were forced to walk single file, and in some places, the canyon was so steep on one side that a stumble could cost a life. Beth heard a man behind her puffing and talking to his companion.

"Curse this wretched road. Wait for a moment, I need a drink."

"This is hardly the place to stop," came a tired, sour response. "We'd better keep moving until we make it to the next fortress."

"Oh relax, didn't you hear? We'll have no trouble on the way, I swear it. That highwayman, Barabbas, has been arrested and taken for trial before Pontius Pilate."

"Good riddance," the other man grunted. "Barabbas was a plague. Judas the Galilean may encourage his followers to punish those too friendly with Rome, but—" the man caught his breath "—when zealousness makes you murder your own countrymen, your revolution has turned."

Beth, watching her step and close on Mary Magdalene's heels, allowed a fleeting moment of relief at the gossip. The famous bandit had been a menace for a long time; she remembered speaking of the man with Reuben years ago when they had been little more than children.

"Please, let me pass," Simon's voice pleaded. Beth saw with surprise that he had turned and was standing before Mary, blocking her way. His eyes were dark, burning coals in his face, and Beth felt a chill move through her despite the sweat between her shoulder blades.

"There's no room," Mary protested, but he shoved past her, his cloak flapping off the cliff edge into the open air. Mary shook her head at him but kept walking.

"Did I hear you right? Barabbas is arrested?" Simon's wild eyes entreated the man behind Beth. She was short enough that he simply spoke over her head. She felt awkward as she was forced to stop on the narrow, dangerous strip of road, trapped between the two men.

"You did," the man said as he stopped, his tone curious. "Did you know the man? Wait, I recognize you." The man's eyes opened wide. "Weren't you Caleb the silk merchant's son? Aren't you from Jericho?"

"I was." Simon's face was dark.

Beth, feeling out of place, looked away. All she could see was the plunging, deadly canyon to her side. She snapped her eyes away. The Jericho man's face was swathed in pity as he looked at Simon. "Caleb was a good man," the stranger sighed. "It isn't right what happened to him and your mother. For us in Jericho, it was their deaths that caused the turn in opinion against Barabbas."

Simon's voice was strangled as he said, "I hope they crucify him before the Passover so I can be there to see it." He spat over the edge.

The other men raised their eyebrows and Beth shuddered. She wasn't sure if she'd wish crucifixion on her worst enemy.

Simon turned away and started to walk again, filling in the small gap that had grown in the procession. Beth shuffled along, the narrowness of the road keeping her just behind Simon's stiff back.

Well, now she knew his secret. It was no wonder he didn't speak of his family. Perhaps they had supplied silk to the wrong people, according to Barabbas. She wondered about what she had learned, yet didn't think she actually wanted to know the details. From what she had heard of Barabbas' brutal reputation, the deaths of Simon's parents would have been painful and slow.

They passed Cypros, a fortress rebuilt in the days of Antipater, grandfather to Herod Antipas. The stone tower overlooked Jericho with an impressive view. It was one of six fortresses that guarded this important road.

The road climbed and snaked on a ridge above deep canyons lined with reddish limestone until it reached a plateau with more fortresses. The people surged forward, eager to escape from the constraints of the narrow road. As soon as she could, Beth separated herself from Simon and went to stand near Peter, drawing deep breaths, her legs trembling. As they stood at this high point they could already see the Mount of Olives. Jerusalem wasn't far, and it was encouraging to lay eyes on it.

They refreshed themselves with a short rest and some food before it was time to move forward. The road dipped downwards now, and while her calves had burned on the ascent, now her shins began to ache as she shuffled down into the Nahal Og Canyon.

Thanks to the winter rains, the area was not as dry as it would be in the months to come. In the depths of the canyons were shallow springs, often the only source of water. Beth passed a nomadic shepherd with his mixed flock of goats and sheep down near a stream that was swollen from seasonal rain. The stubby plants in this Judean desert were tender, with delicate and beautiful blooms. Soon, all that growth would shrivel in the cruel heat of summer, but for now, it was lovely.

They walked upwards again, out of the canyon. They marched west on the Roman-built road with wide steps cut into the slope. The long mountain ridge, the Mount of Olives, was a beacon ahead, encouraging them forward.

As they neared Jerusalem, the Holy City of God, the mood of the procession grew joyous and hopeful. Passover always reminded the people of freedom from oppression. To walk to Jerusalem in company with a prophet made it all seem even more tangible and near. The crowd had walked for over nine hours, but they still found enough energy to rejoice as they neared the Holy City.

As it left the craggy desert area, the road widened and the river of people burst forward as if a dam had broken open. Beth stayed by Peter, feeling safer near his tall, sturdy presence.

Peter laughed aloud at the intoxicating mood. Beth felt a mixture of nerves and happiness as people whooped and whirled around her. She smiled as the people danced, laughed, and sang. She heard quotes from the psalms and the prophets. Many in the crowd went ahead, over the Mount of Olives and into the city. Others took the road that led to the Southern Gate.

Jesus stopped to rest near Bethphage, a village of priests and their families on the eastern side of the mountain. The mountain blocked the view of Jerusalem, but they felt its presence. Beth hadn't been back to Jerusalem for Passover for several years. Her first visit as a child had been painful and harsh. She folded her hands under her chin and prayed that this visit would be different.

Jesus turned and called two of the loyal disciples and said, "Go into the village. Immediately you will find a donkey and a colt there with her; untie them and bring them to me. If anyone protests tell them, 'The Lord requires them,' and they will be happy to help."

"Of course, Jesus," they replied and trotted away.

Jesus found a shady spot beneath a tree and leaned on its trunk. The others found places to rest as well. The gentle breeze was like a caress on Beth's cheeks, and a bit of shade was welcome.

Other pilgrimage groups passed by. The roads were clogged with people going into the city. Jerusalem's population would swell with unimaginable numbers as the days progressed. The city would have been busy for weeks prior—repairing roads, preparing the ritual baths at the Temple complex, whitewashing the tombs so that none would defile themselves accidentally, and the citizens preparing their guest spaces. The inns could not hold all that came from all over the country.

Beth knew the Romans would have made their own preparations. The garrison would be fully manned, and the governor would be on a sharp lookout for any signs of unrest during the politically-charged Passover celebrations.

Peter sat cross-legged. Beth leaned against him. Mary sat near, watching Jesus. James and John were relaxed with the rabbi, but Naomi came and sat with the other disciples.

Naomi leaned forward and spoke in a whisper, her brow furrowed, "Why does Jesus want a donkey? Walking was good enough for him before."

The others glanced at each other without a clear answer, but Matthew's eyes lit up.

"Of course!" he exclaimed, shaking his finger at the sky. Naomi raised an eyebrow. Matthew dropped his hand, "I mean, of course he needs to ride a donkey. He's fulfilling scripture." He cleared his throat before he recited, "The prophet Zechariah said,

"Say to the daughter of Zion, 'Behold, your King is coming to you,

He is just, and endowed with salvation.
Humble, and mounted on a donkey,
Even on a colt, the foal of a beast of burden.'"

Beth pondered the implications of the prophecy. She wondered if Jesus took this prophecy on himself knowingly, and if he expected the people to understand what he did. If so, did this mean he was ready to reveal himself as king?

The two disciples returned leading a gray donkey. Near her side followed her milky white, nearly grown colt.

"It was just as you said it would be, Rabbi," they said.

Jesus went to the colt, preparing to ride it.

"Rabbi," one objected. "The owner said that no one has ever sat upon the colt."

Jesus merely patted the colt's side. It turned and looked at him with large, glossy eyes and batted his eyelashes with curiosity as Jesus took the lead rope and made reins of it.

"Wait, Rabbi," Peter said as Jesus began to mount. He pulled off his coat and laid it on the animal, and others of the disciples did the same.

Jesus smiled at them and mounted the colt. The young donkey turned his head to sniff his foot. Beth realized she was holding her breath, worried that the animal would shy away. She released it in a puff as Jesus directed the donkey to the road and it obeyed instantly. The mother donkey followed with her ears flicking forward and back. Glancing at each other and drawing a collective breath, they arrayed themselves after Jesus on his humble steed as he led the people up the mountainside.

They reached the summit and Jesus stopped as the Holy City spread before them. Once again, Beth stood and looked down over the Temple complex as the gold and white Temple glittered and the courts throbbed with life. This time, she stood as a disciple of a great prophet, a follower of the Messiah. Her heart pounded at the thought.

She felt a pang for her father. She remembered how he had stood beside her with his arm around her, so proud of the Temple's beauty. She reached up and touched her shoulder where his hand had rested. He would have been overjoyed to be here at this moment.

Jesus urged the donkey forward and down the slope as his

disciples followed. The road dipped through the olive groves and into the Kidron Valley. As they emerged to where the road widened and led straight into the city, they were greeted again by the exultant crowd. The people that had gone ahead of them laid their coats on the road, and many were cutting branches and spreading them for Jesus to ride over.

At first, the waiting crowd was constrained and quiet as the Antonia's tall towers hung over their heads, casting shadows that were felt rather than seen.

Then a lone voice broke the restraint and called aloud, "Hosanna to the Son of David!"

Other voices took up the refrain until Beth, in the center of the celebrating crowd, felt the shouts reverberating through her body and lifting the hairs on her arms.

"Hosanna to the Son of David!" the revolutionary cry rose again and again. Beth felt her stomach swoop with fear. Surely Rome itself would hear and come crush them all.

"Hosanna to the Son of David; Blessed is he who comes in the name of the Lord; Hosanna in the highest!"

Everyone smiled, and many of the waiting crowd reached out and touched Jesus as he passed. When Beth saw that no soldiers swept out of the city to stop them, she began to relax. She allowed the atmosphere of the moment to flow through her.

"Hosanna!" she called out. Though her voice was lost in the crowd, it still felt good to say it.

She knew she would remember this day forever; she felt the start of something that would change her whole world. Her senses were sharp and clear, and everything was bolder—the waving people, the eager shouts of joy, the lush crunch of leaves underfoot, the beaming smile on her husband's face, and the heavy, holy presence of the city. Sunlight glinted off Jesus' hair as he entered the gate, and she drew all the images into her heart and promised herself never to forget this day.

Under the Temple colonnade, Jesus dismounted from his donkey and one of the men took hold of its lead. The crowd still followed, adding to the bustling sounds of the Gentile Courts.

Beth's first visit to these courts had overwhelmed her with noise and confusion. Even as a grown woman she found it chaotic. As she stood so near the Temple of the living God, she was distracted by the noisy hawkers and the clamor of sacrificial animals.

Men sat at tables exchanging foreign money for the Jewish coins, the only currency permitted in the Temple. People came away from the money changer's tables with grim faces. They knew the exchange rates were in favor of the Temple coffers.

Nearby, Beth heard two men haggling over the cost of a pair of doves. "Surely that price is too high," the one man was saying, his young wife and infant son beside him. "We're only poor farmers."

The seller's voice was oily as he said, "The price is fair, and you will find none cheaper here. Besides, don't you want the best for your sacrifice to the Lord?"

With the noise, the haggling, and the milling people, it felt more like a market than a temple, and Beth couldn't imagine any Gentile wanting to worship here.

Beth turned away to gaze at the Temple with its pristine, white marble walls and gold trim. The stones used in its construction were enormous, but they had been fitted together with such skill that no seams could be seen. It was truly a marvel. She could see smoke rising from the large altar set before the Temple doors, the altar itself hidden from view by high walls.

A shout and a loud crash made her jump in fear, thinking the Romans had arrived to crush them. As she wheeled around, she had to duck her head as several doves burst free from their smashed cage. Her eyes followed as they escaped into the blue sky and freedom. She whirled around to see Jesus, eyes blazing, grab one end of the dove seller's table, and fling it over. It crashed to the stone floor with a loud clatter. Beth ran up to Peter.

"What's he doing?" she gasped as Jesus grabbed another table and upended it as well.

The dove sellers were yelling and angry, but they noted the large crowd of followers Jesus had with him and didn't fight back.

The money changers saw Jesus storming towards them, his outer robe billowing, and they scrambled to gather up their belongings. The people waiting in line drew back in alarm as Jesus began to overturn tables. The money-changers who weren't quick enough dropped to the ground to protect their gleaming coins as they tinkled and rolled over the tiled floor.

Peter stared wide-eyed at James and John, the brothers rooted to the spot with mouths hanging open. What was Jesus doing? He had been in the Temple less than ten minutes and already the whole city would be buzzing with his presence.

Several men wearing the robes of the Sadducees stormed forward, their folded hands clenched and their chins thrust forward beneath icy eyes, wondering who dared to disturb their proceedings. Temple guards with their long spears flanked them. Beth's stomach turned over as she dragged her gaze up to the Antonia towers. Surely the soldiers there were also watching this disturbance, ready to sweep in and stamp out any trouble.

Jesus held out his arms, encompassing them all, and roared, "It is written, 'My House shall be called a house of prayer'; but you are making it a robber's den!"

The Sadducees were angry and affronted at Jesus' choice of prophecy, but the dove sellers and money changers ignored him as they scrambled to protect their businesses. Beth looked around at the people in the courts. She saw many stony faces of displeasure at Jesus' display, but also nodding heads of approval.

Jesus turned on his heel, away from the Sadducees, and strode further into the Temple Courts to where the rabbis sat with their disciples to teach. The stunned disciples hastened to catch up.

Jesus sat under the colonnade and the people clustered around him. Beth stood back and watched as the blind and the lame came to Jesus, the word of his arrival spreading like fire throughout the city of Jerusalem.

She leaned against a cold marble pillar and remembered well when she had seen the woman with the twisted legs sitting on the hard ground in these same courts. Now, men and women were carried to Jesus and walked out on their own two feet. In the courts of the one true God, all were healed. All were made whole. Today, the children came to Jesus and he smiled and laughed with them, setting his hands on their heads as he blessed them. The money that had been given to Jesus' ministry was given away, the disciples pressing coins into the hands of the poor without reserve. A wall separated the Gentiles from entering the inner courts of the Temple. Yet here, in the common courts, Gentiles came near to Jesus and watched and listened with amazement.

"This is how the Temple Courts should always be," Beth whispered to herself, pressing a hand to her full heart.

From her quiet place by the pillar, Beth soon saw she was not the only one who observed all that was happening. The Sadducees were standing to the side. Some wore the robes of the priests who served in the Temple. Beth saw a Pharisee with a trimmed beard and a thick, puckered scar across his forehead come striding up to join them.

The crowds hung about Jesus even as the shofar blew. Instead of bowing within the inner walls of the Temple, they stayed near him. As one, the people faced the Temple and the courts rang with prayer. In these days leading up to the Passover, the ending phrase was particularity sweet on their lips,

"I am the Lord, your God, who led you from the land of Egypt to be a God to you. I am the Lord, your God."

After the sacrifices, Jesus resumed his work, and everyone's mind was on the freedom promises of the coming festival.

The shadows of the Sadducees and priests stretched long across the courtyard and then vanished as the sun disappeared. They stood in solemn, foreboding contrast to the rejoicing crowds.

Children dashed about in the courts, still shouting the psalm, "Hosanna to the Son of David!"

One of the chief priests snapped to Jesus, "Do you hear what these children are saying?"

Jesus looked back. "Have you never read, 'Out of the mouths of infants and nursing babies You have prepared praise for Yourself?'"

Beth saw the priests frown and mutter to one another. Her stomach swooped. Not content with humbling the Pharisees, Jesus had now made enemies with the priests themselves.

As Jesus rose to leave the Temple, Beth left the column and slid into place beside her friends so she would not be left behind. She passed the glaring chief priests with her face averted, her shawl shielding her face in shadow. As she hastened past, she heard one of the men say,

"How dare he? Who does he think he is?"

"Careful, Simeon," cautioned another. "The crowds are with him."

The man named Simeon scowled. "For now."

Jesus left the Temple on the southern side, taking them through the Lower City. Beth hastened up to Peter and asked, "Does Jesus have a place to sleep tonight?"

Peter nodded. "Jesus has friends in Bethany, disciples of his." He glanced at her and said, "I thought that we would ask your cousin,

Simon, to take in some of us as well."

Beth hadn't seen her cousin since he left Capernaum newly healed and full of enthusiasm for Jesus. Surely, after what Jesus had done for him, he still believed. Surely he hadn't been swayed by the bitterness of the Jerusalem rabbis. At least, she hoped not.

Jesus and his disciples walked past the oldest portion of the city, the part that had stood in the days of King David. Beth wondered if any of them could pass and not wonder if a true king walked the streets once more.

30

TESTING THE LAMB

Reuben sat in the courtyard of Simeon's house scratching the lamb on the knobby bone between his ears. The lamb closed his eyes and leaned against Reuben's hand. The house and street were quiet. The hour was early.

He had chosen this lamb the previous morning, waiting in the Temple courtyard to make his choice from the pens. One of the priests had checked over the lamb with deft, practiced motions. The overwhelming number of lambs to be sacrificed in four days hence called for precise organization—there would be no time to recheck a lamb. Reuben would lead this lamb back to the Temple Courts the morning before Passover and wait with the other men in the Court of Women. When the appointed time came, the gates to the inner courts would swing open, revealing every single priest in the nation; all were summoned for the festival. While the Hallal was chanted, the lambs would be sacrificed in waves.

It was a bloody, magnificent spectacle to witness. Countless bowls of blood were thrown over the altar. The red deluge trickled down, staining the tiled floor and flowing into the gutters. The slain lambs would be hung on hooks, and with skillful cuts, the priests would skin and gut each lamb, then return the meat and hide to the man who had purchased it. The organs and the fat belonged to God. The meat would be taken home, roasted, and eaten entirely in one meal by a large gathering of friends and extended family. The hide was often given as a gift to the host family, for hosts were forbidden to accept money for providing lodging during the festival.

The lamb sitting innocently here, enjoying his head being scratched, was docile and gentle. Reuben felt a twinge of sadness that the lamb would soon die, but it was a noble way for such a beast to end its life.

"There you are," Simeon's voice rang out, startling the lamb and making Reuben jump to his feet. "I have been looking everywhere for you. What are you doing?" Reuben gestured to the water basin and hay that he had laid out for the lamb, and Simeon sighed with impatience. "Leave the beast to the servant's care. We are needed at the Temple."

Reuben scrambled into his sandals and followed on Simeon's heels as the man strode for the Temple, his linen coat sweeping behind him as his feet slapped against the stone road. They crossed the bridge to the Temple and entered through the Western Gate. Simeon didn't seem to think Reuben needed any explanation for their hasty journey to the Temple, and Reuben didn't dare ask while his rabbi was in a black mood.

The reason was soon apparent. There was a battle line of sorts drawn in the Temple Courts. The various parties were arrayed—Sadducees, Herodians, and Pharisees, all standing near one another in unusual unification against the young rabbi, Jesus.

Jesus, however, was ignoring them. He was seated on one of the rabbi seats and teaching the men and women who were gathered around him. Reuben couldn't help but notice Beth in a knot of women near Jesus' feet. He jerked his face away, though he had a hard time swallowing the lump that rose in his throat. He had tried to reason with her. She had chosen the wrong side.

Reuben had heard all about Jesus' noisy arrival in Jerusalem. The man had wrangled a parade to welcome him into the city, his disciples inciting the crowd to call out hosannas in his honor. It was disgraceful how the man tried to push himself forward.

The Nazarene obviously sought to stir up trouble during the Passover Week. He had nearly caused a riot in the Temple Courts within minutes of arriving. Simeon had told him last night that the governor, Pilate, was incensed at the disturbance, and had given strict orders to the High Priest to maintain peace.

Simeon stood with the other Pharisees who had gathered, Reuben on his heels. "Has it begun?" Simeon asked.

"Just about," said a Pharisee lawyer named Jeconiah. "The chief priests would like the first opportunity to show his faults."

"A reasonable request," Simeon said and inclined his head. He turned to face Jesus as the crowd of priests moved forward. The High Priest Caiaphas stepped ahead of the rest, his father in law, Annas, standing nearby in support.

Caiaphas' voice rang out across the courtyard as he said, "By what authority do your miracles come from, and who gave you this authority?"

The crowd looked at Jesus, wondering how he would answer such a pointed question.

Jesus turned in his seat to look the priests and elders full in the face. Jesus gave the chief priests a cold smile, and Reuben frowned. The man was confident.

Jesus folded his hands in his lap. "Well, I have a question for you as well. Was the baptizing John did in the Jordan River of heaven or of men?"

Simeon glanced at Reuben and raised his eyebrows. He leaned towards him and murmured with a faint note of apprehension, "He is not easily baited."

The chief priests withdrew and huddled together. Reuben could hear them arguing about how to respond. Annas raised his hand and silenced them all. With an angry sigh he said, "I hate to admit it, but he's laid a clever trap. If we say, 'from heaven,' he'll ask us why we didn't believe him. If we say 'from men' the people here will be enraged. They see John as a prophet, maybe even more so since his beheading."

"So what should we say?" Caiaphas demanded, putting a hand on his hip.

Reuben grimaced. It was often said among the Pharisees that Caiaphas, though brilliantly charismatic, was not the tactician his father-in-law was known to be.

"Refuse to answer," Annas counseled.

Caiaphas pursed his lips but nodded at his father-in-law. The group went back to stand before Jesus, who was waiting expectantly.

Caiaphas folded his hands and said, "We don't know."

Reuben sighed. It sounded like a silly, politically correct reply to him. Why wouldn't they just answer outright and put Jesus in his place? He was even more frustrated when Jesus took the door they had left wide open for him.

"Neither will I tell you by what I authority I do these things."

The chief priests retreated again, and put their heads together. Jesus rose to his feet and stood before them, apparently deciding it was his turn to attack.

Jesus said, "Let me tell you a story. A man had two sons. He came to the first and said, 'Son, go work today in the vineyard.' The son answered, 'I will not,' but then afterward he regretted it and went. The man came to his second son and asked the same thing. The son replied, 'Okay, I'll go,' but he never went. So, who did the will of his father?"

One of the elders scoffed at the obvious answer and answered at once, "The first."

Reuben clenched his fists by his side. They were playing right into Jesus' hands, unused to the trickery Jesus could do with words.

Jesus said, "You're right. In the same way, the tax collectors and prostitutes will enter the kingdom of heaven before you. John came in the way of righteousness, and they believed him. You saw their belief, but would not soften your hearts towards his message."

Reuben reared up his head, his lip curling in rage. His anger only grew when none of those on his side could come up with a suitable retort. This left them open to a second attack.

"Listen to another parable," Jesus challenged them. "There was a landowner who planted a vineyard and put a wall around it, dug a winepress in it, and built a tower. Then he rented it out to vine-growers and went on a journey. When the harvest time approached, he sent his slaves to the vine-growers to receive his produce. The vine-growers took his slaves and beat one, killed another, and stoned a third.

"Again he sent another group of slaves larger than the first, and they did the same thing to them.

"But afterward he sent his son to them saying, 'They will respect my son.' But when the vine-growers saw the son they said among themselves, 'This is the heir; come, let us kill him and seize his inheritance.' They took him, and threw him out of the vineyard and killed him. So, when the owner of the vineyard comes, what will he do to those vine-growers?"

One of the lawyers called out, "He will give those wretches the punishment they deserve, and he will rent out the vineyard to other vine-growers who will pay him the proper proceeds."

Jesus nodded in clear agreement, and the lawyer looked strangely pleased. Reuben, having heard Jesus speak countless times, felt a trap. He suspected that the tenant vine-growers were supposed to be the priests, lawyers, and teachers of the day—namely the Pharisees and Sadducees.

Jesus asked the lawyer, "Did you never read in the scriptures,

"The stone which the builders rejected,
This became the chief corner stone;
This came about from the Lord,
And it is marvelous in our eyes?'"

The men were affronted and whispered to each other, trying to puzzle out Jesus' meaning as the crowds watched.

Jesus didn't wait for them to understand, but said, "Therefore, I say to you, The kingdom of God will be taken away from you and given to a people who will produce the fruit of it. He who falls on this stone will be broken to pieces; but on whomever it falls, it will scatter him like dust."

The lawyer who had answered lunged forward at the insult, but his companions held him back. The priests and elders huddled together and Reuben heard Caiaphas' sharp rebuke, "Get ahold of yourselves. The people see him as a prophet. We will show his true colors if you fools will just keep your senses and behave rationally. If we start a riot Pilate will have all our careers—maybe our heads too."

They looked up, and Jesus was still standing there, a little ahead of his followers. The twelve men who comprised his inner circle were fanned out behind him, wearing varied expressions. Some appeared bold, a few were exultant at seeing the priests bested, and others looked afraid. Before another question could be agreed upon, Jesus turned and began to teach the people once more.

"The kingdom of heaven may be compared to a king who gave a wedding feast for his son. He sent out his slaves to call those who had been invited, but they were unwilling to come. Again he sent out slaves telling the invited guests, 'Come to the feast, the fattened calf has been butchered and everything is ready!' But the guests made excuses. They were too busy with their own business. Some even took the slaves and beat them, mistreated them, and killed them.

"The king was enraged, and sent his armies and destroyed those murderers, and burnt their cities to the ground. Then he sent out his slaves again saying, 'Those who were invited were not worthy. Go to the highways and invite all that you meet to the wedding feast.' So the banquet hall was filled with all the people the slaves found, good and evil. And when the king entered, he saw a man who had not thought it worth his time to change his clothes for the occasion.

"The king said to the man, 'My friend, why do you insult me like this?' and the man was speechless. The king had the man tossed out into the darkness, where the man wailed and wept at not being included in the wedding feast.'

"So you see," Jesus said. "Many are called. Few are chosen."

Simeon turned to his fellow Pharisees and they huddled close. "Enough is enough," he hissed. "It's our turn. We need a perfect argument, a sure way to expose him to the people." His eyes flicked to the tall towers that hung over the courtyard, and he grinned darkly. "No one would be foolish enough to challenge Rome in sight of the Antonia, not unless he had a death wish. Yet, if Jesus doesn't denounce Rome, how can he be a prophet or the Messiah?"

Simeon whispered his plan to the others. Reuben grinned. Finally, someone had the sense to attack Jesus properly. He was proud that it was his rabbi who had come up with the perfect question to trap Jesus.

Simeon nodded to Reuben as he said to the others, "My disciple will ask the question. Go, Reuben, and get some of the Herodians to go with you. They can report back to Herod Antipas what Jesus says."

Reuben, proud to be entrusted with this important task, gathered some of the Herodians. They laughed with glee when they heard the question Reuben was going to ask. Reuben's nerves were as taut as bowstrings as he stepped forward and felt a thousand eyes turn his way.

Jesus saw Reuben approach, and it was clear he recognized him. Reuben took strength in Jesus' recognition and smiled, because he knew Jesus as well. He was able to let the vast crowds, the chief priests, the elders, and his rabbi all melt away, and face Jesus man to man.

Boldly he began, speaking flattery, "Teacher, we know that you are truthful and teach the way of God in truth. You defer to no one, and are not partial to anyone." Reuben held out his hands, his expression open. "Tell us then, what do you think about paying poll taxes to Caesar. Is it lawful, or not?"

Reuben folded his hands with a smirk. Jesus had no way out of this one. The fact was, it was not lawful to give allegiance to a foreign ruler, and it was even worse to give to a man who called himself 'the son of the divine' as Caesar did. Yet, to refuse to pay taxes was to set yourself up as a revolutionary, which was punishable by death. Either way, the Nazarene would be exposed as a feeble, pretend messiah, or would be dealt with by Rome itself, by no fault of the elders or priests.

Jesus did not look alarmed by the question, unlike the twelve men arrayed behind him. He held out his hand, palm up. "Why are you testing me, you hypocrites?" he scoffed. "Show me a coin used for the poll tax."

Reuben hesitated for a moment, then turned to borrow a denarius from Simeon. Simeon's eyes were dark with disappointment as he set the cold coin in his palm. Reuben swallowed hard as he turned. He placed the coin in Jesus' open palm. Jesus glanced at it and asked, "Whose likeness is that?"

Reuben looked down, "Uh, Caesar's," he answered stupidly. This was not going the way he had anticipated. He suddenly felt naked before the heat of the crowd's scrutiny.

Jesus flipped it over. "And that inscription. Whose is that?"

Reuben spoke through his teeth. "Caesar's."

Jesus smiled and tossed the coin back, which Reuben fumbled in his embarrassment. "Then give to Caesar what is Caesar's, and to God what is God's," Jesus answered.

Reuben licked his lips. His eyes darted around, searching for a rebuttal, but he couldn't come up with a counter-argument—not without sounding more like an idiot than he already did. Jesus had taken their beautifully crafted question and turned it to make Reuben look like a fool. Reuben's ears burned as the crowd whispered with awed expressions. Jesus' reply was perfect. If you were a Jew, you knew that all belonged to God, but if you were a Roman supporter, you heard Jesus say to pay the tax.

Reuben, his face flushed with failure, turned and slumped back to Simeon. Simeon gazed at Reuben coldly and didn't say anything. Reuben felt all the more embarrassed and slipped into the background. Absorbed in his own fumble, he forgot that men greater than he had been bested by Jesus. Instead, all he could think about was the fact that Jesus had publicly embarrassed him. His self-pity turned to anger.

He hardly heard the Sadducees as they questioned Jesus about the resurrection, a fact they refused to believe, and he was not consoled that they too were outwitted in their arguments. Hatred for Jesus was like an overturned inkpot in Reuben's heart, coating everything, and he didn't trouble to mop it up.

The Pharisees sent another man with a question, and Reuben sullenly listened as Jesus again replied with wisdom.

Jesus, seeming tired of these tests, held out his arms and said, "The Messiah, whose son is he?"

"David's, of course," a man snapped.

"Well then, explain how David in the Spirit calls him Lord, saying,

"The Lord said to my Lord,
Sit at my right hand,
Until I put your enemies beneath your feet'.

"If David calls him Lord, how can he be his son?"

Annas came up to the Pharisees and hissed, "Don't answer him. We came to show the people his faults, but he's making us look like children. Ignore him and we slight him as the pretender he is." He stormed away, and the other priests and elders hastened after him.

The Pharisees and their disciples also turned to leave, none wanting to meet Jesus' gaze. They pretended not to see the dumbfounded crowds who watched the religious leaders file away. Simeon strode away without a look or a word to Reuben.

Reuben was left behind in the courts. He sagged. He didn't have the heart to go home and face Simeon's disappointment and displeasure.

So instead, he found a shadowed corner in the colonnade to collect himself. Jesus went back to the teacher's seat, the crowd humming all around him.

The Nazarene had no regard for those in authority! He didn't even seem to want them on his side. The priests, scribes, and teachers would be powerful allies to the true Messiah when he came. Reuben consoled himself that while Jesus was clever in his arguments, his pride was the political mistake that would be his undoing. The man had united the political parties unlike anyone had ever been able to do before—all joined in their hatred of him. What more could Jesus do to make the Pharisees his enemies?

Reuben pricked up his ears when he heard the lesson Jesus was beginning, his tone abrasive and scoffing as he spoke to the people.

"The scribes have seated themselves in the seat of Moses, putting themselves forward as teachers. Do as they say, but do not do as they do. They love to tie up heavy burdens and lay them on men's shoulders, but they will not even lift a finger. Instead, they do all their deeds to be admired by men, even broadening their phylacteries and lengthening the tassels on their garments so they look virtuous."

Reuben made tight fists by his side as Jesus slandered his party and his trade. But Jesus wasn't finished yet.

"They love the honor that goes with their position—the best seats at banquets, the respectful greetings, and being called 'Rabbi.'" Jesus paused and looked at the rapt, wide-eyed crowds. He continued, "Don't ask to be called rabbi, for there is One Teacher and you are all brothers. Do not seek to be raised above others, but lower yourself in service to others. The one who exalts himself will be humbled, but the one who humbles himself shall be exalted." Jesus' voice rang across the courts as he said, "Woe to the Pharisees and the teachers, you great pretenders, you hypocrites!"

Reuben listened in shock and anger as Jesus said, "The hypocrites shut themselves off from the kingdom of God, and won't allow others to enter either! They travel around on sea and land to make one proselyte, but then make him twice a son of hell as themselves. They are blind guides, trying to replace justice with tradition! They tithe so carefully of their herbs, but when it comes to the weightier matters of the law, they neglect justice and mercy and faithfulness! You need to do one without neglecting the other. Blind guides! Straining a gnat and swallowing a camel. They purify the outside of a dish, but inside they are full of robbery and self-indulgence.

"Blind Pharisees, clean the inside of the dish and the outside will be clean too. Woe to you Pharisees and teachers, you are like white-washed tombs, clean and bright on the outside, but inside you are full of dead men's bones and uncleanliness. You appear righteous before men, but inside you are full of hypocrisy and lawlessness."

Jesus drew breath and continued, "You make monuments to the prophets of the past, and say, 'If we had lived in such a time, we would not have been partners in the shedding of the prophet's blood.' Ha!"

Jesus stood up and his voice was like a roiling fire, sending waves of heat over the courtyard. "Your cup is overrunning with the blood of the prophets. You brood of vipers, how will you escape from hell? Watch, I am sending out the prophets, wise men, and teachers to you. You will kill them, crucify them, persecute them from city to city and scourge them in your synagogues so that on you, on this very generation, may fall all the guilt of the righteous blood on the earth, from the blood of righteous Abel to the blood of Zechariah son of Berechiah, whom you murdered between the Temple and the altar."

Jesus threw his arms open wide and turned on the spot, lifting his chin and calling aloud, "Jerusalem, Jerusalem, who kills the prophets and stones those who are sent to her! I long to gather your children like a hen gathers her chicks, but you are unwilling. So your house shall be left to you desolate. I tell you now, you shall not see me here again until you say, 'Blessed is he who comes in the name of the Lord!'"

His heart racing, Reuben recited what Jesus had said, committing the scurrilous words to memory. Simeon was displeased with how things had gone this morning, but with this information, they might have enough to bring a proper case against Jesus—a charge of blasphemy, punishable by stoning.

Reuben laughed mirthlessly. What was more blasphemous than insisting that the entire worship system devoted to God was flawed and corrupt?

His fiery tirade finished, Jesus rose to his feet and strode toward the Eastern Gate.

Reuben overheard someone ask Jesus, "What do you think of the Temple, Jesus? Isn't the construction beautiful? Such large stones, such perfection."

Jesus paused and gestured around himself. "You see all this? Not one stone will be left one upon the other. Every single one will be torn down." The man was left speechless as Jesus strode towards one of the exits, his silenced disciples following with wide eyes and open mouths.

Reuben grinned with indignant delight as he rubbed his hands together. Jesus had *actually* threatened to tear down the Temple. He was making it too easy.

Reuben hastened for home. He found Simeon brooding in the lecture hall, alone. Simeon didn't seem open to conversation, but Reuben knelt and told him all that Jesus had said. When he finished, Simeon bestowed a small smile.

"You have redeemed yourself, my disciple," Simeon said, setting a hand on Reuben's shoulder, and Reuben's heart fluttered with relief.

31

A Woman's Tears

Beth's mind reeled as she followed Jesus out the Eastern Gate. Jesus led them across the Kidron Valley and up the Mount of Olives. As she walked, she looked around herself with a sinking feeling. The number of curious people following Jesus was far less after his accusatory speech in the courtyard. Only yesterday Jesus had been acclaimed as the Son of David. Now, the crowds kept their distance. Jesus strode ahead and the disciples lagged several paces behind.

Beth walked with the other believing women. The women did not speak to one another, and Beth could see the worry on each face. The mood of the other disciples was just as tense. They were all well aware that Jesus had walked into the den of a bear and rapped it on the nose. Of one thing they were sure—the bear would bite back.

"He seems intent on making sure his prophecy comes true," Judas snapped to Andrew as they ascended the slope.

Andrew glanced at Judas and raised his eyebrows. "He's got a plan, I'm sure of it."

"You bet he has." Simon was gleeful. "You heard him, he won't teach in the courts until everyone is singing his praises as one sent from God."

Beth and Mary Magdalene shared a weighted glance.

Thomas looked worried. "I don't think that day will arrive any time soon," he said. "The Pharisees and Sadducees will never accept Jesus, not after what he said today. He just made everything harder for himself."

Peter slowed down and let the others catch up to him. His expression was strained, yet he defended Jesus. "What else could he do? The teachers of the day are corrupt. Should he have tried to curry favor with those who aren't doing God's will?"

Judas was the one to reply, and Beth flinched at his angry tone. "He could have at least kept them happy until he had taken the throne. Then—as king—he could start cleaning up the Temple, establishing the proper priesthood, and correcting the schools."

The whispered conversation continued as they ascended the mount, weaving up the path through the olive groves. If Jesus overheard them, he didn't intervene as the arguments went one way, then another.

Jesus stopped at the summit and peered back over Jerusalem. The afternoon sun shone golden over the bustling city. Beth was one of the last to reach the top, and she joined the others as they gazed down at the Temple complex. The courtyards were packed with pilgrims, throbbing with life. Yet, Jesus had said that the Temple would be torn down and not one stone left atop the other.

She imagined it desolate, a smoking ruin, and swallowed hard. When the Temple had been destroyed generations before, it had been devastating for her people. This place was where God dwelt among them. If He allowed His home to be destroyed, it meant judgment upon them all.

Peter turned to Jesus who was staring down on Jerusalem, his expression drawn. "When, Rabbi?" Peter asked. "How long do we have until the Temple falls? What will be the sign that your time has come and that it's time for the new age to begin?"

Jesus, still staring down at Jerusalem, reached out and put his hand on Peter's shoulder. It was a long moment before he turned to sit away from the main road, gesturing that the disciples should gather around him. The shrunken group of disciples drew close.

Jesus leaned forward. "In the days to come your ears will be filled with talk of wars. Do not be frightened, for while those things must take place, it is not the end. Nation will rise against nation, and there will be famines and earthquakes, but these are merely the beginnings of the birth pangs. They will deliver you to tribulation and will kill you, and you will be hated by all the nations because of my name."

"What?" Judas Iscariot choked out, shaking his head in disbelief.

Beth understood his horrified emotion. She looked around and could see the others were also shaken by this harsh prophecy.

Jesus cast his eyes on each one of them. It was so quiet in the little clearing that they heard every rustle of tender olive leaf. "At that time, many will fall away and will betray and hate one another. False prophets will arise and mislead many. Because lawlessness is increased, most people's love will grow cold. But the one who endures to the end will be saved."

Beth felt her stomach turn over. She turned to her husband and whispered, "Who can endure all that?"

He kept his eyes on Jesus, but reached out and gripped her hand, trying to comfort her in the face of the coming horrors.

Jesus made sure they were all listening before he spoke again with his own hands clutched before him, face earnest as he said, "This gospel of the kingdom shall be preached in the whole world as a testimony to all the nations—and then the end will come. Therefore, when you see the abomination of desolation, which was spoken of through the prophet Daniel, standing in the holy place, you need to flee." Jesus gestured away from Jerusalem with his hand.

Beth clutched her throat as she felt the air ripped from her lungs. Her people clung to the messianic hopes of Daniel, but they also knew the terrible prophecies.

"Forces from him will arise, desecrate the sanctuary fortress,
and do away with the regular sacrifice.
And they will set up the abomination of desolation.
By smooth words he will turn to godlessness those
who act wickedly toward the covenant,
But the people who know their God
will display strength and take action.
Those who have insight among the people
will give understanding to the many;
Yet they will fall by the sword and by flame,
by captivity and by plunder for many days."

Jesus continued, "Don't stop to collect your things, don't turn back to grab your cloak. Flee, escape! For a time of horror such as the world has never seen or will ever see again will fall upon you." Jesus' unfocused eyes stared far away, and with dismay, Beth saw tears run down his face and glisten in his beard. "Woe to those who are pregnant or nursing babies in those days."

Peter squeezed her hand so hard it hurt.

Jesus stood to his feet, his damp face radiating power and hope. His voice rose in pitch and he spoke faster, his prophetic words painting pictures in their minds with snatches of scripture. "But immediately after the tribulation of those days the sun will be darkened, and the moon will not give its light, and the stars will fall from the sky. And the powers of the heavens will be shaken. And then the sign of the Son of Man will appear in the sky. Then all the peoples of the earth will mourn their evil ways, and they will see the Son of Man coming on the clouds of the sky with power and great glory. And he will send forth his angels with a great trumpet, and they will gather together his elect from the four winds, from one end of the sky to the other."

Jesus strode over to a tree. He set his palm against its trunk. "Now learn this parable from the tree—when its branch is tender and it puts forth its leaves, you know that summer is near; so you too, when you see all these things, will recognize that I am near, right at the door. Truly I say to you, this generation will not pass away until all these things take place. My words will last longer than heaven and the earth. You can trust them." Beth looked around at the wide-eyed men and women then swiveled her head to look at the oblivious city of Jerusalem. Within this generation there would be blood and death and horror?

James' voice was hoarse. "But when, Lord, when?"

Jesus gathered himself and sat before his disciples again. "Only the Father knows the hour of that day. The coming of the Son of Man will be like the days of Noah. The people were living their lives, planning for the future, until the moment the flood came and took them all away. Two men will be working in a field, one will be taken and the other left. Two women will be grinding at the mill, one is taken and the other one is left. So be alert, for you do not know which day your Lord is coming."

Jesus wet his throat with a drink from his waterskin and gazed with compassion on their anxious, pale faces. Beth tried her best to understand, but prophecy was difficult—its colorful descriptions mingled seamlessly with fact. Comprehending prophecy felt like trying to keep water cupped in her hands.

Her rabbi gave a small smile. "Take courage my friends, my faithful disciples. Have hope! When the Son of Man comes in his glory, and all of his messengers with him, then he will sit on his glorious throne. The nations will be gathered to the Son of Man, and he will separate them like a shepherd separates the sheep from the goats; he will put the sheep on the right and the goats on the left.

"Then the King will say to those on his right, 'Come you who are blessed of my Father, inherit the kingdom prepared for you from the foundation of the world. For I was hungry, and you fed me; thirsty, and you gave me something to drink; a stranger, and you invited me in; naked, and you clothed me; I was sick and you visited me; I was in prison, and you came to me."

"And the righteous will answer him, "When did we see you, and do these things for you?"

"And the King will answer them, "Truly I say to you, to the extent that you did it to one of these brothers of mine, you did it to me."

Jesus' tone was grave as he continued, "Then he will say to those on his left, 'Depart from me, accursed ones, into the eternal fire which has been prepared for the devil and his angels; for I was hungry, and you gave me nothing to eat; I was thirsty, and you gave me nothing to drink; I was a stranger, and you did not invite me in; naked and you did not clothe me; sick and in prison and you did not visit me.'

"Then they will also answer, 'When did we see you in want and did not take care of you?' Then he will answer them, 'Truly I say to you, to the extent that you did not do it for one of the least of these, you did not do it for me."

Jesus leaned forward, his eyes shining with love as he looked at his disciples. Beth knew without a doubt that he cared about them, and she tried to take heart in the fact that he would not abandon them. Someday the righteous would receive the rewards of the kingdom. She swallowed hard. It sounded like those days of peace were not coming soon.

The afternoon had slipped away and the shadows were lengthening. Jesus stood and stared down on Jerusalem again. They all rose after him, glancing at each other without speaking. Beth stood side by side with the men and women. Who of them would survive the great tribulation Jesus prophesied? Would her husband? Would she?

Jesus turned away from Jerusalem and began to descend the hill on the eastern side. The disciples followed him silently.

They were nearly at Bethany when Jesus suddenly stopped and bent low to the ground. He brushed a delicate wildflower with a fingertip, seeming to savor its fleeting beauty. He drew a breath of the sweet dusky air and turned to face them once more.

"Passover is in two days," he began, but voice hitched with emotion. Gathering himself, he spoke thickly, "My time approaches. The Son of Man will be handed over, and crucified." Tears glistened in his eyes.

The men turned to each other with confusion.

Beth heard Mary Magdalene give a little cry of pain. Beth turned to her friend and saw tears beginning to rain hard and fast down her cheeks. Beth had to blink rapidly to stop her own tears from breaking free. She felt the familiar bands of anxiety coil around her chest and squeeze tight. The destruction of the Temple was a cloudy, vague horror. It was not immediate. Jesus spoke of his crucifixion in two days. Two! She stared at Jesus, a man she had laughed with, learned from, and followed all over the country. She had come to respect and believe in him, and now the prophet prophesied his own death—and soon.

A raven cawed nearby and Beth jolted at the sound. She wrapped her arms around herself as painful memories seared her mind.

She glanced up at Peter. He looked confused and worried, but for once he was silent. She wished he would comfort Jesus and offer him solace as their rabbi grappled with his own, deadly, prophecy. No one said anything. Jesus turned once more and led them into Bethany.

"Jesus!" a voice called. Beth saw her cousin, Simon, striding up to them, his arms spread as wide as his grin. His easy manner felt out of place after the heavy mood on the mount.

Simon beamed at Jesus as he said, "I was hoping to see you. I want to invite you and your Twelve to a feast. I have friends who are eager to meet the famous prophet."

Beth thought Jesus would want to withdraw for private prayer, and was surprised to hear Jesus accept. The rest of the Twelve followed after Jesus, as did Mary Magdalene, Naomi, and Beth. The women were guests in Simon's home for the duration of the festival.

The other disciples walked down the street to their guest lodgings with Jesus' friends.

As the men went to the prepared upper room, the women turned towards the common space where the cooking and chores for the day were already completed. Beth watched the men climb the stairs and felt the urge to race after them. After everything they had just heard, she longed to talk to her husband and let him assuage her fears. Peter never worried about anything. He would know what to say to make her feel better. Instead, she drew a deep breath and sat with Mary as the servants gathered up elaborate, savory dishes to carry up to the feast.

Beth's mind kept turning to her husband throughout the evening as the women ate downstairs. Darkness fell over Bethany as Naomi and Mary whispered of the ominous prophecies Jesus had given them. Beth silently steeped in her anxieties. Naomi was mending a tear in her shawl while she talked, and the simple task was soothing to watch. Beth took a modicum of comfort from her aunt's staid face. It would take more than a prophecy of destruction to rattle her Aunt Naomi.

A scuffle at the door caught her attention. A woman was standing in the doorway with her hair loose about her shoulders and an alabaster vial clutched in her hands.

"Absolutely not!" a servant hissed as she blocked the doorway, a broom in one hand. "You weren't invited."

The woman's whole frame trembled and she drew the expensive white jar closer to her chest. Beth felt emotion roiling from the woman like heat from an oven. She rose to her feet and moved forward to see if she could help.

The young woman's wide eyes turned to Beth, imploring her. "I must do this."

The exasperated servant looked at Beth for help, and the woman used the opportunity to slip past and race up the stairs.

Naomi heaved herself to her feet, her brow furrowed. "What is the girl doing?"

The servant, lips pressed together into a thin line, charged up the stairs. Beth was concerned for the woman and raced up after them both. Naomi and Mary Magdalene were hot on her heels.

She arrived at the upper room. It was the same place where she had slept during her visit to Jerusalem as a girl. The room was brightly lit now, with three low tables arranged in a U shape, and Jesus sitting at the place of honor. The remains of the meal were upon the table, the scent of roast meat still moist in the air. The young woman was approaching Jesus, weeping. The servant hovered near the door, unsure of what to do.

Simon rose to his feet at the intrusion. His eyes flicked to his servant as he pointed at the weeping woman. "Why is *she* here?"

Beth's glance showed several Pharisees at the table, looking alarmed at the proceedings. The other disciples began to whisper while shaking their heads. Peter sent Beth a questioning glance. She shrugged her shoulders and raised her hands.

A sweet, spicy fragrance overpowered the scent of meat and bread. Every voice was silenced, and every eye turned toward the woman. She had opened the alabaster vial and, with trembling fingers, was pouring costly, perfumed oil over Jesus' hair. It trickled over his dark locks, glistening in the light of the lamps. Jesus did not look surprised at this unusual anointing, rather he gazed on the weeping woman with grateful tenderness. A long, poignant moment passed as everyone was transfixed by the emotional scene. Beth realized she was holding her breath and let it slip out, her heart turning over with a strange flutter. Who was this woman, and why was she distressed?

The silence was broken by Judas Iscariot's sharp voice as he leaped to his feet, demanding, "Why this waste? This perfume could have been sold, and the money given to the poor." A few of the other men nodded their heads.

Jesus reached out and took the woman's trembling hands in his own. Her damp face tipped up to him and tears dripped off her chin. He looked around at the gathered men. His voice was hoarse with emotion. "Why do you bother this woman? She has done a good deed to me. For you will always have the poor with you, but you do not always have me." He kissed the back of her hands.

Jesus, his hair shining with the perfumed oil, appeared more at peace than he had the whole day.

Jesus gazed at his disciples, his eyes damp with suppressed tears. "When she poured this perfume on my body, she did it to prepare me for burial. Truly I say to you, wherever this gospel is preached in the whole world, what this woman has done will also be spoken of in memory of her."

The cloying perfume lost its sweetness as Beth was struck with sharp memories of burial spices and oils. She had helped her mother and aunts anoint her infant brothers, and her tears had mingled with the oils as she had helped anoint her father—before they had been sealed away in their tombs.

Jesus truly believed he was about to die. A tear escaped and tracked its way down her cheek.

32

ZEALOT

"Have you seen Jacob?" Simeon stormed into the classroom, tapping a small scroll on his palm. "No one went to answer the door. I had to go myself."

Reuben looked up from his writing-table. The classroom was a quiet oasis amid the hustle and bustle of Festival Week preparations.

"No," Reuben answered, and hesitated. Not wanting to get Jacob in trouble but wanting to be truthful, he added, "I haven't seen him all afternoon, actually. Alexander doesn't know where he is either. Alexander's rather cross that Jacob has skipped off and left them to cover his chores."

Simeon's frown deepened. The house was being scrubbed top to bottom, and all yeast removed in preparation for the approaching Week of Unleavened Bread. Not even a crumb of leaven could remain. Several of Simeon's friends and extended family had arrived for the festival, and so there were guests to attend to on top of the long list of cleaning and preparations.

Simeon sniffed. "I will have words for him when he returns." Reuben spun his pen in his fingers and felt a pang of sympathy for Jacob. Simeon held up the scroll. "A message returned from Caiaphas' palace. He wants to hear what Jesus spoke in the Temple firsthand. Tonight. He is convening an impromptu meeting of the Sanhedrin."

Reuben swallowed hard and set down his pen, his fingers suddenly clumsy. The last time he had stood before these men he had been made to look like a fool. He smoothed his shawl for comfort. He couldn't allow that to happen again.

"I'm sure you will make me proud," Simeon said with a raised brow. It was more of a command than a word of encouragement.

Reuben nodded and Simeon left the room. Reuben was unable to return to his work and instead fiddled with the inkpot and papyrus. In his mind, he recalled everything he had witnessed Jesus say in the Temple Courts. He played the scene over and over again to make sure he remembered everything—every insult, every false slander.

Filled with restless worry, he stood up. Making sure no one was around, he began to rehearse what he would say, pretending that the student benches were full of the stern faces of the Sanhedrin.

He was gesturing boldly, pacing up and down the room when a small sound made him jump and wheel around. It was Michal at the doorway, clearing her throat. She was staring off into the corner of the room, her expression cold and flat. Reuben flushed.

Refusing to meet his gaze, she mumbled, "Simeon is ready to leave. He requests you meet him in the front hall." She spun on her heel and hastened away.

Reuben's shoulders slumped. Though queasy with nerves, he still had room in his heart to feel stung by Michal's continued anger. She avoided him whenever she could, refusing to even look him in the face.

He and Simeon left the house together and strode through the dusk towards Caiaphas' home. It was the largest residence in Jerusalem besides Herod's Palace. It had ornate plaster on the walls, mosaic floors, expensive furnishings, and many rooms for guests. As it was for the High Priest, it boasted a mikveh and a vast meeting room with tiered benches to convene the Sanhedrin. It even had its own prison, a pit where the offender was lowered by rope to keep him secure while his fate was decided.

The palace home was the occupancy of whoever held the office of High Priest. The position was not held for life any longer, but the priestly garments were yanked from one man and thrust at another with little ceremony, and all for the sake of politics. Annas had once been High Priest. Through his shrewd guidance and political mind, his son-in-law now held the title, and his other sons were being groomed in case Caiaphas ever fell from favor.

They were greeted at the door by a servant and led into Caiaphas' meeting room. The other guests had arrived and were holding goblets of wine and clustered in small groups. Several of the men nodded welcome to Simeon. Their glances to Reuben were measuring and he swallowed hard under the weight of their eyes.

Simeon was not a member of the Sanhedrin, not yet anyway. Annas did not seem to like Simeon, for reasons Reuben could not understand. Reuben knew full well that if Annas did not like you, you did not get a seat on the Sanhedrin.

Caiaphas's gaze flicked around the room to make sure all were in attendance. He motioned to his personal servant, who clapped his hands. The servants all departed, shutting the door behind them. The oil lamps flickered as men found their seats on the raised benches. Simeon and Reuben stood a little to the side as the Sanhedrin members awaited instruction.

Caiaphas looked their way and his voice was loud and carrying. "Well, Simeon, let's hear what your student has to say. It had better be worth my convening the council."

"Not all are here though," Annas said, his sharp eyes scanning the room. "Where is Nicodemus? Where is Joseph of Arimathea?"

Caiaphas shrugged. "The scrolls I dispatched returned unopened. Apparently, the two men are in Bethany at a feast."

Annas was displeased, and he thumped his tall, ornate staff on the ground. The silver head of almond blossoms glistened in the light.

"As I was saying," Caiaphas continued loudly with a hint of impatience. "We are gathered to hear what this young disciple overheard. Simeon feels it would assist us in dealing with Jesus of Nazareth."

All eyes fell on Reuben and he froze with fear. He heard an impatient sniff near his ear. He stumbled a little as Simeon pushed him forward. Reuben drew a deep breath through his nose and stood in the center of the room, feeling all the weight of the elder's and chief priest's gaze heavy upon him.

He cleared his throat and began. When he saw the men were all listening seriously to what he said, he relaxed a little and found his stride. He stood tall as he repeated everything he had heard Jesus say.

The priests and elders growled as they heard the words Jesus had spoken against them. Reuben looked around at pair after pair of sharp, narrowed eyes, feeling exultant to have them hanging on every word he said; it was as if he were more than just a disciple.

He heard his voice ring across the room, "If his false words against the leaders of our people are not enough, Jesus himself gave us exactly what we need to bring him down—blasphemy." He let that word hang in the air a moment, and when he saw Simeon looking at him proudly, he thought his heart would burst. "He has prophesied the destruction of the Temple itself. He said that not one stone will be left atop the other, all will be torn down."

The elders and priests stamped their feet in anger, drowning out Reuben's voice. He stood in the center of the thunderous, angry men, and was glad that he was only the messenger.

Annas raised a hand for silence and the clamor stilled. "That is blasphemy indeed. But is it enough to truly convince the people of Jesus' evil intentions?"

Voices were raised all around the room as men argued.

Caiaphas stood up and moved to the center of the room, and Reuben hastened out of the way. "It is true," Caiaphas said. "Jesus blasphemes against God's House, declaring that its leaders are corrupt and that the Temple shall not stand. Still, I don't think the words are weighty enough if we are to publicly arrest the man." Voices began to decry his words, but he held up his hands again. "If we captured him tomorrow we'd have a riot on our hands as we tried to lead him away. We *cannot* cause a riot. Pilate has warned us—any hint at unrest will be met with swift and brutal punishment."

"So we wait until after the Passover then," a priest stood up. "When the crowds have gone home we will take the man and have him stoned for blasphemy. The charges may be weak, but they should stand."

Annas turned in his seat and nodded at the man. "It may be wise to wait, as you say. I think, however, we may want to go beyond stoning the man. We need to make an example of any revolutionary who does not align himself with the Temple and the Sanhedrin." He paused a moment before adding in a serious tone, "We need Jesus of Nazareth crucified."

A collective gasp whispered around the room, and Reuben's gut clenched. He despised Jesus, yet inwardly he quailed at what Annas was proposing. Wasn't death by stoning punishment enough? Just thinking about the barbaric act of crucifixion was enough to make Reuben break out into a sweat.

"We do not crucify like the dogs!" an elder protested.

"Of course not," Annas' voice slid like oil. "We will let the dogs do the deed for us. They will have all the blood upon their own heads, and we shall be innocent."

More mutters moved around the room, and soon heads were nodding in agreement.

"Very well then," Caiaphas said, taking a seat. "We shall wait until after the Passover, then find a way to arrest that wretched Nazarene."

A tiny tap came on the door, and Caiaphas sighed and gestured that Reuben should go and answer it. Reuben opened the door and his mouth fell open when he saw who was waiting.

Scarcely believing his own eyes, he pulled the door wide open and announced, "This is one of Jesus' disciples, one of his Twelve!"

The Sanhedrin leaned forward as Reuben stepped back and let a nervous Judas Iscariot enter the room. Judas walked forward and jerked his head at the assembled Sanhedrin.

"What are you doing here?" Caiaphas snapped as Judas stood in the center of the meeting room, his eyes darting over all those assembled.

"Did Jesus send you to reason with us?" Annas sneered.

"He did not," Judas said, shifting his stance. "He doesn't even know that I am here. None of his disciples do."

Caiaphas rose up and moved forward. He circled Judas, sizing up the man. Judas didn't seem to like the perusal, and he stood taller. Caiaphas asked, "Then what *are* you doing here?"

Judas smiled, his expression becoming open and charming. "I am one of his inner circle. I can help you. I can let you know when Jesus is alone so you can arrest him."

Whispers flew around the room like a breath of wind. Reuben's heart skipped a beat. This was a golden opportunity fallen into their lap when they needed it most, and they all knew it.

Caiaphas' brows lowered and he tilted his head to the side as he ran a finger over his lips. "Just like that, you would turn over your rabbi to us?"

Judas' lips twisted. "His miracles were wondrous, but lately his teachings have become ... distorted. He isn't who I hoped he would be." Judas' expression was bitter. "I was deceived. He told us he is the Messiah, and we foolishly believed him."

Derisive laughter bounced off the walls. Judas shook his head. His next words rasped like a blade sliding over stone. "All the way to Jerusalem, I thought he was preparing to finally make a move for the throne. He always speaks in riddles and parables, so you never know what he's actually saying. Well, tonight he spoke plainly. He has no plans to save Jerusalem from the Romans. He's going to watch it fall and let those who follow him be persecuted and killed."

A long moment of silence followed as the Sanhedrin weighed and measured the Judas' words. Reuben felt a pang of worry for his gentle cousin Beth, but he shoved her from his mind. He couldn't be distracted, not now.

Annas pursed his lips. His tone was sarcastic. "So you're doing this good deed simply to help the people and for no purposes of your own?"

Judas gave a dashing smile and held up a hand as he rubbed his thumb and fingers together. "What would you reward me with if I betray Jesus to you?"

Annas laughed and wagged his finger like a good-natured grandfather. "Ha! I knew it, there is always a price. I never trust a man who does something for nothing." They grinned at one another with perfect understanding.

A scale and coins were brought, and the sum of thirty silver coins was agreed upon.

"I will come and get you at the earliest opportunity," Judas promised, weighing the heavy bag of coins in his hand. His expression faltered for the first time as he said, "Have your guards ready to come at a moment's notice."

"Don't worry about us," Caiaphas sniffed. "We shall be ready. Don't make us wait long."

Reuben held the door open for the traitorous disciple as he hastened out of the room. He couldn't help whispering at the fallen disciple, "Well done. Jesus will finally get what he deserves."

Judas glanced up, and Reuben was surprised to see the disciple smirk, defiance in his eyes. "We shall see."

Reuben shook his head as Judas slipped into the night. He was unsure what had just happened, so he put it out of his mind.

"This shows that God's hand is with us," Caiaphas laughed. "Just when we needed it, help arrived. We shall bring down this false prophet for the good of the people."

Annas tapped his staff on the floor and nodded with a small, sharp smile. "There is little risk to us personally, but everything to gain."

Reuben and Simeon left Caiaphas' house and walked for home by the light of the moon. Reuben's mind was full, and he was lost in his own worries. Try as he might, he couldn't escape concern for his cousin Beth.

"What are you thinking about?" Simeon asked.

"Nothing," he said quickly. He couldn't make it sound as though he had any pity for Jesus' followers. He couldn't let his own emotions cloud his judgment and waver his resolve. He swallowed hard. Jesus had to be dealt with, no matter the cost.

Simeon looked about to say more, but a shout made both men turn their attention down the street. A small crowd was forming. Glancing at one another, Simeon and Reuben hastened forward to see what was happening. Several people held torches aloft, and in the wavering light, Reuben could see two young men in short tunics beating a Jewish man. The onlookers watched in helpless horror. The poor Jew was held fast by the back of his robe while his assailant stood in boxing form and pummeled him in the chest, stomach, and face. Blood gushed from the victim's broken nose and his eyes were swelling shut. Reuben froze in shock. It was a sickening display.

It was a moment before Reuben recognized the battered young man. His heart leaped into his throat. He lunged forward as he cried out, "It's Jacob!"

He tried to shoulder his way through the crowd but hastily stepped back as he met the sharp edge of a sword pointed at his throat. The youth at the end of the blade grinned maliciously.

"Stop this at once," Simeon commanded. "That is my servant."

The man delivering the blows heard him. He paused and smirked at Simeon. He turned back to Jacob and landed three more sharp, rapid punches before he nodded to his friend to release Jacob, who slumped face down to the ground. Still held back by the glint of a sword before his face, Reuben tried to see if Jacob was breathing.

"What is the meaning of this?" Simeon demanded.

With a swagger, the tall, handsome youth waved a roll of papyrus in his bloody fist. "I might ask you the same thing." he sneered, dangling the scroll before Simeon's face. "Why a servant of *yours* is a member of a secret group of Zealots, right here in the city? We broke up a meeting, and caught him trying to flee." He unfurled the scroll. "See here—written proof."

Simeon tried to snatch the scroll away, but the youth was faster. He tucked it into his tunic, clicking his tongue as he shook his head. "I don't think so. I think I will give this to the governor and he can decide what is best to be done to this seditious Jew."

Reuben, trapped by the glint of a sword blade, gritted his teeth.

"You are one of Pilate's men?" Simeon's tone was sharp and torchlight flickered in his dark eyes. "Does he know you are beating men without trial?"

"Of course," the youth replied a little too quickly, his eyes wary. "He has assigned extra men to keep watch during the festival to your ridiculous, invisible god. We are only making sure the peace is kept." The young man sucked his lower lip for a second and eyed Simeon through narrowed eyes. "Since your servant is guilty of sedition to Rome, I see no need to reimburse you for the damage of your man. Your *seditious* servant." He paced the words like a threat. "Go home now, and I won't trouble you for your name. "

Reuben made fists at his side. Though his blood was pumping, he wasn't foolish enough to move. He knew that Pilate might not be happy that the enthusiasm of his soldiers had led to a public, illegal beating on the street. Yet, the young soldier was clever in his insinuations. Simeon wouldn't want the eyes of Pilate delving into his household. Though lacking justice, the deal kept Simeon out of Pilate's courtroom and protected his reputation and the household.

Reuben stared at Jacob, who still hadn't moved. Blood gushed from a cut over Jacob's eye and flowed over the cobblestones, shimmering blackly in the torchlight. Simeon nodded once, and the gang of young men turned and sauntered away, sheathing swords and beginning to laugh with one another. Reuben rushed forward and rolled Jacob onto his back, the young man coughing up blood.

"He's dying!" Reuben cried out. "Somebody help us get him home!"

He peered up at the onlookers, but the crowd was afraid to be seen helping a Zealot. They melted away, taking the torchlight with them.

Simeon came and grabbed Jacob under his shoulders while Reuben lifted his legs. They were heavier than he expected.

"So *this* is what he has been doing all day?" Simeon grunted. "A Zealot? The fool!"

Reuben swallowed hard. He had kept Jacob's secret for years. He couldn't admit that now. As they shuffled towards Simeon's house bearing the bloodied young man, Reuben also carried a burden of guilt. If he had told Simeon what Jacob had been up to perhaps he could have prevented this.

Reuben was soaked with sweat by the time they made it to Simeon's door, leaving a trail of dripping blood up the street. Michal opened the door at his call. When she saw her brother, she screamed a long, sickening wail that echoed throughout the house. The force of her grief chilled Reuben to the marrow of his bones.

Alexander ran into the room at the sound and cried aloud when he saw his son. He hastened forward, trying to take his unconscious son into his arms as if Jacob were still a child.

The four of them bore Jacob to his room and laid him on the low pallet. Reuben stepped back and panted against the wall as Michal ran for water and cloth. Alexander prayed, his keening voice rising and falling.

Mouse-like Tabitha, hearing the laments, came into the room wearing only her inner tunic. She drifted like a silent wraith, her face pale and her eyes glistening orbs. She hovered beside the unconscious body of her son with a look of uncomprehending disbelief that wrenched at Reuben's heart.

"I will fetch a physician," Simeon mumbled as he turned and fled the tumultuous emotions that filled the room so thickly they pushed out the air.

Michal rushed back with a basin, kneeling by the bed to mop up her brother's face. "Who has done this?" she demanded as tears coursed down her face. Reuben told her. Her hands trembled with anger as she pressed the cloth to the gaping head wound. "Romans! They think they can do whatever they like. Where is the justice?" she snapped through her tears.

Tabitha hovered with her hands on her heart, hardly breathing as she gazed down on her only son.

At Michal's command, Reuben and Alexander removed the young man's tunic so she could assess his wounds, covering him with a blanket. Reuben stood back and scrubbed his hand over his face. Jacob's abdomen was purple and swollen.

Alexander whispered, "He is bleeding inside; see where the blood pools?"

"What can we do, Papa?"

"Pray is all, my dear," he said as tears leaked down his face. "The physician will not be able to help. Only the Lord can heal him now."

Reuben swallowed hard, remembering hearing those words long ago as a child.

Michal dropped her head onto the mattress and clutched at the blanket that covered her brother. Reuben longed to comfort her, to take her in his arms stroke her hair.

Her head jerked up. "Wait!" she gasped. "Jesus can heal him."

She turned to her father with a wild expression. "He's been healing people in the Temple—everybody knows it." She turned to Reuben, her eyes brimming and her lip quivering. "Will you go and find Jesus? Will you bring him here?"

Reuben took a step back in alarm and sucked in his breath. "I-I-I don't know where he is," he stammered. The man was wanted by the Sanhedrin. He couldn't bring a blasphemer into Simeon's house!

"Please!" her voice shattered like glass. "You must know where he can be found. Jesus is famous. Everybody is talking about him, someone will know."

Alexander joined with his daughter's pleading, his tone low. "Reuben, please, if you know where he is . . ."

"I don't!" Reuben cut them off, turning away and running a hand through his hair. Their cries were almost more than he could bear. He wanted to help his friend Jacob, he truly did, but he couldn't defy God to do it. His heart ached under this test God was giving him.

"Please, Reuben!" Michal wailed. "He's your friend. He'll die!"

Reuben fleetingly wondered if he could just leave the house, wander the streets, and pretend that he had looked for Jesus. At least that would appease Michal and her father. But Simeon would not approve of encouraging Michal and her father to hope in a lie.

Reuben felt like a heavy stone dropped in his stomach as he said, "I can't, Michal. I just can't. Jesus is a false prophet. We shouldn't have anything to do with him."

She stared at him a long moment, her eyes wide. Time slowed as he noticed every teardrop on her eyelashes. He was jerked back to reality as she charged at him, screaming like a fiend. She forcibly pushed him out of the servant's rooms, slamming the door in his face. He stood with slumped shoulders in the hallway, hearing her sobs behind the door and Alexander trying to comfort her.

Reuben slunk to his room, feeling miserable to the core. He sat on the bed and put his head in his hands. He had seen Jesus heal with his own eyes. He knew that Jesus could heal Jacob, and would do it if Michal asked. Yet the truth was that Jesus' miracles were deceptive, cunning tricks of unholy power designed to lead all the people astray.

Though he knew he was right, when Reuben closed his eyes, all he could see was the look on Michal's face when he had refused to help her.

Reuben balled up his fists and slammed them onto the bed, little satisfied by the muffled thud. He panted as the night's injustices fired his heart. He ached for Jacob. The servant had been a friend, and Reuben would mourn his loss. Somehow though, it was still Michal who overwhelmed his thoughts. Reuben's threw himself back to stare at the ceiling.

In time, Michal might have forgiven him for the words he had spoken months ago. She would have come to understand why he needed to sacrifice their love for the greater love of the law. But after tonight, Reuben knew that she would never forgive him for refusing to bring Jesus to heal her brother. She hated him. He had seen her loathing in every line on her face, felt it in the force of her hands.

He covered his face with his hands and groaned. It wasn't his fault Jacob was a Zealot. It wasn't his fault that Jesus was a false prophet. Rage burned towards the Nazarene whose deceptions had severed all hope of a relationship with Michal. She would blame him forever. Reuben leaped to his feet and paced the room, his heart throbbing with hatred.

Within him was a swirling, hot mass of frustration and pain. All he wanted to do was what was right, and everyone was set against him. He cast aside his own mistakes, and instead threw all his anger and bitterness and loneliness on Jesus. The pain of his father's disapproval, the friendship he missed from Beth, the wall between himself and Michal, the exhausting work of trying to earn Simeon's good opinion ... he balled up all his burdens, bunched them together like a ball of mud, and slung it straight at Jesus, baring his teeth as he pictured it striking him across the face.

33

THE SHEPHERD

Beth wound her way through the thick, jostling crowds in the Holy City, just behind her husband and John. Everyone was in a hurry; the time for the Passover meal was drawing near.

"I still can't believe that you and John were able to find room inside the city," Beth called ahead to her husband.

"It was Jesus who knew where we should go." Peter looked back at her. "Our host has promised us a share of their Passover lamb. All we need are the side dishes."

Beth hitched up the basket on her arm. It was full of provisions they needed to prepare the feast.

Back in Egypt, in the time of their forefather's bondage, the Hebrews had slaughtered lambs and wiped the blood on their doorposts. It was the sign for the angel of death to pass over them and leave the firstborn unharmed. The offering of blood had been the beginning of freedom for the Hebrew nation, and they were commanded by God to commemorate His saving power every year. They kept many festivals, but this one was special. This one held their national identity and symbolized their hope for a better future.

Beth sighed. She did not feel hopeful today. Jesus' ominous words were still sharp in her mind.

They arrived at the designated house in the Lower City, a common, two-story dwelling. Their host greeted them with a bow and showed them to the courtyard where the lamb was already roasting on a spit. His wife was brushing the meat with bitter herbs as was commanded, to remind them of the bitterness of slavery. Beth tried to smile at the shy children who hugged their mother's legs, but her mind twisted with fear as she imagined what these children would suffer in body and spirit if Jerusalem fell.

"You may cook your bread here if you wish," the wife spoke to Beth, gesturing to a clay oven already warm with coals. Beth nodded.

Their host then led Beth, Peter, and John upstairs to the guest room. It was a sparsely furnished space, but large enough for their needs. Beth rested the basket on the low table.

"This looks excellent, thank-you," John said to their host as he set down the wineskins. Their host smiled and left them alone.

"Hello?" a voice called from below, and John answered for them to come up. Mary, mother of James and Joseph, and Mary Magdalene entered, each carrying a basket of her own.

"Whew! I'm glad we went to the market yesterday; it would be insane to try to shop today." Mary Magdalene laughed, but it sounded forced. The other Mary was somber as she ran a hand down the long braid slung over her shoulder.

Peter and John went to fetch water for washing, leaving the women alone. The two Marys gazed around the room looking lost. Beth could see how burdened they were. She impulsively reached out and grasped the women's hands, and they turned to her with wide, questioning eyes.

"I know we're all worried," Beth said. "Jesus wants to share this meal with us, so let's do this for him, okay?"

Mary Magdalene's mouth tipped upwards, and she nodded once. The other Mary struggled with her emotions for a moment, and then she nodded as well. Beth gave their hands one last squeeze before releasing them.

She gestured to the supplies on the table. "We'd better get started. The rest of the disciples will be here soon."

The women began with heavy slowness, but habit took over and they fell into a rhythm. Mary Magdalene borrowed cushions from the homeowner and spread them around the table so the diners could recline. The meal would be long, eaten slowly with many prayers and stories. They set out the dishes and the wine cups. They ground dates into a paste in a pestle, prepared the vegetables and tart dressing, and mixed the dough for the unleavened bread. It was made without yeast in remembrance of their hasty departure from Egypt after the angel of death had passed over the houses of the Hebrews. For the entire Week of Unleavened Bread, no speck of yeast would be found within any Jewish household.

John and Peter returned, each carrying a heavy jar full of water that they set against the wall. John set four of the simple cups in a row and poured in wine and water. The four cups symbolized four promises from the story of the Exodus.

". . . I am the Lord,
and I will bring you out from under the burdens of the Egyptians,
and I will deliver you from their bondage.
I will also redeem you with an outstretched arm and great judgments.
Then I will take you for My people, and I will be your God . . ."

Beth took the unleavened dough and carried it down to the courtyard. The afternoon was waning. The lamb was gone from the spit and taken into the house to be carved. Beth had the courtyard to herself. She began to lay the flat loaves out for baking. She glanced up as Peter came and joined her in the courtyard, and his presence was welcome.

"Nearly done," he smiled, but it did not reach his eyes. "Jesus should be here soon."

Beth felt a chill blow over her despite her closeness to the oven, and she rubbed her arms.

"Do you think—" she hesitated, looking over to where he leaned across the wall with crossed arms. "Do you think Jesus means what he says literally? That he will be crucified at the Passover? *This* Passover?" She swallowed with difficulty.

Peter's face was heavy. "I don't know," he admitted with a sigh. "He speaks of his death, and yet he speaks of coming in glory in our lifetime." Peter tipped up his chin, knocking the back of his head against the wall. "How's a fisherman supposed to understand? I'm a poor spiritual leader for our family."

"No." Beth reached out a hand to her husband. He came and knelt beside her at the oven. She grasped his large hand in her own. "If it hadn't been for you and your decision to follow Jesus, I would never have left the comfort of my home. You know me," she curved her lip. "I would have thought that Jesus was just another dangerous revolutionary and stayed as far away as I could. I wouldn't have heard him teach or witnessed his mighty power and love. You led me to him." Peter did not look comforted.

She leaned over, nudging him. "Besides, it is I who have failed you." She felt tears pressing and Peter looked at her with confusion. "You should have a son or daughter. A child to teach all that you have learned. It's my fault, I'm so sorry, Peter."

"What are you talking about?" Peter shook his head. "How is it your fault? If we had been quiet at home, perhaps you would have conceived by now. We're always on the move, living in rough camps, with hardly a moment to call our own. If anyone is at fault, it is me."

Beth was happy he did not blame her. Yet, she felt blood rush to her face. "Even so, surely we have had opportunity enough for me to conceive. Maybe something is wrong with me, inside. Maybe I am barren."

Peter's chuckled, "Surely not. You are young yet, we both are."

His casual dismissal rankled her nerves. How was he always so confident? "It's been nearly five years, Peter." Peter's eyes searched her face as she struggled to contain her emotions. "I really think something is wrong with me, and I know I should have asked Jesus for healing. But I haven't." She bit her lip, hoping he would understand. "I'm too afraid. It's my selfish fear that has kept you from having a son or a daughter of your own."

"Afraid?" Peter furrowed his brow. "Of what?"

Beth twisted up her mouth in a rueful smile. "You're not afraid of anything Peter, so I don't know if you'd understand." Peter's gaze held her fast, and she struggled to find the right words. "I'm afraid that if I have a baby in these dangerous times it will be born to suffering. When Jesus was born, babies were killed."

Peter opened his mouth but she pushed on before he could sweep away her worries. "Jesus spoke of earthquakes, famines, and war." Tears welled up and spilled over her cheeks as she opened her heart to her husband. Could she make him understand? Her voice hitched as she asked, "What if we have a baby, but it dies? How could I bear to have a child in my arms at last and have to bury it? I'm not strong enough to endure that." She hid her face in her hands.

She felt Peter take her hands from her face, and hold both of them in his own. "Beth, you can't live like that, fearful of pain that might never come. Anxiety is a poor master. It will only lead you and those you love to harm. You need to cast your worries on the Lord, my little dove. Only then will you have a full life."

Beth shook her head, wanting him to understand how hard this was for her. She didn't need pithy sayings, she needed him to *know*. "You just don't get it, do you?" She had held her anxieties like a shield before her heart for as long as she could remember, as if her worries kept her safe and protected her from suffering.

"Beth, you won't have to do this alone," Peter said as he raised a hand to pinch her chin, giving her an encouraging smile. "You have stood by me. I will do the same for you, and any children the Lord blesses us with." She tried to smile, but it wobbled. Peter drew her to him, pressing her against his heart. She felt his hard swallow above her head. "I cannot promise you an easy life while we follow Jesus, but we shall go through it together, all right?" Beth nodded against his chest, drawing deep the scent of his tunic.

Noises from above reminded them of their work, and Peter released his hold on Beth so she could finish baking the bread.

Their host brought them a section of the lamb, cut in such a way that not a single bone had been broken. When the couple went back up the stairs, the small room was full of people and the lamps were lit.

Beth set the fragrant loaves on the table and moved back to find a quiet place to sit with the other women. Beth remembered Passover meals from her past, and this gathering was somber by comparison. The mood of the room was tense as they waited for sunset. As the sunlight retreated from the room no one laughed, no one teased. Even James and John were quiet at the table. John kept casting his eyes at Jesus with concern. Beth thought Jesus was looking drawn and a little pale.

Beth, needing something to break the tension, looked at her cousins James and John, then leaned to Naomi and said, "Your boys have grown into fine men. You must be very proud."

The two boisterous young men had been shaped by Jesus. Though they still loved their fun, their humor was wrapped in a layer of kindness and compassion now. What they had seen and heard and what they had done themselves, had altered them forever.

Naomi smiled a little, but there were worry lines on her brow. "I hope they will grow into old men with grandchildren on their knee. This night though ... My heart tells me that sadness is coming."

Beth swallowed a lump.

As Beth anxiously scanned the men's faces, she noticed Judas Iscariot whispering to Simon, who shook his head, confused. Judas puffed out his breath and leaned away. When he noticed Beth's confused gaze, he turned his head away. She didn't have time to dwell on Judas' behavior; the shofar blast wafted in through the open window.

Jesus indicated that Peter should begin the meal. So Peter took the Kiddush cup and began the benediction, speaking of the sanctification of the meal. Once he was finished, they first ate some green and bitter herbs and the fruit paste.

The conversation was strained as they ate. They all felt the oppressive weight like a gathering storm.

Jesus' somber voice cut the quiet. "Truly I say to you, one of you will betray me."

The room became so still, Beth could hear the neighbors next door. All the disciples stared at one another. Simon narrowed his eyes suspiciously at Judas, who was looking down and picking at the tabletop with a fingernail.

The room erupted with the disciple's protests. They cried out, "Surely not I, Lord?"

Jesus held up his hands and they quieted. His voice was full of sadness. "One of those who dipped his hand with me in the bowl is the one who will betray me." They all glanced at each other with anxious confusion. Jesus said, "The Son of Man is to go, just as it is written of him; but woe to the betrayer! It would have been good for that man if he had not been born."

Jesus looked at Judas Iscariot, who was sitting low and grim in his seat. Judas, realizing all eyes were on him, belatedly cleared his throat and asked, "You mean me, Rabbi?"

Jesus said to him, "You have said it yourself."

Beth stared at Judas Iscariot in alarm. James and John half rose, but Jesus indicated that they should sit and return to their meal. The men shifted on their cushions, all of them staring. Judas Iscariot flushed, but he looked determined. Beth wished that someone would question Jesus and ask what he meant, but it did not seem the time with the Passover in progress. Beth tried her best to focus her mind back on the meal.

The next part of the meal was usually started by a son asking his father a question, but in the absence of a child and his father, John asked Jesus the question, "Why is this night different from all other nights?" The father would respond by telling them the story of the peoples' disgrace and ending with the glory of their exodus.

Jesus was silent a long moment, then a tear slipped down his cheek and he shook his head, unable to speak. Beth's heart pounded as it rose up into her throat.

John said tentatively, "Shall we sing the Hallel, Rabbi?"

Jesus nodded, his expression heavy. They waited for him to lead it, but Jesus was quiet. Peter, as the eldest of the Twelve, began the psalm and the rest responded. As they sang, Peter took the second cup, the Haggadah cup, and passed it around so all could take a sip.

Then Jesus, as was customary, took a loaf of bread and blessed it. He did not pass it, but looked at them all to be sure that they were listening. "Take, eat," he said. "This is my body."

Beth stifled a startled gasp. This was different from the usual Passover, much different. What was Jesus doing?

Jesus passed the loaf, and the disciples obeyed. They all tore some bread and ate it. Eyes flicked around the room as they tried to understand what was happening. Then they all ate some of the lamb as was commanded in the Passover.

Jesus took the next cup, the cup of blessing, and blessed it. This cup was to commemorate their thankfulness for God's work in taking them out of Egypt. Passing through the sea was the moment when their ancestors had felt the joy of being redeemed.

But instead of the usual scriptures, Jesus passed the cup to the disciples and said, "Drink from it, all of you; for this is my blood of the covenant, which is poured out for many for the forgiveness of sins."

Beth's eyes opened wide. His blood? What on earth did he mean? When the cup came to her, she took a sip, the rich wine tangy on her tongue.

When they had all drank from the cup, Jesus said, "But now I say to you, I will not drink this fruit of the vine from now on until that day when I drink it new with you in my Father's kingdom."

Beth was surprised that he would not partake of the fourth cup. The fourth cup was the celebration of the creation of the nation as

God took the people for Himself.

So the fourth cup sat untouched, and they all stole fleeting glimpses at it. What did this strange Passover mean?

They sang the rest of the Hallel as was traditional, Jesus leading them with his eyes closed and his hands extended as if in prayer. The psalm was familiar to Beth. She had memorized it as a child, but the words she had spoken for years in rote became real to her tonight as she watched Jesus sing.

"... I love the Lord, because He hears my voice and my supplications.
Because He has inclined His ear to me ...

The cords of death encompassed me;
And the terrors of Sheol came upon me;
I found distress and sorrow.
Then I called upon the name of the Lord,
'O Lord, I beseech You, save my life!'

Gracious is the Lord, and righteous;
Yes, our God is compassionate ...
I was brought low, and He saved me ...
For You have rescued my soul from death,
My eyes from tears, my feet from stumbling.
I shall walk before the Lord in the land of the living.
I believed when I said, 'I am greatly afflicted.'

I shall pay my vows to the Lord,
Oh may it be in the presence of all His people.
Precious in the sight of the Lord is the death of His godly ones.
O Lord, surely I am Your servant,
I am Your servant, the son of Your handmaid.
You have loosed my bonds ... Praise the Lord!

Give thanks to the Lord, for He is good,
For His lovingkindness is everlasting ...
From my distress I called upon the Lord;
The Lord answered me ...
The Lord is for me ... therefore I will look on those who hate me.

All nations surrounded me;
In the name of the Lord, I will surely cut them off ...
They surrounded me like bees,
They were extinguished as a fire of thorns;
In the name of the Lord, I will surely cut them off ...
The Lord is my strength and my song,

And He has become my salvation.

I will not die, but live and tell of the works of the Lord.
The Lord has disciplined me severely,
but He has not given me over to death ...
The stone the builders rejected
Has become the chief cornerstone ...
Give thanks to the Lord, for He is good,
For His lovingkindness is everlasting."

When the song finished, Jesus covered his face with his hands and sat in silence.

Beth felt like a fist gripped her heart. Mary Magdalene sniffed back tears, and Beth reached out to take her hand. Beth felt someone take her other and glanced down and saw a lined hand in her own. She looked at her aunt Naomi in surprise. She was startled to see tears glistening in those strong eyes, even as the stalwart woman pressed her lips into a thin line. Naomi reached out and grasped the other Mary's hand. Beth took comfort. She was fearful, but she did not feel alone.

John tried to speak to Jesus, but the rabbi shook his head. After a moment, he raised his face and drew a deep breath. He put a comforting hand on John's shoulder.

"I am all right, John," Jesus said. He gazed around at his disciples, rose to his feet, and said, "Come on, all of you."

"We are going out? On the Passover?" Matthew exclaimed, but Jesus was already on his way to the door. The men hastened after Jesus. As one, the woman rose and followed.

"This has been the strangest Passover ever," Mary Magdalene whispered to Beth.

Beth glanced back at the abandoned table with the remains of food and the glistening cup of wine.

Jesus led them into the streets. They were empty—a stark contrast to the bustling preparations of the day. Throughout the entire city, Jews were cloistered in their homes until sunrise.

Jesus and his disciples exited the city, much to the surprise of the southern gatekeeper who tried to convince them to go back to their homes. Jesus was insistent. With a deep sigh, the gatekeeper unlocked the small door and they ducked under the doorway and into the openness. They walked around the sleepy city and up the shadowed

Mount of Olives.

In the heavy shadows of the night, Jesus turned and spoke lowly, "You will all fall away because of me this night, for it is written, 'I will strike down the shepherd and the sheep of the flock shall be scattered.'"

Beth's stomach writhed, and everyone was speechless. She looked around herself but the faces of her friends were shrouded in darkness.

Jesus said, "Remember this—after I have been raised, I will go ahead of you to Galilee."

Peter pushed his way right up to Jesus and declared, "Even though all may fall away because of you, I will never fall away."

Beth's hand twitched as she longed to reach out and pull Peter close to her, to keep her impulsive husband from harm.

Jesus sighed and laid his hand on Peter's shoulder. "Truly I say to you that this very night, before a rooster crows, you will deny me three times."

Peter's next words were vehement. "Even if I have to die with you, I will not deny you."

Beth pressed a hand to her throat as she felt events starting to spin out of control. None of them could die! No, no, no!

"Nor shall I!" cried out James and John in unison, and all the men echoed them, declaring their resolution to die with Jesus.

Beth shook her head. This couldn't be happening now! Even Mary Magdalene cried out her willingness to die. Beth couldn't join their refrain, clawing fear clamped her jaw shut.

The men lit a fire for warmth and made a simple camp in the Garden of Gethsemane. As the fire illuminated the area, Beth saw they were near the olive presses. The familiar sight of presses carved from basalt rock from Galilee should have been a comfort. Instead, Beth felt a painful reminder of how far she was from home.

Beth sat with her arms drawn around her knees. Her eyes followed Jesus as he moved around in the firelight. What expression did she see in his eyes? She knew his moods so well, and this one was new to her. He did not quail or tremble, but his eyes seemed to look into the future and see pain and agony, and he was not eager to go forward to meet it.

Beth sat by the fire and felt no warmth, only an icy chill seeping into her bones. The others were willing to die with Jesus, but now that she was staring down the sharp end of the sword, her resolve melted away into nothing. Could she die for Jesus? For the kingdom he preached? Could she be whipped until her bones were exposed, or stoned with jagged rocks, or suffer the ultimate agony on the cross? The idea made her meal rise in her throat, and it was bitter.

Who did she think she was? She was only a simple woman of no education, humble and meek by nature. She was no warrior. She was gripped by the overwhelming desire to flee. The desire was so strong her muscles trembled. She knew with all of her being that she had to get away, escape before it was too late.

Beth scrambled to her feet and hastened to Peter. She pulled him a little away from the others, into the shadows. Her chest and palms were damp with cold sweat as she whispered, "Peter, I'm afraid. We need to go."

Peter's face was hidden in the darkness, but he reached out and took her hand. His voice was surprised. "Beth, what's wrong?"

"What's wrong?" she repeated as she shook her head at him. "After all we've seen and heard this night, how can you ask me that?"

"Things will be all right," Peter said with confidence, and Beth jerked her hand away with frustration.

"Peter, this is it. Everything is going to come crashing down on us. This is it, this is the moment!"

"Calm yourself, Beth, you're overreacting."

Beth bit her lip hard to try and wake herself from this nightmare. She stared at Jesus and recalled his words, *This is my body. This is my blood.* She was trapped in a nightmare from which she could never wake.

Her breath became short and rapid. She squeezed her eyes shut, pressing her palms to her eye sockets. She tried to remember all the good things that Jesus had said about the kingdom of heaven. She couldn't bring a single one to mind. She tried to recall all the wonders he had performed, but all she could see in her mind's eye was a raven perched upon a cross.

Jesus came up and said in a strained tone, "Peter, come with James and John and be with me while I pray. My soul is deeply grieved this night."

"Of course, Rabbi," Peter said at once.

Beth snatched at his hand, unwilling to let him go.

Peter whispered, "Peace, wife. You are overtired. Go and sleep.

Nothing will happen tonight. Everyone is busy with Passover."

Beth reluctantly released her husband and watched as his shadowy figure disappeared into the darkness. She glanced back at the others. They had found places to settle and rest, and they were much too calm. Bands of fear wrapped around her chest, choking out her breath, and all reason left her.

She turned and fled away from the garden, ignoring the calls of her friends. As she turned towards Bethany, a noise made her jump, and she whirled around to see another disciple leaving the group. Her heart lifted, hoping Peter was coming with her, but the shadowy figure turned back to Jerusalem.

Trying to draw full breaths to calm her racing pulse, she huddled low and ran down the empty road, fearing every shadow, every whisper of the wind.

When she finally reached Bethany and had slammed the door behind her, she fell onto the floor and sobbed at her cowardice.

34

TRIAL OF OPPORTUNITY

The remains of the lamb lay on the table, the bones picked clean. It was nearly midnight. Silence sat heavily upon the dinner guests. Death overshadowed them. Jacob had died late last night, mere hours after being brought home. He had not gone peacefully, but with ragged, blood-filled gasps.

Early this morning, the body had been washed, wrapped in oils and spices, and buried outside the city. Reuben and Simeon had attended the burial, but they had kept from touching the corpse. They did not want to be unclean and unable to participate in the upcoming Festival Week.

Reuben toyed with his silver goblet, feeling overwhelming frustration mingling with grief for his friend. Michal had finally stopped ignoring him. The alternative, he found, was much worse. Whenever she saw him, she froze, staring at him with fiery, accusatory eyes, nostrils flaring, and her disheveled hair wild about her face. He knew she blamed him for not bringing Jesus to heal her brother while there was still a chance.

It was unfair! Reuben took a long draft from his cup. Reuben hadn't hurt Jacob; he had helped intercede and bring him home. Michal should thank him. He rubbed his aching temple with his free hand.

A rap came at the door.

Simeon frowned. "Who could that be at this hour?"

With the staff all in mourning, Reuben took it upon himself to answer the summons. Reuben opened the door and recognized one of Caiaphas' servants, a young man named Malchus.

"It's time," Malchus whispered, his eyes lit up. "We are going to arrest Jesus."

"What, *now?*" Reuben was startled. "In the middle of the night?"

Malchus bobbed his head. "Judas Iscariot reported that Jesus is with only a few disciples, and they are outside the city walls."

Simeon came up behind Reuben and pursed his lips. "Well, if the opportunity has presented itself, I supposed we would be foolish not to take it."

Malchus bobbed his head again. "The High Priest has called for the Temple guards, and there are several other men eager to see Jesus arrested. They are heading for the city gate now. The High Priest thought you might wish to join them."

"I would!" Reuben said at once, pleased Caiaphas had thought of him. He was eager to escape the oppressive mood of the house, and the arrest of Jesus had been a moment he had anticipated for a long time.

As Reuben donned his sandals he asked, "Are you coming, Simeon?"

Simeon held out his hands. "No, this is a task for young men. I shall see you when you return."

Reuben left with Malchus. In the darkness, Reuben jogged with the servant until they caught up with a shadowy mob. They were moving silently, almost secretly, through the city streets, careful not to disturb the people in their Passover celebrations. Lamplight shone from many windows, but no one looked out. Why would they?

The gatekeeper at the South Gate was shocked to see them. "What, *more* people want to go out?" He grumbled as he unlocked the low side door for them, "Where is the respect for tradition?"

One by one they slipped out into the night, Judas Iscariot leading the way. Free of the city walls, they lit torches and the light glinted off a few sword blades. Most of the men were Sadducee or Pharisee disciples, and many carried clubs or sturdy staffs. Reuben wished he had thought to arm himself, but he had no desire to turn back now.

"How will we know it is him?" a man asked. "In the darkness, they might put forward another in defense of their rabbi."

Judas rubbed the back of his neck and thought it over. "I will give you a signal," he said. "The one I kiss is Jesus."

Reuben raised his eyebrows. It was a cold betrayal.

"Come on, men. It's time for me to earn my silver!" Judas said, with only the slightest hitch in his voice.

He led them to the place called the Garden of Gethsemane. As they drew near, they found about two dozen of Jesus' followers, a mere handful compared to the usual crowd he had around him. They had been sleeping by a low fire, and they scrambled to their feet as the torchlight and heavy footfalls awakened them.

"What is this?" a disciple demanded.

The women who followed Jesus pulled back in fear. His glance told Reuben that none of the women were Beth, and he felt a momentary pulse of relief that she would not be present for this. He saw his aunt Naomi but he shrugged away from her narrowed gaze. Reuben's eyes flicked over the other shadowy faces. He recognized many of the disciples, including most of the Twelve. Some were missing though—most importantly, Jesus himself. Had someone tipped him off? He felt a surge of disappointment.

His chin jerked up as he heard Jesus' voice ring through the little clearing and saw the Nazarene stride out from the trees as if coming to meet them. Jesus spread out his arms. "The one who has betrayed me has arrived."

Judas hesitated only a moment, then went forward and kissed Jesus on the cheek. His voice was serious, "Greetings, Rabbi."

Jesus stood and allowed Judas to kiss him, but it was clear from his expression that he knew what Judas was doing.

Jesus sighed, held out his hands palm up, and said, "Friend, do what you came to do."

Reuben was surprised at Jesus' surrender, but he did not miss his opportunity. Reuben surged forward with the mob, surrounding Jesus. Ropes were wound around the rabbi's hands and neck. Jesus did not struggle.

The disciples cried out with panicked voices.

"Stop! What are you doing?"

"What are you charging him with? You can't just take him like this!"

Jesus was jerked by the coarse ropes as they roughly bound him.

"Don't resist," a guard snarled, cuffing Jesus across the head, his hardened leather glove drawing a line of blood under Jesus' eye.

A woman wailed.

"Get off him!" someone yelled, and Reuben jerked backward instinctively as he heard a sharp whistle through the air and saw a glint of metal.

The disciples were armed!

The blade missed Reuben by a hands-breadth, but the clumsy swing struck Malchus in the head. Reuben gasped as blood poured from a jagged wound. The blade had cleaved off the side of Malchus' face. A flap of skin hung loose, his ear was sliced free. Blood gushed and the servant's eyes bulged in horror. It was a second before Malchus reached up to touch his head with a high pitched scream of terror and pain.

Jesus, tightly bound with blood seeping from his face, stood tall and shouted, "Put your sword away! All those who take up the sword shall perish by the sword. Do you think me helpless? If I but asked, my Father would put at my disposal twelve legions of angels. But then, how would the scriptures be fulfilled?"

Reuben could have laughed. The man's delusions would aid in his downfall. Jesus' words sliced through the bravado of his disciples and they fell back, eyes wide in the torchlight. They were simple men after all, not soldiers. Jesus turned back and studied Reuben and the mob with him.

"Every day I sat in the Temple Courts," Jesus said. "Why didn't you arrest me then? Now you come with clubs and swords as if I were a robber?"

Malchus fell to his knees, faint with blood loss as it drenched his tunic. He looked up to Jesus, appealing him with his eyes. Jesus clumsily reached forward with bound hands and lifted the skin back into place.

"Get away from him," Reuben snarled, shoving Jesus back.

He did not want Jesus healing, not now, not in the middle of his arrest! But the moment had been enough. Malchus stopped sobbing and gingerly touched the side of his head. He was soaked in blood, but he was healed.

Reuben growled, "Come on, let's get the Nazarene to Caiaphas."

"What about these others?" a guard asked, swinging his spear toward the disciples hovering just out of the circle of light.

Jesus looked at his disciples, his voice sad as he called to them, trying to make them understand, "This has to happen, to fulfill the scriptures of the prophets."

His disciples scattered as Jesus was taken from them.

They slipped back into the city, the gatekeeper ogling the bound Jesus and the blood-soaked Malchus as they passed. They hurried through the streets to Caiaphas' palace, which was full of bustle and movement despite the late hour. Fires had been lit in the braziers. The courtyard was full of servants preparing refreshments for all the guests. It looked as if Caiaphas had called together almost the entire Sanhedrin.

Reuben's adrenaline was pumping, and he couldn't help but grin as he marched with the mob that had finally taken Jesus. The false prophet—the man who trampled the traditions, stirred up unrest, and spewed poison about the Pharisees—would get what he deserved.

Judas slunk to a corner in a side room, but the guards led Jesus to Caiaphas' courtroom. The double doors were thrown wide and they marched right in. Not sure if he would be permitted to stay for such an important trial, Reuben took the opportunity to slip in with the guards. He did not want to miss a thing. When the double doors swung shut again with an ominous thud, Reuben was a quiet fly on the wall.

Weighted silence reigned as the tiers of men looked down upon the battered Jesus, the torchlight flickering off the stone walls.

"So, we meet again, Jesus of Nazareth." Caiaphas rose from his seat and circled Jesus in a predatory way.

Jesus did not answer but looked straight ahead. The Sanhedrin was an overwhelming presence towering over the lone man.

"Have you nothing to say?" Caiaphas taunted.

The door to the room swung open with a bang, and Nicodemus strode angrily into the room. He took measure of the room and asked in a sharp tone, "My good men, what is happening here?"

"Where are your eyes?" Annas laughed. "Can't you see? We have the Nazarene in our grasp, plucked out of the people without so much of a whisper of protest."

Nicodemus flared his nostrils and asked in a forced, calm tone,

"Are you having a trial? Now? In the middle of the night? This is not permitted in our traditions. We should wait until morning. Indeed, it would be better if we wait until the Festival of Unleavened Bread is passed."

"You question me? Your High Priest?" Caiaphas snarled, storming forward, eyes locked on Nicodemus. Nicodemus bowed before the High Priest, but when he rose up his face was strained.

"Let him go," Nicodemus weighed each word. "You can arrest him again after Festival Week."

Annas thumped his ornate staff. "And allow him to slip away to Galilee again? I think not. God has given us this opportunity, and I do not intend to let it go to waste."

"Then put him in your prison and we shall wait the week," Nicodemus tried again. "There is no harm in waiting for a week."

Caiaphas snorted. "No harm? The people will wonder where he is at the festival assembly. They will look for him. If they find he is locked up in my prison without a sentence they will riot in the streets. For the good of the people, we must deal with this swiftly, at once, even this very night."

Nicodemus shook his head but took his seat.

Reuben, still hidden in the shadows, felt a few pangs of conscience. Traditions were valuable and necessary, and he wondered if this was reason enough to transgress them. He glanced at Jesus and frowned. The idea of letting the false prophet escape was repulsive. He reasoned with himself that Caiaphas was the High Priest and if Caiaphas sanctioned this, what should a disciple have to say against it?

"So," Caiaphas said as he clapped his hands and rubbed them. "What do we have for charges?"

Nicodemus leaped to his feet again. "What? You don't even have charges, and you bring him bound like this?"

Caiaphas swiveled his head and fire danced in his eyes. He snapped, "One more word from you and you shall share the Nazarene's fate." Nicodemus sank back into his seat. Caiaphas straightened his robes. "Charges will not be hard to find."

Caiaphas called loudly, "Malchus!"

The door opened and the servant appeared. He was in a fresh tunic, his hair glistening from a hasty wash. The servant looked at Jesus, then dropped his eyes and stared at the floor.

Caiaphas commanded, "Bring forward the witnesses."

Malchus bobbed his head and brought in a crowd of men. Reuben realized they had been gathered while the guards went to arrest Jesus.

The room rang with accusations against Jesus. Some were just ridiculous; most were too mild. Hours passed. The night was nearly over, and Annas seethed while the Sanhedrin grumbled.

Reuben did not want to put himself forward with his accusation. What if he was scolded for staying to witness? He refused to be shamed before the Sanhedrin. Then again, this could be his opportunity to show his worth. He wished Simeon was here to counsel him. He chewed a jagged nail and shifted his feet.

Jesus stood in the center of the room, silent through it all.

The door opened, and Simeon slipped into the room and made his way to Reuben. Reuben sighed with relief and smiled at his rabbi. Simeon nodded once, his eyes already sweeping the room.

"What is this drivel?" Annas thumped his staff, silencing the cacophony of voices. "We need real evidence. In order to have this Nazarene killed by our laws, the charge must be of blasphemy! Do none of you have such a thing?" He glared at the crowd of witnesses. They shuffled their feet and did not answer.

Simeon cleared his throat and bowed towards Caiaphas. "High Priest, forgive me, but I just arrived. I believe you have had what you needed all along. My disciple is here. He is the one who witnessed Jesus saying that the Temple would be torn down."

All eyes fell on Reuben, and he flushed and nodded. Simeon jabbed him with an elbow.

"It is true," Reuben said, clearing his throat. "He said not one stone would be left atop the other."

"I heard something like that too," said another man as he stepped forward. He pointed at Jesus. "This man said 'I am able to destroy the Temple and rebuild it in three days'. Does that help you?"

Caiaphas gave a short, barking laugh. "At last, we are getting somewhere." He went forward and stood right before Jesus, inches from his face.

"Do you not hear what these men testify against you? Do you have nothing to say for yourself?" He tilted his ear to Jesus, eyebrows raised. Would Jesus take the bait and hang himself?

Jesus was silent.

Caiaphas's shout echoed around the room, "I demand, in the sight of the living God, that you tell us whether you are the Messiah, the Son of God."

Jesus licked his lips, his mouth dry from standing all night without even a sip of water. The entire Sanhedrin leaned forward, waiting to see what he would answer.

Jesus answered, "You've said it yourself." Caiaphas growled, but Jesus wasn't finished. "I tell you, hereafter you will see the Son of Man sitting at the right hand of Power, and coming on the clouds of heaven."

A collective gasp echoed in the room as Jesus made his audacious, blasphemous claim of authority and power.

Caiaphas reached down and tore his robes at this irreverence to God. Reuben felt his heart leap. Jesus had played right into Caiaphas' hands and spoken his own death sentence.

Caiaphas spoke to the Sanhedrin, "You have heard his blasphemy, all of you. This Nazarene not only falsely claims to be the Messiah, but that also that the Temple will fall, and that he will sit at the right hand of God. We do not need more witnesses, do we? So, what do you say?"

"He deserves death!" a man yelled, and soon the whole room was reverberating with the charge.

Caiaphas went over and spat in Jesus' face. Reuben jumped, startled. This was not usual. Another man came forward and did the same. Soon all were clamoring to spit on or slap him, or hit him with their fists, taunting him without mercy. Reuben, feeling a thrill, pushed his way forward and spat on Jesus as well.

Outside the window, the sun was rising. Annas banged his staff on the floor to regain everyone's attention.

"Sit yourselves down," Annas said, with his chin high and eyes gleaming. "We shall do this by our traditions. When the sun has risen, we will charge him formally."

The men found their seats, and the witnesses were ushered out. Jesus was silent in the middle of the room. His eye was swollen, his lip broken, and spittle speckled his face and clothing.

Reuben saw that Nicodemus was no longer in the room. He grinned at the man's cowardice.

"As we discussed previously," Caiaphas addressed the council from his seat. "It would be better for Jesus to be put to death at the hands of the Romans. The charge of blasphemy makes the sentence of death necessary, but the people consider him a prophet. They may rise up if we try to stone him. Let the Romans deal with the angry crowds. We shall inform Pilate that Jesus is trying to make himself king. A revolutionary must be punished under Roman law—by crucifixion."

The council glanced at each other and shifted in their seats. Though Caiaphas had explained why this terrible manner of death was necessary, the mere idea of crucifixion opened old wounds in their national pride. The word brought forth a slew of hatred towards the Romans for all the innocent Jews who had been slaughtered by the pagan's barbarous ways.

Finally, heads began nodding agreement to this plan.

Caiaphas continued, "We must deal with this quickly. There is no time to wait for the usual second day of deliberations. It is for the protection of the people that we do this."

The men agreed.

The morning shofar blew, and Caiaphas rose to his feet. Reuben stood with the other men with their feet drawn together and their hands held palm up. They prayed the Shema facing the Temple. As the last word echoed around the room, all eyes were back on Jesus.

"The court of the Sanhedrin is now in session. Who is the accused?"

"Jesus of Nazareth," Annas answered.

"And of what is he accused?"

"Blasphemy."

"Do we have witnesses present who attest to this blasphemy?"

A chorus of voices replied, "We do."

"Very well," Caiaphas said. "As High Priest, it is my duty to sentence Jesus of Nazareth to death."

35

THE LAMB

The dawn shofar blew in the distance. Beth knelt facing the Temple and whispered a prayer as tears trickled down her cheeks. The silence of the house was oppressive. She was all alone, Simon and the servants were with friends within the city walls. Her mind roiled with fears for Jesus and the others, even as she prayed. She had slept little, her slumber disturbed by nightmares. When she finished praying the Shema, she sank back on her heels and stayed there for a long time.

With a small shake of her head, she roused herself. She couldn't wallow in her cowardliness. She had to rejoin the others. Trying to strengthen herself, she ate a bit of leftover bread and drank a cup of water.

As she chewed without tasting, a memory rose up in her mind unbidden. She was reminded of the feeling of fear she had felt in Magdala when Mary Magdalene had been convulsing on the ground, blood trickling down her cheek. Jesus had come and told her, *"Your faith is great, Beth."*

Beth's chin sunk to her chest in shame. Where was her faith now? She was painfully aware of her faults. She was a worrier, anxious over every little thing. Despite her shortcomings, Jesus had commended her faith. He must have seen something in her she could not see in herself.

Wiping her cheeks with both palms, she rose to her feet, hardening her resolve. Fear still fluttered in her stomach, but she knew that she could not hide in the house while Jesus and all her friends were out trying to do the work of God. Yet, as she stared at the doorway, her feet were rooted to the floor.

She shook her head and tried her best not to think. "Just go out the door," she whispered. When she stood outside in the fresh air, she whispered again, "Just go to the edge of town." On the outskirts of Bethany, she had to order herself once more, "Just make it to the Garden of Gethsemane."

Somehow, despite her fear, she set one foot before the other and made it to the garden. Breathing out a puff of breath, she peered around herself, and her heart sunk when she found the garden empty. Not a soul was around. The olive trees swayed in the breeze, and birds flitted from branch to branch. The garden appeared peaceful and serene, but her instinct told her that all was not well. Feeling lost, she walked through the trees. She found a bag tumbled open with its contents damp in the morning dew. An outer robe lay forgotten in the thin grass. A glint caught her eye and she moved to investigate.

A sword! She gasped and jumped back as if it were a coiled viper. She pressed a hand over her racing heart and stepped forward to look closer. The sword looked old, like a relic handed down from another war, but on its sharpened edge was dried blood—still red as though it was recently used. Something was horribly wrong.

Beth wrung her hands and looked around herself. "Peter?" she called as she turned on the spot. Only the wind answered. Something terrible must have happened to the others. It was the only answer for the scattered belongings and the bloodied sword. Beth realized with a sinking feeling that the protection of the Passover had not been enough. Her heart in her throat, she rushed into the city.

Jerusalem had returned to the previous bustle, the streets packed with people exploring the Holy City. Beth bent her steps to the house where they had celebrated the Passover. The crowd jostled her. Without Peter to make a path for her, she floundered like a boat without its sail, trying to push her way through the press of people. She stumbled up to the right house and pounded on the door.

Their host from the night before answered the door and looked surprised to see her.

"My friends?" she gasped. "The rabbi? Are they here?"

"No, they're not," he snapped. "Why did you all leave in the night? And who will clean up the mess you left behind?"

Her heart sunk. Beth didn't answer, but fled for the Temple. A large family was heading the same way, and she fell in their wake, letting them break through the tide of people.

"Jesus will be teaching in the courts," she whispered to herself. She tried not to think of the blood-stained sword. She tried to make herself believe that her husband and friends were safe.

Her sandals slapped on the steps leading up to the Temple Mount. She passed a seated man and came up short, turned, and ran back to him.

"Peter!" she called, relief flooding her.

His head was bowed so low it rested on his knees, his hands were folded over his hair, and his hat had fallen on the ground before him. He was sobbing. Beth, overjoyed at seeing him unharmed, threw her arms over him.

"Peter, oh, Peter!" she cried. Still, he wept. She shook him a little and asked, "What happened? What's the matter?"

Peter's voice was muffled as he answered, "I denied him like he said I would. Three times I said that I did not know him. I thought I was willing to die fighting at his side, but it all went wrong. So terribly wrong."

Beth felt fear creeping up her spine and shivered. "Where's Jesus? Where are the others?" Beth lifted her head and looked around, searching. She saw many people, but not a single one she knew.

Peter's voice was muffled as he said, "Jesus was arrested last night. A whole mob of men came, and Judas Iscariot was leading them."

"Judas!" Beth gasped. It was as if someone had yanked the rug from under her feet and she was falling backward with no one to catch her. She pressed her palms into the cold stone stairs to steady herself. She remembered the shadowy figure that had left the same time as her, heading back to the city. That must have been Judas.

"Why, Judas, why?" Beth shook her head in shock and turned to her husband. She demanded, "How could Judas do such a thing? He is one of us!"

Peter shook his head, groaning with suffering.

Her mind flitted like a sparrow in a storm, trying to find a safe place to land but finding none. Passionate Judas, so desperate for a Messiah, the man who had saved her from the soldiers, who had traveled and ate and slept with them for three years, their friend—*he* would hand Jesus over to the jealous priests?

She whispered, "Did I even know him?"

Peter cried out, "Don't say that! Otherwise you might as well say you don't know me either. Judas had Jesus arrested, but I am no better. Didn't we all abandon Jesus when we turned and fled, leaving him with the soldiers?" Beth felt shame wash over her again as Peter continued, "How can we call ourselves Jesus' disciples or his friends? Three times I said I didn't even know him!" He lifted his eyes to implore her, and her heart broke when she saw his despair. He whispered, "What kind of a man am I?"

Beth sat numbly beside her weeping husband, staring ahead and seeing nothing. Jesus was arrested. His prophecy was coming true. She felt as if a boulder sat on her chest, making it hard to draw a full breath. Perhaps Jesus would still overcome. Hadn't he bested the priests and lawyers before?

Beth looked at her husband for reassurance, but he was still hiding his face. Peter was the brave one. It had been Peter who had stepped out of the boat. It had been Peter who had cried out that Jesus was the Messiah, the Son of God. When everyone else was fearful, he had faith. His despair shook Beth to the core.

She reached over and rubbed her hand over his back, trying to rouse and comfort him so he could comfort her in return.

"I am more a coward than any of you," she whispered. "I was the first to flee. Peter, you lost faith for a moment, but I know you love Jesus."

"I do love him! But what can I do now?"

Beth felt her heart wrench at the utter sadness in his gaze. His eyes pleaded with her to give him counsel at this perilous moment in his discipleship. She wavered. Right now, he was safe. Her heart wanted to soothe and comfort him, but without putting her husband in mortal danger. She could advise him to go home to Capernaum and write Jesus off as another failed revolutionary. The words were like sour grapes on her teeth and she shook her head.

She remembered the promise she had made to the Lord, that she would never try to pull Peter away from following Jesus. Did that promise still hold now that Jesus had been arrested?

Her conscience won over her fears. "I don't know what we should do, Peter, but—" she swallowed hard, "—we can't abandon him." She looked up the steps towards the Temple, trying to feel hopeful. "When is his trial?"

"It's already over," Peter said flatly.

Beth gasped. "Impossible!"

"The Sanhedrin didn't even wait overnight but have been questioning him since the arrest. I followed him to Caiaphas' palace and waited in the courtyard. Within minutes of the sun rising, he was sentenced to die. They've taken him to Pilate now, hoping to get him sentenced to crucifixion."

"No!" she cried out, drawing her hands over her mouth, her hands forming fists so tight her fingernails dug into her palms. Peter nodded his head, silent tears running anew into his beard.

"He knew this would happen, he said so himself!" Peter cried out, pounding his leg with his fist. "Why is he doing this? Surely even now he can escape!"

Beth felt a sudden urge to do something, anything at all, rather than sit and worry. "Come on," Beth said, leaping to her feet. "We have to know what is happening. You said he's been brought before Pilate? Let's go to the Antonia."

Peter looked doubtful, but he heaved himself to stand. They made their way to the square fortress that flanked the Temple, the bulky Roman garrison with its tall, overbearing towers. When they arrived, Beth saw a crowd filled the front courtyard, packed shoulder to shoulder. Beth could not see over the mob.

"Is Jesus there?" she asked her taller husband.

"I see soldiers," Peter said and swallowed hard. "But I don't see Pilate. He must not have come out yet."

Beth chewed on her lower lip as she scanned the crowd, wondering if any of their friends were here as well, perhaps with more information. Turning on the spot, she saw an armored centurion passing behind them and moving for a guarded side door.

"Marcus!" Beth cried out. He turned and saw her, recognition in his eyes. Her fear for Jesus gave her courage, and she ran forward, Peter scrambling to catch up.

"Beth, what are you doing here?" Marcus said with wide eyes. He looked at Peter, sizing up his distraught appearance. "You should take her away from here. There may be trouble."

Beth pleaded, "Please, do you know what is happening to Jesus?"

Marcus glanced over his shoulder and murmured, "I can't talk here. Follow me."

Marcus marched up to the guarded door, and a guard held the heavy door open for them, revealing a shadowed hall. Beth hung back with uncertainty as Marcus went inside, suddenly fearful again. What if it was a trap and the Roman arrested her husband as well?

Marcus leaned out the door and beckoned again, and Beth sucked in her breath as she entered the Roman garrison. The door slammed behind them and she jumped. Beth felt a chill as they walked down narrow, stone hallways. Marcus stopped in an empty passageway and turned to face them. His mask of authority melted into frustration and sorrow.

"It's not good for Jesus," he rubbed a palm on his cheek and then over the back of his neck. "It would take a miracle to get him out of this mess. The scribes and elders have brought forth charges of sedition. The first revolutionary, I think, to be brought forth by a fellow Jew." He shook his head at the idea. "Your rabbi is a good and powerful man. I don't understand how he can let this happen."

"You believe he could stop all this if he truly wanted to?" Beth asked, looking up at the tall, armored man. How could this Gentile have faith when her own people did not?

"I think he could, yes," Marcus said.

Beth sighed, "I do too."

Peter cried out, "I don't understand why he won't."

Marcus eyed them both. "There may still be hope. I'm going to watch what remains of this sham of a trial. If you promise not to cause a disturbance, I will bring you to the upper level with me. You can see clearly from there."

Beth nodded, and Peter promised, "We will be quiet."

With a grim expression, Marcus marched further into the fortress. He led them down hallways and up a flight of stairs. They went through a small door and emerged on a walkway that surrounded the courtyard below.

Beth went with the two men to the balustrade and set her hands on the cold stone. She looked down. The milling crowd below filled the entire space, and Beth could see the chief priests in a group near the front. On a platform was a backless, hard chair facing the crowd —the judgment seat. It was empty, and Jesus was nowhere to be seen.

"They must have taken him inside," Marcus said. "Perhaps for private questioning."

The double doors swung open and a tall man marched out wearing a frown, gleaming armor, and a sword at his narrow hip. His close-cropped head was bare. Flanked by guards, Jesus emerged, and the crowd hissed at his arrival. Jesus looked exhausted. A cut under his puffy eye had dried with crusted blood. Beth gasped at the sight of him, and Peter groaned.

Pilate glared over the crowd, and like students before a strict teacher, they quieted. He shouted, "It has been our custom to return a prisoner to you during the feast. Who shall I release to you? Barabbas, or Jesus who is called the Christ?"

"Barabbas?" Beth gasped. "Not that murderer!"

The noise in the crowd began again as everyone spoke at once. From their high vantage point, Beth saw men elbowing through the crowds, spreading themselves out. They began chanting, "Barabbas! Barabbas!" until others began to join in.

Beth saw a scuffle starting below. With alarm she recognized Simon the Zealot, struggling against a guard that kept him from getting to the chief priests. Andrew and Thomas came up behind Simon, trying to pull him back to safety. She was relieved to see the men were safe and unharmed, but for how long?

"Barabbas killed my parents," Simon choked out a cry as Andrew and Thomas pulled him away from the guard. Simon shouted hoarsely, "He's an animal!"

Simon's desperate cries were drowned out by the chanting of the crowd. Beth felt sick. In a choice between Jesus and Barabbas, they would choose the brutal highwayman?

Pilate shook his head with frustration, held his hands up, and asked the question again.

Again the crowd began to shout, "Barabbas! Barabbas!"

The chief priests were smug, but Pilate appeared disgusted with the whole crowd. He did not relish releasing a criminal. He again held up his hands.

When Pilate finally quieted the crowd, he said, "Then what shall I do with Jesus who is called the Messiah?"

"Release him!" she and Peter called, forgetting their promise to Marcus to be quiet. It didn't matter anyway, because the crowd was louder.

"Crucify him!" the lackeys in the crowd yelled, and many others shouted agreement.

"What evil has he done?" Pilate shouted back.

"Crucify him!" more and more shouted. The crowd began to mill.

Marcus shook his head. "We're about to have a riot on our hands."

Pilate saw it too. He spoke to a servant, who disappeared into the fortress and returned a few moments later holding a basin, with a towel over his arm. Pilate began to wash his hands, and the crowd stopped shouting to see what he was doing.

He snapped the towel off the servant and dried his dripping hands. "I am innocent of this man's blood. See to that yourselves." And he tossed the towel back at the servant, turned, and walked back into the fortress.

A man in the crowd yelled, "His blood shall be on us and on our children!" and others took up the grisly chant.

Beth clutched the balustrade for support, her knees weak.

Jesus was led back into the fortress. Shortly afterward, two guards emerged and tossed a ragged man out into the crowd. Beth's lip curled as the foolish crowd pulled back, wanting nothing to do with Barabbas. The murderer cackled like a fiend as he ran away from the Antonia, enjoying his unbelievable good luck.

"Where will they take Jesus?" Peter asked Marcus in a strained tone.

Marcus was hesitant to answer. "They will take him into the inner courtyard. As is customary, he will be scourged."

Peter groaned again, and Beth felt bile in the back of her throat. Marcus looked at them with sympathy.

"I can take you to where you can see," Marcus' eyes flicked between them. "But it is a horror to witness."

Beth and Peter looked at each other. Beth tried to find some reason or understanding of what was happening to their rabbi in Peter's eyes. They mirrored her own confusion and despair.

"Take us there," Peter said.

Marcus led them through more passageways and they emerged over another courtyard. This one appeared to be a training yard. Beth saw a crowd of soldiers, all laughing and jeering and standing in a circle. Tied to a stake was Jesus, stripped to his waist, his back gushing blood as the whip's jagged tails were raked across his skin.

The gore was so sudden, so shocking, Beth had to stuff her fist in her mouth to stop from screaming as tears of anguish drenched her face.

Jesus writhed in silence, a silence that felt louder than a thousand screams.

"I can't watch this," she sobbed. She turned and saw Peter heaving against the wall, emptying his stomach. Marcus glanced at Jesus, but quickly jerked his face away with a hard swallow.

"Can't you do something to stop this?" Peter gasped at Marcus.

Marcus shook his head. "I have no power to stop it."

"Take us out of this wretched place," Peter groaned.

Marcus took them inside and led them back through the cold halls of the Antonia. They emerged back on the street. Beth and Peter stood together in a daze, sickened and horrified at what was happening to their friend.

"I will leave you here," Marcus said, his face twitching with suppressed emotion. "Be careful." He turned and went back inside.

"Oh, Jesus!" Peter choked out the words. "What can we do?"

In the shadow of a nearby inn, Beth saw women she recognized. Among them were Naomi and Mary the mother of Joseph and James. Mary Magdalene was supporting Jesus' mother. John was there too, telling the women what had happened in the courtyard. All of them were weeping openly.

Beth took her husband's hand and moved towards them. Peter's hand yanked out of her grasp and she turned in alarm.

Peter cried out, "I can't bear it, I just can't!" He turned and ran into the busy street, soon lost in the crowds. Beth stood halfway across the road, jostled by people, wavering as to whether she should follow her husband or go to her friends.

As horrible as it was, she found she couldn't leave yet, not until it was finished. She went to the women.

"Oh, Beth!" Mary Magdalene sobbed and threw herself at Beth. They embraced for a long moment, holding each other tight.

Together they stood and watched the door of the Antonia. The minutes felt like hours before guards came out from the Antonia leading a stumbling, blood-soaked man. The women cried out as if one voice.

"How can they treat him like this? He has done nothing wrong!"

Mary Magdalene choked out a sob. "They mock him, even as they take him to die."

Beth saw Jesus wore a cruel crown of twisted thorns.

"How can he even walk?" John whispered, staring in horror.

They all gasped aloud as a soldier hoisted a heavy beam on Jesus raw and bloody back, making him carry the object of his death. Jesus began to walk.

Crowds gathered as word spread about who had been arrested and sentenced to crucifixion. It was difficult for the women to stay close to Jesus. Beth and Mary Magdalene clasped hands to keep from being separated as they pushed their way through the jostling crowd. Jerusalem women who saw Jesus began to cry out, their lamenting wails drawing more people.

Onlookers drew near and gasped when they saw Jesus' bloody frame. Behind him trailed dark, glistening footprints.

"What did he do?" Beth heard over and over as she pushed forward to keep up. "Isn't that the rabbi people were talking about? The one that healed in the Temple?"

The heavily armed Romans kept the curious crowds back. Even when many hurled insults at the soldiers, they did not leave their post but kept Jesus moving onward, painful step by painful step.

John kept calling Jesus' name, trying to let Jesus know that they were here with him, but Beth couldn't tell if Jesus heard them over the clamor of the crowd. As they turned a corner, Beth bumped up against Matthew and James in the crowd, both men staring as Jesus walked past. They were like horrified statues and wouldn't reply to Beth as their friend shuffled by on his way to the cruelest death the Romans could offer.

Mary Magdalene pointed an accusatory finger across the crowd. "Look! There is the traitor, coming to see the fruits of his lies."

Naomi spat on the ground, and Beth saw Judas's anguish as he beheld his former friend stumbling and suffering on the way to his death.

"I think he regrets it," Beth whispered. She remembered her crushed husband and felt a moment of pity for Judas. He had loved Jesus—why had he given him up? Had Judas expected this to end differently?

"Too late," Mary said and shook her head.

They pressed on, forcing their way through the crowds so they could keep up with Jesus. Halfway, Jesus crumpled to his knees. He was unable to rise, even as the guards screamed in his face.

"Please!" Beth pleaded with the guards. "He can't go on."

The guard ignored her and kept screaming at Jesus. Coming out of nowhere, Marcus was at Jesus' side, pushing the soldier aside. His eyes caught Beth's and she held out her hands, silently begging him.

Marcus spoke to a man in the crowd, "You there, carry the cross." Beth thanked Marcus in her heart for this small gift, the only act of mercy he could give Jesus.

The man shrank back. "I can't!"

"Do it for him, please do it for the rabbi," Beth begged again.

The man recoiled again, but at Marcus' insistence, he shouldered the heavy, blood-smeared beam with a look of revulsion. Beth couldn't fathom how it would feel to carry the instrument of another man's death.

They came out of the city and to the place called Golgotha. Marcus walked with the other soldiers, keeping near Jesus' shoulder. Crosses loomed in the barren place, burdened with decaying corpses. The stench was overwhelming and people covered their noses. Two more men were being prepared for crucifixion, and they were sobbing, cursing, and begging.

Jesus arrived at the place of his death and sank to his knees. Not a word nor a cry did he utter. The women stayed as close to him as they could, until they were chased back by the guards.

Marcus came up, a cup in hand. He held it to Jesus' lips. "Drink," he said, and Jesus sipped. "It will numb the pain."

Jesus turned his face away and would not take any more. Marcus tried again, but he had to turn sadly away when Jesus refused. He went to stand guard, his gaze averted. Beth saw his Adam's apple bobbing.

The women disciples huddled together as Jesus was stripped bare. Beth choked a cry as the garments she had helped weave with her own hands were torn from him, stained with his blood. She jumped with each hammer blow as with cruel spikes he was fixed to the cross. His arms were stretched wide, and his raw back pressed against the coarse wood. He writhed as the nails pierced him, his face contorted in agony.

Beth bit her lip so hard it bled, and she tasted blood as she watched Jesus' flow into the ground.

Then the cross was raised for all to see the trembling, wounded, humbled man. The women huddled together, grasping at each other.

All they could do was wait for him to die.

Beth heard the other women crying on either side of her, and she felt tears dripping off her chin.

The guards cast lots to see who would get Jesus' clothes, callous to the suffering man above them. Beth wanted to cry out in protest as his clothes were claimed by strangers, but the words were choked off in her throat.

Beth glanced to the side as the chief priests arrived in a procession. They were haughty and triumphant. Beth felt her hands shaking in anger as they mocked Jesus even as he was dying.

A scribe yelled, "You were going to destroy the temple and rebuild it in three days! Let's see you save yourself!"

Another man yelled, "If you are the Son of God, come down from the cross." His friends laughed with him. As she looked at the men with revulsion, she recognized a dark-robed man in the jeering crowd.

It was Reuben.

She felt as if she had been slapped across the face.

His face was contorted with hate, a look so vile she hardly recognized him. Her heart, already full to breaking for Jesus, still found room to ache for the friend of her childhood.

She whispered, "Oh, Reuben. What have they done to you?"

Caiaphas turned to the other chief priests and sneered, "He saved others, yet he cannot save himself. If he is the King of Israel, let him come down from the cross and we will believe in him."

They all laughed and jeered.

"He trusts in God, so let God rescue him now if He delights in him, for he said, 'I am the Son of God!'"

The caw of a bird shook Beth to the marrow of her bones, and her chin jerked up. The ravens were circling.

Jesus' head lolled from side to side in silent agony. She noticed something had been fixed above him.

"They have written something above his head," Beth whispered.

"It says, 'This is Jesus, the King of the Jews'," John answered, wiping a hand across his eyes. A cruel title, meant to insult their whole nation.

A raven landed on the cross of the man next to Jesus. Too greedy to wait, with sharp jabs the bird pecked at the criminal until it plucked out his eye, all while the victim screamed and feebly twisted his head, trying to escape.

Beth could not cry out in horror or look away. A strange sense of unreality was descending on her, smothering her. A hush fell over the world as if she had ducked her head underwater. A terrible ringing hurt her ears. She stood in the center of her childhood nightmare, and it was worse than she could have believed. It was not a nameless man on the cross, parched with thirst, suffering from wounds, torn muscles, hunger, and exhaustion. It was a dear friend and a good man, one that she loved.

She wished he would survive. She wished he would die and end his suffering. She wished she could close her eyes, walk away, escape the pain she saw and felt within her heart.

Jesus' mother could not take any more. She wailed, "My son! My precious boy!" The others tried to comfort her.

Beth felt Mary Magdalene clinging to her arm, pulling her to the little knot of disciples. The women supported each other, keeping vigil for Jesus when so many of his followers had fled. Beth's mind felt sluggish. Where had the others gone? Where was Peter?

The sky fell dark, and Beth blinked in a daze. Had so much time passed that it was night?

The soldiers who guarded Jesus looked at the sky in alarm. She heard one say, "It is only noon! What evil is this?" They sharpened their stance and clutched their spears.

The crowd was uneasy, and the jeers ended.

It was not the natural darkness of night, with stars and moon to comfort. The sky had a sickly hue that stopped the birds from singing and made animals cower. Torches were lit, casting flickering shadows that danced with lives of their own. The priests and lawyers muttered among each other, their volume smothered by the darkness. Beth caught the word, "eclipse", and "completely natural", though the men were wary and watchful.

For three hours the sky was dark, and Beth watched Jesus' chest struggle to rise and fall. She stared as if his next breath was the only thing left in the world.

He drew in a long, rattling breath, and he cried out, "My God! My God! Why have You forsaken me?" He slumped down again, twisting his weary head as if to turn from the pain.

Beth felt her knees wobble and choked out a sob. Oh, Jesus! How often had he turned to his heavenly Father in prayer and came back restored? Her heart cried out. God, help him!

A man, feeling pity, went forward with a sponge on a reed and held it up so Jesus could drink.

"Leave him alone!" another jeered. "Let's see if Elijah will come and save him."

"Oh, Jesus!" Mary Magdalene whispered to the others. "He feels forsaken."

Beth saw a Pharisee approach and she stiffened instinctively. Then she saw it was Joseph of Arimathea, one of the men who had dined with Jesus at Simon's house. His robes were torn and his beard was wet with tears.

"It is a psalm," the scholar said. He chanted aloud,

"My God, My God, why have You forsaken me?

Far from my deliverance are the words of my groaning . . .
In You our fathers trusted; They trusted and You delivered them.
To You they cried out and were delivered;
In You they trusted and were not disappointed.

But I am a worm, and not a man,
A reproach of men and despised by the people.
All who see me sneer at me; They separate with the lip,
They wag the head saying,
'Commit yourself to the Lord, let Him deliver him;
Let Him rescue him, because He delights in him.'

Yet You are He who brought me forth from the womb;
You made me trust when upon my mother's breasts.
Upon You I was cast from birth;
You have been my God from my mother's womb ...

I am poured out like water, And all my bones are out of joint;
My heart is like wax; It is melted within me.
My strength is dried up like a pot shard,
My tongue cleaves to my jaws;
And You lay me in the dust of death.

For dogs have surrounded me;
And a band of evildoers have encompassed me;
They pierced my hands and my feet. I can count all my bones.
They look, they stare at me; They divide my garments among them,

And for my clothing they cast lots …

You who fear the Lord, praise Him;
All you descendants of Jacob, glorify Him,
And stand in awe of Him, all you descendants of Israel.
For He has not despised nor abhorred the affliction of the afflicted;
Nor has He hidden His face from him;

But when he cried to Him for help, He heard —"

Joseph of Arimathea was cut off as Jesus pushed himself upwards to draw a full breath, and released a long, painful cry. His head slumped forward as he died.

Tears gushed down Beth's cheeks and speckled the dust. She heard the shofar blow. It sent a shiver down her spine. It was time for the sacrifice.

Before the trumpet blast died away, a great tremor shook the earth. Beth cried out as the ground beneath her convulsed. She struggled to stay on her feet. Naomi fell over, and the other Mary wailed in fear. The crowds shouted as the large rocks in the valley cracked in two.

Beth, looking at Jesus' limp body, saw the centurions stumbling back in alarm. Marcus stepped forward and declared, "Truly, this was the Son of God!"

With those words in their ears, the crowd dispersed. They did not wish to stay to watch the other men die on their crosses. The scholars, lawyers, scribes, and priests drifted away like a putrid mist, leaving behind those who truly mourned.

After a long moment of silence, Mary Magdalene whispered, "What will become of the body?"

Beth's stomach turned over. Criminals were not accorded a proper burial but were usually left to rot. How could that happen to Jesus?

"I will ask Pilate for it," Joseph of Arimathea said, and he turned and went back into the city.

Beth stared at the cross with gritty, dry eyes. All her tears were spent. Her throat was parched. She felt like a wrung cloth. Now that Jesus was dead, exhaustion swept over her. She shuddered, feeling faint.

"I'm going to go find Peter," she said woodenly to the other women.

She did not reenter the city, but took the long way, stumbling around the city walls. It was nightfall by the time she made it to Bethany, and she found her husband in the house with many of the others. Beth's eyes swept the room. Fear and despair were on every face.

Peter glanced up as she stood in the doorway. She wavered, groaning. Peter leaped to his feet, wrapped his arm around her, and led her to a quiet corner. He tucked her in a blanket as if she were a child.

"Where were you? I was worried," he said. She could only shake her head. Peter continued, "Jesus has been buried. Joseph of Arimathea took Jesus' body and laid it in his own tomb."

Before she drifted off, he brought a cup of water and held it to her lips. She gulped it down and felt sleep wash over her like a wave. It was in sleep that the nightmare ended.

36

THE SCAR

The Temple was like a broken anthill, men scurrying every which way without knowing what they should be doing. It was early in the day, the first day of the Week of Unleavened Bread, a High Sabbath to the Lord. The people were commanded to gather for an assembly in the Temple today, and yet nothing was as it should be.

"So it's true?" Reuben asked the lawyer, Jeconiah, who was standing in the Court of Israel watching the chaos in the Court of Priests over the balustrade.

"Torn from top to bottom," the lawyer shook his head. "It happened last night, right in the middle of evening sacrifices. The men inside the Temple nearly died from fright. They ran out shouting at the priests who were in the middle of sacrificing the lamb. 'The veil between us and the Holy of Holies is torn!' they wailed, and none of them have been willing to go back in. Another veil needs to be hung, but that will take some time. I'm not sure how we will manage the assembly today."

Reuben looked at the Temple with a furrowed brow. The veil was tightly woven by skilled weavers using the finest materials and replaced yearly. It would take more than an earthquake to tear the fabric of the veil. What did this mean?

He could not ponder it long, because Simeon came up beside him. "Come with me. There is a meeting with Pilate," he said and strode off without a backward glance. Reuben hurried to catch up.

Despite the chaos in the Temple Courts, Reuben felt a sense of inner peace. It felt good to know that Jesus of Nazareth would trouble them no more. The people would go back to their old ways. When Reuben returned to Capernaum someday to visit friends and family, it would be as if Jesus had never lived. Revolutionaries came and went, and the people had learned to move on and forget.

They took the stairs to the Antonia and found men gathered in the front courtyard. The chief priests were there as well, speaking in their tight group.

Pilate came out of the fortress, looking cross. "Why must I always come to you?" he snapped.

They shuffled their feet, and Caiaphas, speaking for them, was appeasing. "It is no slight to you, I assure you. It is because it is a Festival Week, and we must keep our purity."

"You Jews and your wretched purity," Pilate growled and snapped his fingers. A servant scurried to bring him a tray with fruit and wine.

Reuben had the feeling that they had interrupted the governor's breakfast.

Caiaphas' face darkened, but his tone stayed deferential. "You know that a man was crucified yesterday, a Jesus of Nazareth."

"Of course," Pilate said with a noisy slurp from his cup. "What of it?"

"Well, while he lived, this Jesus made ridiculous claims. The deceiver said that on the third day he will rise again."

Pilate paused with a mouthful of wine, stared at them for a long moment, and gave a loud swallow. "Indeed?" His tone was mocking. "Oh dear me." He turned and whispered loudly to his servant, "What are we doing in this backwater, Festus?" The servant smiled at his feet.

Caiaphas continued as if he had heard nothing, "We ask that you give orders for the grave to be made secure until the third day. Otherwise, his disciples may come and steal the body away and say to the people, 'He has risen from the dead,' and the last deception will be worse than the first."

Swirling the cup, Pilate looked at them as if trying to understand a creature he had never seen before. He swigged the last of his wine, set it on the tray, and heaved himself to his feet.

Already walking away, he called over his shoulder in a careless tone, "Fine. You may have access to my soldiers. Send some of them to the gravesite and make it as secure as you know how. Joseph of Arimathea collected the body, you can find the location from him." He paused and turned back at them, his tone sharp as he added, "This better be the last I hear of Jesus the Messiah."

"Of course, Governor," Caiaphas said, inclining his head. Pilate nodded and went back into the fortress, the servant pulling the door shut behind him with a bang.

Reuben turned and raised his eyebrows to Simeon, who pursed his lips and went to join Annas, Caiaphas, and the others.

Annas noticed them. "Ah, Simeon and your disciple ... Reuben, isn't it?" Reuben was pleased Annas had troubled himself to learn his name, and he stood a little taller. Annas sighed and turned to his son-in-law. "That was unpleasant, but at least we have what we need."

Annas' notice of him emboldened Reuben to speak. "Please, if it would help you, I can take the guards and oversee the securing of the tomb." Reuben folded his hands behind his back and stood with confidence.

Annas raised his eyebrows, but Caiaphas winked at Simeon. "This one is eager, isn't he?"

Simeon smiled. "You have no idea."

The two men shared a little laugh. Reuben's face warmed, but he was able to laugh at himself too. Caiaphas looked at his father-in-law, who was nodding.

"Very well," Caiaphas said. He slipped a large ring from his finger and held it out. "This is my family ring. Use it on the seal." Reuben took it and noticed the ornate engraving. "Speak to Joseph of Arimathea about the location of the tomb. I believe he is staying with a friend in Bethany." Caiaphas frowned, his look full of dark meaning. "I think we shall need to speak with him soon."

Reuben felt a prick of pity for the Pharisee who had cast his lot with Jesus. Annas and his five sons were all of the Sadducees, and Reuben felt a certain loyalty to Joseph for being of his party, even if he had been deceived by Jesus.

Caiaphas turned and led his group of priests away, leaving Simeon and Reuben alone in the courtyard.

"Bold," Simeon turned and said to Reuben, his eyebrow arched.

"Perhaps too bold, but if you do well at this I am certain more ways to serve will open to you."

Reuben suddenly felt nervous, and he asked his mentor for advice.

"Take four guards with you," Simeon said. "And also a length of cord and some soft wax for the seal. Have the guards take turns sleeping so that no one may come on them unaware."

"I shall stay with the guard, as well," Reuben said, drawing up to his full height. "To make sure that all goes well."

Simeon raised an eyebrow again, but nodded. Reuben had a second, private reason for wanting to spend the next two days sitting in front of a tomb. It would keep him well away from the grieving, fiery Michal.

"Will you send me a bag of provisions?" Reuben asked. "I would buy from the market if it weren't the Sabbath."

Simeon nodded and left at once.

Reuben met with a centurion and gave him the orders. Reuben felt an unfamiliar sense of authority when the centurion bowed his head. The centurion summoned four foot-soldiers accustomed to working with the Jews to go to the tomb with Reuben.

Reuben's eyebrows shot up as the soldiers approached. He nearly laughed aloud as he recognized three of them. They were the youths who had forced him to carry their baggage. He saw they recognized him as well. The broken-nosed leader had the decency to look a little worried.

The centurion told them to follow all of Reuben's orders, and Reuben stood a little taller. They shifted and looked at each other, and Reuben smirked at their discomfort.

Reuben looked the men up and down, trying to imitate Simeon's critical eye. He questioned them, making sure they had packed enough supplies so they wouldn't need to leave the tomb unguarded.

Alexander arrived with a small bag for Reuben. The steward didn't speak a word or look him in the eye. The man's withdrawn attitude checked Reuben's pleasure, and he fell silent. As the wordless steward turned and left, Reuben slung the bag over his shoulder. He felt a little odd as he did so. A man wasn't supposed to carry supplies or travel on the Sabbath. However, this was for the good of the people.

"Let's go to Bethany," Reuben said, and the armed soldiers fell in behind him, their hobnailed sandals loud on the cobblestone. The sound made people draw back and watch as they passed. Reuben suppressed a grin as the crowd gazed at him with respect.

They left the city and made their way to Bethany. They inquired after Jesus' disciples and were directed to a house. Reuben rapped on the door. It opened a crack, and Andrew peered out.

"Reuben?" he asked in surprise. He didn't open the door further but looked past Reuben to the four soldiers. "What do you want?"

"Reuben is here?" someone inside the house called out, and Reuben recognized Beth's voice.

Reuben took a breath to bolster himself as Beth swung the door wide. Her brown eyes were sharp as she stared at him with an expression he had never seen Beth wear before—accusation. It reminded him of Michal, and he cleared his throat uncomfortably. Beth's eyes took in the soldiers, and he was surprised when her gaze did not falter. Her only hint of fear was a hard swallow. Peter came up behind her, and Reuben saw many of the other disciples in the room.

Reuben gathered himself and demanded, "I need to speak with Joseph of Arimathea. No harm will come to him if he answers my questions."

Beth shook her head. "You're not yourself, Reuben." She leaned forward and whispered with narrowed eyes, "I saw you. At the crucifixion."

Reuben's face heated as he remembered the pleasure he had felt in hurling insults at Jesus. Sharp images of Jesus' broken body pushed their way forward, but he stamped them down. Jeering at a dying man was not something he felt particularly proud of, but the death had been necessary, a good for the nation.

"Is he here?" Reuben pushed on.

"I am," Joseph said, and he came forward. He stood with chin high. Reuben knew he assumed he was about to be arrested.

"Good. Where did you take the body of Jesus?" Reuben asked.

"What?" Peter interjected while Beth's eyes widened. "Why do you need his body? What more can you do to him?"

"We wish to make sure that *nothing* is done to him," Reuben said coldly. "We know that Jesus claimed he would rise after three days. We just want to make sure that no one decides to ... help him rise."

"We would never!" Peter jerked forward, and Beth put her hand on his arm.

Joseph ducked out the door, seeming to want to calm the

situation. "He is laid in my own tomb," Joseph said. "If you promise not to disturb the body, I will take you there."

Reuben held out his arm and gestured for Joseph to lead the way. Joseph's stride was clipped, angry. Reuben followed, and the four armed men brought up the rear. They came to a quiet tomb on the Mount of Olives.

"I'll need to see that the body is there," Reuben said.

Joseph frowned, but he had no choice but to let the soldiers roll back the heavy stone that covered the opening.

Reuben stood in the doorway. The tomb looked new. Reuben could see cut marks where the tomb had been chiseled from the rock. It was obvious Joseph had made this tomb for himself, and likely no one had laid here until Joseph had given it to Jesus. Reuben did not want to go inside during the week of Unleavened Bread, but he had to be sure he was securing the right body. Resigning himself to a week's impurity, he sucked in his breath as he ducked inside.

A wrapped body was laid on a stone shelf, the face covered by a cloth. Reuben's hands shook as he gingerly reached forward and lifted the cloth. The crown of thorns had been removed. The blood had been washed away, revealing cold, waxy flesh, with blueish lips set in a peaceful expression. It was Jesus; Reuben would recognize the man anywhere. He hastily replaced the face covering and escaped the tomb.

"Seal it," Reuben said, his tone rough as he tried to shake off the tremble in his hands. The soldiers obeyed and the stone was moved back into place. They placed a seal over the door and Reuben pressed the High Priest's ring into the wax. If anyone tried to open the door, the seal would be broken and the grave-robbers would have to answer to the High Priest.

"Are you certain that is enough?" Joseph's tone was sarcastic.

Reuben turned away from Joseph. "You may go."

The man hesitated, but then turned and walked away. Reuben felt another flicker of pity for the Pharisee who had chosen the wrong side.

"Wait," Reuben called. Joseph paused, and Reuben went to him. Away from the soldiers, Reuben whispered, "You should expect a summons from the Sanhedrin."

Joseph pulled back, eyeing the younger man up and down. "Is that a threat?"

"No." Reuben shook his head. "A warning." He didn't go so far as to suggest that Joseph leave the area for a time, but he thought the man would understand the hint. Reuben wanted Jesus gone, but he did not want good men and women who had been tricked by a charismatic deceiver to be punished.

Reuben returned to the soldiers. They had found places to sit. It was a pleasant spring day, and the men enjoyed lolling on the grass and playing at dice. Reuben sat aloofly apart. Simeon had packed a few scrolls in the bag, and Reuben stretched out to read, trying to forget the accusatory look Beth had given him.

Surely she couldn't still believe Jesus was a Messiah now? In a few days, she would understand why Jesus' death had been necessary.

The High Sabbath ended at six at night, but Reuben stayed at the tomb. He ate a simple supper of dried fruit and unleavened bread. When night darkened the sky, he made sure that the men were prepared to take turns keeping watch, then rolled himself in his cloak and went to sleep.

"Another earthquake!" a voice cut into his dreams.

Reuben felt like he was being shaken awake, but quickly realized it was the ground trembling beneath him. He stumbled to his feet in the dimness. The sky was pale gray in the east.

The soldiers were pointing upwards and crying out in alarm. Reuben looked up and threw a hand over his eyes, for a figure was descending from the sky, bright like lightning, wearing garments as white as snow. Terror gripped him as he cowered, and he heard a grating sound of rock sliding over rock. He chanced a peek at the heavy stone. It was moving from the tomb entrance, breaking the seals they had placed. The terrified soldiers fell like dead men, and Reuben fled into the trees in a panic.

He was crouched and trembling when he heard the voices of women. He tentatively lifted his head and saw them through the tree branches. They clutched at each other, and he recognized the curly-haired woman who stood in front. She was speaking with someone, and he realized with a jolt that she was talking to the bright figure who was now seated on the large rock. With his heart pounding in his ears, he could not make out the words.

The women crept to the tomb and looked inside. Was that Beth with them? The dazzling figure vanished, and Reuben could hear the women crying out in astonishment. As one they ran back the way they had come.

Minutes passed. The only sound was the rustle of leaves, the chirping of birds, and the pounding of Reuben's heart. He felt frozen, transfixed, and terrified. His mind could not comprehend what had transpired, and he sat dumbly for a long time.

When his pulse finally slowed, he crept toward the tomb. The soldiers were beginning to stir, but he went past them. With great fear, he peered into the tomb. It was empty. His heart turned over and his mind flew. How could he explain this?

The broken-nosed soldier came up with a groan, rubbing his head as if it hurt him. He glanced around himself. "If I had been drinking last night, maybe I could explain what it was that I saw, but I can't. I would call it a nightmare, except we all saw it happen."

He walked up to Reuben, who still stood at the tomb entrance. The soldier also looked inside. He swore.

"What happened to the body?" he said, his face paling. When Reuben didn't answer, the soldier grabbed him by the front of his robes and roared in his face, spittle flying. "WHERE IS THE BODY?"

Reuben tried to wriggle free as he panted, "I-I-I don't know! I saw the same—the same thing you did, and then some women came."

"Women?" the man scoffed and pushed Reuben backward so he stumbled and landed on his seat.

The other soldiers came forward and all four of them scowled down on Reuben. One began cracking his knuckles in a threatening way. Reuben scrambled to his feet with as much dignity as he could muster.

The broken-nosed soldier crossed his arms. "*Women* came and carried the body away?"

"No! They ran away with empty hands," Reuben said, annoyed at the note of fear that tainted his voice. "They came and talked to—" he swallowed hard at the memory of the indescribable creature "—then they left in a hurry."

The soldiers shook their heads and looked at each other with worry. "Pilate will have us scourged for this."

"It's his fault," said one as he jabbed a thick finger towards Reuben. "He's the one in charge here."

They were right. He had taken the authority on himself willingly, and he had reveled in it. Now Reuben felt nauseated as he pictured the angry faces of Simeon, Annas, and Caiaphas.

Reuben, thinking fast, stepped forward, his hands outstretched. "Come with me. We will talk to the chief priests. I will tell them everything that happened and make sure you don't get into trouble."

Reuben didn't dare go back and tell the story of what he had seen without others to back him up.

The five men gathered their belongings. Reuben stuffed the broken seals into his bag, and the men jogged away with nervous glances.

Reuben took them to Simeon's house first. Alexander saw the soldiers storm into the house and fled from the room, calling for his master.

"Reuben?" Simeon said, rushing down the stairs. "What are you doing here? Why are you not guarding the tomb?"

Reuben told what he had witnessed. The words tumbled from his mouth as if he knew that if he dwelledon what he had witnessed, he would have to process and try to understand it.

Simeon paled and reached up and touched his scar with trembling fingers. It was the first time Reuben had seen him acknowledge the scar.

"The chief priests must be told. We can get ahead of the rumors if we act fast." Simeon struck one hand against the other. He frowned at Reuben with concern. "We must handle this delicately. Luckily, you are young and your mistake can be blamed on your inexperience."

Reuben hung his head as Simeon led them all to Caiaphas's palace, the nervous soldiers following with hands wrapped around the hilts of their swords.

In a small side chamber, Reuben told stony-faced Annas and scowling Caiaphas everything he had seen. When he came to the figure in white, he struggled to find the correct words to describe it. When he finished, Annas, his lined face purple with rage, rose up, clutching his staff.

"Lies!" he cried out, and Reuben's heart stopped.

With a lightning-quick move, Annas swung his staff at Reuben. Reuben tried to duck out of the way, but the ornate staff struck his face, slicing him from brow to cheek. Reuben cried out and stumbled, stars dancing in blackness. His hands cupped his ruined face as blood gushed over his eye and down into his beard. His whole face burned and throbbed. Reuben cried out again in pain.

"For your failure," Annas snarled. "The disciple truly has followed in his rabbi's footsteps." He glared at Simeon and resumed his seat, and Reuben flinched away from the priests in shock.

Simeon, his face grim, came over and removed Reuben's shawl and pressed it to his bloody face. "Really, Annas?" Simeon snapped. "Still striking disciples? Hopefully you have not cost him his eye. Hold it tighter, Reuben. We will have to take you to have this sewn."

Reuben looked at his teacher miserably through one watering eye. Simeon led him to a corner and seated him before Reuben could faint from the pain. The sympathy on his mentor's face was a drop of balm on his sore heart.

He looked up at Simeon's forehead. Painful realization dawned. He finally understood where his rabbi had received his scar. What had Simeon done that had displeased Annas?

Simeon went back to the others, and the discussion and planning began. Reuben, his head feeling like Annas had split it open, sat in silent misery.

When the meeting was over, Simeon came back and led him to a physician near the Large Market. Reuben managed to choke down a bitter drink that made him feel woozy and unable to stand. He drifted in and out of consciousness. When he was awake, he cried out in pain as he felt thread pulling the edges of his skin back together. Then everything faded again. A cold and smelly paste was spread over the gash and his face was wrapped in clean linen, leaving his good eye free to see.

The physician washed his bloodied hands as Simeon helped Reuben to his feet.

"I think I might vomit," Reuben gasped, and the physician calmly held out a basin for Reuben to use.

"That might happen for a while," the physician said to Simeon. "Give him only broth and watered wine for the next few days. Reapply the salve every day, and hopefully in a week we can remove the stitches."

"And his eye?" Simeon asked as Reuben hunched over the basin.

"I think it will heal. The area around it is swollen now, but the cut skipped from his brow bone to his cheek." The man eyed Reuben. "What happened anyway?"

"We would rather not say," Simeon replied delicately, and paid the man.

Simeon gripped Reuben around his waist and pulled his arm over his shoulder. It was a slow, agonizing walk back to Simeon's house.

When he was home and able to lie down on his bed, Reuben felt the world stop spinning, but his face burned all the more.

Simeon left and returned with an empty basin, a jug of water, and a cup. He also had a folded prayer shawl over his arm to replace the bloody, ruined one. He passed it to Reuben, who clutched it to his chest, running his hands over the smooth weave.

"I'm sorry," Reuben said between gritted teeth, his eyes smarting. "For letting you down."

Simeon patted his arm. "Whatever happened at the tomb, I do not blame you. If four armed soldiers were unable to stop the disciples from taking the body, what could you have done?"

Relief surged through him, but he furrowed his brow. It made his gash burn, and he winced. "But Simeon, the disciples didn't take the body, it was just ... gone."

Simeon raised a hand. "I think you are a little muddled from that blow to your face. The soldiers fell asleep, and when you all woke up, you saw Jesus' disciples had stolen the body in the night."

Reuben pressed his hands to his throbbing temples. He knew that was not what had happened, but he pressed his lips together and swallowed.

Simeon folded his hands. "The story of the disciple's deception is already being spread through the city by our people, to head off any rumors they might want to start."

"And the soldiers?" Reuben asked.

"Caiaphas is telling Pilate what has happened, speaking up for them to keep them from blame. We paid them a tidy sum of money to ... compensate for any loss they might suffer at having fallen asleep."

Reuben understood the money was a bribe, to keep the soldiers from speaking of the ethereal sight they had witnessed at the tomb.

"You should sleep now, I think," Simeon said, turning to go.

"Wait," Reuben said, then hesitated.

"Yes?"

Reuben summoned his courage. "How did—how did you get your scar? Did Annas strike you?"

"He did," Simeon nodded, fingering the puckered line across his forehead. "Shortly after he had been deposed. He was terrible to be around that first year, and I lost an important scroll he needed."

Reuben felt sympathy, and also a comfortable sense that he shared something with Simeon. Then his gut wrenched. Because of Annas' anger, Simeon had never been allowed to rise to his proper place. His wise rabbi had been denied his seat on the Sanhedrin for simply losing a scroll. What would happen to the disciple who lost an entire body? He felt like he might vomit again.

"Will this ruin my standing with the chief priests permanently?" Reuben's voice shook. Had he lost everything?

Simeon clasped his hands before him, and his smile was the gentlest Reuben had ever seen on that wise face. "No, at least not completely." He reached down and patted Reuben's arm. "You may not rise as high as we had hoped, but Annas will not live forever. He will not stand in your way of becoming a Temple scribe or teacher. With my guidance, I am sure you will achieve all I could not."

Simeon left then, and Reuben was left alone with his thoughts. His head pounded too strongly for sleep to come. He heard soft footsteps in the passage, and for a moment his heart leaped as he thought Michal was coming to look in on him. The footsteps passed, and his heart sank. She might have forgiven him once for the cruel, false things he had said, but she would never forgive him for letting her brother die.

He fingered the bandage over his ruined face and felt tears of self-pity prickling his eyes. Who would want him now, disfigured as he was? The unfairness of it all overwhelmed him. He choked back more tears, and the salt burned under his bandage.

"Curse you, Jesus," he hissed to himself, clutching his shawl to his chest. "Even after your death, you are causing me pain."

37

DAWN OF A KINGDOM

Beth pulled her blanket up higher on her shoulder to ward off the pre-dawn chill. She opened her eyes, trying to hide from the memories of Jesus' broken body that rose too clearly beneath the shadow of her eyelids. How could that be her last memory of him?

All around her she heard even breathing. It had been late in the night when the disciples had finally laid down to sleep. They had all wept for their rabbi and talked until they were exhausted. The house was full, and the close air was rank with fear, doubt, and sorrow.

Nicodemus had been to see them. He had brought a gift of burial spices, and then he had gone back into the city.

Joseph of Arimathea was staying with them, as were other of the faithful disciples from Jerusalem, Bethany, and Galilee. Jesus' mother had left her sons and had instead cleaved to the disciples as she grieved her firstborn. John had devoted himself to her comfort, trying to get her to eat and sleep.

Beth thought she heard footsteps, and she lifted her head. In the shadowy dimness, she could see a woman moving towards the door. The silhouette of thick curls told Beth that it was Mary Magdalene.

Worried for her friend, Beth untangled herself from her blanket and tiptoed after her, grabbing her sandals from the pile by the doorway.

"Mary!" Beth called in a loud whisper as she stepped outside. Mary paused. It was too dim to make out her face, but Beth could see the weary slump of her shoulders. "Where are you going?"

"To the tomb," Mary said flatly.

Beth reached out to brush her friend's arm. "I'll come with you."

"So will we," another voice said.

Beth turned and saw Mary, mother of Joseph and James, coming out of the house, along with Naomi. Mary nodded silently. Together, the woman began to climb the Mount of Olives. Beth fell in behind the others who had been there when Jesus had been laid to rest in Joseph of Arimathea's tomb.

It was a relief to escape the stagnant air of the house and breathe deep the fresh, dewy scent that preceded the rising sun. As the handful of women walked, the sky paled above the Mount of Olives.

Lost in her reflections, Beth nearly ran into the back of her friend. Mary Magdalene murmured, "There are guards at the tomb."

Beth looked around her friend's shoulder and her stomach sunk. Roman soldiers were gathered before the large stone that closed the tomb's entrance. Two slept, and two were keeping watch. Beth wrapped arms around her middle as fear and indignation took turns in her heart.

Before the women could decide what to do, the sun rose. As the golden light broke into the sky, the earth began to tremble and Beth was thrown off her feet with a sharp cry.

"Another quake!" Mary Magdalene gasped, reaching out to clutch a tree branch for balance.

A piercing light shot down from the sky, and Beth threw a hand before her face. She peeked through her fingers and saw a figure like that of a man. He was as bright as if made from lightning, and his clothes shone as purely white as freshly fallen snow.

Beth trembled with fear and lay prostrate upon the ground, her face pressed to the damp grass. As she shook with fear, she heard a grating sound. Then the earthquake ceased and it was silent.

Beth's rapid breath sounded loud in her ears, and she lifted her face from the ground. Naomi and the other Mary were also sprawled on the grass, terrified. Only Mary Magdalene stood before her, still clutching the tree branch with white knuckles. They all stared at the celestial figure sitting upon the large stone. The open tomb yawned darkly beside his brilliance. The figure beckoned.

Mary Magdalene paused a moment before stepping forward. Still laying on the ground, Beth's mouth was dry with fear, every muscle tense. She began to flee from the celestial creature. As she turned her face towards Bethany, she remembered the last time she had abandoned her friends and the shame that smote her the next morning. She had to do better this time. Her knees felt like water, but she rose to her feet and followed the other women towards the tomb. Beth saw the soldiers laying motionless on the ground. She couldn't tell if they were dead. She wrung her hands.

"Don't be afraid," the angel spoke, and his voice sounded like rushing water. "I know you are looking for Jesus who has been crucified. He isn't here. He has risen, just as he said he would."

Beth's mouth fell open, and Mary Magdalene mumbled a prayer aloud.

The angel gestured to the open tomb. "Come. See the place where he was laid. After you have seen, go quickly and tell his disciples that he has risen from the dead. Behold, he is going ahead of you to Galilee; you will see him there."

Mary Magdalene glanced back over her shoulder and reached out a hand to Beth, who still hung back. Mary gave her a tiny smile of encouragement, and Beth took the offered hand. The women drew together and went forward in a huddled group. They ducked into the tomb.

Beth blinked in the dimness. The tomb smelled earthy. A shelf the length of a man was cut into the rock, but all she could see was a pile of linen. She looked around the tomb. There was no corpse. Beth clutched Mary Magdalene's arm, her mind reeling.

"I saw his body laid here," Mary Magdalene whispered, and her voice hitched. "Now it's gone. Has he truly risen?"

The other Mary looked at them with wide, amazed eyes. "What else could have happened? We saw the angel and heard his proclamation."

A smile broke on Mary Magdalene's face, illuminating her beauty from within. "We need to go to Galilee, right away! Come on, let's tell the others!"

Beth's heart leaped within her, a mixture of fear and joy. Could it be true that Jesus was alive again? It was too amazing to be possible, but what else could have happened?

The women burst out of the tomb into the bright dawn. When they emerged, the angelic being was gone from the large stone. The women fled from the tomb together, Mary Magdalene and Beth still clutching hands. As her feet flew, Beth's heart pounded with exultant fear at what she had witnessed.

They were half-way down the mount when they came upon a figure on the road. They slowed to a walk. The man was dressed in a simple robe with sandal-clad feet. At first Beth thought he must be the gardener, but then he turned and smiled at them. They all stumbled to a stop. Beth felt the air sucked from her lungs.

"Good morning," Jesus smiled at them. "Peace be on you!"

"Oh!" Mary gave a choked gasp, and she ran ahead of the women and fell at his feet. "Rabbi!"

Beth's feet moved forward of their own will. She could scarcely believe what she saw. She cringed when she saw the holes in his hands where the spikes had been driven. Yet, despite the scars, the man was not standing like one recovering from crippling scourging and crucifixion. Her eyes drew up to his face, and she saw his happy expression. She looked in his eyes and joy poured into her soul.

"Rabbi!" she cried out as she fell on the ground at his feet and worshiped him again, the way she had so long ago on the Sea of Galilee. The other women knelt before him as well, all of them watering the soil with happy tears.

Jesus spoke to them, "Don't be afraid. Go and take word to my brethren to leave for Galilee, and there they will see me."

The women rose to their knees.

"I don't want to leave you," Mary Magdalene cried, reaching out and clutching at the hem of Jesus' robe.

Jesus laughed and said, "There is no need to cling to me. Go, tell the others."

Beth rose to her feet, and the other women followed suit. They walked a few steps down the path, and when they looked back, Jesus was gone.

Beth blew out her breath. "Did that just happen?"

"It did!" Mary Magdalene looked at her with wide, shining eyes. "Jesus has risen! He is alive!"

Mary squealed like an excited child and reached out to hug Beth. They skipped in a circle with their arms tight around each other.

Beth stepped back and shook her head, grinning foolishly and trying to understand what had happened. "Who will believe us when we tell them Jesus is alive? It seems impossible. They're going to call us fools."

They ran back to the disciples. Mary Magdalene was the first in the door. She let out a rolling laugh, and her curls danced around her face as she shouted, "He has risen!"

The other disciples did not believe all at once. When they were finally convinced, they gathered their belongings and started north for Galilee.

Beth was quietly happy as they walked, trying to understand everything that had happened these past few days. The earth was resplendent in its new spring garb, and everywhere Beth looked were signs of new life: a delicate bud, an airy butterfly, a bird carrying back food for its chicks. She thought of the risen Jesus with a thrill in her heart.

Beth paused at the rise of a hill and gazed back at Jerusalem. The Temple Mount glinted in its white and gold magnificence, the Antonia stood tall with its attitude of oppression and might, and within the thick city walls the people lived out their lives, oblivious to the wonder that had transpired.

Peter noticed Beth had fallen behind and came back to stand with her. Together they looked over the city and Beth felt a sudden pang of sadness. Reuben lived there. Her cousin had thrown his lot in with the Pharisees and would share their fate. God had affirmed Jesus by raising him from the dead, fulfilling the prophecy Jesus had spoken. So that must mean that all of Jesus' prophecies would come true. Her stomach turned over as she remembered Jesus saying that Jerusalem would be left desolate, and she swallowed hard as she pictured the glorious Temple torn down.

"Are you all right?" Peter asked, leaning to see her face better.

Beth turned away from the city and her brooding thoughts. "I am. Though, I still feel as if I am in a strange dream."

"At least you've seen Jesus," Peter said. "I long to see him for myself." Peter reached out and took both her hands, his face serious. "I have something I want to share with you. Remember months ago, when Jesus took James, John, and I up the mountain and the cloud descended on us?"

"I do." Beth nodded. "I asked you what happened, but you said you couldn't tell me, not yet."

Peter smiled. "I can tell you now. We'll tell all the others too, but I wanted to share this with you first." He gripped her hands tighter, and Beth's pulse quickened. "When we were on the mountain, Jesus was transfigured before our eyes. His face shone like the sun. His clothes were as white as light." Beth was reminded of the angel, and she could picture what Peter had seen. Peter looked at her, wonderment in his eyes as he said, "Moses and Elijah appeared."

"Truly?" Beth gasped.

"They did, and they were talking to Jesus. I was overcome. I even offered to build three tabernacles for them, one for Jesus, one for Moses, and one for Elijah." Peter shook his head, twisting his mouth. "As I spoke, a cloud came down and hid them from my sight, and I realized I had made a terrible blunder. A voice spoke to me out of the cloud and said, 'This is My beloved Son, with whom I am well pleased. Listen to *him*!'" Beth's heart faltered, imagining how Peter must have felt at a heavenly rebuke. "I fell flat on my face, and James and John did too. I was utterly terrified. Then I felt a hand on my shoulder. I looked up, and Jesus was holding out his hand to me, appearing as he used to. 'Get up,' he said. 'Don't be afraid.' I looked around, and we were alone again. I could scarcely believe what I had witnessed. As we came down the mountain, Jesus told us not to tell anyone else what we had seen, not until the Son of Man rose from the dead. I didn't understand what he meant, until now."

She marveled at what Peter had seen. Moses and Elijah had come to speak with Jesus. Those two men were towering figures in her faith. Yet, the heavenly voice had placed Jesus above the other two great men, higher than both the giver of the law and the prophet who had been swept up into heaven by a chariot of fire. She grappled to understand Jesus' mighty authority.

Jesus was their Messiah, their king, and prophet, and Beth wondered if he would take the position of High Priest upon himself too. She had longed for God's presence to come and dwell among them since she was a girl, and all her people prayed for the same. Jesus' resurrection was the start of this movement, the beginning of the kingdom of heaven.

Beth and Peter stood silently for a long moment, contemplating the glories of God. A bird sang out and wheeled overhead and the wind whispered through the spring grasses. Beth stepped forward and wrapped her arms around her husband, laying her cheek upon his chest.

Peter's hand rested on her back. He hesitated a moment, then asked, "Now that he's back, will you ask Jesus to open your womb?"

Beth felt the familiar flutter of fear in her heart. The kingdom would not come without tribulation. Part of her still recoiled at the idea of bringing a baby into a troubled world. She looked back at the Temple. The city of Jerusalem would someday fall, and her people would suffer.

Like a wave, her fear began to rise. She was prepared to be swept away by her emotions, but for the first time, the crushing weight of her anxieties refused to wash over her. Her eyes opened wide in surprise when the fear in her heart receded, and her mind became like a calm sea. Truth shone like a beam of sunlight over the water.

She had knelt at the feet of a risen Jesus. How could she fear? Joy and peace swept in like a gull, hovering over the calm sea within her. Jesus was to be their king, and when the trials were over, the blessings would flow in. She felt the yearning for a child rise stronger than ever inside of her. She could bring forth a new citizen for Jesus' kingdom—another believer. She could raise a whole family to abide in the kingdom of heaven. A feeling of love and peace like she had never felt overflowed within her.

Beth looked up at Peter and smiled. "Yes, I will ask him." She glanced ahead to where the others were rounding a bend in the road. She laughed, "Come on, we're falling behind!"

Three days later, they were near the mount Jesus had designated. The sun was setting as they climbed the grassy slope near Capernaum. Spring flowers bobbed their heads, and bees worked busily as the last rays of the sun warmed the earth.

Beth looked around at the disciples. She knew these men and women so well. They had followed Jesus for three years, had rejoiced in his power, and wept at his death. As they ascended the mount she recognized the mingled hope and anticipation in their faces. Their faith had brought them to the mountain top. Their eyes swept for the first sight of their rabbi.

As they reached the summit, they saw a man waiting for them. His dark hair was tousled by the breeze and he wore simple white linen that offset his sun-darkened skin.

"Rabbi?" Peter called. "Is that you?"

"Come and see for yourselves!" Jesus laughed at them as they paused, eyes searching his face.

Beth's heart turned over as she looked at her risen rabbi again. He was the same man, and yet he was different. Jesus had often been weary in the days of his ministry, and it had shown around his eyes and in the slope of his shoulders. In the days leading up to Passover, he had been weighed down with sorrow, knowing the pain and suffering he would soon endure. She trembled when she remembered how he had looked on the cross, broken and bleeding.

Now his face was free of any weariness, laughter was in his eyes, and he stood strong and straight. Authority and power radiated from him. The disciples began to go forward one by one, bowing at his feet. Some hesitated at first, but soon all were on their knees before him. Beth knelt beside her husband. As she bowed low she smelled the sweet, earthy scent of grass.

Jesus' mother bowed low, then stumbled to her feet and lunged forward. She wrapped her arms around her son's waist, sobbing into his chest. "It's you, it is truly you!" Her voice was muffled in his robes.

Her open affection loosed the rest. The other disciples rose to their feet and clamored around Jesus, touching him, all talking at once with laughter and amazement.

The sun glistened on the horizon, painting glowing hues across the Sea of Galilee as the talking slowed and they sat down in the spring grass, gathered together as they had before.

"So, what happens now, Jesus?" Peter asked.

Jesus' face was triumphant as he answered, "All authority has been given to me in heaven and on earth. So, go! Go and make disciples of all the nations, baptizing them in the name of the Father, and the Son, and the Holy Spirit. Teach them about the kingdom, teach them to observe all that I commanded you."

"You sound as if you are leaving us," Mary Magdalene protested. "We just got you back, you can't go!"

Jesus laughed, and his face was lit from within as he said to them all, "I am with you always, even to the end of the age."

38

Not Peace, but a Sword

"Do you think we have waited well?" Beth asked her husband. Her tone was purposefully light and playful. "Do you think we are like the wise virgins who brought extra oil?"

Peter chuckled, and the silver in his beard caught the flickering light. "I hope so, my dear. His coming hasn't been as quick as I expected."

Beth understood and nodded in agreement. "It has been over thirty years since we saw him depart in the clouds. At that time, I thought he would be back in a few years, now—now I understand how little I truly know."

"And yet how the time has flown," Peter said, his voice richer than it had been in the early years of marriage; it had a gravelly tone to it now. "The things we have done. The things we have seen." They smiled at each other, sharing the memories.

"Would you have ever believed that we would bring the Gentile Christians and Jewish Christians together?" Beth shook her head. "The battles we have fought! I sometimes wonder if Jesus is watching us somewhere, chuckling as we try to make the oil and water mix."

Peter's tone was thoughtful, "And yet they are starting to blend. The Christians are becoming their own distinct group, enough that we are no longer protected in Rome under the banner of Judaism."

Beth sighed and was lost in her thoughts for a time.

The persecution they had faced since the disciples declared a crucified Messiah to the world had never stopped. There had been moments of reprieve, but always there were those who sought to destroy Jesus' disciples and stamp out the good news of Jesus' resurrection.

Things were at their worst now. Through a series of misconceptions, the Romans believed the Christians were cannibals. They completely misunderstood the meal Christians shared to commemorate Jesus' last supper.

The idea of worshiping a man who had died the most pitiable and humblest of deaths was absolutely ridiculous to the outsiders. And yet, the number of Christians had grown among the Jews, and in incredible numbers from the Gentiles. With the growth had come considerable challenges. The apostles were busy ensuring that the new churches that sprung up were teaching the true message that Jesus had left with his disciples. Many false teachings had arisen about who Jesus was, and if he had truly risen bodily.

The believers had searched the scriptures and found confirmation of Jesus everywhere, and shared that information with as many as they could. The apostles themselves had much to sort out in their own minds. Many details of Jesus' mission on earth had been talked through, their understanding growing through plenty of discussions, study, and prayer. Beth remembered the most difficult questions. Should they continue sacrificing in the Temple? Should the Gentiles be circumcised and live under Jewish purity law? Were they indeed living in the kingdom now, and if so, why was there still so much evil in the world?

When the persecution in Jerusalem became too great, Peter left to travel the country and show others the Way.

Beth had gone along with Peter on most of his missionary journeys. She had witnessed her husband thrown in prison, and she had prayed for his release until he miraculously showed up at the door. She had tended to the bloody stripes on his back, lashings he had gotten from preaching the good news. She had comforted him when he was brought low. Together they had wept as many of their friends and allies had been killed for refusing to deny that Jesus had indeed risen from the dead as the Messiah. The memories of her friends pulled at her heart.

"I miss the others," Beth whispered to her husband, the one who understood her best. "It seems like it was a lifetime ago. Remember? Sitting around the fire, laughing and joking with Jesus. We were children then. We didn't understand. Yet, I treasure those memories."

She could see the men and women disciples around the fire with the light flickering on their smooth faces and dancing in their happy eyes. How many of those eyes had closed now, waiting until Jesus should return?

Beth swallowed hard. The years had been hard on them all, the suffering and deaths of Jesus' disciples a testament to their faith in a risen Lord.

"Are you content with your life, dear wife?" Peter asked, his voice sadly earnest. "Did I do right to take you away from Capernaum, your mother and siblings, your home?"

"Oh yes!" Beth was quick to answer. "I wanted to be with you, Peter. I always want to be with you." The look of love in his eyes warmed her. "Of course, I had to give up my dream of a quiet life, of us sitting snugly in the evenings with our children surrounding us."

To turn away from that pleasant future to one of uncertainty and hardship had been one of the hardest decisions of her life, yet she did not regret it. She continued, "I have lived a new dream these thirty-some years, the dream of the kingdom of heaven. Evil may lash against us, pain and suffering are still fighting strong, but we know that Jesus has been made Lord of all, and the victory belongs to him! How could I let that pass me by?"

Peter picked up a scroll and turned it round and round. Many of the apostles had taken to writing letters to the churches, because in this way, the words could be reread in times of question and shared with their neighbors.

Beth watched the spinning letter in his hands and said, "Your deeds will live on in your letters, dear husband. You shall not be forgotten."

"Nor you," Peter said, gazing at her. His eyes spoke volumes.

Beth laughed, proud she could still do so. "I have lived in the background, and that's where I shall remain, I think. I don't want fame or public recognition."

"Still, you will live on in the hearts of the church, in all the men and women you taught and counseled and loved. Mark especially has been like a son to us. He will never forget your kindness to him all these years."

Like a son. Beth's heart swelled, and she felt a bittersweet emotion wash over her. She had never felt a baby kick within her, never brought forth a child of her blood. Before Jesus had ascended, Beth had, at last, asked him to heal her womb. She had been stunned by his answer. She could hear it as if he had spoken only yesterday.

"You shall have children beyond count," Jesus had said with a gentle look in his eyes. *"But not of your womb."*

Beth remembered how she had been taken aback at Jesus' words, hurt and shocked as she had wondered what he meant. She struggled for years trying to understand.

As she had poured her love into the young men and women who flocked to Jesus' banner, she had been rewarded with their affection and respect, and then their overflowing love. She had been the ear they turned to, and the shoulder they cried on. She had knelt and prayed with them all. She had planted Jesus' words on their hearts. With pride filling her eyes with tears, she had seen them go out into the world to proclaim Jesus.

One day, as she had knelt in prayer, lifting up the many young men and women, she had finally understood what Jesus meant. Now, she truly felt as though she had raised a hundred children, and all were as dear to her as if she had borne them herself.

Tears burned as their many faces swam before her. She prayed for them day and night, that they would stand firm as persecution hit the church like a hammer's blow.

Peter leaned as close as he could to her and whispered fervently, "Should all the world forget the mighty deeds you have done in serving Jesus and me, I should never forget. Jesus will not forget. He will remember everything, Beth. All of it."

Beth felt a tear slide down her cheek.

A clang of metal made her jump. She looked up and saw her prison door was opening. She lifted her shackled hands together and dashed the tear away. She stood to her dirty bare feet, turning a brave face to her husband through the bars that kept them separate.

"I love you, Peter," she called, her tone hitched as harsh hands reached for her and pulled her from the prison.

"And I love you!" he called after her as she was jerked into the low dark hallway. "Be strong, dear wife!" he called out, his voice breaking.

She was dragged by the guardsmen through the underground prison until she emerged into the sunlight. She had to fight to keep her eyes open. The light burned after so much time below ground. She breathed deeply her first breath of fresh air in months. She didn't want to miss anything in this moment.

She thanked God for the blue sky above, its beauty was not lost on her today. It was the only thing of beauty she saw as she was led far from the prison over a stony path. Rome, the magnificent city of opulent architecture and overwhelming depravity, was behind her. Deep in that enormous city was a house where her friends met, one of the little churches that met in secret while Nero sought to stamp them out. Did they know that today was the day? Would they come and witness?

She arrived at the execution grounds, and Beth saw a crowd had gathered. She took courage when she recognized the faces of those she knew. Their tears comforted her.

She turned and faced her greatest fear.

Her hands trembled, blood rushed in her ears, and the corners of her vision were dim, but she did not scream in terror or weep. She faced her ultimate nightmare but had learned the faith and inner strength to take it head on.

Rough wooden poles, with dried blood on their splinters, were struck into the ground permanently, and the cross beams lay ready for use. She saw with a lurch the long spikes, still filthy from their last victim. Slaves, insurrectionists, enemies of the state—they were all brought here to die. On some of the crosses, she witnessed victims in various states of dying and decay, left to rot where all could see and remember not to anger Rome. Ravens pecked at their faces. She felt a touch of the unreal. Was this truly her fate?

Pulling her gaze away from the hanging corpses, she clung to the image of the resurrected Jesus. He had gone through this, indeed he had endured worse. The Spirit he had sent her had suffered crucifixion, and he had come out victorious on the other side. So would she.

Death was not the end, not for her.

She struggled to keep Jesus firmly in her mind as the soldiers turned to her and unshackled her trembling hands. They began to tug at her clothes, and she instinctively fought back as they tore her tunic from her body. They responded by hitting and kicking her, and she forced herself to yield as she was stripped bare and the crowd laughed and mocked her. She was dragged to the cross and her whole body shook as she felt terribly, terribly cold.

Her eyes bulged as the first spike was driven, and she writhed under the hands that pinned her, the shock making her unable to cry out. The second spike ripped a plaintive wail from her lungs, and as she was hoisted by her arms up to the stake she screamed in agony. The third nail was driven through her heels and she wished she would faint, but she did not. She sobbed from pain.

Yet, in the agony, she could still taste the victory that was already won. They would kill her body, but her soul was kept safe in God. She could see Jesus before her, weeping with her, as the evil forces fought bitterly against the kingdom of heaven.

She was there, trembling, when Peter was brought before her. He cried out in anguish when he saw her, pulling at his clothes.

"Be-be-be strong, dear husband," she stammered encouragement to him as tears poured down her face.

As they prepared to nail Peter to the cross, he begged, "I cannot be crucified like my Lord Jesus. I denied him at his moment of trial. I am not worthy to die in the same manner. Hang me upside down, I beseech you!"

The guards laughed at him but were willing to comply. Beth sobbed as her husband cried out as the spikes were driven.

It was not long before he was beside her on a cross of his own, and they were again side by side, as they had been through life. They spoke and prayed with each other. They knew death was coming for them soon. As the blood pooled in Peter's head, he fell in and out of consciousness. Beth continued to weep in pain, though even her tears had left her.

Hours passed, and Beth felt like her shoulders were being pulled from their sockets; they burned with searing pain. To draw a full breath, she had to push upwards with her feet, ripping the tendons against the sharp spike. Her mouth was a parched desert, her tongue thick. She looked over at a nearby cross. A raven was there, picking at the carcass. Her stomach swooped and she turned her face away.

She did not fear the raven, she told herself. She would not fear death. She looked over to where the soldiers kept watch, to ensure their friends would not rescue them. Through bleary eyes she saw a

Pharisee, a thick puckered scar marring his face, running from his forehead to his lower jaw, splitting his beard. She remembered that face before the scar, when it had smiled at her and they had shared their hopes and dreams for the future.

He was close enough for her to see that he was uncomfortable. She felt a stirring of hope at the hint of compassionate emotion. Not all was lost in him. He had chased them all the way to Rome, intent on stamping out all twelve of the Apostles and those who followed the Way. She had seen him at the trial. She knew he had not only discovered them, but he had informed Nero himself.

"Reuben!" she rasped.

Reuben came forward a few steps, his face was grim. Beth had to let him know. She worked her leather-like tongue in her mouth, and her speech was slurred as she said, "I forgive you, Reuben."

His eyes widened a moment, then he scoffed and walked away.

Peter died as the sun set, choking and gasping with blood dripping from his mouth. Beth struggled on her wounded feet and cried out hoarsely for him, but he was gone.

Beth hung beside the body of her husband all through the night, shivering uncontrollably with cold, writhing in agony, and clawed with thirst and hunger. Beth whispered to herself, a word, a bit of prayer, each time weaker.

The sun rose the next day, and with it came the cawing of ravens. She felt like a stranger in her own body, every sensation fading. Was this it? Was this death?

She lifted her heavy head to look up, but she did not see the birds circling overhead. She saw the clouds and smiled one last time, the pain falling away and the joy rushing in.

39

FLIGHT OF THE RAVEN

"The Temple has fallen, the Temple has fallen!" Reuben's grown son yelled out as he burst through the front doors. His face was covered in soot, his hands blistered, and his cheekbones sharp beneath his wide eyes.

Reuben heaved his shrunken frame to his feet. He left his dying wife with his seventeen-year-old daughter, Atara, and stumbled past his son to look out the front doors. From his courtyard in the upper city of Jerusalem, he could see the Temple Mount, but the glorious white marble Temple was completely obscured by black, billowing smoke.

Reuben tore his clothes and wailed.

Jerusalem had revolted against Roman occupation four years ago when the governor took money from the Temple and killed the innocent civilians who protested. Thousands of men had died in the revolution—even women had been whipped and crucified.

The Zealots had moved in and took control, driving the Romans out of the Holy City. The Romans had dug in their heels and set up their forces around the city, trapping the people within.

The siege had starved them all. The city was thick with the stench of corpses. Yet, above every other horror, the destruction of God's

Temple was the worst tragedy of all.

Reuben's son, named Simeon after Reuben's rabbi, was panting. "The Romans have breached the walls and are flooding the city. I ran as fast as I could—they are slaughtering all that they see. Our soldiers are falling back to the Upper city, preparing a new barricade here."

Reuben's tried to grapple with the words his son was speaking, but his thoughts were tossed like chaff before the wind.

The Temple! The Temple! His mind wailed, even as he tried to focus on what he must do.

He saw Simeon's mouth moving, but the only sound in Reuben's ears was a sharp ringing. Reuben stared at the thick smoke and was paralyzed by memories. He had achieved all his dreams in the view of the Temple.

He had seen his chance for recognition in stamping out the Christians that were infecting the Holy City like vermin, spreading their blasphemy like a disease. His zeal had taken him out into the world, chasing them down, arresting them in their homes and so-called churches. He had dragged them before the courts so they could be sentenced to prison, flogging, or stoning. His passion had not gone unnoticed. He had been ordained as a full Pharisee at a young age, to the pride of his rabbi.

Rabbi Simeon had even helped Reuben find a beautiful and wealthy bride, Rebekah. Reuben and Rebekah had raised two children in his new home in the Upper City. He had everything he ever wanted—a family home, recognition for his intellect and zeal for the Lord, and the approval of Simeon, the Pharisees, and the entire Sanhedrin.

Reuben shakily fingered the scar that marked his face, making him easily recognizable as a feared character among the Christians. He was over sixty now. His hair was silver and his beard was flecked with gray.

Despite the passing of time, he had not felt his years until he beheld Beth upon that wretched cross. Then all the years had piled on him at once, and it had been the end of his career. He had returned to Jerusalem seeking peace and rest—but had found war and death.

The memories of Beth made his eyes burn. Oh, Beth! Why did she choose a life like that? She should be safe in Capernaum with her grandchildren bringing her wildflowers. He could see her as she would have been, see her silver hair framing those sweet, expressive eyes.

He wished he had not gone to the crucifixion. He had thought himself immune, but she was not another nameless Christian, she was his cousin, his childhood friend. Seeing her small, naked frame suffering in agony had hurt his heart more than he cared to admit to anyone. Her eyes had found him, and she had done the ridiculous and forgave him for nailing her and her husband to the cross.

Reuben shook his head. The death of Peter had been necessary. Reuben would have spared Beth if he could, but Nero was eager to make a public display by killing them together.

He remembered the ravens flying overhead, waiting to feast on the flesh of his childhood best friend. The memory was too painful, and he fled from it.

He turned to his son, coming with a jerk to the present. Atara hovered nearby, her clothes hanging loosely from her frame. She was the crown of his life, but it hurt every time he looked at her. She should be in the flower of womanly beauty, not sickly and pale. She should be nursing a baby, not her dying mother.

"We must go. We cannot survive in the city any longer," Reuben spoke, laying his wrinkled hand on his son's starved, skeletal shoulder. He cringed at the feel of his son's bones. Simeon and Atara stared at their father with fear and confusion.

"How will we get out?" Atara gasped. "We're trapped!"

"There is a secret passageway beneath the city that leads out into the valley," Reuben said, and his children looked at each other with wide eyes.

They must think he had gone mad, he realized. He saw their doubt, for if there had been a chance of escape, why hadn't they taken it before? Oh, why hadn't he taken it before!

He knew why. He had stayed to suffer because of the Temple. He had trusted that God would not let it fall. His heart wrenched inside him as he looked once more at the billowing black smoke. He choked back tears and tried to smile at his children. "Come, leave everything, we must go now!"

He and Simeon each took a side of Rebekah's blanket and picked her up. They shuffled with the precious load, and the family left the house for the last time.

Their movements were painfully slow. Reuben had to shout for the gate to be left open so they could exit out of the Upper City before they were barred and trapped. Reuben saw the fear on his children's sunken faces as they passed through the barricade, but he could not let them starve to death as the siege continued.

The Lower City was a putrid slope of ruined homes, the dead lying on the streets where they had fallen, birds and insects feasting on the swollen corpses. He prayed that the house he needed was still standing. The entrance to the passageway was well hidden, and the secret of its location known only to a few.

Reuben sighed with relief when he saw the building, and he entered the obscure house. Setting down his wife, he lifted a mat. He grunted and heaved open a trapdoor in the floor. A ladder led into the earthy darkness.

Simeon looked at it in surprise. "This leads outside the city?" the young man gasped. When Reuben nodded, his son grabbed his arm. "We must tell the others! Our friends will die in the city." He turned to go, but Reuben grasped his tunic.

"Son! We will not be able to get back to the Upper City, the gate will be sealed." He swallowed hard. He had known that he was leaving his friends to die, but haste was necessary to save his family.

"We must tell people. We can't slink away protecting only ourselves," Simeon said hotly and wrenched away from his father. As he ran out the door he called, "I'll be back!"

Reuben cried out as his son ran from him into danger. Soldiers would have flooded the city by now. Atara was crying, and Reuben brushed a hand down her cheek and spoke words of comfort to her, though he hardly knew what he said.

He picked up his wife, a feat he would not have done so easily if she was not skin and bones. Grimacing, he heaved her over his shoulder. With Atara to guide him, he somehow made it down the wooden ladder.

He stood at the bottom gasping, with sweat running into his eyes, and all he saw was darkness. With his wife over his shoulder and Atara grasping the back of his robe, Reuben crept into the tunnel. Soon he could see nothing at all.

"You must go in front," Reuben panted, his legs trembling. "Run your hand along the wall and guide me."

The young woman moved around her father in the narrow, low passage and began to lead them along. The air was thick and cool and pressed on them, and Reuben listened with all his might for the return of his son. It wasn't long before he did hear voices, many voices, all panicking. He realized the danger the moment before it happened.

The press of rushing people racing through the utter darkness knocked him forward. He dropped Rebekah, and Atara screamed as she was thrown to the ground. He managed to keep his feet, but he was jostled, pinned to the wall, elbowed and his feet trod on. Atara screamed but he couldn't move from where he stood, so thick was the passing crowd of panicked people. Eventually the flood of people stopped, and he stood in silence.

His heart hammered. "Atara?" he called. There was no answer, no noise. With trembling hands, he lowered himself to the ground and felt for his wife and daughter. His hands felt warm wetness and he began to weep as his fingers found a face. He lowered his head and breathed the scent of his wife's hair. He cried aloud, the noise pressing back on him in the close space. He could feel no moment of her lungs, no beat of her heart. He crawled forward.

"Atara! Atara!" he sobbed.

His hand brushed against a bare foot, her shoe was gone. His hands fluttered and felt her chest for a heartbeat. He felt none. He sat and wept, rocking back and forth, lost and fearful.

Where was his son? He must wait for Simeon.

He did not know how long he waited in the dark with the empty bodies of his wife and daughter, their life crushed from them. He heard noise coming and realized it was another flood of people. He scrambled to his feet, and with tears washing down his face, he pressed onward before they could overtake him. Stumbling, with his hand dragging against the wall, he finally saw a dim light ahead of him. He crawled from the tunnel into a small cave where moonlight felt as bright as day.

He was near the Mount of Olives, and he could see thousands of torches flickering from the Roman armies. The olive trees had been razed, leaving jagged stumps like broken teeth. Siege engines were flinging rocks the soldiers had dragged from the broken, eastern wall. The city was ravaged, fires spreading as smoke rose blackly into the sky.

Turning from the horrific sight, Reuben crawled through the grass, scraping his hands and knees on sharp stones. Twice, he had to fling himself to the ground and hide from patrols. The soldiers discovered others and dragged them away crying for mercy, but somehow he was never found.

He crawled away from the city he loved as the Temple burned and pagans killed his people. Finally, far from the city, he wobbled to his feet and began to walk. He did not know what had happened to Simeon, but surely his son had escaped. They would meet back in Capernaum, the town of Reuben's youth, far from the destruction of Jerusalem.

He carried nothing but grief on his journey. He snatched moments of sleep in ditches, unwilling to seek refuge among strangers

His mind was numb as he arrived at Capernaum. For the first time in many years, he looked upon the sparkling waters of the Sea of Galilee and saw the square-sailed fishing boats bobbing on the water. The summer grasses were tall, waving in the breeze. It was like he was transported back to the days of his youth, and he fell to the ground weeping uncontrollably. Weak with hunger, grief, and thirst, he lay on his face in the road.

He awoke in a strange bed, with an oddly familiar face over him.

"Peace, Reuben," the woman said and held a bowl of broth to his lips. He gulped it all. As he struggled to keep his eyes open, he groggily thought that Beth had returned to care for him.

When he woke again he was alone. He looked around himself and tried to learn where he was. He was on a small cot in a little room. A window was open and he could hear the call of birds from without. Footsteps approached and he saw the same woman as before. She appeared younger than him by only a few years. When she smiled he gasped, for it was Beth's smile.

"Hannah?" he asked, his voice raspy in his ears.

"Yes, it's me," Hannah said, and came and knelt beside him. She gave him another drink of broth. "Would you like some bread?"

The smell of real, fresh bread was like a whiff of heaven. He breathed deeply and she broke off a small piece and held it to his mouth. He ate from her hand in the silence, his eyes searching her face for any hint of hatred. Did she know what he had done? Did she know that he had been the one to find and send Peter and Beth to their deaths?

Sated but exhausted, he leaned back against the bolster and sighed. "My son, has he come to Capernaum?" he whispered to the ceiling. He knew before she answered that Simeon had not come, otherwise he would be here with him.

"No," Hannah patted his arm. "But keep up hope."

"There is no hope. The Temple has fallen." He felt hollow inside. "My wife and my daughter are both dead, likely my son too. What hope can I have?" Tears leaked unchecked down the sides of his face.

"I am sorry," Hannah said, and when he looked at her, he saw that she truly was. She held his hand as he wept, and when he closed his eyes he could imagine it was Beth's.

He didn't remember falling asleep, but when he woke up he was alone. The sound of singing came from another room. He listened a moment, and then, curious, he rose from his cot on shaky knees. The broth and bread gave him enough strength to walk from the room with wobbly steps. He was in a hallway with a window, and he peeked out. The sunlight told him it was early morning, and it shone on a courtyard he recognized.

This was Peter's house. The thought made his stomach lurch.

He made his way to the staircase. Using the wall as support, he went down toward the singing. He made it halfway before he was forced by his weakness to sit. He could see the room he remembered well. He recalled the feeling of welcome and love he had felt when he had sat and eaten with Beth and her family so long ago. Now the room was filled with strangers, all of them singing. When the song finished, they passed around bread and wine, speaking of the blood and body of Jesus.

Reuben was stunned. He, a great persecutor of the Christians, the man who had been responsible for the death of one of the great Christian leaders, was being nursed to health above a church.

He feared that someone would notice him, recognize his scar, and know who he was. He tried to creep back up the stairs, but he slipped and fell, and the noise was enough for heads to turn. He stared at them and shrank against the wall, feeling his vulnerability. He was old, he was weak. They looked back, and he was surprised to see a few smiled at him in pity. A man in about his fifties came forward.

"Reuben, it's me, David," the man smiled, and Reuben tried to trace the features of the boy he had known.

David reached out, and Reuben held out a trembling hand to shield himself, not believing that these people did not want to drag him out and stone him. David grasped Reuben's hand and helped him to his feet. David led him back to bed.

David settled the bedclothes over him. "Sleep, you are still weak from your flight from Jerusalem." He left Reuben to the pounding of his heart.

They must not know! He realized in shock, and then he said it to himself firmly. They must not know.

Weeks passed, and Reuben waited and waited for his son who never came. Did he die in the city walls, trying to show others the way to freedom? Was he now being led away to slavery? It hurt not to know.

When he was well enough to move about, Reuben liked to sit in front of the house and watch the boats on the water. He often cried as he sat, remembering his family, remembering the days of his youth and all the hope he had held for the future. He had not pictured a future such as this.

Hannah and David were always kind. Both had married Christian spouses, had children and grandchildren, and the two families lived together in the large house Peter had built for Beth on their marriage. Tamar had passed away, but they spoke of her like they would see her again someday soon. The children in the house were Reuben's cousins, but they called him 'grandfather' out of respect, and it made his eyes burn.

Despite being back in his hometown, Reuben did not return to the home of his brothers. Reuben and Ebenezer had not made peace before the fisherman had passed away. Reuben hadn't seen Zeb and Ben since the gathering of his mother's bones many years ago. He had only been invited because it was his mother's dying request that the brothers be reunited. His mother's wish had been impossible. Reuben had realized their brotherly affection had been as dried and empty as the bones they placed in the urn.

No, Reuben could not go to his brothers and beg for a place at their hearth. The last time Reuben had seen his brothers, he had been successful, wealthy, and renown, with a wife and two children. Now he was alone and broken. He did not try to reason why he felt more at home in Beth and Peter's old house.

Ruth, Hannah's granddaughter who was about five-years-old, came out of the house and crawled into Reuben's lap. He could smell sunshine in her hair and he remembered his daughter at that age. Oh, Atara!

Ruth turned and looked at him. When she saw him weeping, she wiped away his tears with her little hands.

"Don't cry, grandfather," she said. "You'll see your family again someday. Jesus was the first," she spoke innocently, and he jerked slightly at the name. "He was the first to rise in the new kingdom. He is our king. His death bought us all and we are no longer slaves to sin. He'll come back and bring everyone back to life again, and we'll all live together and be happy."

Reuben knew that in those few sentences she had spoken the entire Christian hope. Jesus, the man crucified, was alive. He had dealt with sin, and he was coming back for them.

Ruth nestled against his chest, and together they watched the boats on the sea.

It was strange living with a family of Christians. They prayed different prayers than Reuben was used to, and they sang different songs. Always, they spoke of Jesus like he was coming back any day now. Reuben had persecuted dozens and dozens of Christians, and yet those here were all kind to him. They smiled and asked after his health. He wanted to warn them of who he really was, but the words stuck in his throat.

The day came when Reuben could not stand it any longer. He was sitting at the table, in the same spot where he had sat on that wonderful night of visiting with friends some forty years ago. Hannah was mending, as her sister had done, and David and his brother-in-law were repairing a net in the corner. Reuben's heart broke inside him and he knew he had to confess.

"Hannah," his voice wavered. "I must tell you. I was a great persecutor of the church. I put many Christians in prison, dragging men and women from their homes without mercy. I looked on and approved when they were stoned or scourged."

The words were like bile in his throat. He realized he had come to be ashamed of his actions. How could that be? Hadn't he done it all for God?

Hannah and David glanced at one another. Hannah set down her mending and reached out with one hand to pat his arm. "We know that, Reuben. You were quite famous for it." She drew a hand down her face, mimicking the line of his scar. "Everybody in the church here knows who you are."

He sat back, shocked. They all knew who he was, and yet they were all so kind? It reminded him painfully of Beth forgiving him even as she hung on the cross. He shook his head at the haunting memory. They couldn't know everything, otherwise he would not be sitting here in this home, fed and safe with little children calling him grandfather.

"Hannah, I—" he had to gather himself "—I had your sister arrested. I am responsible for the terrible way she died. She was ... crucified." He stared at Hannah as he spoke, waiting for her expression to change to one of horror and hatred. "She was crucified outside of Rome beside her husband."

Hannah's face did not show hatred. She looked sorrowful, and her voice was thick as she said, "We know, Reuben. We know that too."

Reuben felt as if he had been struck across the face. "You know?" he gasped. "How can you have me here in your home? How do you not hate me?"

Hannah leaned forward, "It is easy to hate, to desire revenge. Jesus asked more of us. He asked us to love our enemies, and to do good to those who hate us."

Reuben remembered sitting on a hill with the other Pharisees years ago, when he had heard those words himself. He hadn't imagined he would see those words play out in his own life.

Tears began to rain down his face. The weight of Beth's death sat heavy on him. He looked at Hannah with pained confusion. "She was dying, and she told me she forgave me," he sobbed. "How could she do that?"

Hannah put her arms around Reuben, and David left his nets with his brother-in-law and sat beside him. They spoke to him, words of comfort and the forgiving power of Jesus. Reuben remembered how he had been so angered to hear Jesus forgive people for their sins. He had seen it as blasphemy. Now, witnessing Hannah and the other Christians living out that forgiveness, he felt a stirring in his heart.

Months passed while Reuben lived in Peter's old home, the meeting place of the church in Capernaum. His health returned in full and he began to help around the house by mending nets for David, minding the children, and doing odd chores.

His training in languages and transcribing was put to use as well, for many letters passed through the house. The Christians had a great network of letters of teaching that they read aloud when they met. It felt awkward, as a Jewish scribe, to copy a Christian missive as accurately as he transcribed Scripture. Yet he found the process a balm on his soul as he sat in the quiet and listened to the familiar sound of his pen scratch against the papyrus. Once, a letter came into the house written by Peter himself. Reuben wept as he copied what Peter had written about the virtues of a gentle and quiet spirit, seeing Beth described in all the words.

His grief settled over time. It always present, but he could bear it. The day came when he shared a real laugh with the children at their game and it felt good.

As he observed these Christians from within their midst, he witnessed their generosity to the poor and the sick, their strong sense of community, and their unfaltering faith even in the face of great danger. All those characteristics were Jewish to the core. Their Christianity was based on the law Reuben loved—the same law that commanded charity, faith, and brotherly love.

In quiet moments, Reuben reflected on everything he had heard Jesus say, and all he had seen him do. He dredged up the memory he had worked so hard to suppress—the morning at the tomb, the miracle he had seen with his own eyes.

For the first time, he was able to look at Jesus' life through the eyes of his disciples, and he began to doubt his original conclusions. He shrank back from the truth, but it grew in his heart until he realized that he had been wrong to deny Jesus.

One balmy evening, David found him weeping for the shame of his sin, the part he had played in the death of Jesus.

After a long talk, David took him down to the sea. For the first time Reuben was baptized, not by washing himself, but by someone doing it for him. He was plunged into the Sea of Galilee in the name of the Father, the Son, and the Holy Spirit, and was risen up into the sunshine, born into new life.

As the water trickled down his gray hair, he clasped his hands before his heart and marveled at the road he had traveled to finally find the Way.

A shadow wheeled overhead, and he thought he heard the cry of a raven as it flew far away.

MORE BOOKS BY KATRINA D. HAMEL

as the stars

45 BIBLE FICTION SHORT STORIES

From the tears of Eve to the bond of Priscilla and Aquilla, this Bible Fiction Devotional takes you on an immersive journey through the pages of scripture.

Deepen your familiarity of biblical figures and find inspiration for your own journey in theirs. Written for lovers of Christian Fiction, this devotional pulls the emotion from the gripping stories of the Bible while staying grounded in scripture. Rally your 300 men with Gideon, brave the king's displeasure with Esther, and rust in God's acceptance with Rahab.

It's time to travel through the biblical world and discover the amazing events that are woven into God's plan for all mankind.

ACKNOWLEDGMENTS

This book would never have come to be without the encouragement, patience, and support of my husband, Chase. I love you, honey.

Huge thanks to my dad, Lee, for setting my feet on the path of writing again. You woke up my long-sleeping desire to be an author, and I will be forever grateful!

Thank-you also to Gary Collier who first suggested this book and helped me turn a short story into my first "real" book and gave me access to some amazing study resources at Coffee With Paul.

Joni, I appreciate your careful insight and helpful edits. As kids, you were my first and favorite critic.

Thank-you Alison and Desiree for agreeing to read my earlier drafts, and suffering through hefty descriptions and terrible typos.

Thank-you, dear reader, for choosing to share your precious time with me. I pray that this journey through Matthew has left you inspired to dive deeper into your faith.

About the Author

Katrina lives in Alberta, Canada with her husband, Chase, her four children, and their two cats. She considers herself blessed to have grown up hearing the gospel in her home with believing parents. Because of their examples in faith and teaching, she was baptized at the age of twelve and is proud to call herself a Christian.

Katrina welcomes comments and questions at her website:
www.katrinadhamel.com

Printed in Great Britain
by Amazon

37136570R00260